Living in Love Here and Now

To John
May you always live in Love
Rafael

Ralph DeGruttola

ISBN 978-1-68570-568-8 (paperback)
ISBN 978-1-68570-569-5 (digital)

Christian Faith Publishing
832 Park Avenue
Meadville, PA 16335
www.christianfaithpublishing.com

Printed in the United States of America

I would like to dedicate this book to my daughter, Mary Ann Tabaro. May she rest in peace. She lived in love.

Acknowledgments

This book contains ideas I've read, heard, studied, and experienced over the course of a lifetime. The ideas of philosophers, psychologists, scientists, and theologians are explained and used to address questions of concern to people. I am grateful to all these scholars who have touched my life and upon whose shoulders I stand in writing this book. Most of all, I would like to express my gratitude to God whose words were the guide and inspiration for answers to fundamental questions about life; answers that give insight into the meaning of life and perhaps our salvation.

Contents

Part 1

LIVING EXISTENCE

Introduction

Since the dawn of civilization, when men and women became aware of their existence, they asked themselves three very important questions: *Who am I or what is my identity? Is there a purpose in my being here and now? What is my destiny or what happens when I die?*

All of us want answers to these questions, and because we want them, we are afraid; afraid we will not find the answers we so desperately want. Fear produces anxiety, which is painful. Even if one knows the answers, there may still be anxiety depending on the answers. Without answers, we can get discouraged and break down because knowing our identity, purpose, and destiny makes us whole and holds us together as human beings.

The mind searches and needs answers. If it can't find them, the mind will fabricate them. People often describe their identity in terms of what they do, which can also satisfy their purpose in life. I'm a policeman, and my purpose in life is to protect people. I'm a teacher, and my purpose in life is to teach children. As for their destiny at the time of death, many people have doubts and are afraid, so they try not to think about it.

→ How would you answer these three questions?

→ Do you think of yourself in terms of what you do?

What motivates us to act? Do we act to maintain a state of balance, reducing tension within us, producing a feeling of pleasure and well-being? Perhaps it's the urge to grow and evolve that is the primary influence on our behavior. Maybe it's survival, the most basic instinctual motive of all. We seek what is needed to survive. Perhaps it is not so much physical but a psychological need such as self-esteem and self-realization, or maybe spiritual needs such as a need to know there is a God. Ultimately, happiness is a factor in motivating us to act and do whatever we think will bring us happiness. It could be pleasure, growth and evolution, survival, or something else called love or God.

→ What motivates you to act?

In looking at the identity and nature of people, we must ask ourselves, do we have a free will? Or are we at the mercy of genetics? Or perhaps conditioned by environmental forces? How do the energies in our bodies work? Is our being determined by early events in our lives? Or can experiences and activities in later life influence our identity, purpose, and destiny? Is the identity of each person unique? Or are there universal patterns of behavior that are a part of every person? *Ultimately, what is the mechanism inside us that produces specific behaviors under certain conditions or circumstances?* Finally, *what is existence*? Who are we really?

We seek to answer these questions. Yet, even with the answers, we often struggle on life's journey! We want to change, to be more of what we think we were put here to be, but we often fail. We confess our sins and admit our mistakes. We repent and resolve to amend our lives. Yet we struggle to do so, returning to confess the same sins and make the same mistakes over and over again.

We struggle with temptations and do not seem to have the discipline to overcome them. So we become discouraged and disillusioned with ourselves. We give up only to courageously try again and eventually fail once more. It is when we know the true answers to these questions, believe them, always keep them in mind, and act upon them that our struggle in life becomes meaningful.

This book is written to help those who are struggling on their journey. We draw upon religious revelations, theology, psychology, scientific and philosophical information, and thinking about our own internal and external experiences to answer our three basic questions.

The Divine Truth

The Divine Truth

To answer the basic question of who we are, we must look at our interior intellectual activities and our exterior physical actions. *This is because our interior intellect influences our exterior behavior.* Thoughts influence actions and give us clues to our identity. Reading the Bible with faith, science, psychology, philosophy, and our own experiences help provide answers. They are all important in identifying who we are, why we're here, and where we are going.

To determine the specific causes of our behavior, we must analyze ourselves. We must recognize our mental and physical behaviors, break them down into parts, and determine how they relate to each other to produce our behaviors. For example, a car moves passengers from one location to another. To determine how it does this, we would have to break it down into parts and determine what they do and how they relate to each other to produce the energy to move the car.

A car is a complex mechanism that transports objects. Some people think the identity of a person can be determined in a similar fashion, but we will see people are much more than complex machines, although some scientists would disagree. They believe someday we will make a robot with artificial intelligence that will be better than any man or woman! The sum of a person is much more than his or her parts. Unlike the robot with artificial intelligence, our intellect and free will can freely and consciously influence our behavior, and in so doing, our destiny. We will see how this can be. *We will learn to control our minds with thoughts, which determine our behavior. This enables us to effectively live our true identity to obtain the destiny we were designed and created to have.*

Let's focus our intellect now upon our experiences to see what they reveal about us. We all experience our own existence. We all know by firsthand knowledge and without any doubt that "I" exist here and now. Another way of saying it is "I am" here now. To get some idea of our identity, let's break down "I am" into parts and relate the parts. First, we focus upon the "I."

"I" is all parts of the body, including the intellect and free will capable of controlling our bodies' actions. It is the sum and substance of who we are encompassing, everything we have been, are now, and someday hope to be. The "I" contains everything significant about us. Next is our "am," which is all of our physical and mental behaviors, and it too is a part of our identity. All of our acts are contained in the action verb "am." Acts or "am" are the product of our "I."

In the Bible, God revealed His name to Moses. God's name is Yahweh, which translates to "I am." In Biblical times a person's name sometimes revealed something about their identity, specifically the "am" of "I am."[1] For example, a person named John Carpenter was more than likely a person who worked with wood. Clearly, our identity is similar to God's identity! We both refer to ourselves as "I am." We are both beings who are living existence. ***Like God, we are energy, which is living existence expressed as ideas and feelings acting in the here and now.***

God did not use the words "I was" or "will be" but "I am," a living being who is continually in the present. God is unlimited eternal energy expressed in the action of being. ***God is living existence.*** To the theologian, this is the *divine truth* about the identity of God. The biblical revelation about God and our own self-evident experiences about ourselves are similar.

Made in God's Image

It has been revealed in Genesis that we are made in the image of God: "Let us make humankind in our own image according to our likeness."[2] When He says this, the creator is consulting with a heavenly court of angels. As the psalmist noted, God made man in His image "a little lower than God."[3] To let us become masters of earth and all its diverse creatures.

This declaration about our God like nature or identity is truly amazing! Our nature is synonymous with our identity. *Like God, we are energy expressed as living existence who can proclaim "I am."* The revelation clearly makes us the benefactor of the abundance of creation. It implies that between the creator and His creation, humanity, there is a link that would indicate an almost unlimited potential in us.[4] God pronounces what He has made "very good"[5], so we are very good by virtue of the creation of our existence.

If we believe these revelations concerning our identity are true, then the study of God in the Bible should provide insight into our nature. Likewise, the study of people in science, philosophy, and psychology along with our own experiences should provide some insight into the nature of God, or at the very least confirm some of the truths revealed in the Bible.

As an example, much of what we know and feel about divine attributes may have begun with our knowledge and experiences involving our human attributes. As children, we often idolize our fathers and incorporate many of their good attributes into our minds. When we learn about God the Father, it is easy to ascribe many of these good attributes of our biological Father to God the Father. Likewise, when we read divine revelations and learn about the attributes of God our Father, we gain insight into the good attributes our biological fathers have or do not have. The revealed word about God the Father can provide a greater understanding of our worldly father and vice versa. *Since our identities are similar to God, then perhaps our purpose for existing should also be similar to God's purpose or mission.*

2

Personality and Identity

Psychologists use the word *personality* instead of *identity,* and personality just like our nature is synonymous with identity. The psychologist Gordon Allport gave us a good definition of our personality. It is "a dynamic organization within the individual of the psychophysical systems that create characteristic patterns of thoughts, feelings and behaviors which determines our unique adjustment to our environment."

Within this definition, we see the action words dynamic, create, thoughts, feelings, and behaviors. We also see that our personality is a series of psychophysical systems, and these systems exhibit a definite organization. In psychology, the word *psychophysical* refers to traits that are permanent universal mental dispositions or habits. The mind determines the consistent behavior patterns with these traits or habits. They make up systems of traits that are within an organization. So we see traits are universal mental habits that are a part of every person's mind.

The following are some examples of psychophysical traits within a person that are opposed to each other:

- Some people are submissive, obedient, mild, accommodating; others maybe dominant, assertive, aggressive, and competitive.
- Another set of opposing traits are social concerns: people are socially untutored, unconcerned, boorish, as opposed to socially concerned people who are socially mature, alert, and self-sufficient.
- Still another set of traits involve people who lack social action. They do not volunteer for social services, experience no obligation, and are self-sufficient. While others are dedicated to a group with a sense of inadequacy, they are concerned with social good works, not doing enough, and joining in social endeavors.
- Finally, there are people with traits that are low energy tension: relaxed, tranquil, un-frustrated, and composed as opposed to people who are high energy tension: they are frustrated, driven, overwrought, and fret.

Traits have also been identified with the concept attitude. An attitude is not an opinion for or against something. It is a predisposition to act or react in a characteristic manner of response to a given situation. It is either "inward" or "outward" directed acting with the energy of existence.

The organization of systems is energetic and always changing by acting upon the environment as well as being influenced by it. To some psychologists, these traits within organized systems explain the adjustment of people to their environment. Adjustment to our environment is essential to our survival. Unless these traits can satisfy our animal and psychological needs of our bodies, we cannot survive physically or psychologically. Unless these traits and our faith can satisfy our spiritual needs, we cannot survive spiritually. We are more than intelligent animal beings; we are human beings. According to Allport, these energetic organized systems of traits constitute and influence our identity or personality. They are part of our "I," which constitutes our identity.

→ Can you recognize some of the traits listed as belonging to you?
→ Can you see them as habitual tendencies or habits that influence your behavior?

Our personality involves using the energy of life within, causing us to act upon our thoughts and feelings with exterior actions. It is the organized systems of traits within our "I" that direct the energy of life with our "am," which includes the action verbs in Allport's definition. The acts are manifestations of the energy of life. Allport's definition of our identity has some similarities with the identity of God as the great "I am" or the infinite energy of life expressed in the action of being. We are the lesser "I am" made in His image!

3

Trinitarian Nature of God and Man

Allport indicates that within us, we have organized systems of traits. Psychologists have identified some of these systems. One in particular was identified by the psychologist Eric Berne who was studying and classifying verbal interaction between people. The psychologist identified three systems within an individual. Each system is called a person! The systems or persons within a man or woman are called parent, child, and adult! Each person is a distinct personality with its own being! Yet, the synthesis of the three personalities make up one identity encompassing all three! The three personalities are found in every person. It has been revealed in the Bible and to church fathers that there are three persons in one God! Each system is a person we call God the Father, Son, and Holy Spirit.[1] *The three persons within a man or woman are similar to the three persons within the one divine God!* Isn't it interesting that what a triumvirate God revealed to the church Fathers was similar to the triumvirate human being discovered by a psychologist? One should not be surprised since it has been revealed we are made in God's image. Revelation into the nature of God is sometimes reflected in the psychological discoveries in the nature of people.

Like the three persons in one God, the three persons within us are dynamic and organized interacting within themselves and with people outside themselves. The three personalities having their own distinct traits, are different parts of the one intellect within each individual. We can be taught to identify these persons within ourselves by their traits. By looking within, we can observe which person may be occupying our inner thoughts at any one time. We can also observe our exterior interaction with others, identifying which of the three persons within us is engaged in interacting with them. We can learn not only to identify but select which person(s) we use to interact with others. We can also learn to identify which person(s) the men or women interacting with us are using.

For example, we may be using our parent when interacting with a man, and he may be using his child in his response to us. Psychologists call this activity Transactional Analysis. This involves classifying our conversations into the parts of parent, child, and adult. It involves deliberately watching and using one of the three in our conversation with others and within ourselves.

Transactional Analysis is a part of our interpersonal relationships. Since three divine persons are in one God, when one of the three is interacting with us, the other two are present. Jesus said that He and the Father are one[2], and whoever interacts with Him is also interacting with His Father. In order to recognize three persons within us, we must know their distinguishing traits. *Not surprisingly, the distinguishing traits of the three persons within us are similar to the traits of the three divine persons in God.*

Made In God's Image

Existence	Personality		
God	Father ↓↑	Son ↓↑	Holy Spirit ↓↑
Humans	Parent	Child	Adult

God the Father

God the Father and our biological father or any authority figure in our lives give us rules and laws for living. Authority figures can be our parents, relatives, friends, clergymen, teachers, or coaches, anyone we respect, admire, and believe. The rules can be the Ten Commandments given to us by God the Father or the man-made rules sometimes derived from the Ten Commandments. They are given to us by word of mouth, written, or by a personal example. Parent figures give us rules for our protection and benefit. The laws of God are always beneficial to humanity. One can't say the same for man-made laws because we are human and subject to error. Our abortion law is an example of an evil man-made law.

→ Can you think of any rule your parents established when you were young that you rebelled against? Was it beneficial for you?
→ Can you now think of rules your parents established that you followed because you knew they were beneficial for you? Perhaps you follow them here today!
→ Were there any rules your parents established that were similar to the rules of God the Father?

God the Father is the creator of heaven and earth. Our biological parents cooperated with God the Father in our creation. All our parental figures as well as God the Father nurture us with understanding, protection, judgments, and punitive actions to enemies who threaten us. The psalms provide us with many attributes or traits of Father God such as generous, just, persistent, faithful, compassionate, truthful, and most of all, loving and forgiving, causing His children to feel safe.

Psychologists have also identified traits we also associate with our parents or parental figures that may also be found in God the Father. These traits are self-assuredness and security, resourcefulness, assertiveness, a controlled exacting power, social precision, and self-discipline. All good traits are exhibited perfectly in God our Father, and our own parent figures may lack some or have some they may exhibit perfectly or imperfectly. Nevertheless, they are traits of an ideal father.

One of the traits of our parents that can diminish or harm us is our inner critic. Breaking God's law, it can punish us for thinking, acting, and feeling imperfect and so being imperfect. Our judgmental parent can be extreme, making severe negative judgments about ourselves and becoming a tyrant within us.

→ Have you ever considered similarities between your parents' traits and those of God the Father? Or between God the Father and your parents?

The essence of the Franciscan movement began when Saint Francis of Assisi experienced the Fatherhood of God. Francis rejected the inheritance and wealth of his biological father when he said, "Now I have no father except God, my Father in heaven." In short, he was ridding himself of all the earthly security his father could provide, trusting completely in God the Father. Embracing poverty, he relied completely on the mercy of God the Father; however, he was aware he did not deserve it.

God the Son

The God who is Jesus loves, respects, and admires God, His Father, as any child does when the biological father is good. Maybe even when the father is not so good! As a good Son, Jesus complies with His Father's rules and wishes graciously and without delay because of the respect and admiration for Him. This love of His Father has the Son sacrifice for us. His sacrifice was not only for us but because it was the wish of His Father. As Jesus said, *And*

I lay down my life for the sheep. For this reason, the Father loves me because I lay down my life.[3] On the night before His death, He said to His Father on the Mount of Olives *not my will but yours be done.*[4] *The sacrifice of His life is the supreme and perfect act of love for the Father inside Him and for us!*

Within many of us is a child who may do the same, obey our parents' wishes because we love them. Others may have a child within who rebels against their rules and does not obey them or obeys them grudgingly or with procrastination. Jesus seeks power and counsel from His Father within so He can provide service to others. Our child within us may seek power and counsel from our parent figures so we can provide service to others like Jesus. Others may seek materialistic wealth and power from their parents for personal enhancement.

- → How many children expect money and property when their parents die and feel cheated when they do not leave them any? They expect an inheritance, and if they don't get it, they are bitterly disappointed. Are you one of them?
- → How many children are bitter because they think their parents were not fair in the distribution of their wealth among family members? They fail to realize their parents, with the help of God, have given them the greatest possible gift of all, *life!* Are you one of them?

Children are curious and creative creatures. Older children can improve human relationships by educating people. Psychologists call these child traits within us our little professors. As the Son of God the Father, Jesus is a creative radical who taught groups of people in parables. The child within us can do the same, especially with our own children. In addition, psychologists list traits such as adventurous, sensitivity or tender-mindedness, imagination and concern with social good works in describing the child in all of us. These are similar traits you would find in the Son of God.

→ Can you think of a time you sacrificed for your parents' wishes? We are not talking about rules but wishes.
→ Were you content and at peace? Or did you experience regret and dissatisfaction?
→ Can you think of a time you rebelled against what your parents did or said or wanted? At the time, how did you feel? How do you feel now when you think about it?
→ Can you think of anything you did as a child that your parents wanted, and you still do it here and now?

Jesus could have been a son or daughter to Father God. It has nothing to do with gender. Jesus was born male by virtue of the conditions and position of women in the culture and society in which he was born. Jesus was born male so he could fulfill His mission in His society. Under different circumstances within a different society or culture, the Son, Jesus, could have been a daughter!

God the Holy Spirit

The Holy Spirit is similar to the "adult" the psychologist says is within us. In the Bible, the Holy spirit could be thought of as being wisdom in the Old Testament. This is one interpretation of wisdom. We think of the female gender pertaining to wisdom because in the Bible, wisdom is referred to as "She" or "Her!" Since God is both male and female from now on, we will use the pronouns He or Him and She or Her when referring to God. Of course, you will realize when we use the words *He* or *Him*, we may be referring to God the Father or Son, and when we use the words *She* or *Her*, we may be referring to wisdom or the Holy Spirit!

Incidentally, since God is male and female, and since the Holy family of Father, Son, and Holy Spirit is within one God, we have a family within us! The adult in us is female as wisdom is within God. The adult female within each of us helps us survive by gathering and processing information This information is acquired by revelation from God found in the Bible, parental authority figures, and from experiences in our lives.

Our adult can be thought of as an analyst who judges or analyzes. This is a valuable role for the adult that thinks. With an awareness of our flaws and with an understanding of the consequences of such flaws, we can acquire the determination or perseverance to correct them. Psychologists use traits such as persevering, mental capacity, and analytical and free thinking to describe the adult within us. They are all traits of the Holy Spirit. In short, the Holy Spirit is like a counselor who helps us, one-on-one, to make the right decisions and do the right thing.

→ Have you ever been in a situation where you felt anger, injustice, and you wanted to strike out, but you put aside your feelings and acted reasonably? This was probably your adult intervening with the help of the Holy Spirit.

Of course, all the positive traits or attributes of God our Father, Son, or Holy Spirit recorded in the Bible and by psychologists are found in all three persons of the Blessed Trinity. It is all a matter of focus, which is what we choose to emphasize or view God as being. *Father God is viewed as the Creator and giver of life and the law; His Son is viewed as the Savior and creative activist who fulfills the law and teaches it; the Holy Spirit is the divine person who is the wise counselor helping us interpret and implement the law and live the life of Christ upon His resurrection and departure from earth.*

Another Look at the Trinity

It may very well be that every man and woman has the same traits and attitudes, and either one can fulfill any role. Their only difference is physical! It would seem our God is gender neutral and may be a combination of male and female as psychologists interpret us to be. We can account for the three separate persons within the one God without any reference to their gender. It may be a matter of focusing upon specific traits or attitudes, which were just mentioned. One person in the blessed Trinity may have a greater focus on some particular traits than others and by their actions fulfill some role. For example, Jesus focused on the trait of obedience to the person who begot Him and fulfilled the role of teacher, healer, and creative activist here on earth. On earth, the role of a person is often determined by environmental and circumstantial conditions.

A psychologist, Martin Buber, developed an ideology of personality consisting of I, Thou, and We. Buber's theory of personality like Eric Berne's theory of Parent-Child-Adult is derived from created human reality and common sense and not from divine revelation found in the Bible and from prophets. The Thou (Son) is begotten not made from the I (Father), and the We (Holy Spirit) proceeds from the "I" and Thou.

The Trinity is a mystery we will never completely understand. If we could, we might suspect it was conceived by a human being and did not come from God's revelation. We move from divine revelation to philosophical and psychological interpretation of this mystery using reality and human experiences. It must always start with our faith in the truth of the Trinity revealed in the Bible and not with our psychological or philosophical interpretation of reality.

Living and Nonliving Existence

Since we are created in the image of God, our identities are similar. Both God and His creation, human beings, refer to themselves as "I am," which represents all that they are. Like God, we are living beings with energy that generates mental and physical behaviors moment to moment. Like God, our living existence is similar to Hers in some ways and different in others. Like other living and nonliving beings, we are similar in our togetherness but quite different in many other ways. How are we similar and different from God and other living and nonliving beings?

Similarities and Differences

- All living people, animals, and plants are different from nonliving beings, such as gases like oxygen, liquid like water, and minerals like rocks. Like God, living beings can use energy to move themselves both mentally and physically; nonliving beings can't. As living beings, we use living and nonliving beings such as oxygen, water, and minerals to generate energy to move; nonliving beings do not, and God does not. God is the infinite energy of life. We are created reflections of His energy and must generate energy from living and nonliving beings. We breathe air, drink water, and eat plants and animals to generate energy.

- We are interdependent on living and nonliving beings as well as being totally dependent upon God for our existence. God is not dependent on any of His creations. Within God, the Father, Son, and Holy Spirit are interdependent on each other.
- All living beings with the help of God can reproduce their own species; nonliving beings cannot. God shares with us His ability to create. On the other hand, God would not create Himself; there would be no point to it!
- All living beings use the energy of life to grow; nonliving beings don't, and God doesn't because She is infinite.
- All living beings physically evolve and change, adjusting themselves to a changing environment. Nonliving beings do not evolve or change themselves but can change physically or chemically if acted upon by outside forces. God does not evolve or change. She is always present and constant. Of course, when the Son of God became man through the incarnation, He assumed all of the characteristics of human beings being fully human while at the same time being God!

Like our living God, people have a mental awareness of their existence. Plants have a primitive or dark sort of awareness while animals have a much greater awareness of existence than plants. An animal, however, is not self-aware and cannot think in the way people can. People are self-aware, which means they can see themselves, thinking, feeling, and behaving. We know, we exist, and we are aware that someday, this existence will end.

Since we are aware of our existence and that existence is good, we can proclaim to all humanity as God proclaimed to Moses, "I am." The question now is what in us is aware of the thoughts, feelings. and behaviors of our existence and ourselves? It is our consciousness. I am conscious of myself and that "I am." This conscious awareness of myself is similar to God.

It is our consciousness and intelligence that comprises our intellect. It is our intelligence that causes us to rationally think. Our intellect generates new ideas by thinking and uses them in creating new beings in new relationships. God gave us this gift of our intellect, which contains the awareness that produces understanding and the ability to act upon this understanding with a purpose. This intellect is infused within our animal bodies and makes us a little less than Herself. So in seeking our identity, we can summarize at least part of it in the following manner. We are:

- Beings in a material body consisting of energy expressed as *living existence;*

- Beings who can use the energy of life to move, reproduce ourselves, grow, and physically change and evolve adjusting to our environment;
- Interdependent on living and nonliving beings for our existence as well as being totally dependent on God.
- Made in God's image with a trinitarian nature;
- Beings with an intellect with traits or habitual tendencies organized into systems that create distinctive patterns of thoughts, feelings, and behaviors. This can help us adjust to our environment and survive;

The Essence of Existence

Since our identity is living existence, the question arises: What is existence? Put another way, what is the essence of our existence? Essence is what makes a being that exists unique and different from all other types of beings and different from nothing. We have demonstrated how human beings differ from nonliving beings, and yet, both still exist. What is the essence of existence in both living and nonliving beings? Scientific investigation has answered this question. ***The essence of existence is moving energy forms that must be united by forces that establish a relationship with each other to create a being that exists.***

Energy forms can be thought of as either a solid particle or as a wave of energy moving as a unit. These forms make up the atom, the smallest entity in existence. Within the atom, the energy forms, called electrons, circle a center consisting of forms such as protons and neutrons. Energy such as electromagnetic, gravitational and centrifugal forces hold the electrons to the nucleus. A nuclear force holds the forms inside the nucleus together and are extremely strong. These energy forces hold the energy forms together.

Within existence, energy forces and energy forms or matter are the same energy, only different in appearance. Energy cannot be created nor destroyed by any natural force of science. *Energy can only be transformed* by natural forces from one appearance of energy to another. Only God can supernaturally create energy from nothing or completely destroy energy to nothing

Distance Within the Atom

The space the atom occupies is miniscule. So small, in fact, it cannot be seen by our most powerful microscope. Yet, within this infinitesimally small space, the distance between the energy forms of the atom are vast. If we could increase an atom to the size of the earth, the electrons circling the center would be proportionally the size of cherries! The neutrons, protons, and other particles that make up the center nucleus would be the size of a house! A vast sea of empty space fills in the rest of the atom! The atom is like a miniature solar system with the electrons representing planets and the center nucleus the sun. Like a solar system, most of the atom is a vast sea of empty space.

Atoms and Humanity

How do we relate this atomic existence to our living existence? All people are made up of atoms that form molecules that make up cells. Cells form tissues that combine to make up organs. Organs unite into systems such as the nervous, circulatory, or skeletal systems that operate together, establishing our existence. We consist of almost an infinite number of atoms or solar systems in the universe we call man or woman! Since an atom is a vast sea of empty space or almost nothing, and we consist of a universe of atoms, how do we account for the huge solid energy form our existence appears to be? There are two reasons we appear to be a solid mass, which we are not. First, there are trillions of atoms in the universe we call our body. Second, the extremely miniature electrons travel at tremendous speed (almost 186,000 miles per second) in an infinitely small space, so they appear to be everywhere at the same time! This is why much of existence appears to be a solid mass, but isn't!

There is no existence without relationships between energy forms, and there is no relationship without the energy forces that relate the energy forms, thus creating atoms that occupy a specific space. This process is true at all levels of existence! It is true at the subatomic level with forces used to draw electrons inward, uniting with the nucleus to create an atom. It is also true at the molecular level when forces push an atom outward to unite with other atoms to create a new existence called a molecule. What is true at the atomic and molecular levels is also true at the human level with the energy forces of two people pushing outward to find each other. They unite in a marriage relationship, forming a new existence, a family. At the same time, these two people have some of their energy turned inward to maintain their individual existence within the family unit.

Two Kinds of Energy

We see here and now that there are different kinds of energy forces at work. One force unites inwardly, maintaining our existence as separate beings. It's called *individualization.* Another force has energy pushing atoms outward, uniting with other atoms, creating molecules that are a new, more complex beings. It's called *socialization.* In both cases, we have energy forces that create relationships that unite. There is a force at all levels of being directed "inward," creating relationships that unite atoms, molecules, cells, tissues, organs, systems and, finally, human beings holding us together, forming our own separate existence. There is also a force at all levels of being directed "outward" that seeks out other beings and unites with them while still maintaining their own individual existence. This happens with atoms uniting to form molecules and at more complex existences right up to men and women uniting to create teams for different purposes such as athletics, work, friendships, and families.

So these principles of energy are used to explain all levels of existence from the simplest to the most complex.

What could produce such a beautiful, well-organized, and designed system that applies at all levels of existence?

→ Do you think the same principles that happen at all levels of existence occurred by chance?

or

→ Do you think a creative super mind designed and created the energy forms united by energy forces at all levels of existence from the atom to humanity? The possibility of this happening by chance or statistical probability is infinitely small if not impossible!

The Bible provides a good example of these energies in one case directed outward and, in another case, inward. It is found in the story of Martha and Mary.[1] Martha directs her energy outward, doing the cooking and serving. Mary directs her energy inward, sitting at the feet of Jesus, listening to Him speak.

For Christians, the contemplative life of listening precedes and motivates the doing of corporal works of mercy. Jesus stated that Mary had chosen the better part, and it would not be taken from her. What does this mean? Perhaps Jesus is telling us our active life in this world ends at death because in heaven, all our needs and desires will be satisfied. There will be no need for corporal works of mercy!

On the other hand, our contemplative prayer life, which begins here and now on earth, continues in heaven to a much greater clarity and intensity. This is because here on earth, we see God in shadowy form, but in heaven, we will see our Lord face-to-face. *Communication with God through prayer is the one thing we do on earth that we will continue to do in heaven.* Perhaps this is why what Mary chose to do was the better part.

There are times when people must be alone, focusing their energy forces inward, engaged in solitary activities such as prayer or reading. There are other times when the forces are focused outward to socialize and unite with other human beings. Without these two energy forces maintaining and sustaining our existence, we could not survive as individuals. *Life is a balance between these two energy forces.* Sometimes it's a challenge and struggle trying to maintain this balance and reduce tension.

- → Do you focus on individualization, preferring to keep to yourself and engaged more often in solitary pursuits? If so, some people would call you an introvert.
- → Do you focus upon socialization, preferring to be with others, interacting and uniting with them in activities? If so, some people would call you an extrovert.
- → Or are you able to maintain a satisfying balance, reducing the tension between withdrawing and exploring as needed?

Creativity

Having been made in His image, creativity is at the heart of existence, and God who creates existence has placed within us this wonderful gift of creativity. God's creative energy can be seen in all His creation. It can also be seen in the words and works of His incarnate Son, Jesus Christ, as revealed in Holy Scripture. Like God, our intellect uses mental energy to create new ideas, relating and uniting these ideas, attaching them to feelings, which the will uses to produce behaviors. Behaviors in turn create new and interesting forms of existence that reflect these ideas.

With new ideas, people created the airplane, a house, and a shovel. We can also create a baseball team, work gang, church, friendship, and family. Every day, we can create new and different experiences, artwork, as well as activities and products that enhance our existence. Most of all, people with the help of God create and raise their own children, which requires creative actions. It's easy to destroy creative work and hard to produce it. It is easier to kill than to create and maintain life.

We can now add to our understanding of our identity. We already know we are energy expressed in rational living existence created by God. We know we are beings with an intellect consisting of intelligence that thinks and a conscious awareness of ourselves as living existence. This intellect can produce ideas, which are used in the creation of new beings. We now know our identity also includes the following:

- Our existence is moving energy forms in relationships held together by energy forces.
- Our energy forces are directed "inward," holding our energy forms together, maintaining our separate individual existence. Without our energy forms held together by energy forces, there would be no existence.
- We want to maintain our own awareness of ourselves as separate thinking, feeling, and acting individuals. At the same time, we have energy forces directed "outward" because we also want to unite with other people establishing a new and different kind of existence. This is the creative component to our nature. We can satisfy both desires by balancing the energy forces.
- We are able to use our intellect to generate ideas from which we can create new beings;

Process of Existence

As we've seen, the energy forces of life are directed in two directions: "inward" to hold a being together as individuals, and "outward" uniting beings together. As we know, this happens at all levels of existence! Science has explained how these energy forces accomplish this union at subatomic and atomic levels.

Individualization

At the subatomic level, an electromagnetic energy force is directed "inward," causing the electrons to circle the center nucleus, holding the atom together in a union that maintains its own individuality. The electrons have a negative electrical charge while the protons in the nucleus have a positive electrical charge. Since opposites attract, the negative electrons are pulled inward toward the center or nucleus with the positive protons by electromagnetic forces. The electrical charges within the atom are balanced since the number of electrons equal the number of protons. This balance of electrically charged electrons and protons along with centrifugal and gravitational forces keep the electrons circling the protons in the nucleus at a fixed distance. The integrity of the individual atom is maintained. This is the mechanism of individualization.

As we know, this process of individualization happens at all levels of existence, including the human level of being. At times, we want to be alone, engaged in solitary activities. We pray, read, watch television alone, and play solitary video games. We focus our thought inward with our energy used to meditate upon questions concerning our identity, purpose, and destination. We search for answers because the answers give meaning and direction to the energy of individualization and socialization. The focus of energy on the answers holds us together psychologically and spiritually. This is just like the electromagnetic centrifugal and gravitational forces that hold the electrons and protons together to make an atom.

When we do not know the answers, we are afraid and rush in all directions because we don't know who we are and where we are going. It is at this time that our inner self, our "I," is collapsing. When we cannot find our meaning for living and what sense there is in all this existence, we experience within ourselves feelings of despair, cynicism, and depression. This is why if we cannot find the true answers, we create false answers, but often, we will find they do not sustain us in the face of adversity and death.

Without a true understanding of who we are, why we're here, and where we're going, we sometimes face what we perceive to be irreconcilable and insurmountable problems that can lead to suicide. We turn to death because we do not see any other way to solve our problems. It all seems meaningless and hopeless. Suicides do not see that even if they cannot solve some of their problems, they could live with any problem if they understood and believed in the true answers to our three basic questions.

Socialization

Even when the force is directed "inward" and we think we're alone, it is necessary to have a relationship with God through prayer and meditation. To focus this energy force exclusively on one's self without any meaningful relationships with others is not the proper use of it and results in problems living as we were meant to live. *We are social beings by nature, and so much of our energy must be directed "outward," uniting with others physically, socially, psychologically, and spiritually if we are to grow and survive as human beings*. Psychological research demonstrates social contact is essential to intellectual growth. As we know, the way we use the energy of life individually or collectively requires balance.

→ Do you think people, especially our youth, are focusing too much of their time on individualization by their use of the computer to play games?
→ Do you think this could produce an imbalance of energies that could be to their detriment?

Mechanism of Socialization at the Atomic Level

How does the energy of existence establish this union or connection between beings whether they are living or nonliving? Science has answered this question as well. *An atom unites with another atom by giving part of itself, an electron, to another atom who receives it.* This is called Ionic Bonding. This causes an electrical imbalance creating a force of attraction uniting the atoms so they become molecules.

Why is there an electrical imbalance in forces? This is because some atoms give and therefore lose negatively charged electrons, and other atoms receive and, therefore, gain negatively charged electrons. This loss and gain results in the loss of an equal number of negatively charged electrons and positive protons within each atom, causing an electrical imbalance. One atom becomes more positive with the loss of a negatively charged electron and the other becoming more negative with the gain of a negatively charged electron.

This electrical imbalance between two atoms results in their attraction and union. A sodium atom gives one of its electrons to a chlorine atom who receives it, and bonding together, they become sodium chloride or a salt molecule. Some properties of salt molecules are different from sodium and chlorine atoms. If being positive is better than being negative, then as the Bible says, it is better to give than receive! What do you think?

Atoms can also unite by sharing a part of themselves, their electrons with other atoms. This is called Covalent Bonding.

Two hydrogen atoms can each share a part of themselves, their electrons, with an oxygen atom who receives by sharing them and becoming a molecule of water. In both cases, the molecules of salt and water are different forms of existence from the original atoms that went into making them. Their physical properties such as color, odor, taste, and density differ from the original atoms. Since only a small part of an atom is given or shared with another atom, they maintain the essence of their identities within the union.

To demonstrate this more clearly, if we separate the salt and water molecules back to the atoms used to constitute them, they return to their original state with their own identifying properties. This indicates the atoms of sodium, chlorine, hydrogen, and oxygen are not assimilated, completely losing themselves in their union to make salt and water. This explains how atoms can unite to form a new existence, yet each atom within the union keeps its own individual existence. Existence, whether its individualization or socialization, involves forces that unite energy forms. *Our individualization coexists with socialization! This is how we can unite with another person or group of people and still maintain the essence of our identity or who we are.*

Ionic Bonding (Giving and Receiving Electrons)

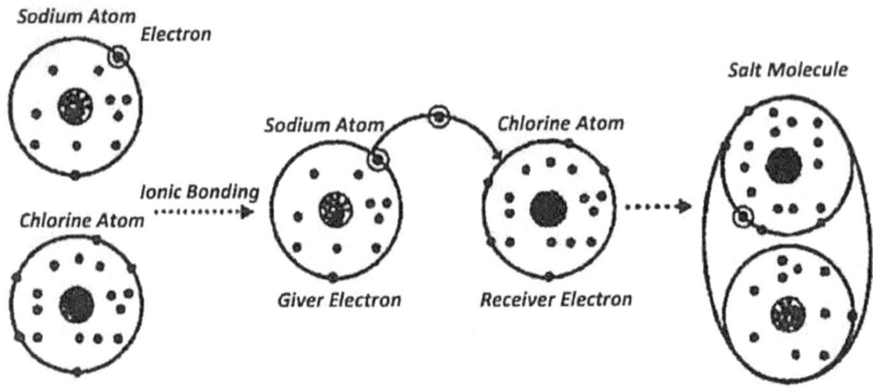

Covalent Bonding (Sharing Electrons)

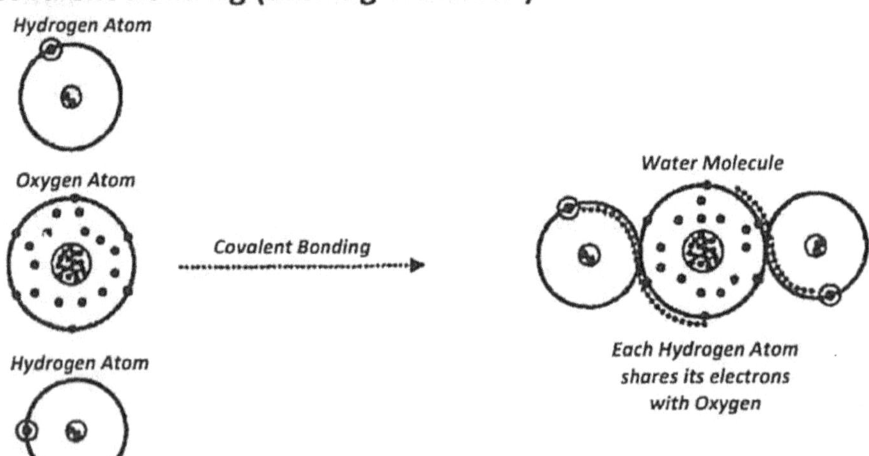

Mechanism of Socialization Between People

The acts of giving, sharing, receiving, and accepting to establish a union of new existence occurs at the atomic and molecular levels, right up through the most complex of organisms, human beings. This is the process of existence. *In socializing, people unite with others by directing their energy outward in the acts of giving and sharing while others accept their generosity.* At lower levels of existence, it is not a matter of willingly accepting, giving, or sharing. Giving, sharing, and accepting implies choice with an ability to reject. With lower forms of existence, it's a matter of acting without choice. Animals at lower levels of existence do not have the intellect nor the free will found in people, so they cannot choose. They receive, give, sharing or rejecting instinctively, responding to physical drives, but do not freely give, share, receive, or reject.

We can use our voices to give a compliment and can use any of our material possessions as a gift. We can also use our time and talents as gifts. All our gifts must be received and accepted by another if there is to be a union or connection. We can give an idea to another person. The people we give it to must accept it. By this, we mean that inside their intellect, they must open their minds by pushing their ideas to one side and making room for the idea from the giver.

We can also unite with others by sharing any of our activities, our goals in life, enjoying the joys of living together, sharing and giving everything we possess with each other, including ourselves. This is why generosity is an essential ingredient in Christianity. Isn't it interesting that the process of existence is similar at all levels of existence?

→ Do you realize that in giving or sharing a part of yourself or receiving from others, is really uniting with them? The union can be physical, psychological, or spiritual.

→ Do you think this similar process that happens at all levels of existence happens by chance? Or was it created by God?

7

The Control of Energy

Types of Energy

Between people, there are energy forces of an erotic nature and forces associated with all kinds of desires. There are forces of a creative and spiritual nature. They are all different aspects of one and the same energy. Our energy within must push us "outward" to socialize with people by uniting or connecting with them so we can grow and survive.

Balance of Energies

Too much socialization can be detrimental to our well-being. There are those who perform for a crowd or audience and are very concerned with being accepted by all the people who watch them. They spill out their energies and burn themselves out, trying to please everyone. There are people, especially some teenagers, who want so much to be accepted by a group that they focus most of their energy "outward" to achieve it. It can be an illusion that can never be achieved because very few of us, if any, will be liked and accepted by everyone.

As we have seen, life is a balance between the forces, inward and outward. Both are necessary. Too much of one, however to the neglect of the other can result in dire consequences. Jesus balanced these energies in His life. There were times when He withdrew from people to be alone to commune with His Father. At other times, He was engaged in His social ministry, going amongst the people, feeding, healing, instructing, and forgiving the sins of His flock. Mankind must do the same, but it's not easy. People search for balance, which is determined by how we use our energy to exist.

God does not create nor give us life by using energy from His existence like sodium giving a part of itself, its electron to a chlorine atom to create a salt molecule. Nor does God share His energy with us. Instead, He gives us the energy to exist by creating it out of nothing! When you think about it, all our energy is really His. With His gift of creation, we exist whether we like it or not.

Once we exist, we decide whether we use His energy appropriately or not. *Our spirituality or kind of relationship we have with God is determined by how we use the energy.* Receiving this energy, we can establish a relationship if we so choose. It is amazing that the union of energy forms is similar at all levels of existence! It would seem all existence created by God to some degree resembles His image. We are, however, the closest resemblance because we are aware and have some control over the energy of life so we have a special relationship with the Creator. We were made a little less than God.

The energy from God emanates from our natural sensory drives, such as erotic energy. These inborn drivers are called instincts. Energy can also emanate from passionate rational desires for sex, survival, power, fame, fortune along with a passion for creativity and spirituality. As stated earlier, different types of energy are really different expressions of one and the same energy created by one eternal God and patterned after His own energy. These forces are powerful, can be unfriendly, and are capable of taking over and having us display all kinds of constructive or destructive behaviors. *The question is, how can we discipline ourselves to contain and control this energy, enabling us to access and constructively use God's gift to us?* To effectively control the energy is a great challenge facing all people. Can we effectively use it to influence our final destiny?

→ How do you control your instinctual or passionate energy forces?
→ Can you recall times when these forces were constructive? Destructive?

The problem is many people think they can control these energy forces all by themselves; they can't! Often, teenagers think they can control their sexual passions, which involve raging hormones within them. They are naïve. Unfortunately, many today do not try to control them, so fornication and sex as an extension of dating is commonplace. Sex without solemn commitment too often leads to unwanted pregnancies and abortion. As long as we have casual sex, abortion is inevitable!

It is impossible to control our passions without strong convictions, without prayer, without God and without the taboos of society that were prevalent years ago but are now gone. There was a time if a girl became pregnant out of wedlock, the taboos of society would consider it a disgrace. If possible, she would leave the community to have her baby if she could not get married. She would feel guilt and, even worse, shame, but no more! There was a time young girls and boys were taught by their parents that there was to be no sex without marriage. To do so would bring displeasure and sorrow to the family, to themselves and to God because sex outside of marriage is sinful. Nowadays, this is seldom the case. For many who don't want the baby, society encourages them to have an abortion. It appears killing an unborn child is an acceptable form of birth control for many people!

This energy cannot be controlled without beliefs and virtues that must be lived with the support of Christian families and friends. In addition, we need and will always have the support of God if we sincerely ask for it. Unfortunately, the fruits of naivete can be seen in the promiscuous society of today. It is seen in our violent culture, pornography, the large number of divorces and unwed mothers raising children without fathers resulting in the destruction of the family. It can also be seen in the large increase in fornication, adultery that leads to the greatest evil of all time, abortion. This resulted in the slaughter of more than sixty million unborn innocent children in our country to date and counting.

Faculties of Our Identity

Our identity has two essential faculties, an intellect and free will. They are found in the "I" when we profess our existence, "I am."

Intellect

An investigation into our mental life reveals something about our true identity. As mentioned earlier, **the mind has an intellect with two parts, intelligence and consciousness**. Let's investigate them now in greater detail.

The intelligence of our intellect thinks, and our consciousness is aware of our thinking. Thinking or intelligence is a process of reasoning using logic, analysis (breaking apart), synthesis (putting together), comparison, judgments, and conclusions. There are lower forms of thinking, which people and some animals can use such as association, conditioning, trial and error, and imitation.

Since consciousness sees or is aware of thinking, it must be separate from thinking! In addition, with consciousness, we can remove ourselves from our bodies and watch our bodies moving and talking, just like our ability to watch ourselves thinking. It's like having a third eye to see with. If we can watch our bodies moving and thinking; our consciousness must be separate not only from intelligent thinking but also from our bodies! In short, there is a conscious self, separate from our thinking and our bodies, which exists, and functions differently, yet is housed within our intellect and physical body.

→ Have you ever observed yourself thinking? If so, what was observing?
→ Have you ever had an out of body experience, observing your body acting? If not, why not give it a try?
→ Have you ever said to yourself, "I like myself"? Who is the "I ?" Is it separate from myself?

Both intelligence and consciousness acquire knowledge of our identity. We experience the difference between them by seeing how they function differently to acquire knowledge we use to exist.

Intelligence

We have seen that intelligence acquires knowledge with the process of thinking, such as reasoning. What this thinking process does is relate ideas acquired from images received from our senses and stored in our memory. In logic, we compare these ideas for similarities and differences to arrive at conclusions and judgments. In judging, we compare the observation of our ideas with a standard. If our idea is consistent with the standard, then it is right or correct. If not, then our idea is wrong. *Since reality is the standard, then when our idea is consistent with reality, we have truth, and it is right and good.*

In conditioning, we learn to associate certain rewards with specific behaviors. When the behaviors are exhibited, we acquire the rewards. Certain behaviors always acquire the desirable ends or rewards we seek, so they are repeated and can become conditioned habits. We acquire habits by learning to associate. As we know, habits are like Allport's traits. Some people think we are born with traits that perhaps can be enhanced with learning. Others think we learn the traits of child, parent, and adult personalities. What do you think? Certainly, God does not learn. She has no potential; She is complete actualization!

For many of us, it is seldom a matter of using the higher processes of rational thinking. Instead, we often use the lower forms of thinking such as conditioning or habitual thinking, and often, we imitate or use the ideas parent figures place in our memory! They are used as solutions to problems that crop up in our daily lives.

An example of using ideas placed in us by parental figures would be as follows: a girl is asked to spend a night with a gentleman friend. She immediately remembers the words of her mother: "Good girls don't sleep with a man unless there is a sacred commitment like marriage in which both parties promise to be faithful and live together until death." So she rejects his offer.

On the other hand, making this decision with a higher form of rational thinking would go something like this; I want desperately to get married and have a family of my own. I like this guy and think he would be a good husband and father. If we sleep together, this may make our union in love and friendship a lot stronger. It may lead to marriage or a child. With a child, he may decide to marry me. Besides, we both want to know, or at least I do, if we are sexually compatible. If we are not and got married, it would probably lead to divorce. The only way to find out for sure is to sleep together. So she sleeps with him.

As one can see, she established a positive list of arguments for having premarital sex. As we also see, she didn't list any negative arguments such as the poor reaction she might get from parents and friends. The fact is, if she has a child out of wedlock, she may have to support that child, which may alter her future plans. The fact that it may be harder to find a nice guy to marry with a child, not to mention that it is not consistent with her religious beliefs. In such cases, considering both positive and negative arguments of an act is essential in making an informed decision or judgment.

Of course, sexual frustration can also play a role in the decision. She may want a child regardless of marriage, thinking this will be her family. It will be a damaged family because some believe every child needs a father and mother, and without both, the child will suffer. Others believe a grandfather, an uncle, a big brother, or even a faithful boyfriend can take the place of a father in what may be called an extended family. Of course, there may be young girls who do not have a good extended family and try to raise their children alone with little support. This can be a real problem.

She could also use her religious beliefs and her higher order thinking skill of logic to reject his offer of sex in the following manner:

> People who love God obey His laws because God makes laws to help us.
> Fornication is a sin against God's law.
> Since I love God, I will not sin, so I must reject this guy's offer.

Consciousness

Consciousness acquires knowledge that deals with situations in life by awareness and doing. *With consciousness, we know by seeing and doing, not thinking!* The seeing is the doing. For example, if we are lying on the ground and see a tree falling upon us, we move. We do not think to ourselves, should we move or stay? We do not ask what the arguments are for and against moving. We simply see and move. Athletes within a game such as basketball do not have time to reason or think but only spontaneously see and act. They are consciously acting or reacting to situations in the game.

In his book, *Proof of Heaven*, Eben Alexander MD establishes beyond any doubt he was brain dead. Yet, he was still aware of himself and what he was experiencing! He describes his after-death experiences by consciously knowing in this way, "To see is to know, thoughts entered me directly, immediately with instant understanding and with consciousness; there is no distinction between experiencing something and understanding."

Dr. Alexander refers to consciousness as an entity or being which makes us human beings; however, it can also be thought of as a process of knowing within the entity we call a human being. It is the entity with this process of knowing that survives after death. If the process survives, then perhaps the process is the entity. Or if this process of knowing survives, so does our entity or true being that possesses it. For human beings, consciousness can be considered an upper level of mental life by which we are aware and enables us to be conscious of ourselves.

→ Have you ever been involved in a situation where you directly or immediately saw what had to be done and did it? You did not think or go back into memory for a solution. Conscious knowing happens many times in your life. Now you are aware of it.

Being self-conscious, we are aware of our mortality. It is often self-consciousness that uses the energy of life for socialization and individualization.

Comparing Intelligence and Consciousness with Respect to Change

Consciousness and intelligence both involve our knowing, but we now see that consciousness is a different way of knowing than the intelligence of thinking. Another difference between intelligence and consciousness involves the ability to change. We can measure intelligence with written tests such as intelligence and achievement tests. The social science of psychometrics deals with the intelligence aspects of the mind and can measure it because intelligence can grow and change. It can be investigated by the mathematics of statistics. We learn with intelligence.

On the other hand, consciousness does not change or grow in this life. It can never be investigated by social science and its handmaiden mathematics because it is within us, and *we are only consciously aware of ourselves by subjective internal experiences. It is that part of us that never changes.*

Changes Upon Death

Consciousness is that part of us that we are most afraid of losing at death. Aren't we most afraid of losing our awareness of who we are and entering the dark oblivion of nothingness? The great Greek philosopher, Socrates, when faced with this problem, said he would not be afraid! Before taking the poison hemlock that killed him, he maintained it made little difference if life continued after death or he entered the dark oblivion of nothingness. If the latter be the case, he would not know it. How do you feel about it?

→ Don't you want to go on after this life? Are you afraid you will not? Does faith play a role?

Comparing Intelligence and Consciousness with Respect to Memory

Another difference between the two is memory. Consciousness does not need nor use memory. When we consciously know by clearly seeing directly and acting immediately, we do not retreat into memory for prior ideas to use. When we see with consciousness, there is a clarity in seeing reality or what is. With consciousness, there is no choice, no thinking, and no conflict. On the contrary, thinking is needed when we don't see clearly with our consciousness and struggle in conflict for a solution. Unable to find answers in ideas stored in our memory or habitual thinking, we turn to higher order thinking skills, such as logic or reason to make a choice if we know how. Here and now on earth, however, many of us use our consciousness or lower order thinking rather than higher order rational thinking.

→ How many of your behaviors do you think are free? And how many are from conditioned thoughts, habits, and ideas stored in memory?

The following is an example of a boy making a decision that he regrets. A young man who is a senior in high school wants very much upon graduation to enter the military and fly jets. His parents and girlfriend want him to enter the family business because his parents are getting old, and he is the only child. He loves his parents and would like to help them out, but he dislikes business, and his dream is to fly. It is an extremely successful business that can provide him with the great lifestyle he has grown accustomed to.

What should he do? He doesn't use higher order thinking skills, habitual thinking is not helpful, and he rejects parental advice because this decision involves his life. He must choose because he does not consciously see a solution. *With choice, there is always conflict.* The young man finally decides to enter his father's business. At first, there is relief because the anxiety he experienced prior to the decision is gone. Several years pass, and he regrets. Whenever a forced choice is made, the mind often plays the game "What if." "What if I selected the military, followed my dream, and failed to get my wings? What if I joined the military and did get my wings?"

We will find that if we do regret, it usually indicates a forced choice that is wrong because of the conflict within us. It results from the two options and our struggle to choose one. As a poet once wrote, "The saddest word of tongue or pen, no sadder than these it might have been." He might have been a flyer, but his choice was forced, and it was the wrong choice.

→ Do you think the creator needs to use intelligent thinking to acquire knowledge?

We must always remember God's intellect is perfect and fully actualized. Our intellect is imperfect with a capacity limited by our human nature. Our intellect is constantly seeking truth and knowledge while God's consciousness sees infinite truth and knowledge. She sees and knows everything. She does not have to think or use reason as we do. She has it all instantly with Her perfect consciousness in the eternal present.

Our consciousness is imperfect but is created in the image of God's consciousness. As Dr. Alexander experienced in heaven, he did not have to think or use his memory. He knew with consciousness similar to the way God knows.

→ Have you ever had to make a choice in which there was conflict and struggle? It is always an important choice, such as getting an education, a job, or a spouse.

→ How did you make the choice? Did you use higher order thinking skills or some idea placed in your memory by parent figures? Perhaps it was an idea from past experiences that was conditioned into you.

→ How did you feel prior to the choice? After the choice?

→ As time passed, did you ever regret your choice? If so, it was a forced choice and it was probably wrong!

→ How did you come to believe in God? Was it a choice?

Memory and the Intellect

To think efficiently and effectively, our intelligence requires a good memory. A good memory recalls relevant facts and prior solutions used in similar situations in our past; when we think, we can use ideas of things in memory. We can analyze them along with ideas from present experiences. In analyses, we can break these ideas expressed in sentence form down into parts, comparing the parts, and then synthesizing or combining them in new and original ways to create things and solve problems. This is creative thinking, and it uses memory.

Tyranny of Memory

Memory is an important component of the intellect's thinking, but it can also be a serious problem. Within memory, we store conditioned responses and habits that we often live daily along with ideas placed in us by parents and authority figures. This can prevent us from creatively and spontaneously responding to the present situation.

There is also stored in our memory the images of people in our past as well as images of ourselves. Associated with these images may be good or bad feelings. We can think about people or actions of the past. Such thoughts can produce feelings such as sorrow and resentment or feelings of joy and happiness. An example would be a past betrayal we cannot forget or forgive.

Betrayal is the worse feeling to deal with. It haunts us not only with resentment but, even worse, with thoughts of injustice resulting in the feeling of being a victim. Without intervention of some kind involving understanding and compassion, it could terminate in aggressive behavior toward the betrayer. Injustice is the cause of many revolutions. *The answers to our three basic questions can provide us with an understanding of ourselves that enables us to deal with betrayal or, for that matter, any sin or injustice we experience!*

→ Have you ever experienced betrayal? How did you feel? What did you think or do?

These ideas and feelings prevent us from being in the present. The present is reality; nothing real exists in memory. When we look through images of the past to see someone, we will never see them as they are in the present moment. What we now see of them may be similar to past images, but they are different. One thing is certain: We all change with time and experiences.

Tyranny of Comparing

The ability to compare is needed to think, but it too can be used to prevent us from fully experiencing the present moment. For example, we experience a sunset, and in thought, we compare it with a prior sunset we saw in Key West and is now stored in our memory. We lament that it is not as beautiful, and we long to go back to that prior sunset in Florida, remembering how we felt and what we did. In so doing, we are lost in thought and out of the present. In looking at the operation of our intelligence, we see that using our memory to compare can keep us from being in the here and now.

Memory and the Future

Our memory also contains thoughts of the future, which are not real. We want to know our future. In the future, we may want to be someone else or be somewhere else or have something else. We all dream or have dreamed about our future, what we will do, what we will be, and what we will have. We make plans of what we must do to achieve our dreams. This is good. We must know, however, that with these dreams can come fear; fear that our dreams will never come true or perhaps fear they will! Be careful. Fear can motivate us to act to fulfill our dreams; however, it can also have us commit terrible sins to achieve them, and even when we sin, our efforts are not always successful.

We must also know that if we dwell too much upon our dreams, we may resist or become confused or refuse to accept who we are, what we are here for, or what we have here and now. When we dwell too much upon our dreams, we remove ourselves from the present moment, which is the reality of who and where we are. *Memory can be one of the greatest tyrannies in our lives, preventing us from being who we truly are or enjoying what we have.*

→ What are or were your dreams? Did any of them come true?
→ How much time did you spend basking in memory, thinking about your dreams? Do you think it was helpful? Or did it keep you from truly experiencing the here and now?

My father would advise me saying, dream about the goals you will achieve in the future, make plans on how you will achieve them, work hard here and now to achieve them, and someday, your dreams will come true. I believed my father and did what he said, but in living my life, some of my dreams didn't come true! I dreamed, set my goal, planned, and worked hard, yet some of my dreams were not fulfilled. So I went to my father for answers, and his response was that perhaps my plan was wrong or maybe I didn't work hard enough.

As I thought about my father's advice, I realized it was good advice, but he left out one important warning. It was simple: you can dream, set goals, plan, and work hard and still not obtain your dreams! Why? Because in life, shit happens. Things such as sickness, disasters, or perhaps we don't have the mental or physical skills that may be needed. There can be a host of factors we have no control over, including luck!

We must be aware of the teachings of authority figures stored in our memory. We must examine them. This must be done because upon examination, we may find they are sinful and decide not to use them in our daily lives. The parent in our personality is the authority figure within us and is a composite of all the authority figures in our lives who influenced us.

→ Do you know what parental ideas or beliefs that come in the form of advice or judgments reside in your memory?
→ Are you aware of using them to solve problems in your life?
→ Can you think of one thing you do now that was taken from an authority figure's ideas, opinions, or beliefs?
→ Have you examined them to determine their veracity for you here and now?

Of course, *the greatest moral teacher of all time is Jesus Christ.* Have we examined His teachings? And can we interpret or explain why we believe them, other than the fact that the Son of God told us to do so? For many people, it is enough to read in Second John, "Everyone who does not abide in the teachings of Christ but goes beyond it, does not have God, whoever abides in the teachings have both the Father and the Son."[1] For those who believe Jesus is the Son of God, they will obey all of His teachings because He told them to do so, and for them, this is enough.

- → Do we, as Christians, know His moral teachings?
- → How many can we list?
- → Have we examined them, other than the fact that the Son of God told us to obey them? If we believe Jesus is the Son of God, then we must believe what He said is true and should be lived.

Free Will

The first faculty of our identity is the intellect. The second is free will.

→ Do you have free will?

Many people think they are physically and psychologically free. In general, freedom means the absence of any restrictions upon our actions. There are several types of restrictions. There are *physical restraints* upon our movement, for example, when a person is in prison. There are *moral restrictions,* which involve obeying the law. When we are morally free, there is a lack of moral restrictions or any obligation to obey the law. *Psychological restrictions* involve drives that force us to do certain things or not do them.

A dog, for example, is forced to eat in the presence of food when he is hungry. Not by any laws or moral obligations but because of the physical drives within him. The dog is not psychologically free, but a human being is! A person can refrain from eating when hungry, and a soldier can remain at their post in the face of danger and fear. We call psychological freedom "freedom of choice" because a person can choose from different courses of action.

Freedom is an attribute of the will whereby we can act or not act or we can act in this way or that way. Most of us would acknowledge the existence of freedom by our everyday personal experience. Freedom of the will is self-evident. Every act of self-control is an implicit manifestation of the free will. In experiencing such events, we are conscious of the fact that a tendency or trait in us can be held in check by a higher tendency. This higher tendency is the will.

Some psychologists, like B. F. Skinner, are deterministic, believing we do not have a free will. To these people, our behavior is the result of conditioned thoughts and habits or our biological drives with little or no say on our part! Common sense tells the person on the street we must have a free will because without law and the free will to obey the law, chaos would reign in our society. It is only a small group of intellectuals that accept determinism as true! Humanity for centuries has believed we are free, responsible for our actions, and in control of our destiny. If we are wrong in this belief, how can there be order in our world?

If there is not free will, there can be no justice as we know it. In most countries, the administration of justice is firmly based upon the belief in the freedom of human action. Before making a judgment, the judge and lawyers try to determine the degree of deliberation, and freedom in committing a crime. In most cases, the degree of freedom determines the degree of punishment. If a person was not free when committing a crime, they would not be punished. A case in point would be the criminally insane. If there is no free will, there is no responsibility, no virtue, no merit, no moral obligation, no duty, no morality, and most of all, no love!

Freedom

We've established the existence of the will. We here and now know any exhibit of self-control is an implicit manifestation of the will, but what about freedom? Is it only an absence of restraint? Or is there something more? We live, believing it exists, but what is freedom? For most people, freedom involves alternatives to choose from. The more alternatives to choose from, the freer we are. Choice appears to be implicit in our concept of freedom; but is it?

An eastern ideology of freedom is that it has nothing to do with choice! It has to do with freedom in action. We recognize this as the activity of our consciousness. Let's explore this ideology a little further. We've seen that whenever we have a choice, there is conflict. Remember the young man who had a choice between a military career and the family business? Prior to his decision, he was in conflict; he was confused with doubts about what to do. There was a great deal of anxiety and mental anguish. He had a choice, but was not truly free? Why was there internal conflict? Isn't it because he did not see clearly what was before him? If he consciously saw directly and immediately what is, none of the alternatives would exist. He would know what to do because his consciousness knows by seeing and acting.

There would be no choice. He would be free from choice. The young man would know without any doubt that he must follow his dream whether he succeeds or not as a flier. He knows now that since he didn't, he lives with regret. His forced choice made with internal conflict was the wrong choice. Although there was immediate relief, eventually, he lived to regret it, and with the regret, he knows without a doubt he made the wrong choice.

God has a free will, but do you think She makes decisions on what to do by choosing from alternatives? Of course not. As we know, God consciously sees clearly and acts; why would She have to choose? As Dr. Alexander explained, he knew in heaven with consciousness and did not have to choose or struggle with decisions. God sees and knows what is truly good, so She "voluntarily" acts to do the good She sees. God would not sin, even if She could choose to do so because She consciously sees the act is contrary to Her nature. To act contrary to Her nature is to act contrary to Her existence because as we know God's nature is living existence.

Unfortunately, with our free will, we are free to act contrary to our nature or identity. Our consciousness is not perfect. God's is. To act contrary to our nature is sinful, and if we persist in sinning, it could lead to the death of our spiritual existence. Why would God give us a free will if this is possible? Do we know why?

11

Proof of Our Spiritual Existence

The next issue to address is to look deeply into conscious knowing to see what it truly gives us. To address this issue, we must look into the nature of conscious knowing. What is the nature of consciousness? We know how consciousness acts within a person, but specifically, what does the process produce with respect to this knowledge? To answer this question, we must look at the product of the conscious process. *It is the product that gives us some understanding of what the nature of consciousness is.* We are looking at the product now, not the process we've already addressed.

Since we can't study the nature of consciousness directly, we must study the product or ideas it produces. *If the product or ideas of our consciousness are spiritual or immaterial, then the nature of our consciousness must also be spiritual and immaterial.* This is because as a being is in nature, it can and will act and produce. The identity of "I" can be expressed in our acts of "am." This does not mean our acts are who we are. Our identity is located in our "I."

As we know, the *essence* of a class of beings is that which makes the class different from any other class of beings. The essence is the foundation of our identity or nature. A being with a purely material nature can only produce material concepts. It can't produce an immaterial spiritual product or concept. *Consciousness can produce concepts of things that do not exist in the material world!* Within our conscious imagination, we can create monsters and superheroes that do not exist in the real world and never will.

If our intellect can create things that do not exist in reality, it must be immaterial. Material knowing with the senses can see, hear, touch, or smell specific things. We can only look at images of a specific oak, pine or elm tree. On the other hand, conscious knowing 'sees' well beyond a specific tree. Perhaps intelligence does a comparative analysis of the similarities between the images of each tree, and our consciousness takes the analysis and synthesis of intelligence to produce the general concept of "treeness."

Although this could happen, it is most likely not the mechanism that produces the general concept. More likely, our consciousness merely sees the images of the trees and extracts the general concept of "treeness" without the help of intelligence. This is more likely the case because consciousness does not use nor need thinking. Love is also a general concept. Love and "treeness" are examples of general or universal ideas that do not exist in the material world. How can the mind produce something that is not real and does not exist? Can a mind that is material produce something that is immaterial or spiritual? Can a mind produce something it is not capable of producing?

To summarize, we start with specific beings in the material world entering our minds through our senses to form images like a camera would. The universal idea, which consciousness extracts from the images, is the essence or identity of trees that applies to all specific trees that exist. We call the universal idea "treeness." This is a spiritual process which produces spiritual or universal ideas that represent the spiritual essence of a being's identity. These universal ideas within people do not exist in plants, animals, or in the real physical world.

To say it another way, since we are consciously aware of the spiritual universal ideas of a being's identity, then our consciousness must also be spiritual. This is because the essence of our consciousness within our "I" is reflected in what it produces in our "am!" This is what the Bible says with respect to knowing with our spiritual intellect:

> "Now we have received not the spirit of the world, but the Spirit that is from God so that we may understand the gifts bestowed on us by God. And we speak of these things in words not taught by human wisdom but taught by the Spirit, interpreting spiritual things to those who are spiritual."[1]

Since the material organ we call the brain cannot produce an immaterial universal spiritual idea, then our consciousness is not dependent on the material brain and can exist without it! In short, *we are spiritual beings because we have a spiritual intellect within material bodies but not dependent on our bodies for our intellectual existence.* As spiritual intellectual beings, we will exist after our material bodies are transformed back to the elements from whence they came. People who do not believe in our spiritual existence experience two deaths. A death occurs when the body dies or falls apart, returning to its original elements. A second death occurs when the last person who retains an image of them in their memory dies. Unless, of course, they are famous. For those who believe in their spiritual existence, there is no death in their awareness and spiritual intellect. Scientists may be able to create artificial intelligence equal to or greater than humans, but they will never be able to replicate consciousness and its way of knowing.

→ Do you believe the essence of your identity or who you are is spiritual and never dies? Think about your universal ideas.

Dr. Alexander experiences this eternal spiritual existence in heaven when he writes "consciousness is the basis of all existence." Of course, it is the basis because the intellect of God and human beings use the energy of life to establish spiritual ideas used to create relationships, and relationship is existence. We have seen there can be no living nor nonliving beings in existence without energy forces uniting energy forms in relationships. Therefore, there can be no energy forms in relationships that establish beings without either the divine or human intellect creating and maintaining them. It is our consciousness within our spiritual intellect that generates spiritual ideas that can establish relationships between people by using our gift of the energy forces of life! Spiritual ideas establishing relationship will be addressed in Part Two of the book.

Jesus said, *It is the Spirit that gives life, while the flesh is useless.*[2] Our creative intellect is at the very essence of our identity. It is essential in establishing spiritual relationships for existence. It is the consciousness of the Creator, God the Father, who created and maintains the forces that establishes relationships by uniting forms whether living or nonliving beings, enabling them to exist. God's consciousness is spiritual existence, and He created us with a spiritual existence which is our consciousness. This is consistent with God's revelation of His name "I am." God is existence with consciousness, and so are we by His creation! Therefore, we have the potential ability to see as God sees and to love as God loves.

We must always remember God's intellect is perfect with an infinite capacity. Our intellect is imperfect with a capacity limited by our created nature. Our intellect is constantly seeking truth. This involves knowledge in this life using intelligence and consciousness, but we are never satisfied. *God does not seek truth. She is truth!*

In the life to come, our limited capacity could be completely full, and we will be perfectly satisfied. Or we could continue to seek truth and knowledge for all eternity but never achieve all truth because if we did, we would be God! As we saw previously, God's consciousness sees infinite truth and knowledge. She does not have to think or use reason to get it. She has it all instantly in the eternal present.

12

Living Existence in Time

As living existence, we occupy space in a sea of nothingness, but what about time? How does time relate to existence? God's existence is in the eternal presence. God does not have a past nor beginning nor does He have a future. People as created beings have a beginning in this life on earth. With our thinking, we create psychological time. Within and outside us, we experience the movement of objects from moment to moment, exhibiting change that we use to measure time. *One truth that many believe is certain in this life is that everything changes.* Time moves on.

As we know, if we are to seek past experiences, we would find them in the storehouses of our memories. The future also resides in memory. Isn't the future merely the experiences of the past used to project what we want or do not want to see happen in the future? There are past experiences we would like to see happen in the future and others we would like to avoid. Living existence is always in the present. *The past and future exist only in our thoughts.* When we live totally in the present, there are no thoughts of past or future, and certainly, we are not in time. As a person living here and now, we lose all sense of psychological time, and time passes with no awareness of its passing.

All of us have had experiences in which we become so involved in doing something, we lose all track of time. When we live in the present, there is no separation between the individuals and what they are doing within the environment that surrounds them. The individuals and their activities are one. Athletes experience this type of union with the game they play.

As stated earlier, athletes have no time to think in the game. They only have time to spontaneously see without an awareness of any spectators shouting or yelling in the stands. When a musician composes a song, an artist paints a picture, or a craftsman is hard at work, there is no separation between the artists and their creative work. Creators and their works are one without any awareness of the passage of time. When Michelangelo created and painted the ceiling of the Sistine Chapel, in a sense, he became his painting for the period of time in which he painted it. Artists who paint holy icons experience this union with their work as they pray and meditate before each time they paint.

→ Have you ever been so involved in what you were doing in the present moment that you lost all track of time? You said to yourself, "Where did the time go? Time flew by."

Peak Moments

People can experience peak moments, which can occur even when doing ordinary work. Suddenly, for no apparent reason, we are filled with a sense of goodness, beauty, and the joy of just living. We can feel our hearts, minds, and bodies. All at once, we are aware of our connection to everything around us and spontaneously proclaim, "God, it feels great to be alive!" Go to any school playground and observe it on the faces and hear it in the voices of young children who come running out of school to play. It's a spontaneous response to the goodness and beauty of life.

When we experience these peak moments, we are not in the past or future of psychological time. It is at these times when we experience the goodness of creation and the joy of living in the present that we forget time. *We are aware of our being as God is aware of Her being in the eternal present and we are happy.*

→ Although you live in the present, how much time do you spent in past or future thoughts?
→ Do you think there will be an awareness of time in heaven?
→ Have you ever experienced peak moments?

Sometimes older people do not like to experience young noisy children enjoying themselves playing. Perhaps it reminds them of the joy of living they once had and now seem to have lost. Here and now, there are those who often spend time in memories, trying to find the joy in living by basking in the thoughts of past peak moments that are gone. To the extent they do this, they miss out on the joy of living in the present where they may find peak moments again if they only knew how to recognize and embrace them.

To Change or Not to Change

How does this eternal present differ from this world of change? We know the apparent truth that many believe, and this is that everything in this world is changing. This includes parts of our identity! As we know, the intelligence as part of our intellect can and does change with education. Our traits, which influence the way we do things, can be modified by the intellect with a great deal of work. We can also change minor incidental parts of our identity like our appearance or physical skills. We have some control over their existence. They are not essential to our true identity.

As we know, our true identity is our essence and makes us different from any other class of existing beings, including God. We can be consciously aware of our identity or who we truly are. We are aware of what we are doing, what we have done, what is happening to us, and what possibly could and will happen to us like getting old and dying. *It is wonderful to be consciously aware of our true identity. This is the part of us that will always be in the eternal present. It will not be transformed at death.* Once we are aware of who we truly are, this awareness and our true identity never changes.

Things that Don't Change

We are all changing physically and psychologically, second by second. Since we are changing, how can we know our true identity? Do we have a self we can know? We can now answer this question in the affirmative. We have a conscious awareness of our existence and the existence of everything we see with our universal ideas. *We know true universal ideas will never change or be transformed in death. Nor does the consciousness of our intellect that produces the awareness of these universal ideas change.*

Truth can never change nor can God who is truth. These same ideas have existed in the minds of people since our creation. A big question is whether the awareness of our identity is true or false? Another way of asking this question is, do the ideas in our awareness capture the entire essence of who we are? Unfortunately, for some people, the answer to this question is no! Ultimately, we will find that if we know our true identity, then it leads us to our purpose, our mission in life, and our final destination. Our purpose, our mission, and final destination do not change. We may not achieve them, but they are our objectives, and these universal ideas never change and are achievable.

Since universal ideas apply to our purpose and identity, they always exist in the eternal presence. Some might ask, how can this be? After all, we were created, and being born, we had a beginning. We may not achieve our purpose or destiny, and even if we achieve our destiny, it won't happen until we are transformed at death.

The answer is simply that the universal ideas of our identity, purpose, and destiny always existed in the mind of God. As the Bible tells us, She knew us before we were born.[1] It was a matter of actualizing God's ideas. We are a creation of His idea of us, and our purpose and destiny existed in His eternal mind long before we were born. We began to be conscious of our existence at birth.

When a farmer plants the seed of corn, he knows the corn exists. It exists in the rain that waters the seed and soil, the sun that warms the air, and the minerals of the earth. They are all a part of corn. It is merely a matter of having them actualize into an existence we can recognize as corn. It is the same with us. We existed as God's universal idea of us until such time as we were actualized into our present existence.

To summarize, we continue to expand our ideas of our identity. We now know the following:

- **The process of existence is our energy forms using energy forces in giving, sharing, and receiving parts of ourselves to each other, establishing a relationship that is a union with a new existence.** The energy forms we call men and women give, share, and accept individual parts from each other, establishing a union in marriage, family, and friendships.
- Made with an intellect consisting of intelligence that thinks and with a consciousness that is aware of ourselves thinking, feeling, and acting;

- We are spiritual beings existing in the present with a spiritual consciousness and intelligence within a material body but not dependent on our body to exist.
- Our identity has a free will enabling us to act or not act or to act in one way or another, and so we are responsible for our behaviors. Perhaps real freedom is freedom in seeing and acting with consciousness.
- With our spiritual intellect, we are able to produce spiritual ideas used to create new kinds of existences with God's help.
- We are constantly changing physically and psychologically, but not the spiritual essence of our identity. The elements that comprise our material body will be transformed in death, but the conscious awareness of ourselves will not.

Acts for Ends

We know when we assert our existence by proclaiming "I am," the "am" contains all our acts of our identity. "I" brings forth these acts. Let us look into our acts to see what they can mean, how they specifically relate to our identity and destiny. We need energy to act, and acts may be a manifestation of our traits that cause deliberate behaviors, but why do we act?

People act to acquire an end. The end is the objective of our acts. The end can be something we need to survive physically, psychologically, or spiritually. Perhaps it's a state of being that we want. Regardless of what end we seek, the end motivates our energy to act in order to get it. So we see the end we seek is first in the intention of rational thought or instinctual drive but last in acquisition. We may desire getting an A in math. This end is first in our thoughts. To get the A, we must act with our traits or habitual tendencies. If we have the trait of low energy tension, we will act to get the A relaxed, satisfied and composed. If our trait is high energy tension, we will seek the A by being driven, frustrated, overwrought, and fretting about the work. In any case, the A will be last in our acquisition if we get it but first in our intention or motive to act.

Good Ends

The Greek philosopher, Aristotle, defines the end as "that for the sake of which a thing is done," and he defines the good as "that at which all things aim." Aristotle is telling us that every end is good or the good is the end we seek. ***We seek an end because we perceive it to be good and act to obtain an end for the sake of its goodness.*** Unless we perceive the end as having some good for us or others, we would not act. We do not seek anything we perceive to be totally bad. We must see some good in it.

Can this be true? Don't take Aristotle's word for it; just look into your own thoughts to see if it is true. With consciousness, watch your desires for an end and see how this motivates your energy to act in an effort to get what you want. And when you get it, how do you feel? Aren't you happy that you have reached the end of your quest? And don't you think the end you acquired has some good? You're happy and satisfied because you now possess the good or end you wanted. It may or may not be something you possess physically, but consciously, you are aware you have it, did it or can do it and so you are happy. Look into yourself and see if this is true from your own experiences.

What if shit happens, and circumstances prohibit your pursuing the end you dream of having? This was the case of Saint Therese Lisieux who was a cloistered nun. She dreamed of working in the foreign missions. Unfortunately, a severe illness prevented her from going. She prayed about it to Jesus who answered her prayer, revealing to her that "her desire was enough." This tells us that our intention or motive is essential, even if we can't act. Motive can be a blessing or a curse. Jesus taught that we can commit a sin with our intentions and desires. In Matthew, Jesus said, *You have heard that it was said "You shall not commit adultery." But I say to you that everyone who looks at a woman with lust has already committed adultery with her in his heart.*[1] This raises the bar substantially if we wish to live as Christians. We can sin not only with our physical acts but with intellectual acts such as our intentions or motives!

Final Ends

Yet we also experience with the possession of some good ends that there always seems to be another good we wish to possess and then another and another. We wonder if there is some final end or ultimate goal that would make us perfectly satisfied and happy, a final end that would stop our constant search. When we think to ourselves we're never completely satisfied, there is always a longing or yearning for something more or something better. Perhaps it's a lasting peace and joy that will never end. We say to ourselves there must be a final end, a supreme good for us, but what is it?

→ Have you ever experienced this? Asked yourself these questions and wondered what would make you supremely happy and remain with you always?

From our knowledge of God, we know God created this yearning and desire within us, and He would not do this to frustrate us. *We all want the supreme good or ultimate end, and when we achieve it, we will be perfectly happy. All people want it because it's a part of the identity of every person.* Why would God create this yearning in our nature if He did not plan to satisfy it? God who is truthful, wise, and good loves us and would be incapable of such cruelty.

Homosexuality

A homosexual man or woman could make the same argument. They think they were born with these cravings and yearnings for the same sex and it is a part of their nature. If this is so, it was placed in them by God. God would not create them with these cravings if they were designed to lead a person to evil or did not intend to satisfy them. Others believe these craving and desires are learned, not inherited, or merely a hormonal imbalance that can be treated. They maintain gay sexual behaviors are sinful. This was made clear in the Old Testament, the writings of Saint Paul, and 2,000 years of tradition. In any case, when the cravings occur, we must not give in to them but resist these temptations and behaviors. What do you think? Regardless of what you think as Christians, we accept homosexual people with kindness, compassion, and friendship!

To Act or Not to Act

To act or not to act; that is the question? To answer the question, we must remove any uncertainty about the end we seek that causes the will to mobilize our energy to act. Yet, experience tells us, we can become uncertain and confused about the good we seek because of our imperfect intellect.

All Kinds of Good Ends

Something may be good for one person but not another, or a good may not be right for us at a particular time. Sometimes in acquiring a good, there are evil consequences or collateral damage we do not want. The confusion also comes with the fact that there are all kinds of good things. Some are truly good while others may appear to be good but in reality are not. Some ends only give pleasure. Some may be good in the short-term but may be deadly harmful in the long run.

A drug addict takes a drug for the pleasurable experience; it makes him feel good. More important, it helps him forget all his problems. A calmness and peace come over him, and all his fears and anxieties are gone. Unfortunately, it doesn't last; the problems always return, so he needs to fix it again and again with drugs. Sadly, his function in the real world deteriorates, and eventually, the drugs may kill him. The drugs appear to be good, but they are not. It is only an "apparent" good.

→ Have you ever acted for an apparent good?

We see there are good ends that may help part of our being but may be deadly to our whole being. Truly good ends are constructive to our lives as opposed to "apparent good ends," which can lead to our death; or worse, it could lead to our destruction as a human being and result in spiritual death.

We can now see that to act or not to act is not as simple as it seems. There are times we clearly and consciously see the good and act to get it. Other times, we do not see clearly, and there are times we may mistake the "apparent good" for the "true good" or seek an end, which may be good, but not for us here and now. Playing basketball may be good, but not on the night we are studying for a final exam the next day. *We need a norm or standard we can use to determine if our acts are good or bad, truly good or apparently good.*

Finally, there are times we know what is the true good we should seek but don't. We settle for an immediate lesser good, which may ultimately be destructive to our souls. This may be because we may have a false concept of a final end or we don't believe or are uncertain of it. We don't see because we don't want to see. We will take the immediate lesser good than some greater good that may not exist. In the end, any act that prevents us from getting to our final end is bad.

Morally Good Acts

We often hear people talk about a good person, a good act, and a good end, but what do we mean when we say, "This is truly a good person." We know the end we seek is good, even if it's an apparent good; however, all God's creations are good because God doesn't make junk! We are good by virtue of our existence as well as our identity, purpose, and destiny God created all of us to be and have! We exist, and life seems good, but it is not necessarily the moral good.

Some evolutionists think not only are we evolving physically but morally as well! As we gradually evolved from the savage existence, our moral ideas also evolved, and ways of acting that worked developed into customs. They were gradually modified and improved into our present system of morals. All morality is based on custom. The problem with custom is some customs can never be eliminated, and some acts can never be made customary. Suppose murder, lying, and stealing were made customary; how long would we last as a human race? *Some acts are right or wrong by their very nature, and no custom or positive law established by human beings can change them.*

Standard of Morality

Standard of Morality

The good in everyone's life is not necessarily the moral good. *The moral good is always our true good because it always contributes to the goodness of the whole human being.* The moral good is the spiritual good that gives us the identity of a human being. What is the standard or norm by which we compare our acts to determine if they are constructive and morally good? How do we determine what is morally bad or destructive to our well-being?

Immediate Standard

Good acts lead us to good ends and ultimately our last end. The problem is we have little experience with our last end, but we can determine what ends are good or bad by studying our identity or human nature. God created our identity with all its parts and relationships. Therefore, God must want us to act in ways that preserve the right harmony in these relationships and parts of our identity. Acts must conform to our internal organs, our animal and rational parts as well as our body and soul. We find our truly good ends leading to our ultimate last end by studying our identity. God directs us to good ends by our identity. To live in accord with our true identity is to acquire the goodness and happiness we seek! Living in conformity to it directs us ultimately to our true destiny. *Our entire human nature or identity is the immediate standard we use to determine the morality of an act.*

If we were creating a robot to produce a product or end which was good, how would we make the robot? Wouldn't we construct it with an identity or "I" needed to produce the good acts of "am" to get the job done. Wouldn't God do the same thing? Wouldn't He create our identity to be capable of acting in such a way that we could achieve our final end?

We know without relationship, there is no existence. Our intellect is the basis for establishing our relationships as human beings and we must look to all the relationships of our identity as our immediate standard. We use all of the relationships of human nature to determine if our acts are constructive or destructive in getting us to our true resting place: heaven, our highest good.

The Three Basic Relationships of the Immediate Standard

When we say the relationships of our identity as human beings, we are dealing with both the physical and spiritual aspects of our nature. Since we have a human identity, there are several aspects to it. We have acts that are physically good and acts that are spiritually good. There are acts that are both physically and spiritually good, but there are acts that are not. An act can be bad, physically, but good, spiritually, or vice versa. Acts can be indifferent, which could mean they are neither good nor bad. However, any indifferent act can be made good or bad based upon our intention. Washing dishes can be an indifferent act, but if it is done to honor God and for the service of others, it becomes a good act.

We are animals with physical and instinctual drives we must learn to control. It is necessary to acquire the things we need to survive as an animal, and this is good. We are also a spiritual being with an intellect consisting of a conscious awareness and reasoning that we must use if we are to survive as a human being, and this is also good. When we talk about our survival as a human being, we are talking about the survival of the essence or core of our identity as spirit. We must live in accord with our true identity as *spirit.* When we do not, we are moving away from our destiny and diminishing our spiritual nature's ability to establish good relationships.

With the animal part of our human nature, we are dealing with relationships that involve our primary physical needs such as food and shelter. With the spiritual part of our identity, we are dealing with social activities involving all our relationships with other human beings and God. We can use the things we primarily need, our achievements, and our actualized potential abilities in our relationships. In fact, we can use everything we have to establish relationships, including ourselves, with the only exception being the spiritual essence of our identity or who we are.

Our immediate standard is our nature with all its relationships. We have an animal body with inner physical organs and our spiritual intellect. We must have an inner harmonious relationship of the physical and spiritual parts that make up our inner being or individualization. We are not only solitary but social beings, and as such, we are part of God's creation. We must have harmonious relationships with all His living creation with the kind of identity He gave us. The three key relationships in our interacting or socialization with all His creation are as follows:

- First, as created human beings, we have a relationship with God.
- Second, as social beings, we must have relationship with our fellow human beings.
- Third, God made us masters of the earth, so our relationship with living and nonliving things below us is our possession of them!

God, however, created all people equal in nobility by virtue of their creation. He created all of us with the right to justice. God's creation of the earth and everything in it belongs equally to all of us! We are all responsible in helping God protect the nobility of all people and His earth. All living and nonliving beings that make up the earth are deserving of fairness and entitled to our respect. They all have an existence of their own and are not just an environment we can act upon or possess. When it comes to the earth, our American Indians had a relationship with it, which is much closer to God's intentions!

The two aspects of human beings' *nature, both the instinctual animal and spiritual intellect, should be in harmonious balance.* Often, they are not. If a conflict does arise, the higher spiritual behavior must prevail over the lower instinctual animal behavior. For example, in sexual behavior, our intellect must prevail over animal instinct if we are to behave as spiritual human beings. Our spirituality is the higher priority.

In summary, we can say the conduct of a person is morally good when it is suitable to our true nature as human beings or the nature of God. We are spiritual beings with our nature created in the image of the nature of God. We must live in the right relationship with God, humanity, and everything else in our environment. Our rational spiritual nature must consciously control our instinctual animal appetites. *Our relationship with God must hold priority over all other relationships. Our relationship with our fellow human beings must take priority over everything else in our environment.* Unfortunately, we live in a world where priorities are often confused!

For many, the possession of vast amounts of gold, natural resources, or stocks in the stock market that translate to wealth and power take priority over anything else. Why do people seek power and wealth? Perhaps they have lost their sense of God or maybe they don't know their true nature, purpose in life, and destiny.

Ultimate Standard

Our ultimate standard is the nature of God found in the revelations of the Bible! Our identity resembles the divine identity; therefore, God intends that our activity resembles His activity. *Our acts are morally good and lead to our highest end when they resemble Biblical doctrine and Jesus's acts and so are in conformity with His nature.* Our acts are bad when we misuse our intellect and free will and do what God cannot do, and that is *not* conform to His identity, which is sin. In determining the morality of an act, the question would be, "What would Jesus do?"

- → What relationship is your highest priority?
- → How much do you value your relationship with people?
- → What kind of relationship do you have with the Lord?
- → Why do you think people seek power and wealth?

Life: A Mixture of Consequences or Ends

To act or not to act, it can be confusing at times. Life is full of good or indifferent acts that can have evil consequences along with good ones. Are we expected to ensure that all results associated with morally good or indifferent acts have only good or indifferent consequences? This means we could never act if there was collateral damage or evil consequences along with good ones! To attempt to live with such expectations would significantly limit our activities and make living unendurable.

A Mixture of Consequences

Many activities in life result in a mixture of good and bad consequences. When we do certain good things, there always seems to be collateral damage by virtue of the laws of nature or other people involved in the act. A doctor who treats a deadly contagious disease may put his life in danger. The treatment is good, but the loss of the doctor's life is physically bad.

A company makes a new product that is significantly better than the product of their competitors. This results in the closing of factories and laying off thousands of workers. The product is good, the layoffs bad. Or we get a job, which means another person who desperately needs it doesn't. It's good we got the job but bad the other fellow who desperately needed it didn't get it.

This produces a problem for us; how can we live our lives in a way God intended while voluntarily compelled to do evil? Many people may want to do the right thing, yet in so doing, they are faced with bad consequences they do not want. We would like to give more money to the poor, but we don't want the bad consequence of making the sacrifice of going to fewer restaurants, buying less clothing, cigarettes, or vacations.

How do we solve this problem and make the decision to act or not act? That is the question. The answer may not be as simple as one might think. For an evil consequence to be voluntarily permitted to accompany a good end, we must consider several factors in deciding to act or not act.

First, to begin with the righteous person does not voluntarily cause an evil consequence. The evil consequence must be an incidental and unavoidable by-product of a good outcome a person is rightfully seeking. *As Christians, we cannot want, will, or intend an evil end, even with a good or indifferent act.* For example, a person may work hard, which is an indifferent act, but the evil end the person seeks with her earnings is to buy and use drugs.

Second, any act for a good end must be a good act in itself or at least an indifferent act, which is neither good nor bad. *We can never achieve a good end with evil means.* For example, we may want very much to pass a very important class to graduate, so we steal a copy of the exam or we cheat in class with a hidden paper with answers. This means acquiring the good end of passing the test by the evil act of stealing or cheating can't be condoned under any circumstances.

Of course, if one lies to save lives, the circumstances might be different. Let's say we were helping Jews escape and the Nazis enter our home and asked if we helped any Jews leave the city. We lie and answer, "No." Of course, we could refuse to answer, and the good Christian would say this is the way. Clearly refusing to talk is not lying, but are we courageous enough to pay the price of terrible torture? Is the evil act of lying justified by not merely saving our lives but the lives of all the Jews we may help escape now and in the future? *Can doing a little evil for a much greater good be justified?* We leave it in the hands of God.

As we can see, it's not an easy decision. We prefer not to make the judgment, but we must! Some people may think civil disobedience with violent protest and lying, which are evil acts, are justified by a good end. This good end may be victory and the acquisition of power for a political party. It may mean the advancement of a political ideology. The moral principle in this matter is as simple as this: *an evil act can never be justified by a good end.*

Third, *the good and evil ends must at least be equivalent.* It would not be right if the evil consequences are significantly greater than the good ends or when the evil consequences are proportionally favored over the good. If in any good act the evil consequence significantly outweighs the good end, it should not be done. In the example given above, feeding the poor is significantly more important than our vacation or cigarettes.

A female soldier jumps on a grenade thrown into a foxhole, saving the lives of three fellow soldiers while losing her own. The act of jumping on a grenade was an indifferent act. Her intention was to save lives, which is good along with the good consequence of the lives she saved. The good consequence of saving three lives outweighs the physically bad end of losing her own. This situation is comparable to a man going into a burning building to save a child or jumping into a raging river to save a life. It is also comparable to a poor man working long hours at a menial low-paying job to support his family, reducing significantly the quality time he can spend with his family.

In each case, the good and bad ends are at least equivalent or the good outweighs the bad. A person runs into a burning building or jumps into a raging river to save a dog. The bad end of possibly losing one's life outweighs the good end of saving a dog. Would we advise our teenage son or daughter to do it? A human life is far more valuable than any animal. Would you risk your life to save an animal? Would you be willing to die for an animal? Some people might, but you can't say their lives are equivalent.

To Bomb or Not to Bomb

One final and very controversial example has to do with the dropping of the Atomic bombs. The Second World War had been raging for four years, and the Japanese were beaten. Their Army, Navy, and Air Force were defeated along with the loss of their island empire in the pacific. To end the war, we would have to invade the main island of Japan with a tremendous loss of American and Japanese lives. It was estimated that upward of two million American lives would be lost and 10 million plus Japanese.

The Japanese were fanatical with many civilians and the military living by a code of honor that required death rather than defeat or surrender; therefore, requests to surrender were always ignored. We had a bomb that would end the war quickly and save millions of lives. It meant, however, the death of innocent young children and civilians not directly involved in the war. But many, however, would be willing to fight to the death if their homeland were invaded.

Is dropping the bomb that was so destructive it had the potential of destroying all of humanity a morally good act? It was clear the number of lives saved by ending the war quickly and without an invasion was far greater than the deaths caused by dropping the two bombs. We warned them a bomb of mass destruction was on the way, but people would not leave their cities. Obviously, we dropped the bombs and ended the war, but should we have done it?

The Bible says "You shall not murder,"[1] but at what cost? Could this be considered an act of self-defense? It's not an easy answer, is it? But often, life is not easy, and human beings are complex beings.

- → Can you think of a time you acted for a good end that also had evil consequences?
- → Was the act good?
- → Did the good end outweigh the evil consequences?
- → Have you ever committed an evil act to achieve a good end?

All Kinds of Ends

To find or not to find our true destiny, that is the challenge that has immense value for us. We seek something that leads to an end we want. In some cases, the thing we seek, which leads to an end, is merely a "means" to that end and not the end. It lies between us and the end we seek. For example, we may work at a terrible job to get the money to buy a car. Work is not the end, it is only a means to get the end we want, which is the car. There are some things that are means and others that are ends.

Intermediate Ends

On the other hand, there are some things we may seek for their own sake because they are good, but also for the sake of something else, a greater good. We seek an education because knowledge is good to have, but we can also seek an education to get a good job. In this case, education is called an "intermediate" end. Another example is eating a meal we thoroughly enjoy; it is good. However, eating enables us to physically survive, which is a greater good.

We can also have a long series of intermediate ends before we reach a final end. Life can be a series of intermediate or subordinate ends or merely a means to get to an end. We want A to get to B and B to get C and so on. We may seek a last end because it closes a series of means and ends. We call this end a relative last end because it closes a series of ends, but the relative last end is directed to a greater end or good. For example, finishing education, military service, or a summer job are relative ends that lead to a greater good. That good might be a job we will do the rest of our lives or perhaps even some greater good!

Final Ends

We seek "our truly last end" for its own sake and for the sake of nothing else. It is the conclusion of "all" the series of means and intermediate ends that make up our lives. In this case, we are talking about our absolutely last end, which does not lead nor is directed to any other end. In fact, everything we do, every intermediate series of ends, is directed to this true last end. It is the destination we arrive at when we live, perceiving and acting in accord with our valid identity or with the divine personality of Jesus Christ. *Those who do not know Jesus through no fault of their own can still reach their true last end if they live in accord with their true nature.*

We have seen that any end we seek is always perceived to be good; therefore, we could say our last end must be our highest good. We know the moral goodness of our acts is determined by our acting in agreement with our total human nature or true self. It is our true good because in so acting, we reach our final end, the highest good. *Our valid identity not only directs us to our last end, but since our identity is spiritual and continues after our physical death, its existence is involved in our final end.* To determine if an act is morally good is to not only see if it's in accord with our true identity, but to realize the acts and the intermediate good ends they produce lead us to our all-inclusive destiny or last end.

→ Do you see and understand that living should be morally good because it leads to your last end or final good?
→ If people truly see and understand this, wouldn't they always seek to do what is morally good?

Same Identity, Not Necessarily Same Destiny

We know all people have the same identity with an intellect that has the same needs and desires craving satisfaction. We have observed enough people to know this is a self-evident truth; therefore, it would seem all people should experience the same last end. They do not! All acts of a rational human being should be for their absolutely last end; they are not! God created us with the same identity and to have the same last end. Since we can think and act freely, the question is, can we influence our identity, and in so doing, change our last end?

Catholics believe if we are consciously aware of what we are doing and we freely do what is evil without repentance, we can determine our last end. We can determine a final end, which is not good and not what God intended.

God created us with a free will, and it is an essential part of our identity. We must be free to exercise it. God can change it, but if He does, He is changing our identity or who we are. God knows our final end because She exists in the eternal present. Because She knows does not mean She determines or wants us to have a bad final end. *Preknowledge does not mean predetermination.*

Existentialists

As we know, the essence of our identity never changes. *Our free and conscious actions do not determine who we are but can determine our last end. This is why Christians can love the sinner but hate the sin!*

Existentialists disagree. They believe we determine our identity by our actions. They think that first we perceive our identity, then we act upon the perception, and finally, we become the perception. If we perceive ourselves to be a dog and so act like a dog, we become a dog. As we have seen, the consciousness and so the perception and thinking of a dog is different from that of a person. We are consciously aware of ourselves and can act freely; a dog cannot. A dog can be conditioned to act or imitate another's acts or possible act by trial and error to get what it instinctively needs to survive but cannot rationally think. Dogs can't freely decide to act or not act, so they cannot be held accountable for their actions.

We cannot change our identity into something it is not. It is true we may perceive our identity as being a dog. Or for that matter, we may perceive ourselves to be a waiter, beggar, criminal, doctor, rich man, or even a king or queen, but it is a false perception. *What we do is not necessarily who we truly are.* We can perceive ourselves as being a dog and behave like one, but it does not mean we become one. This acting like a dog comes from a false perception of our identity. Of course, we are not speaking specifically of a dog but animal behavior. We are part animal and can allow the animal part of us to be in control, but it is not who we truly are.

Nevertheless, our consciously free acts do affect our relationship with God. It is our relationship with God which affects what we are capable or not capable of receiving from Him with respect to our final end.

→ Do you think your perceptions can change your identity?
→ Can you positively or negatively influence your identity by acts that could determine the kind of destiny you will have?

Of course, there are people who only act for intermediate ends and goals. They desire proximate ends without thinking about a last end or the supreme meaning or purpose for living. These people are opportunists who can go in any direction for what they perceive to be what is good for them and their family. They are not limited by any moral principles or responsibilities. They act whenever the opportunity presents itself.

A moral rational person does not act this way. It is certainly not the conduct of a human being. The final end for people like this is wandering or aimlessly moving from one end to another. They have the same last end God intends for every person. However, they make the mistake of thinking wandering is their last end and sadly give up searching any further. It is an irrational way of living, and their behavior is not righteous or in accord with the true nature of human beings.

→ Do you know opportunists who make wandering their last end?
→ When you talk to them, do they appear satisfied and happy?

We can now summarize with our focus upon our identity dealing with the morality of our acts and their relationship with our destiny.

- We all seek a final end. It was placed in our identity by God.
- God directs us to our destiny by our morally acting in accord with our true nature and the divine nature revealed in the Bible.

- Our nature involves our relationship with God, our fellow human beings, and all living and non-living beings below us existing in our environment.
- We determine our destiny with our "I" containing our intellect and free will which acts with our "am."
- We can act for a good end, which also has a bad consequence by always intending a good end, by acquiring the good end with good or indifferent acts, but not with evil acts. The bad consequences must be unavoidable, and the good end must be at least proportional to the evil consequences.
- People can have a true or false understanding and awareness of their identity. What we do is not who we are.

→ Do you see your true identity? We considered twenty-one ideas associated with our identity, but there is more to come.

Many who live in Africa, the Middle East, and parts of central and South America live under miserable conditions. Many of these people look for a better life to come in heaven. However, they are willing to give their lives to a cause which promises them a better life here and now.

Life in North America and Europe is much better than many other places in the world. To many of these unfortunate people, it is the promised land, the end they seek here on earth. For we who are fortunate to live in these promised lands, we live under conditions the unfortunate people may consider heaven like. Under such good conditions, many of us enjoy life and look to make it as good as possible. Others may not appreciate the wonderful life we have, even the poorest among us, because we have never experienced life under a truly totalitarian, oppressive, or terribly poor country. For many of us who have this good life, we are reluctant to leave it or sacrifice our lives for any future existence in heaven or risk doing anything that would jeopardize our lifestyle.

18

Searching for Our Destiny or the Final End of Our Existence

People will not agree upon what is or may constitute our last end and highest good. One thing is certain: life as we know it here and now will end. The final end should be the same for everyone because we all have the same identity, but it isn't. We all seek our true end which is the last end God intended. Some people may never find it.

This may be because their universal idea or perception of their identity is wrong or incomplete. So they live a false identity and reach a final end God did not intend. Or they may have some awareness of their identity, know what they are doing is wrong and really contrary to who they are, but still freely do it. As mentioned earlier, they may settle for a lesser good in this world instead of the greatest good in the life to come. They may have doubts about a heaven they are not sure exists.

→ Do you truly believe there is a heaven? Or do you have doubts? At times, we all have doubts but never stop believing or doing what is morally right.

They may deliberately convince themselves that their motive for acting sinfully is more important than the hurt they cause or the damage to their perception of themselves and their relationship with God. *Our destiny is determined by the awareness of our nature, the divine nature, believing in this awareness, and living in conformity to it.* Of course, our awareness of God's identity is limited by our created nature.

→ Do you think a person acts differently when he or she has doubts about heaven, does not believe it exists, or never thinks about it?

→ Do you think there are advantages to acting morally in accord with your true identity and Jesus's teachings, regardless of whether there is a heaven or not?

Our Destiny-Transformation of Our Bodies

We are living existence within a material body. Eventually, our bodies will be transformed at death into another existence. It's a fact that cannot be disputed. Thousands of years ago, a Roman put it this way: "When I die, the material that make up my body here and now will come apart, disintegrate, and return to the soil as elements.

The plants will use my elements to grow, and then my elements will be part of the plant. A cow will eat the plants, and now my elements will be a part of the cow. Someone will eat the plants or the cow, and now my elements become a part of this person."

So living existence is cyclical, moving from living existence to nonliving existence and back to living existence. We go on but in different forms. Some will say this is our final end and highest good. We should take comfort in knowing our existence will continue in another energy form. Others might say it's a beautiful process, and we must accept it without fear or reservation because we have no choice.

→ Do you think this is our final end?
→ If you did, how do you think you would feel? How would you act?
→ Would you want it to be your final end?

The important question for most people would be, will we continue to exist after we die? Will the essence of our identity, which is the awareness of our existence, continue after our death? Many of us do not want to lose ourselves in some different form of existence. We want our identities, which means our awareness and memories of ourselves, to continue to exist after we die.

→ Be honest in your answer. When you die aren't you really afraid of losing your awareness of yourself much more than your physical body?

Perhaps like Socrates, you don't care one way or another. You may think this now, but what about at your hour of death? We want to know what we are doing and what is happening to us. We want to know the here and now in this continued existence after our deaths.

Once again, we know our conscious awareness of our individual existence can continue after we are transformed by death. We know it can continue because by its very nature, it is spiritual. As we demonstrated earlier, our intellect can produce an awareness of universal ideas that are immaterial and do not exist in reality. If our intellect can create and be aware of spiritual immaterial ideas, then it must be spiritual. If the product is spiritual, the producer of the product must also be spiritual. We once again briefly repeat, this explanation, in an effort to get you to see and believe in our spirituality. Because we are spiritual does not mean we see it and understand it. Perhaps we only casually look and do not see, hear but do not listen. Maybe it takes more than a logical argument! Perhaps it requires experience or a gift from God! In Matthew, Jesus tells His disciples why He speaks in parables. It is because we often look and do not see and hear but do not listen and understand.[1]

We have learned that in examining our identity, we find universal desires in all people that can never be completely satisfied in this life. People have universal spiritual desires such as perfection, perfect happiness, total goodness, absolute peace and eternal life with a concept of heaven where all these desires will be satisfied. Previously, we have seen that these desires or longings for perfect happiness and goodness were placed in the identity of every person by a benevolent creator. He must intend to fulfill them or else He would not have placed them in all of us! All these universal ideas and the desires that emanate from them are addressed in the Bible.

- Perfection: Jesus encourages us *to be perfect, therefore, as our heavenly Father is perfect.*[2]
- Peace: Jesus says, *Peace I leave with you, my peace I give you.*[3]
- Eternity: Jesus said, *In my Father's house, there are many dwelling places. I go to prepare a place for you, and I will come and take you to myself.*[4]
- Goodness: in Psalms we read, "No good thing does the Lord withhold"[5]
- Happiness: God reveals to the prophets, "who fears the Lord will have a happy end."[6] There is nothing better for us than to be happy"[7]
- Eternal life: Jesus announces to us *everyone who lives and believes in me will never die.*[8]
- Finally: in Romans, God entreats us "do not be conformed to this world, but be transformed by the renewing of your minds, so you may discern what is the will of God, what is good and acceptable and perfect."[9]

→ Do you believe in these revelations concerning you and these universal ideas about your eternity, peace, happiness, goodness, and perfection?

Heaven on Earth

We know we can influence the essence of our identity by a false and incomplete awareness of it, which in turn affects our behavior and thus determines our destiny. In short, we can influence our "I," which affects our "am" which results in our destiny. *A key question is what could bring us the greatest amount of goodness and happiness in this life?* Many people may think our lives here and now are our destiny! Perhaps we were built to create heaven for ourselves here on earth by living in a way that achieves the greatest possible good. After all, it was revealed that God is living existence, and He created us with the identity of living existence as close to His as possible. So if we live our lives as close as possible to His, we have found our heaven here and now on earth.

There are people who think we are all afraid of dying. Religions are aware of this fear and use it. They promise a heaven after death to alleviate this fear, but there may not be a heaven. Maybe this here and now is all there is. If this is true, then we must find our heaven in this life. Those who believe this have a hard time believing we are spiritual in nature. This is because if we are spiritual, then there is life after death, and in this case, this life may not be our heaven. It would certainly not be our final end.

What does finding our heaven in this life mean to some people? What is their perception of heaven here and now? Where can they find it or get something that will bring them as close to heaven as possible in this life? All of us would like to know our destiny. We are afraid of an unknown destiny or future, so some of us find one here and now on earth.

The essence of our identity is the same for all people, but we differ in our intelligence, traits, upbringing, and education along with our experiences as a person. This is why we will find different final ends and different good things we conclude will bring us as close to perfection as possible here and now on earth.

→ Do you think your life is as good and happy as it gets? If so, do you think you have found or will find your heaven here and now because there is nothing else for you?

19

Our Destiny Is Happiness

The Greeks have defined happiness as "desire satisfied by the conscious possession of the good." Happiness occurs when our intellect is in possession of an end we perceive as good. There must be an end if we are to be happy. As we learned earlier, we all desire the good end we seek, and when we acquire it, we are satisfied and happy. Whenever you acquire something you want, aren't you happy? All people desire happiness, and this basic desire is embedded in all other desires. Does this mean happiness must be our last end or highest good? In fact, happiness is a fundamental motive in all we do. Search your own mind and emotions to see if this is true.

Happiness cannot be our last or final end. If we are not happy, we want to be, and if we are happy, we want to be happier and we want it all the time. It seems we are not satisfied with some degree of happiness. If we think something will make us happy or happier by possessing it, don't we crave it? We may have craved the good ends of having a wife or husband, children, a college education, a job, or perhaps a house that will become a home. When we possessed any of these good ends, weren't we happy? But it didn't last, did it? We always seem to crave more, so how could happiness be our last end or final good?

This is a truth we experience in reality. *Nothing we can possess or wish to avoid because we perceive it as harmful, will completely satisfy us here and now.* Would a benevolent God make us continually search for a lasting completely satisfying happiness we can never find? Could this endless searching, finding an end only to search again, be our last end? Could searching again and again sometimes finding, sometimes not finding be our heaven? No, it couldn't be God's intention and most certainly is not heaven here and now.

Yet, we all know people who are miserable. How can this experience be reconciled with our understanding of happiness? Some people may seek the sadistic pleasure they get from being miserable. Others may believe it is impossible to be happy because they lack the means to acquire the good they desire. Believing it's impossible, they despair and wallow in misery. Still others may feel it is better to experience this present misery rather than work hard to acquire what they desire. They may think hard work or taking risks will produce greater misery, so in their fear and laziness, they live in misery. If one desires misery for its own sake, it would be considered a perverted condition and quite an unnatural desire.

Happiness may be a basic motivation in all we do, but it may not be the only reason we act. We may act because we intensely desire an end for the well-being or benefit of a good end, regardless of any happiness we may experience in possessing it. For example, suppose we want an education for our child because we care for her and know it will benefit her. We work to finance her education. This is our primary motive. If our child succeeds in getting educated, of course we will be happy, and happiness may be a by-product of the end achieved.

The most important motive is the education of the child and its benefits to her. Even if we suffer in our efforts, we may still do what is necessary because what we achieve is a true good, and true goodness is of immense value, regardless of any feelings of happiness. *As we know, by their nature, all people seek goodness and its collateral benefit happiness.* It is a desire for goodness as well as happiness that motivates us. Everyone wants it, but many may not know where to look, perhaps seeking an apparent good instead of a true good, searching in all the wrong places!

→ What good ends bring you happiness?
→ What did you have to do to acquire those good ends?
→ Do you think it is an apparent or true good? How do you know?

Remember, we can be happy with an apparent good end, which is not the true good. On the other hand, we may not be happy with a truly good end because of the collateral evil associated with it.

Our Destiny: Pursuit of Perfect Happiness

It's true that most people are not satisfied with some degree of happiness. From the partial happiness we experience, we can infer or conceptualize the spiritual idea of perfect happiness. We all want more, and we want it to last and be with us forever. In short, we all have a craving for perfect happiness, which is natural and deeply ingrained in the identity of people. So we see it is not just happiness or peace we crave but perfect happiness and peace.

As we now know, these cravings are for things that are spiritual. Perfect happiness and peace do not exist in our present reality. God put this craving for perfection in happiness and peace into our nature. He would like to satisfy it. Of course, the capacity of our identity will limit the total amount of goodness, happiness, and peace we can possess. On the other hand, God's capacity is not limited. We must always keep in mind our limitations in the creation of our identity; it helps in our humility. Nevertheless, unless we mentally and physically act freely to consciously possess goodness, we will never be happy. If we can ultimately possess something that is totally good, goodness itself, then we will be perfectly happy.

→ What do you think would make you perfectly happy?
→ What do you think would make you as happy as possible here and now?
→ Are they the same answer?
→ Do you ask God for help in your search for happiness? If not, why not?

Perhaps you feel you do not deserve happiness. No one deserves it. This is what is so amazing. God helps us even when we do not deserve it. Do you know why?

We know that perfect happiness can be obtained because it was created in us to be satisfied, but is it obtainable in our lifetime? Search as much as we possibly can, and we may never find anyone who desires nothing because they possess all they desire. We seek to possess all that is good because we want to be happy all the time. We want to consciously possess as much goodness as we possibly can so we can be as happy as we can be, but it's not perfection. *It is self-evident from our own personal experiences that perfect happiness is not possible in this life.*

Although we will never find anyone in this world who possesses all the goodness that can make them perfectly happy, we do know people who possess more of it than others. We know some people are happier and more satisfied than others. We say to ourselves, "We want to be as happy as possible. We may not be perfectly happy, but we would like it as perfect as we can have it here and now."

→ Who is the happiest person you know?
→ Ask this person, "What makes him or her happy?"

Our pursuit of the highest good is the goal of human life. When we find it, we will be perfectly happy. The possession of it is our last end. There are those who seek perfect happiness and believe that someday they will find and acquire it in this life. They keep searching, possessing, and searching some more. It's an illusion! Total goodness and perfect happiness are not real here and now. They are spiritual realities. Yet, we know everyone wants as much happiness as possible. We search for an object or end to possess that is as close to the highest good as possible so we can be as perfectly happy as possible. An end, which is close to the infinite good, should perhaps guide us to our absolute last end.

We know God intended us to consciously possess the highest good and be as perfectly happy as the capacity of our identity will allow. We can't completely achieve this in this life; therefore, Her intention must be fulfilled in the life to come. *The question is, what is the greatest good that we should seek and consciously possess in this life?* If we can find and possess it, we will experience our greatest happiness here and now.

→ Where do we find the greatest good in this life? Perhaps possessing it will lead to our highest good and perfect happiness in the next life.

We will never find the answer to this question by only looking within ourselves. To find it, we must search both outside and within ourselves. Unfortunately, some people only search in one direction!

21

Our Destiny: Material Good Things and Goods of the Body

Much of the world has a surplus of basic goods needed to survive. Most think it is good to have more than our needs require. It ensures a higher material standard of living. To many, the possession of material good things is the greatest possible good in this life. It brings power, respect, and a style of living that will provide the greatest degree of happiness here and now.

If we can acquire great wealth and possessions, we will be free to do what we want, go where we want, and possess anything money can buy. Many of these people think everything has a price. For many of us, those with great wealth are admired, and we strive to live the American dream of going from rags to riches. Many in our "throwaway culture" are always searching for more and never seem to be satisfied. They seek bigger and better homes, more and better food, cars, and vacations. *They are more concerned with having, not being.*

This is evident in a society that has a weight problem, enough clothing to outfit much of the third world, and takes endless vacations. Others seek the power great wealth can bring and the prestige that goes along with it. This is the only way to getting as much happiness as we can expect here and now. Most people who have been poor and now are rich or living comfortably will tell us it's better to be rich or comfortable than poor, provided other things in life such as one's health is good. Sometimes, these things are not.

Counterargument

Material wealth can come without happiness, and many wealthy people know this from experience. With some who have worldly fortunes, there is a longing for something else or something more. It could be a longing for a goodness and peace they've never known. This is because we are not merely material but spiritual beings. We long for spiritual things that will last forever. Some call it a longing for God.

→ Do you have such longings?

Eastern ideology tells a story of a very poor man in India who asks God to make him rich. God instructs him to go to a road and wait for a monk who will be traveling on it. The poor man should ask him for a very precious gem in his possession. When the monk appeared, he asked him for his valuable gem. The monk smiled and gladly gave it to the poor man.

As the poor man, now rich, was returning home, he became aware of an insight and quickly turned around to find the monk. When he found him, the monk asked him, "What would you like now?" The man said to the monk, "Please give me what you have that enables you to give me such a valuable possession."

→ What is your most valuable possession? Is it your family, your wealth, or something else?

Often, there is a great desire to keep our goods of fortune, and with it comes the fear of losing it. This fear can bring a great deal of psychological and even physical pain. In the end, we lose all our material possessions at death. Jesus said, *Do not work for the food that perishes but for the food that endures for eternal life.*[1] Goods of fortune can never bring the greatest degree of happiness and satisfaction we are seeking in this world or the perfect goodness and happiness that can only be found in our spiritual life to come.

The atheistic Communist will say this wonderful destiny in the hereafter is a pie in the sky. It is used by the rich people to keep the poor people from seeking their fair share of the pie here and now. They believe this wonderful destiny in the hereafter is used as an excuse by weak people who doubt themselves or they are afraid to rise up and take a fair share of the wealth they need to live. A wonderful destiny could also be used as an excuse to stop working all together.

Some early Christians stopped working because they believed Jesus's return to earth would happen at any moment! There may have been some truth in what the communist preached, but keep in mind the true communist does not believe in God or eternal life. So they do not believe Jesus is the Son of God or in the promises He made. Jesus said, *Take care! Be on your guard against all kinds of greed, for one's life does not consist in the abundance of possessions.*[2]

Jesus also warned us about false prophets who preached a false ideology like the true Communist who is an atheist. In Matthew, Jesus says, *Beware of false prophets who come to you in sheep's clothing but inwardly are ravenous wolves.*[3]

Chris's Story

Chris was attending an alternative high school for delinquent teenagers. As a school administrator, it was my job to visit the school, so it was not long before we became friends. Chris came from a poor single parent family. He was a poor student who disliked school, an angry boy with a chip on his shoulder who was always ready to fight. One morning, he came to school in a new car.

I asked him, "Whose car are you driving?"

He said, "It belongs to me."

I asked him, "Where did you get the money to buy it?"

His response was, "Wouldn't you like to know."

My response was, "You're dealing drugs in Bridgeport."

(This is a city next to our town that was once my residence.)

His response was, "So what if I am."

I asked, "Why are you doing this?"

His response, "Why are you asking me this question? You know I'm from a poor family, I don't have much of a future. I'm not good in school, so where else am I going to get the money to live the kind of life I want to live? I'm no fool. I watch TV and see the lifestyle of the rich and famous. Everyone tells me it's better to be rich than poor. Well, I was poor and want a better life being rich."

My response was, "You'll probably be dead by the time you are thirty. Do you want this?"

His reply was sad when he said, "To tell the truth, I would rather have twelve years of the high life and take my chances. I don't want to be struggling to make a skimpy living at a crummy job like digging ditches or working at a machine the rest of my life."

I warned Chris to stop dealing drugs because I cared about him and didn't want to see him get hurt. For the sake of others, I had to report Chris to the police, asking them to keep him under surveillance. At the same time, I counseled and tried to convince him to stop his illegal activity that hurt people because sooner or later, he would be arrested.

When we think about it, there is some truth to what Chris said. Getting a job involves negotiation, and when negotiating, you must have something to negotiate with. Chris could negotiate if he had a good education or sellable skills; he had neither. He could negotiate if he were a member of a union, but he didn't know anyone connected to a union nor did he have any skills many unions required. His family was poor and had nothing to give or offer him like working or inheriting a family business.

The hard truth is without an education, skills, union membership, or a family business or inherited wealth, and when the only thing you have to negotiate with is your time and manual labor, you are at the low end of the food chain.

→ Wouldn't you prefer to have your child a successful doctor or lawyer rather than a garbage collector?
→ Which one of these jobs would you prefer telling a friend your child has? Why?

Many of us might say we don't care what our child does for a living as long as it's honest work. But do we really mean it? We live in America, the land of opportunity for everyone, the land where everyone has a chance at upward mobility. For some, like Chris, there is a slim chance of rising in status or class. What does it mean to rise in status? In America, this means a better lifestyle. Perhaps it is acquiring a profession or a lucrative business, which can mean a rise in social status. It means buying all the good things we want with our new wealth, going from rags to riches.

There is another American Dream that does not entail a rags to riches story. It is working hard to buy a nice family home with a nice backyard where the kids can play. It is located in the suburbs with a good school system and safe neighborhood. Both dreams provide the motivation to drive the economy and lift us out of poverty.

→ What is your image of the American dream?

→ Do you think achieving the American dream will bring the greatest happiness possible? Many work very hard for it.

As Chris would say, "I've been poor and I've been rich. It's better to be rich!" The Bible places Jesus's presence with the poor, not the rich. To find God, we should go amongst the poor as Jesus did and help them. The Bible warns us of the psychological and spiritual danger in being rich and privileged.

What is Chris's real problem? It isn't his lack of skills, lack of union membership, or family business or any goods of fortune. Chris does not think the goods of fortune he acquires are only means to an end. He thinks they are his final end or ultimate good. If necessary, he would sacrifice his life for it. He thinks goods of fortune will bring him the greatest happiness possible in this life. It's an illusion. *His real problem is he lacks the awareness of his true identity. He perceives his value as a person is associated with money and what money can buy.*

If he lives long enough, he may learn material fortunes may bring temporary pleasure, but it never lasts. Because Chris does not know who he truly is, he does not understand his purpose in life or his destiny. It is the same with many poor young people today, especially those living in our city ghettos with a single parent and without a strong authority figure in the home. Many of these young people have very little if any moral training. They have adopted the values and priorities of a materialistic society.

→ How important are goods of fortune to you?
→ How impressed are you with people who have great wealth?
→ Do you know people who believe in God yet see their highest priority in life as goods of fortune? Perhaps this is because they see it as their greatest good and the fulfillment of the American dream.

Goods of the Body

Some people look at their bodily endowment as their greatest good here and now. They believe it brings them as close to perfect happiness as possible. Beauty, strength, physical skills acquired in athletics or the arts and professions are highly prized and proclaimed. Those without gifts of the body do not get the opportunity to use them and do not receive recognition.

As we grow old, we must lose them often to the consternation of those who once possessed them. They are temporary ends we once achieved and now watch as they slowly die. There are those who are reluctant to let them go and sadly try to hang on to them when they are gone. Some become delusional. They think they still have them when in reality, they are gone. The truth about our world and all of our animal being is that it is changing. To try to live otherwise is living an illusion.

We must learn to live with these changes. *If we do not live in accord with our identity and the changes that happen, we are living a lie, which can have tragic consequences.* It's sad to see an older man or woman acting and dressing like a teenager because they valued their youth and beauty. They considered it their greatest asset, their highest good, and could not let it go.

→ How do you feel when you see this kind of man or woman? Does it remind you of anyone?

Each morning, we wake up to a new day. All our yesterdays are gone, and our tomorrows may never come. Some of what we may have wanted and dreamed of having we will never get. A great deal of what we had and wanted to keep is gone through no fault of our own; it's just a part of life. Perhaps we dreamed of being a great athlete or professional, successful businessman, or priest. We finally realize we will never fulfill all our dreams. Maybe we were endowed with great physical skills. We were young, healthy, with loved ones who cared about us, and there was the stable church prior to Vatican II. Now it is all gone, our skills, youth and health, and even the church we knew. *Unless we accept these changes and let them go, we are not accepting reality. We are living an illusion.* We are stuck and unable to move on into the new life, we are now living without them.

→ Have you had to let go of a dream that never came true?

→ Are you trying to keep in your mind something you had or wanted, but here and now, it is gone or will never be?

It is like the woman who was trying to hold on, not wanting to let go of her youth, or a man who dreamed about being a major league athlete, which would never be.

Unless we let go of our past and all the dreams that failed to come true and unless we embrace our present existence and see all the good we have here and now, we will not be happy or find any peace in this world.

Our Destiny: Individual and Altruistic Pleasure

Individual

We do what feels good, and it is either sensuous or intellectual pleasure. Some people believe sensual pleasure is our highest good here and now. If an act produces pleasure, it is considered good. The Greeks taught happiness is synonymous with pleasure, and today, many people use the word *pleasure* for happiness.

Sensual Pleasure

Sensual pleasure is slightly different than happiness. It involves the reduction of tension by gentle motion while pain is rough motion. For these people, the wise person lives life to get the greatest sensual pleasure or gentle motion and the least pain. Many of them don't believe in

God or have serious doubts about a hereafter, so they seek the greatest amount of pleasure here on earth. This pleasure can mean feeling as good as possible with sex, even if it results in infidelity and betrayal. Or it's about feeling good about your lifestyle with great possessions and vacations. For others feeling good is about their joy in power and fame. For still others, it's food or drugs. Does this sound familiar in some people we may know? Perhaps ourselves?

Intellectual Pleasure

A variation of this aim of living for a last end is not sensual pleasure but is intellectual pleasure. These people call intellectual pleasure happiness, which is an abiding peace and a tranquil calmness. They acquire intellectual happiness by using their thinking to solve problems on their job, within their family, and for the community. They seek a peaceful happy end by keeping personal problems to a minimum and in so doing alleviate a great deal of suffering for themselves and others. *The end of physical and psychological pain is the most natural desire, and a more peaceful existence happens when pain is diminished.* They work hard to solve problems so there will be the least pain and fear, even the fear of God and death. For them, this way of life brings us as close to perfect happiness as we will ever get. The solution to a problem is good, and the conscious possession of it brings happiness, and that's all there is. They give little thought to anything else.

→ Do you recognize such people? They are usually very smart problem solvers.

We can also have smart problem solvers who do not think our greatest happiness is solving problems to eliminate and reduce physical and psychological pain. They solve problems to accomplish this goal but for a much greater purpose that involves perfect happiness to come in a life hereafter. Many people who seek pleasure as their aim in life think that a combination of sensual and intellectual pleasure is the one true end or goal. In this combination is found the greatest degree of happiness here on earth.

→ How important is physical and intellectual pleasure to you? Is it one of your highest ends and greatest priorities? It can be but under certain conditions. Do you know what these conditions might be?
→ How often do you aim for sensual or intellectual pleasure and get it?
→ Do you know people who believe in God, yet their highest priority in life is physical and intellectual pleasure because they see it as their greatest good here on earth?

Counterarguments

It is important to understand some kind of pleasure is a necessary ingredient to happiness. Without pleasure, people cannot be satisfied because they desire it. In fact, pleasure is our first good. Young children use feeling good as the standard to judge every act. For us, there is a natural relationship to pleasure. In this life, pleasure can be acquired by our faculties or natural abilities from people or things that surround us. We do not merely enjoy. We enjoy doing or experiencing something or someone. No faculty is designed exclusively for pleasure. The faculties we use to experience pleasure have other purposes.

For example, our sexual ability is for reproduction of our species, yet it has pleasure. With our intellect, we seek the truth, solve problems, and live the life of a civilized person and yet there is also pleasure in solving problems. We eat to live, but food can be enjoyable. *The pleasures and enjoyments entice us to exercise our natural abilities to act for a primary purpose, and pleasure is the lure.*

Some people would never get married were it not for the pleasures associated with being married. It is clear nature intended pleasure to be an intermediate end. It provides sensual and intellectual pleasures for a person but also lures a person to use his natural abilities for a greater purpose. We may seek pleasure as our last end or greatest good, but if we do, we are opposing or contradicting our human identity. In so doing, the act is not only unnatural but immoral.

Pleasures are not acquired by all people and at all times. To acquire some pleasures, we must give up others. We can't exercise our natural abilities continuously, so pleasure doesn't last. Too much pleasure can bring pain, and with old age, it decreases. Pleasure is most certainly not our last end nor will it bring us as much happiness as possible.

It is a feature of happiness and an inducement for getting us to do the right or wrong things.

Altruistic Pleasure

There are people who believe pleasure is our last end, but the focus cannot be on personal pleasure. They believe it comes from seeking the greatest happiness for the greatest number of people. It is known as the Greatest Happiness Principle. They think the morality of an act is determined by its ability to promote the common good. *The common good is the standard used to determine the morality of an act.* For them, the prosperity or happiness of the people is the standard of morality.

Personal pleasure and the avoidance of pain is subordinate to the general prosperity and happiness of the entire community. Many people and some politicians think this. They believe the goal or last end for human action and the standard of morality is for all humanity to be free from pain and as rich in enjoyment as possible. They dream of a utopian state. Pleasure is for the whole community and not necessarily for the pleasure or happiness of the individual person.

It is true there is a great deal of satisfaction and happiness when individuals contribute to the common good, even at a high cost to themselves. They think this is virtuous, which is a factor in making us happy. This kind of pleasure-seeking becomes altruism because it seeks the common good of freedom from pain and enjoyment for all the people. Perhaps you've experienced such people in your life. They are selfless and always willing to make others happy, even if it means losing their own. Always thinking and acting for the common good and not necessarily themselves; they believe the pleasure of others brings them great happiness. You may have heard them referred to as virtuous people.

→ Do you know people like this?
→ Do they appear to be happy most of the time?
→ How important is the common good to you?
→ Would you sacrifice things important to you for the common good?
→ Is the happiness of the majority of people more important than your own or your family and friends?

Counterarguments

There are critics who do not believe these altruistic people have found the highest possible good in this world. They do believe, however, that works of charity, helping others with gifts, relieving pain and distress brings the purest and best happiness we can experience, but it's still unsatisfactory. There will always be ingratitude and misunderstanding of someone who receives the help. Often, their efforts to do good by helping people can result in bitterness and disillusionment. Besides, they argue if helping people become better is our last end, what about the people who receive our help? What is their last end or highest good? They seem to suggest a person who is willing to receive is not as good or maybe of less value than the giver.

23

Our Destiny: Virtue and Holiness The Only True Good

There are many people who believe virtue is our last end and the only true good. For them, virtues are good moral habits of the will while vices are evil habits and all the rest are indifferent. A habit is a tendency we have; it is like a trait we considered earlier. We acquire a habit by the constant repetition of the same act. We can lose it if we do not continue acting with it or perform an opposing act.

A habit is not an act but an inclination to act. It rests between our potential to act and the act itself. Habit does not give us the power to act. Our identity or nature provides us with the power to act. When we exercise this power, we are aware that each time we perform the act, we find it easier to repeat it. We realize this is how a habit is formed. A habit contributes to our power to act by making it easier to perform the act. The act enhances the habit, and the habit makes it easier to act. We all have these traits or habits; God does not! God does not have potential and does everything with absolute ease.

→ Are you a creature of habit?
→ Are your habits good or bad?

Habitual thinking can be useful to us when habits are used to address routine tasks so we are free to use thinking to address the more serious issues in life. However, habitual thinking and conditioning can be detrimental to our lives if it dominates our thinking. It is detrimental if it prevents us from addressing a problem with creative thinking and consciously seeing. We can also think or do habitual acts that are sinful. With intellectual activity, we can imagine or focus upon good spiritual things, which bring ecstasy. Or we can imagine evil things, which brings apparent goods but ultimately agony.

Virtues

Moral virtues are morally good habits. The most important moral virtues are *prudence,* which is freely choosing the right means for a good end; *temperance,* which involves controlling our appetites for things that are good to have or good for our bodies and preventing an overindulgence of them; *courage,* which enables our facing necessary danger; and *justice,* which involves treating people fairly ensuring they get what is due them. Two of the most important intellectual virtues are *wisdom* and *understanding.* Wisdom is the ability to think and act using truths from experience, common sense, insight, and understanding. Understanding is the ability to make truthful interpretations and decisions concerning situations and especially people. *To understand people is to be sympathetic, empathetic, tolerant, and aware of the primary self-evident truths about them and ourselves.*

Self-evident moral and intellectual virtues are directly involved in good living. They are good habits, which are a part of our consciousness that can direct our will and control the passions of our sense appetites. With moral and intellectual virtues, we not only know what to do and how to do it, but it makes it easier to do. It enables us to select the right course of action, which is the means between two opposing extremes of too much or too little.

Rational thinking or reasoning is often not needed with virtues. People who believe virtue is the only true good thing are making a big mistake. They claim virtue is not only the way to happiness; it is happiness! Virtuous people are the happiest people in the world! To get some idea of what this means to some people, we must gain insight into what they think about the origin of existence, our identity, and God.

Origin of the Species

A question related to the three basic questions in our lives is simply this: what is our origin? Where do we come from? An answer to this question points in the direction of answering our three questions of identity purpose and destiny. We are all self-aware of our existence. The origin of our existence can only come from one of two sources. We always existed in different forms of energy or we and all that we see and experience were created by an individual creator. If we were created, the Creator had to create us out of nothing or use a part of Himself in His creation. Revelation tells us there is an individual Creator, and He created the universe and all that we see and experience out of nothing. Sirach states "all human beings are dust and ashes."[1] Dust and ashes can be interpreted as nothing or from created nonliving basic elements. To be created from a part of God is to be God, and if we know anything, we know we are not God.

Pantheism

There are those who believe in the ideology of virtue as the only true good, they usually do not believe in creation. They believe all the universes, everything that is in them, and the natural laws that govern them always existed. For them, all the universes taken together are God and are therefore eternal. It is an ideology called Pantheism, and many people today believe in it. According to them, our human identity is a small part of the world's universal nature and its soul. Our identity and destiny are found in nature, which is our fate. We must develop a resignation to our fate by controlling our irrational emotions.

We must act in accord with reason by discovering the immovable unchangeable laws of nature. The universes and their laws of nature are the true and only good. This is where virtue plays an important role. Virtue is the true good and only happiness for us because with it, we can live in accord with the nature of the universe and, in so doing, survive. These pantheists who focus upon the goodness of virtue believe the essence of virtue is self-sufficiency in which a person is independent of everything and everybody.

Counterargument

It is self-evident truth, and scientific fact indicates, we are not independent. Our being, which can act with virtue, is dependent on other living and nonliving beings for our existence in this world. For those of us who believe in God, we know both the material and spiritual parts of us are dependent upon God our creator. It is also a scientific fact that from nothing, nothing comes. Empty space cannot spontaneously produce anything. In studying the universe and its laws, many scientists think the design and function of the universe could only come from the intellect of some great mind. The mathematics of statistics' does attempt to account for events of the universe and the existence of its beings. As previously mentioned, the chance of these events happening or its more advanced beings coming into existence using the mathematical laws of probability are astronomically small. It's almost impossible to believe. It has to be the handiwork of a Creator.

→ Do you believe all existence here and now is God or a part of God? If so, you are not a Christian, Jew, or Muslim but a pantheist.
→ Do you believe acting with virtue is self-sufficient? Or do you believe that acting with virtue has some other purpose? Virtue is a valuable tool for those who believe in God.
→ Do you know where you came from and where you are going? Jesus said to the Pharisees, *Even if I do testify on my own behalf, my testimony is valid because I know where I came from and where I am going.*[2]

Holiness

The philosopher, Emmanuel Kant, attempted to reconcile the ideas of happiness and virtue by uniting them into a process he called "holiness." Holiness is a feature belonging to our identity, which entirely achieves the purpose of our existence, and therefore, we are completely one with ourselves. Kant maintains that virtue is the pursuit of holiness. Our last end is holiness, and the highest good for us is the virtue of pursuing holiness so we can be worthy of happiness. Although we strive for holiness, all eternity is needed to possess it if we ever can or will possess it. This is because strictly speaking, only God is holy. It is an overwhelming mysterious holiness which is "utterly other" than His creation.[3] It is a holiness beyond description.

Our worthiness to be happy is partial, just as our happiness is partial and not perfect. We pursue holiness by acting with virtue moment to moment. Virtue is superior to happiness because happiness is a by-product of the virtue of pursuing holiness. The virtue of pursuing holiness is a duty we pursue for its own sake; however, it may be a pursuit of an unreachable goal or end.

To summarize what this ideology believes is that holiness is the true end we seek, but our last end may be the pursuit of it by virtuous acts, and in so doing, we are worthy of happiness. We may never get to the truly last end or it may take all eternity to reach it!

→ Do you think a God who created and loves us would make the true last end He wants us to have unreachable?
→ Do you believe our pursuit of holiness is the highest good we can expect and is most likely our last end?

The Bible tells us to be holy because God is holy.[4] Holiness is an unfathomable feature of God; it is a special state of being or existence. *Holiness is existence without sin which is a pure existence.* Holiness may be an attribute of our final true end, but it is not the end. We'll make this clearer a little further along.

Our Destiny: Virtue and Knowledge

Happiness is found in the intellect, and therefore, it is a subjective state. We know rational knowledge is from the intellect, and virtue is from the habits of the intellect and will; they too are a subjective state. It would appear we have found our last end. Perhaps virtue and knowledge are our last end and the highest good, which produces happiness, we seek here and now.

Objective of the Intellect

The objective of our intellect is total truth and goodness. The free will informed by the intellect of what is good seeks total goodness. When we talk about wanting complete satisfaction of an insatiable desire for an ultimate end, we are talking about knowing all there is to know that is real and truly good. When we possess all of it, we are perfectly happy. Our intellect is constantly seeking knowledge and truth. It won't stop if there is more to know. Aren't we always looking for knowledge in school, on the Internet, in the news media, TV, books, movies, and from experiences in daily living? Isn't life about knowing more each day. Can anyone say they know all there is to know or want to know? Can we say we don't want to know more about God or ourselves, family or friends, business, events of the day, or even the weather?

Knowing People

We are, by nature, social beings. We are not created to live alone, and loneliness can be a terrible feeling. This drive to reach out to people and to know all that is true about them is not only instinctual but rational. Our intellect is unlimited in our desire to know all human beings we encounter. This is because all people have some goodness within them, and remember, we are all good by virtue of our identity as rational living existence. And more, we all have the potential for getting better and better in our goodness. Our intellect can look at ourselves as well as others. We see not only the good we possess but the greater good we can become. In reaching out to people, we want to know their hopes, dreams, needs, and fears. As we listen to their stories, we are searching for the goodness and truth that can be found in everyone. We want to find and know the goodness no matter how small it may be.

→ Do you look for the good in everyone, no matter how small it may be?
→ Do you see not only what a person is but what the person could be?
→ Do you see the good you possess as well as the greater good you can become?
→ How do you respond to the goodness or potential goodness you see?

It is true we want to know the goodness in everyone, but for what reason? Why is it so important to know about their goodness? Do you know the answer to this question?

All people have the same human nature, needs and desires that come from their faculties of intellect and free will. Now we see our nature includes an insatiable universal appetite that craves and strives for virtue, truth, and goodness. Like the longings for happiness and peace, this craving lasts a lifetime and won't stop because they are not satisfied. We know we desire total truth, yet even when we possess a limited amount of truth, it is good and can bring us happiness.

Once again, desire for truth is placed in our nature by God, so it must be obtainable. Saint John refers to Jesus who is the light that brings truth: "The true light which enlightens everyone was coming into the world."[1]

He goes on to tell us that Jesus said to the Jews who believed in Him, *If you continue in my word, you are truly my disciples; and you will know the truth and the truth will make you free.*[2]

If your children desire something that is truly good for them, and if it were within your power to satisfy their desires, would you deny them? Not if you love them, especially since you had a hand in creating them with these natural desires of truth and virtue, and so it is with God, our Creator.

Counterargument

To dedicate our lives to the pursuit of truth and virtue is an excellent way to live because they are important in obtaining our last end, but they are not our last end.

Can possession of total truth result in the highest good and make us perfectly happy not only here and now but in a life to come? We must keep in mind total truth for us is limited by our capacity to know, and this is determined by our nature. We cannot possess absolutely all truth because to do so is to be God! We could have, however, an almost infinite capacity for knowledge.

Our knowledge is not perfect; therefore, it is subject to error and is often not perfectly clear. Rational knowledge involving thinking and remembering can only be acquired by the hard work of study, at least in this world. We can never acquire enough of it. We have people who never desire a great deal of specific knowledge in fields such as science, mathematics, or history, etc. Some knowledge we acquire can be disappointing due to the fact that knowledge can be used for good or evil. This indicates it's a means, not an end. People who seek and acquire knowledge can be happy, but we are fooling ourselves if we think it will produce the greatest happiness here on earth. We'll never get enough of it and can use it for evil. Since we can use it for evil, it could never be our final end.

As we know, virtues are morally good habits. The exercise of acting with these habits can lead us to our last end, but they are not the last end. Unless they can lead us to an end or a good we seek, they have no meaning or value. The good that any virtue has comes from the end. *What is the value of knowing and the habit of acting morally if it does not get us to our final end?* Is it worth knowing or doing? With knowledge, we must see an end as the greatest good, which is presented to the will. The will with traits and virtues or morally good habits drive us on to our final end and greatest good. The virtue of the pursuit of Holiness has little meaning or value if it does not get us to our true last end.

Our Destiny Is Evolution

The theory of evolution indicates the unlimited progress of humanity and people's ability to develop themselves. Many people today use this ideology to find their ultimate purpose in life and their final end. *To these people, the process of evolving is far more important than an unknown last end.* To some people, life is merely a matter of adjusting internal mental activities with the external universe.

For their own good, we must adjust people's desires with the altruistic desire for the common good. We must adjust our cooperation with the universe without any activities interfering with it. Adjustment brings happiness, and lack of adjustment brings pain. The psychologist, Allport, who defined personality believed his system of traits create patterns of thoughts, feelings, and behaviors that enable us to adjust to our environment. The adjustment determines our physical survival.

If you are an evolutionist, you believe your last end, which is your destiny, and that of all humanity is to evolve toward a higher state of living beings. Consider this: if everything is evolving, then everything is changing. This is a truth we discover in experiencing reality. We experience change daily in our lives. It's a scientific fact. Our bodies and minds are changing second by second. If everything is changing from moment to moment, how can we be aware of ourselves? How can we know who we are? Eastern ideology says we can't!

Survival

There are two kinds of survival, one physical and the other spiritual. Both are parts of our identity. There is physical and spiritual dying or transformation. We can die physically, but as we know, our conscious spirit will go on. There is also a spiritual death determined by whether we live in accord with our identity. Spiritual death does not mean we will no longer exist as a spirit. We have determined that the spirit never dies, so what does it mean to die spiritually? Do you know?

We have established, as spiritual beings, the conscious part of our identity never changes. This is consistent with our self-image, which was made in the image of God. God is total actualization of all that is good and true. She never changes in the eternal presence. Our destiny can change from what God intended. We can rebuke Her intentions. With a free intellect and will, we can change our destiny to a final end that is not good. Our identity in this final end will continue to exist after our material body is transformed at death into its base elements, but it will not be an existence God intended. This is spiritual death. We will discuss it in greater detail later in the book.

According to the evolutionists, presently, our adjustment is imperfect, but we are evolving into a synthesis of individual and common goods. *The individual good involves the energy we turn inward to keep ourselves together as human beings. The common good is the energy we turn outward to help others. The evolutionist believes our last end is either evolving energies for ourselves, for the common good, or a synthesis of the two.*

Our Destiny: Evolving Energy for Ourselves

One version of evolutionism believes self-actualization is the ultimate goal, our greatest good, and as happy as we'll ever be. To these people, self-realization is one's awareness of their full potential. Being all, we can be. Another way of saying it is the actualization of all our potential. Since we are made in the image of God, we have within us undeveloped talents and abilities God has given us. When people develop their talents, there is a self-actualization that results in our satisfaction that produces happiness. Self-realization of our actualized talents and abilities is our happiness because it is good.

→ Have you developed any of your talents and experienced satisfaction and happiness?
→ To what degree do you wish to develop them?

→ How important is their development to you? Why?

For people who believe in this ideology, self-actualization is our true and ultimate end. Many people believe they can be better versions of themselves by actualizing their potential talents. These ideologists believe *the idea of further self-actualization of one's potential is the moralizing influence in life.* It is their moral standard, and when one acts to self-actualize their potential, they are good. People's morality is identified with their final end, which is self-actualization. Many people live to actualize their potential to be all they can be. Women as well as men see self-actualization as a high priority, and some are willing to sacrifice much of their lives for it. Unfortunately, in some cases, women would even sacrifice their service to their children to be all they can be at work or in their professions.

→ Do you know people who believe in God but think self-actualization is the greatest possible good at least in this world?
→ Do you think they are as happy as it gets here and now? They are totally dedicated to their work and talent. There are many people who develop their talents and are successful and appear to be satisfied and happy.
→ Why do you seek self-actualization?
→ Do you think it is the greatest good possible or a lesser good?

If we actualize our potential for our own sake and personal satisfaction, most of our energy is turned inward, focusing primarily upon our own self-development. Those who believe this is our destiny maintain either a universal nature, or God provides us with these potential abilities and wants us to develop them.

Counterargument

The problem is the desire for self-actualization can be with mediocre talents, and their development is never perfect. In the end, we lose our talents to old age and death. Even if we develop a great talent to a high degree, can we be truly satisfied with ourselves and the recognition we may receive? People who are extremely talented or successful in a profession or business are not always satisfied and happy. This is because all they truly care about is the actualization of their talent to a great degree, often for the fame it brings.

When Babe Ruth walked down the street, people would say, "There goes Babe Ruth, the best baseball player there ever was or will be." Their identity becomes their talent or profession. It becomes their "I am." I am an actor, teacher, fireman, or soldier, etc. They may get married, but foremost in their life is the product of their talent and work. In many cases, with such people, divorce is inevitable. We see it in movie stars and professional athletes.

It is true self-development can bring us happiness, and sometimes, it is accompanied by fame, fortune, and worldly power, but it can never make us perfectly happy. In fact, it is not the happiest we can be in life. *We were never made to be satisfied with ourselves!* The energy that drives us inward to self-development can lead to significant reduction or even exclusion of the energy pushing outward to relate with others for the common good. This can be detrimental to our well-being. Self-development is a good end, but it is not our last end or highest good. It can and should be directed to our last end.

Our Destiny: Evolving Energy for the Common Good

An alternative to self-development for the individual is to develop one's self exclusively for the common good. In this case, much of our energy is turned outward, focusing our self-development primarily for the whole human race or nation. People with this ideology maintain the last end of the individual man or woman is to contribute to the good of all people or the nation. This determines the value of a person.

This was the ideology of Nazi Germany and a lot of other totalitarian nations. These despotic nations think that morality comes from the state and consists of obeying civil laws. In Nazi Germany, laws which stripped Jews of their citizenship, the right to education, followed by the loss of their businesses, homes, and ultimately their lives were considered moral and right! It was evil. There are acts, however, the state must order and other acts the state must forbid because our identity as human beings require it. As we know, there are acts that are morally right and others morally wrong by their very nature and existed long before customs or the state!

This ideology believes as individuals we are only capable of a little happiness, but our race and nation are evolving into a race of supermen and women with a great deal of happiness. Millions of people liked it. We want to be as happy as we can be in this life as well as make others happy. We don't want to wait for some future that may never come. We want things that benefit us and the nation here and now as we live. This happiness involves the evolving race of people and the nation. It will bring greater material goods of fortune and a higher level of culture with an increase in talents. This can provide greater cultural experiences, including fame, prestige, and power to the nation of people as a whole. It does provide some benefits to the individuals who share in this ideology and contribute to it, but our final end is not the good of the nation.

→ Do you like this ideology? What do you like or dislike about it?

Counterargument

This ideology and its implementation will not bring the highest good and can't produce complete satisfaction, which is perfect happiness, or even come close to it. If individuals exist for the whole race, and this is our destiny, then what is the goal of the whole nation or race of people? *Men and women were not made to live exclusively for the state or common good!* We must live for the common good, but we must also live for ourselves. We don't want to completely lose ourselves or our identity and the awareness of our existence within the state or even within God, for that matter. To lose our own identity and separate existence from God is to be assimilated into God, so we become God or a part of God.

We know for sure we are not God or even a part of God because God is an infinitely good being who is perfectly happy; we are not! Most certainly, the state is not God. *Nor will we be completely satisfied or happy with an unknown destiny that is evolving toward something we will never experience.*

The evolutionist claims progress for the sake of progress, but it's pointless. How can we progress or move without a known goal? The United States' liberal ideology of the utopian state and the advancement of civilization has merit, but it is not our goal or final end. The utopian state is an illusion. It will never be achieved because of the imperfection of humanity. As the Son of God revealed, the poor will always be with us. Jesus was not only referring to being physically poor but spiritually poor since sin and evil will always be with us in this world. We can strive for a better state, but it will never be perfect or ideal. Utopia is a spiritual idea, not a physical reality. The utopian state is most certainly not our last end or highest good.

→ What is the highest priority that directs your energy? Is it "inward" for self-development and actualization? Or is it "outward" for the common good? This may account for your earlier response of being an introvert or extrovert.

→ Is there a balance of the two in your life?

→ How do these answers compare with your previous answers on individualization and socialization?

Self-development for ourselves and the common good are both good intermediate ends. As we know, there must be a balance of both energies in our lives, but they are not our last end or highest good. They can and should be directed to our last end.

Our Destiny: The Evolving Energy of Pragmatism

A second version of evolution believes thinking is a tool that motivates the will to solve problems and seek a satisfying life. In the world of experience, most of the time, we do what is most satisfying. Don't you seek to do what is most satisfying? And when you are satisfied, aren't you happy? Life offers all kinds of good things. The good we choose is the greater good, and the good we reject is the lesser good or evil. We choose the greater good based on our abilities, what satisfies us, the requirements of the situation, but most of all, what we perceive will bring greater future satisfaction.

If it works to solve our problems and satisfy us, it's the greatest good for us. *What works to satisfy is good.* This is pragmatism, and it is very practical. It is the ideology of John Dewey. We don't need an end to drive us forward.

When satisfied, we seek another new experience for another satisfaction. With satisfaction in solving problems or dealing with a situation appropriately, we are happy. In evolution, we need no end or destiny; it is the process of moving the energy force that pushes us outward to find what works right here and now. This is most important, not the end.

→ Do you believe you do not need an end to motivate you?
→ Do you think a satisfying experience is enough to drive you and everyone else forward to search and acquire more?

Pragmatic people seldom make long-term plans or think about ends but live day by day. Their concern is the process of moving forward, not in the destination. There are people who some may call pragmatic who make very few plans, live day-to-day, spend most of what they earn, and often will borrow to live in the present. They give little thought to their increasing debt and how they will have to pay it back some day. They live in the present, satisfying their immediate needs and desires to buy without any thoughts of the past or future. Their primary concern is being happy and satisfied in the present.

Moving from one moment to another, they experience as much satisfaction and goodness as possible. If they vacation on a ship, they don't care about the destination, only enjoying themselves onboard and encourage friends to join them because it increases their enjoyment. Not all pragmatists are debtors, but they all seek to solve problems associated with their desires so they can acquire the greatest amount of satisfaction and happiness in this life. They do not think about the long-term future, and their motto is "If it works for me now, it is good."

→ Do you recognize some of this pragmatism in yourself?
→ Is there some good or truth in pragmatism? If so, what could it be?

A Summary of Ideologies

All evolutionists believe our existence is evolving toward a state in which all human problems will be solved. This would be the utopian state that some politicians say they are working to achieve. Self-actualization of our potential abilities or the pragmatism of finding what works to satisfy us can be for the sake of the individual person. It could also be for the sake of the common good, the state, or the entire human race. It could by a synthesis of both alternatives.

Synthesis of the two is the logical choice because within every person's identity is the desire for individualization and socialization. We must balance a union or synthesis of egotism and altruism, and often, this is hard to do. As we know from personal experience, we were never made to be satisfied with ourselves. Nor were we made to live exclusively for the state or for the common good. To do so and expect to be satisfied is an illusion.

Pragmatism as well as all the other ideologies deal primarily with our temporal welfare. It is our welfare in time, our physical presence here on earth with little to no thought given to our spirituality. All these pragmatic ideologies which deal with our destiny make temporal welfare our last end and highest good. Indeed, people should be as satisfied and happy as can be here and now, and whatever works to make them satisfied is good. We should have as much pleasure and as little pain as possible in this short time we have on earth.

With our discussion of the different destinies that people believe in, it is clear that goods of fortune or what is below man and man himself cannot make us perfectly happy. These ideologies along with their destinies will never completely satisfy us by themselves or in combination with others. They are transient and uncertain, and over all of them looms the specter of death. *Death alone is a sufficient argument to show these ideologies could not be our last end or highest good.* We dealt with these different ideologies to help you see how some people make them their last end, their highest good, and the be all and end all of their lives.

Some people may ask, we are finite beings, why can't we be satisfied with a finite good? Why must we seek total good and perfect happiness? To answer this question, we start by realizing there are two types of capacities for goodness and happiness. There are proximate and remote capacities, and in God, they are identical, but not in human beings. In dealing with a proximate capacity, we are dealing with a capacity at a particular moment. Remote capacity deals with the full potential of the human intellect, which is never reached in the present moment. As we know, the intellect is finite in its nature, but in its range of operation, it is unlimited. It always wants to know more and possess more good, even though the human intellect can never know all truth or possess all goodness. Only God in a life to come can completely fill our proximate capacity, which is finite by nature but has an unlimited reserve of truth and goodness for our remote capacity.

26

Our True Last End or Greatest Good

We've seen that all the ideologies we've considered are not our last end or highest good. We have considered them so we could see and understand how so many people can lose their way in searching for it. Perhaps you are one of them. Even when we honestly think we believe in God and go to church, there may be doubt and confusion about who we are, where we're going, and how to get there. So we reach out for immediate goods often found in one of these ideologies, but none of them are completely satisfying. These ideologies will not provide us with the greatest amount of good in this life. Nor will they ever provide us with as much happiness as possible, even if we managed to acquire the goodness they offer.

Many of these ideologies claim our temporal welfare is our greatest good and last end. By temporal, we mean our physical and psychological well-being in our present existence. For those who do not believe in God or eternal life, these ideologies seem reasonable. We should get as much happiness with the least amount of pain as possible. For those who believe in God, these ideologies may fulfill some of our temporal needs but will miss our spiritual needs and final end.

Our True Last End is the Possession of God

We all want to possess the greatest possible good so we can be as happy as possible. It can only be found by living in conformity with our true identity and accord with the divine identity expressed in the Bible. We have eliminated all things below human beings and humankind itself. Our destiny is to possess God. *We believe humanity will only find as much goodness and happiness as possible in this life, and the greatest good and perfect happiness in eternal life by possessing God!* This is because God is infinite goodness and happiness. If we wish to possess as much goodness as the proximate capacity of our nature allows so we can be as completely happy as we were designed to be, we must possess God. Keep in mind in our union or possession of God individualization coexists with socialization. We unite with God by giving of ourselves, but not our identity or who we are. In the possession of God, we are not assimilated or lose our identity in the union. If we were totally absorbed into God, we would become God and we know we are not God.

Only a being that can fully satisfy all our desires for total truth and goodness can make us perfectly happy.

God is the only being that possesses total goodness and truth.

Therefore, only the being of God can satisfy our desire for total goodness and truth and make us perfectly happy, and hence, possessing God is our last end.

How to Possess God

We possess God by living as perfect a relationship as possible with Her in this life and a completely perfect relationship in eternal life. As we know, life is relationship, and the objective of this relationship is union within ourselves and outside ourselves with God and others. *If we do not have a relationship with God, then we cannot possess God.* If we do not possess God, our destiny could be quite different from what God intended. Another way of explaining this is if we live in conformity to our identity, we possess God. God directs us in our possessing Him by our living in conformity to the identity He gave us. Or we can act in a similar way Jesus's identity compels Him to act. Only spirit can unite and possess the Holy Spirit. God is spirit, and those who worship Her, must worship in spirit and truth.[1] In this union, we possess God as much as the proximate capacity of our identity will allow and with an unlimited reserve for our remote capacity. This is our destiny and the final end God intended.

Questions

Some questions will arise.

→ We are finite human beings; God is infinite; how can we hope to possess Her?

We must understand not only our possession of God but the way we possess Her. Certainly, God is infinite, but we do not possess Her in an infinite way, the way the Father, Son, and Holy Spirit possess each other in the Holy Trinity. In eternal life, we will be perfectly happy in a way in which our created nature will be completely satisfied, but we will not be infinitely happy! We will know and relate to God as much as our created nature's capacity allows. Our possession of the infinite is finite. If this is the case, then we would know that a greater goodness and happiness exists.

→ Since we know there is a greater good to possess, how can we be perfectly satisfied if there is more good to possess?

We possess God by the fullness of the proximate capacity of our nature, and so we can be perfectly happy. In eternal life, our proximate capacity could differ according to size. Some may be bigger than others, according to the condition of our spirit and the way we've lived our lives in relationship with God. The nature of the God of justice demands it. In heaven, our souls will know saints that will have a larger capacity for good and a much greater degree of happiness than many others. Will we be envious or dissatisfied with our own limited condition of perfect happiness? We can't be envious or dissatisfied when we are perfectly happy because to be in such a state of happiness, we must be in conformity to God's will. We know that God's will is just and best for us.

How We Direct Energy

We know now that we can possess God by establishing a union with Him, but how do we establish this union? For many people, God's presence is not seen or felt in this world. We know that nature establishes a union of existence by the process of giving, sharing, and receiving parts of one's self with others, but how do we do this with a God who is not present to us? How do we use our spiritual energy to possess God by spiritually uniting with Her? We must look within ourselves and without to scientific knowledge and divine revelation for answers. From revelation and our own personal introspection, we know God's and our identities are spiritual; for us, it is spirit within a body. Therefore, spiritual energy results in a spiritual union expressed in our living existence.

To possess God, we must look to how we use our spiritual energy to existence as well as establish the existence of new beings. How do we direct this energy? Scientists and evolutionists give us some idea of how to direct this energy. We know science teaches us that our energy forces are directed "inward" to maintain our own existence. They can also be directed "outward," uniting with other human beings to establish new existence, such as a family, friendship, or giving birth to a child. Or we can unite nonliving beings to create a new existing being, such as a car, furniture, and electricity.

We have seen that one theory of evolution has us actualize our potential abilities for both ourselves and the common good. Both objectives are accomplished by balancing our energy. We direct some of the energy to actualize our abilities inward to benefit our individual existence and outward to benefit the common good. We possess God in a similar fashion in how we use our energy. We can use our energy to establish a relationship with God through individualizing and socializing. Our inward individualization and outward socialization forces are different from all lower forms of existence, even though the process is similar.

Internal Focus

The essential difference between the existence of human beings and the existence of all other beings in this world is our spirituality. We turn our spiritual energy inward to be aware of ourselves, our thoughts, feelings, and actions. We are aware of our thoughts and feelings and can focus them upon our Creator. We focus upon the Creator and so relate and possess Him, Her, or the universal God through the process of communication. We communicate with God by prayer, the Bible, using methods of meditating or contemplating. We will be more specific about this relationship by communication in the second part of this book.

Our awareness and relationship with God provide us with a true understanding of our identity, purpose, and destiny. This understanding brings meaning and value to our lives so that we are able to hold our psychological and spiritual existence together. As we have seen, without meaning, life is unbearable; we can fall apart, and suicide is a possible alternative.

External Focus

Our spiritually conscious intellect and free will also uses the spiritual energy of life directed outward to create the relationship that establishes a union with others. This is done by using our spiritual energy to give and share with love parts of ourselves and our possessions, which unites us with others and God! As Jesus taught us, *Truly I tell you, just as you did it to one of the least of these who are members of my family, you did it for me.*[2] Jesus was telling us that when we feed the hungry, clothe the naked, and shelter the homeless, we are not only doing it for the least of *His* family; we are doing it for Him, the Son of God. This is the way we establish a union with God, and in so doing, we decide to possess God. Keep in mind in our union or possession of God individualization coexists with socialization. We unite with God by giving of ourselves, but not our identity or who we are. In the possession of God, we are not assimilated or lose our identity in the union. If we were totally absorbed into God, we would become God and we know we are not God.

Unless we communicate with God first with an internal focus on prayer followed by an external act of uniting with others, we cannot relate to God. If we do not relate to God, how can we hope to unite, and in so doing, possess God?

Conclusion

In short, we can use our energy to maintain our existence and help others to exist. They in turn help us exist for the sake of God and Her will. When we do this, we relate to God, and with Her help, we can diminish our sinfulness and enhance our holiness. As we know, holiness is pure existence without sin. This attribute of existence can only be perfect in heaven. On earth, our holiness is a potential that can be slowly actualized by the proper use of energy here and now. It will not be fully actualized until our final end in heaven.

Who are we? As we have seen, we are spiritual living human beings existing within a physical body, created by God in His image with an intellect and free will that enables us to direct our spiritual energy to unite with God. In this union is the relationship that allows us to possess God. We are, however, much more! God's intellect like our intellect requires a motive that will energize Her actions.

What is God's motive for turning Her energy "inward," uniting three persons within one God? What is the motive for turning His energy "outward" to save us from our sins so we survive as spiritual human beings for all eternity united to Him? What is our motive for using our energy inwardly or outwardly to relate? It is the motive that determines our use of life's energy. ***God's only motive for Her actions is the motive of love. Made to Possess God, it must be our motive as well!***

Part 2

LIVING IN LOVE

27

Needs and Love

Needs Influence Behaviors

The essence of God and human beings is life. A fundamental question is what motivates the movement of life? Some psychologists focus upon our needs and consider them the primary motivators of life. They regard them as the building blocks of our personality. There are primary or physical needs and secondary or psychological and spiritual needs. They are motives that generate the energy to act so we can survive physically, psychologically, and spiritually in this world.

How do needs work? To answer this question, we must look inside ourselves and see that our motive for striving or searching is for things we need or desire. We seek to satisfy our needs and desires by consciously possessing things within our intellect as well as things we must physically possess such as food and shelter. When we possess what we need, our search is over, and we have achieved our intermediate end; it is good, and we are happy. We see our motive for striving and searching is to satisfy our needs and desires that have been placed in our nature by God. *To see that needs and desires motivate the energy to search and seek is to see a truth about ourselves.*

Strength of Need

One attribute of need is strength or intensity. The amount of energy used to satisfy a need is demonstrated by the intensity of the behavior. A need considered of great importance will result in greater energy expressed in the intensity of the behavior to acquire it. The intensity is exhibited in the vigor, enthusiasm, or thoroughness with which a behavior is done. "Need strength" can also be observed in the priority of a need. A high priority need can be seen in what we do first. If it's important, it is usually done first.

→ How much strength does your need or desire for God have?
→ Do you devote time to Him daily? Do you frequently talk to Him?

Primary Physical Needs

Our basic natural needs, such as food, water, sex, shelter, and safety must be satisfied repeatedly over time. As time passes, basic needs gradually become more intense, and we act so the need is satisfied. For example, with the passage of time, your body starts to need food. Eventually, when the need gets strong enough, we'll do something to get food, which diminishes the need state. Clearly, the motivation to act for basic needs stems from our efforts to maintain a physiological balance and survive. It keeps stress to a minimum and ensures a sense of biological well-being. It is an important motivation but not our greatest one!

Providing for Primary Needs

We are fortunate because in our country, we have a surplus of supplies to satisfy our primary needs. We are not afraid because we have more than enough. Unfortunately, this is not the case in some Third World countries where starvation rears its ugly head, and people die and live in squalor. Imagine waking up each morning, wondering if you can get enough food to eat. It is immoral for countries like ours to have a surplus of material goods while people in other countries lack the necessities to survive as human beings. The world and its natural resources, including food, belong to God. Jesus blessed those aware of this fact, calling them poor in Spirit.

When we are poor in Spirit, we know that everything belongs to God. Therefore, everything we have is a gift from God, including our lives. We are grateful for the good things He has given us and we thank Him. Since this is so, we should see that we are not enough. Nor do we have or know enough to deal with the demands and problems of life. We should understand life forces us to depend on God to survive each day. God trusts us to be good stewards of His precious gift of life. He trusts us to spread His message of love with acts of compassion to the poor, the sick, immigrants, and even those who have harmed us the most. It is an expression of our love and gratitude for Her many gifts. Some Christians do not act in ways that indicate they are aware of this truth or perhaps choose to ignore it.

→ Are you poor in Spirit?

God wants us all to have an understanding that we are to be poor in spirit. We are to love each other and share Her resources so that all might survive and live in dignity. It is not a matter of charity but of justice. Justice is one of the primary virtues of love. A just act is an act of love. Unfortunately, people have exploited the poor by owning and controlling the world's resources. They use these resources to enhance their existence and power at the expense of people who suffer and die.

We read in Micah, "Alas for those who devise wickedness and evil deeds. They covet fields and seize them; houses and take them away, they oppress householder and home, people and their inheritance. Therefore, thus says the Lord, 'Now I am devising an evil against this family.'"[1] The few with power and wealth exploit the many. As my father would say, "The big fish eats the little fish." With little regard for God and His creation, they take not only their share but what rightly belongs to others, including their rights. This is not justice.

As Martin Luther King said, "We can never have peace without justice." It has been this way since the beginning of recorded history. One of the reasons people go to war is for resources. For the Christian, the common good takes precedent over private wealth and ownership of the world's resources.

- → Are you just?
- → Do you thank God for your good fortune?
- → Do you pray for those who are less fortunate and share some of God's gifts with those in need?

Secondary Psychological Needs

Secondary needs require a rational intellect and free will to function. The intellect does not spend a great deal of time on basic needs in those people who are fortunate enough to live in countries with a surplus of material supplies. People in these countries are more aware of their psychological or elicited needs. Elicited needs evoke the intellect to be aware of things, such as achievement, self-actualization, power, self-esteem, dominance, and affiliation. They are often called higher order needs.

We do not need to satisfy our psychological needs to survive physically. However, in satisfying psychological needs, we acquire ends necessary to maintain a healthy psyche. Our psyche deals with our mind. Imagine trying to live without self-esteem or if our efforts to actualize our potential talents are frustrated or we struggle in our efforts to achieve or belong. Mentally, we would be severely handicapped, and it could influence our spirituality. To focus upon secondary needs requires an intellect and free will. Animals do not have the intelligence, consciousness, nor the free will of people; therefore, they do not experience the secondary needs.

Intelligence and free will are also required for the need to love and be loved, which is the highest need resulting in the cardinal or greatest motive. In the hierarchy of needs, psychologist placed the need for affiliation or belonging, which some call love, between our primary and secondary needs. Love is the linchpin that can be involved in all other needs. Love is an end in itself while both physical and psychological needs are intermediate ends that can be used in the process of love. These intermediate ends can motivate us to act so we can satisfy the need to survive physically and psychologically.

→ Do you think our motivation to act is only a matter of physical or psychological survival?

These needs can also be instrumental in the process of possessing God in love, which is our final end. It all depends upon whether we act with the motive of love. We must see that all our needs, which involve surviving here and now, can have a spiritual value when used with love in serving God by serving our fellow human beings.

PARTIAL LIST OF PRIMARY and SECONDARY NEEDS

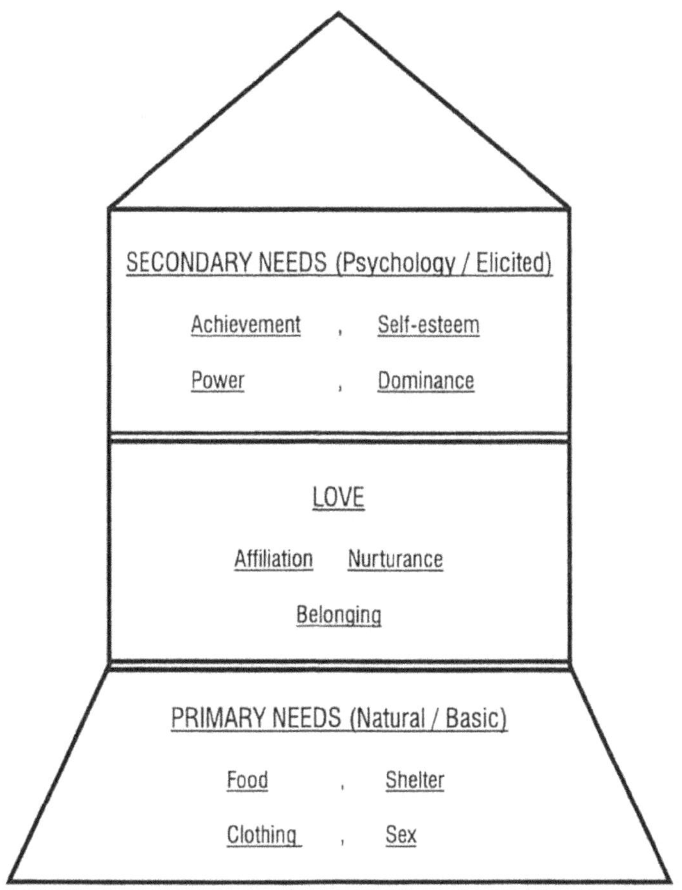

Difference Between Need and Desire

We should not confuse need and desire. Desire motivates us to get what we want but do not need to physically survive. We need food to stay alive. We do not need the secondary needs of power or achievement. Both primary and secondary needs can be desired; however, primary need is necessary for physical survival. If there is a dire need for things to survive, the strength to acquire them can be much greater. Any secondary needs such as success or power can be thought of as desires using this distinction.

Needs Can Fuse and Compliment

Our needs can fuse and reinforce each other. This attribute of needs is fusion or interrelating. It can get difficult because needs can stand alone or can fuse with each other to be reflected in the same act. For example, a woman may have a high need to nurture her child to alleviate her loneliness but can also dominate the child, which is her need for power. She nurtures in a way that enables her to dominate her child. Or a teacher may have a need to exchange information and dominate her children. She may deliver information to her students in a teaching approach that directs their behavior in an aggressive or authoritative manner.

Why do we need to know and to exchange information? As we know, the objective of our intellect is to acquire information and truth because information can be power! It can be used to help us and others or it can be used to hurt or destroy others in the case of gossip and spying. Information can be used to take advantage or treat unfairly those without it.

In addition to fusing a need, we can also interrelate needs having them complement and reinforce each other. For example, a person's need for exchanging information can support and work to benefit the need to nurture and love. One of the reasons Jesus came into the world was to deliver information to us concerning heavenly matters. It was information about the heavenly kingdom to come that only the Son of God could reveal, and He did it out of compassion and love. He related our need for information with our need for nurturing love. We needed this information to survive as spiritual human beings. *Many of our needs can complement, reinforce, or fuse with our spiritual need to love.*

Love Is a Great Spiritual Need

Love has both physical and psychological aspects to it. We call it a spiritual need. Love is like a secondary need because it requires a rational intellect and will. It is like a primary need involved with our physical survival. It is also essential to our spiritual survival as human beings.

If God did not love us, we could not survive physically. Love is an essential need when we live in accordance with our nature. When we love, we are following in the footsteps of Christ, and we begin to live a heavenly existence here on earth, which continues into a heavenly life to come.

Motivation by Needs

Psychologists think both primary and secondary needs operate through a concept termed "Motive." People of faith include the spiritual need for God as the cardinal need. *A motive is the reason that impels a person to act.* We can be aware or unaware of the reasons, and in many cases, we are unaware.

Press

Motive involves both need or desire and an environmental influence called press. A press is an external condition that creates a desire to obtain or avoid something. Press brings into play motivation just as need does. Both needs and press involve the ends we are motivated to achieve by our acts. An example of how press works with a need for food is when we just finished a wonderful dinner and are completely satisfied. Along comes someone with our favorite ice-cream cake, and all of a sudden, we don't feel as satisfied. The motive to eat has been revived not by need but by press.

Another example of press for secondary needs is our effort to keep up with friends concerning our home, car, clothing, or vacations. It all involves fear and competition. We get a new expensive car not because we need or want it but because it is better than our neighbor's car. Competition of this sort can have a serious effect upon our generosity. Instead of concern for the social good, our focus is primarily upon ourselves and how we can be better than others.

Press can also work with other secondary psychological needs when we see someone receive a reward for achieving something. It can increase our own motivation to get a similar reward by replicating their achievement. Teachers use press with students. They have unmotivated students observe classmates receiving rewards for academic achievements, hoping they will be motivated to replicate the achievements for similar rewards.

→ Can you think of a time when you were motivated to act by environmental press?

A woman who decides to have an abortion can be persuaded by press. It may not only be a matter of satisfying her own individual desires, such as the baby preventing her from developing her talents or the lifestyle she seeks. It may also be pressure from the family, friends, or boyfriend. It may be pressure from society as a whole, which says, "It's your body, do what is best for you. Get rid of the baby." After all, the civil law says it's okay! It may not be just her own personal sin but the sin of people in a society who help push her into it!

Press can be used to enhance the generosity of love for the common good! The apostles watched Jesus's acts of love demonstrating His compassion for the hungry and sick by feeding and healing them. They saw the love, respect, and admiration He received from the people and His love for them. Jesus served the people with and without miracles. The washing of feet is a service without miracles. Jesus used miracles to demonstrate His love so that people would believe the teaching He received from His Father. The apostles were motivated to serve by watching Jesus serve the people with love. They wanted to love and be loved like Jesus. The importance of press is seen in surrounding our children with good examples in their formative years.

Bartering

In our interaction with others, we often barter for what we need. This interaction is not sinful in itself. We interact by giving and getting, but some of us always try to get more than we give for our own selfish reasons. Some get pleasure out of their winning and others losing. The ecstasy of victory to some is a matter of competition and greed.

→ Can you recognize these motives for bartering in some people you know? Perhaps in yourself?

How often do we barter with the thought of getting the most and giving the least? Some will see it as smart business. Others enjoy it, seeing it a game with winners and losers. If it is unfair or unjust, it is not love. If we love, we do not take advantage of another's weakness, ignorance, or helplessness. The good act of bartering becomes sinful by the intentions of some people. The important idea in bartering is fairness. This does not mean we should not try to get the best value for our money.

Affiliation and Nurturance

The need for belonging, affiliation, and nurturance are built into our nature by God. People call these needs love because they are usually associated with love; however, they do not have to be. In fact, all of our basic needs and many of our psychological needs may be associated with acts of love. When they are, they contribute to our spiritual survival as human beings. *The motive for acting to satisfy needs or desires is a key to love.* There are psychological needs, such as dominance, aggression, and blame avoidance. They may be used to enhance our physical or psychological existence but are not good for our survival as spiritual human beings. In fact, they will hinder our survival unless they are kept under control.

The motive of love is used to help people survive by living in physical, psychological, and spiritual reality. Aggression and dominance can corrupt and hinder life. We must live with the power of love, not with the power of dominance or aggression.

We seek to satisfy our need to relate with others, but for what purpose or reason? A need may be involved in a relationship of love. Nurturing is needed to physically survive, but motives for nurturing can vary. There are many reasons to nurture, besides the motive of love. A mother and father may nurture and care for their child for the work an older child can do or for security in their old age. Maybe they nurture their children for their desire not to be lonely or so that they may dominate or live vicariously through their children. They may even do it because they perceive their children as a way of achieving their own immortality. The hard truth is parents may not love their children!

As we can see, there are motives that drive our actions to fulfill our needs, but they are not necessarily the motive of love. If our only motive for relating with others is to save and benefit ourselves with no concern for anyone else, this is not love. By relating without the motive of love, one can survive physically and psychologically in this world, but spiritually, it's another story. *When we act, we must act with the motive and intention of love if we are to survive spiritually and live as human beings.*

Almost all elicited psychological needs are not needed to survive physically; however, the exceptions are affiliation and nurturing. They are essential for physical survival. Nurturing is much more than providing primary basic needs. It involves holding, stroking, talking to babies, listening, and training children. Without affiliation and nurturing, a baby dies. Perhaps this is why some people consider them needs of love. The child, the weak, infirm, and old need caring people who will nurture or help them acquire many of these basic needs. The commandment in the Old Testament to "honor your mother and father" means not only obeying them as children but nurturing them in their old age.

→ Do you nurture and provide for your parents in their old age? Will you if the time comes?
→ Have you ever nurtured a child, the weak, infirm, or the old? Why?

Sometimes the old are reluctant and even refuse to have their needs satisfied because they are too proud. Sadly, they may be denying someone the opportunity to love by nurturing them. We are born into this world as babies, and if we live long enough, we return to being babies. Babies need to be nurtured and loved. Sadly, some old people are not willing to accept their return to childhood in old age.

All of the basic and many of our psychological needs can be used by our intellect to motivate acts of love. As stated earlier, it all depends upon our reason for acting. How do we perceive these needs we strive to achieve? If the acts to achieve the need emanates from the motive of love, then the need or desire is spiritual because it is involved in the process of love and contributes to our final end. Eating can be done for love. We eat to live so we can love by helping others to live physically, psychologically, and spiritually! We do not live to overeat exclusively for pleasure and self-gratification, which is the sin of gluttony.

→ Do you think you include the motive of love in acting to satisfy the needs or desires of others? Perhaps you are still only focused on satisfying your own needs, even when you help others.
→ What secondary psychological needs are most important to you? The need that generates the most energy and when possible is acted upon first.
→ How important is your affiliation with family, friends, strangers, immigrants, and beggars?
→ Are they all of equal importance? Should they be? Why should they be or not be? What would Jesus say?

Summary

As we now know, some psychologists consider our needs the building blocks of our identity and the underlying determinants or motivation of our behaviors. *The greatest and most important need is love.* The essence of our identity is spiritual life. The spirit is in the "I" of our intellect that is expressed in the "am" of our deeds. All our physical and psychological needs are intermediate ends. They are not necessarily spiritual and associated with the motive of love and our final end unless our intellect makes them so. ***These needs or desires can and should become spiritual by our intellectual thought providing the motive of love in acting to satisfy them!***

Needs and Desire Cause Fear

People are afraid of many things. We're afraid of being lonely or losing security. We're afraid the good feeling of yesterday will not occur today. We're afraid of losing our job or source of income, losing fame, fortune, youth, health, and our lives. We're afraid our loved ones will stop loving us, or even worse, we might stop loving them. There can be great fear in loving, but in perfect love, there is no fear as the Bible states "perfect love casts out fear."[1] *Fear lives in thought; in fact, it is a thought.*

The Cause of Fear

Fear is a feeling of anxiety or dread caused by approaching danger. When we look into our thoughts of fear in our daily lives with introspection, we see its effects of anxiety and dread and ask ourselves what is the cause of fear? *We observe that when we act to obtain what we need or desire, the good we perceive, we are afraid. We are afraid we will not get what we need or desire or we want to keep something of value, and we are afraid we will lose it!* For example, we want this job; we're afraid we won't get it! Or we want to keep this job; we're afraid we will lose it! With insight, we see fear is linked with needs and desires.

The Effects of Fear

Let's suppose in our relationship with another person, we want something. Perhaps it could be only that they like us. If we pay attention, we notice we may change a little. It may be in our voice or perhaps our body becomes a little tense or we may become anxious. This is a product of fear. With fear, there is psychological danger similar to physical danger we may experience when we are about to fall! Fear may become so intense we cannot learn, take tests, make rational enquiries, and there may be times the intensity is so great it becomes terror, and we can't even move.

With fear, we are not really free. If we are pleasure-seekers, we realize fear is not pleasurable but painful. We move from pleasure to the fear of losing it or not getting what we think will bring happiness and pleasure. Fear can motivate us to act in a positive manner, getting us what we need and want.

Fear can also motivate us to act in a negative manner, causing us to do terrible violent things to get what we need or desire. It can place us in a state of psychological or physical violence. The violence is experienced in the uneasy feeling in our bodies and minds, which is disagreeable with panic and ultimately suffering. *Fear often results in sin to acquire what we desire and diminish the suffering.*

Our Standard of Success in the World

We are conditioned to produce in the culture we live in, to be all we can be so that we can become successful, which usually translates to power, fame, and fortune. Most of all, we want our loved ones to be proud of us, whether it be in school with good grades, in sports by playing well, or successful in our jobs or in our marriages. Often, we determine our success by how well we do in competition with others and the goals we set and achieve. To be a good person comes from the achievement of our ambition, our beliefs, or ideas of what it means to be a success and the goals society and parental figures have conditioned into us. *Desire, ambition, beliefs, fear, and violence are all a part of us, a part of living we act out in our daily lives and they are all related.*

Fear is thought that works with needs and desires, and we project them into the future. The past resides in our memory. With the past, we perceive the good we have experienced or would like to have experienced. We desire these good things in the future. When we are engaged in such thoughts, we remove ourselves from the present. We can be afraid we will not acquire the future we desire, and there is a lot of violence and suffering here.

Dealing with Fear

There are two ways to deal with the ideas of fear. With introspection, we can clearly see where fear comes from. It comes from needs and desires. We see what it does to us with all its dangers in trying to live with this violence and pain. We see how it can take us out of being in the present. To understand the truth about fear is to be free of it. Understanding provides us with the ability to live with it, without struggle, and to move away from it.

Another way of dealing with fear is the religious way. This involves replacing all our destructive beliefs, desires, and ambitions with ideas that come from the Word of God made flesh, Jesus Christ. It is no longer what we desire but what God desires and we trust Her. Of course, to do this, we must learn to love Her as perfectly as possible.

Eastern thinking maintains if we do not need nor want anything, we will not be afraid. Aren't we, however, merely dealing with desire, the desire to want or need nothing? But we do need things to physically survive, and wouldn't we desire them if there was any doubt of our not obtaining them? We're in love today and want to keep it tomorrow, so we try to do all we can to secure it, and we're afraid we'll fail. Our desire is to live forever, and we're afraid of death we know is inevitable. *To see fear in our daily living, to see what it is, what causes it, and what it does to us is to see the nature of fear and much of the thought within us.*

→ What is something truly important you desire or need? We're talking about important things such as a job, promotion, education, a spouse or friend, fame, fortune, or a substantial achievement.

→ What is the feeling that accompanies your desire? Why do you think you have this feeling?

→ If you truly loved someone, would you be afraid? If you loved God, would you be afraid? Why? Why not?

Traits and Love

Traits Influence Behaviors

Some psychologists do not focus upon needs as the major influence upon our behavior or the most important building blocks of our identity or nature. For these psychologists, the major building blocks of our identity or nature are traits. This ideology was inferred by observing that people display consistency or continuity in their thoughts, feelings, and actions. As we saw previously, according to Allport, traits are relatively permanent neuropsychic structures which initiate and guide human behavior. They guide us to our ends. We know traits are stable. Some think our motive for acting is because of these traits or permanent dispositions, which are habits or tendencies.

Core Traits

Earlier, we considered some of these traits. Hans Eysenck, a psychologist, identified two super traits within our identity: introversion/extroversion and emotional stability/instability. As stated earlier, introverted people focus upon individualization, turning their "psychic" energy inward, orienting their energy within themselves. The extroverts focus upon socialization, turning their psychic energy outward, orienting their energy to the world outside themselves. The psychologist Harrison Gough maintains that certain traits that influence behavior are common to every culture and society because they are naturally developed by social interaction. However, some Christians believe they were placed in the nature of human beings by God, which is a religious interpretation of their origin. Harrison Gough calls these traits self-concepts.

Core Traits of Love

One self-concept trait in particular is social responsibility, which is a tendency to keep in mind and work for the common good and not to act out of selfishness. This core trait has been associated with love and is common to every culture and society. Still another psychologist, Jerry Wiggins, and his associates maintain that traits influencing the quality of interpersonal experiences are the basic foundation of identity.

One of Wiggens' core traits is the extrovert who is warm and agreeable. This is a core trait he labels love. *The core traits of love should influence the dynamic interaction between two or more people.* The traits of social responsibility and the warm agreeable extrovert become love traits if they are motivated by love. The trait of social responsibility could be exhibited solely for personal political gain. The trait of being an agreeable extrovert could be solely on display to sell a product for profit. In such cases these traits would not be considered acts of love. To be love traits they must have the motive of love when exhibited.

Isn't it interesting that they are common in every culture and society? To the believer, it leads one to conclude these traits were designed and placed in human beings by a very intelligent Creator. Or perhaps the "potential" traits were placed in us. They just need to be actualized by discovering a motive. The motive for interacting with other people may be found in biblical revelation and introspection of ourselves! We now know this motive should be love.

There are other core traits such as dominant/submissive, which can also influence the dynamic interaction between people. The important thing to keep in mind is that none of these traits are necessarily traits of love. We can give or share with another person using the traits of warmth, agreeable, and extroversion without love! Acting upon traits or acting to satisfy needs become part of the process of love by our reason for acting. With these acts, what is the end we seek? If the motive is love and the end is heaven for all, then it is a trait or need of love.

Traits Interacting with Situations

Our environment and situations can also influence the traits involved in our dynamic interaction, just as needs or desires can be influenced by our environment. The idea is that *the core traits of our identity and the situation in which we find ourselves can interact with each other to influence behavior.* Sometimes the core traits have the overall affect upon the behavior of people, and at other times, the situation has the overall affect. Sometimes it is possible that both the core trait and the situation interact to have the effect.

An interaction means that variation or changes in situations affect some people in one way and others another way. For example, two men may experience a situation which is pleasant and without stress surrounded by kind honest people. Under these conditions, both men are warm agreeable extroverts. Suppose the situation becomes stressful and unpleasant and full of sinful people in a corrupt decadent community. The first man will remain faithful to his motive of love and the core traits of being a warm agreeable extrovert. The second man changes with the environment, becoming coldhearted, calculating, and corrupt. His motto is "When in Rome, do what the Romans do."

How do we explain the difference between the two men? One might say the motive and core traits associated with love in the first man were not as firmly established in the identity of the second man. Perhaps the second man did not have the experiences in his life that strengthened and reinforced this motive of love. *True love will always prevail in a real Christian, no matter how bad the situation or environment may be.*

The Trait of Self-Monitoring

Another factor that can explain the behavioral difference between the two men is the psychological trait of self-monitoring. Some people who are "high" self-monitors are greatly influenced by their situation and surroundings. They like to fit smoothly into whatever situation they encounter. They look to others in the environment for clues as to what actions are appropriate. The "high" self-monitors have a motto, which is "to get along, you have to go along with what others are doing," even if what they are doing is wrong and the high self-moniters know it!

Unfortunately, this motto is often used by many of our politicians. Without following this motto, many would not survive politically, and for most politicians, political survival is the most important rule, survival at almost any cost. For example, as a junior legislator, you are placed on a legislative committee. The senior member on the committee from your political party asks you to vote as the party wishes you to vote on certain issues. If you don't vote with the party, it gets back to your party's leadership in the House or Senate. Suddenly, you will not get money from your party for your next campaign. Or a challenger is selected and financed to run against you in the next primary election. Suddenly, your district fails to get any money that is being distributed to districts for projects. Suddenly, a bill which you have written or support fails to come out of committee and brought to the floor for debate and a vote.

Failing to go along because you were true to your conviction, you may have to pay a price, which is not surviving politically. There are politicians who compromise their convictions for money from lobbyists for their next campaign. The word for politicians is *compromise. As Christians, we can compromise on strategy or different approaches but never on conviction and basic beliefs or principles.*

The "low" self-monitors are more focused upon their motive of love along with the core traits, experiences, beliefs, and faith which strengthens them. In situations that may be contrary to their convictions or teachings that guide their lives, their actions will be in keeping with their convictions. Usually, "low" self-monitors have a clearer understanding of their identity and purpose in life. This provides the motive for their conviction, which becomes a post to hold on to in times of trouble and change. This enables them to remain consistent in their behaviors during troubled times.

Peter was self-monitoring when he took action in the garden by drawing his sword and cutting off the ear of one of Jesus's adversaries. He looked to Jesus for help, approval, and a clue as to whether it was appropriate behavior. Clearly, it was not as Jesus explained *for all who take up the sword shall perish by the sword.*[1]

In this situation, Peter was trying to accommodate to the situation. After all, he did see Jesus overthrow the tables of the money changers. He needed Jesus's physical presence to give him strength and direction. After Jesus was arrested, He was no longer in Peter's presence. Peter was alone and amongst people who were not supporters of Jesus. In this situation, Peter may have accommodated to the needs of the situation by denying Jesus and preventing his own persecution. Peter was a "high" self-monitoring apostle! That is why he was not consistent! He was much stronger in a situation with Jesus present. Alone, he did not fully understand his identity and purpose. Another way of saying it is without a strong motive for being, he accommodated to the situation.

Certainly, it was Peter who identified Jesus as the Son of the Living God. At the time, he did not fully understand the true purpose of Jesus coming into the world. He didn't understand what Jesus came to do or how He was to accomplish it. Peter may have thought Jesus was the Messiah who was going to rid Israel of the Romans by His mystical powers. In addition, Peter may not have been sure of his purpose or the role he was to play as one of Jesus's disciples.

As a "high" self-monitoring apostle, Peter needed Jesus for support when life got tough. Most "high" self-monitoring people need a post to hang on to outside themselves. It could be power, prestige, highly developed skills, ancestral heritage, a leader, friends, a group of friends bound together in a common cause, etc. It was not until Jesus rose from the dead and the apostles received the Holy Spirit that they clearly understood who Jesus truly was, what His purpose was in becoming man, and where He was going. They clearly understood that He was the fulfillment of the scripture prophecies.

With this enlightened awareness of God, Peter and the other apostles and disciples understood their own identity, mission, and destination. With this new awareness of God and themselves and the presence of the Holy Spirit within them, Peter become a "low" self-monitoring apostle. He no longer needed an exterior post to hang on to when he experienced the evils that come into every life. He now had the understanding and love within himself. This enabled him to die on a cross as his Lord did.

→ What posts do you hang on to in tough times?
→ Are you a "high" or "low" self-monitor?
→ Can you become like Peter, no longer needing an exterior post?
→ If you were a German Catholic in Nazi Germany, would you go along with what was happening to the Jews and others so you could get along with the majority of your countrymen? Or would you resist at your own peril?

Some of us might say, "We know what is the right thing to do, but we don't know or doubt whether we would have the courage to do it."

→ What do you think would give you the courage?
→ Would you go along to get along, even if it meant having to live with injustice and corruption?

Psychological research has shown behaviors associated with dynamic interactions are often influenced by more than one trait. *We as Christians believe the dominant traits influencing the interacting of people are those core traits that relate to the intention to love.* The foundation of our identity are these traits because they influence the behaviors of interpersonal relationships. We know that relationship is the foundation of life. *To live our true identity, the traits that are the building blocks associated with love must dominate.*

Traits and Needs

We've considered both traits and needs as influences upon our behavior. It has occurred to some psychologists that both traits and needs are similar things! Some psychologists focus upon traits that are tendencies to act. Others focus upon needs and desires which motivate acts. Regardless of the focus, both are the building blocks of our identity. The cardinal building blocks are both love traits and love needs and desires that are involved in the process of love. Both love traits and needs must dominate because love must dominate if we are to survive as spiritual human beings.

Summary

Let us now summarize the ideas discussed concerning needs and traits that provided additional insight into our identity. All primary and secondary needs are intermediate ends. This means they are ends but can also be means to a final or greater end. The immediate end satisfies the physical and psychological needs. If our needs and their intermediate ends are used in the process of love, they help us obtain our spiritual end. They also satisfy the spiritual need for love not only in the present but for all eternity. Traits are tendencies like habits that influence our behavior. We believe the core traits of responsibility for the common good and warm agreeable extroverts when motivated by love should dominate our personality. They are essential to living in accord with our true identity, purpose, and destiny.

What is this good end we seek with our interaction of love? To answer this question, we must look to our needs. The psychologist Abraham Maslow answered this question with one need, *belonging* We want to belong and be loved with traits and virtues in the process of love. We want to be accepted and affirmed by a person, a group of people, but most of all, God. This gives purpose and meaning to our lives when we belong and are accepted by God in a love relationship in which we possess Her.

→ What is this thing called love?

31

What Is This Thing Called Love?

More songs, poems, and stories have been written about love than any other subject in history. The Beatle's sang, "All we need is love." Nate King Cole sang, "The greatest thing you'll ever learn is just to love and be loved in return." Cole-Porter asks the question in his song, "What Is this Thing Called Love?"

Earlier in this book, we asked some important questions we did not answer but left with you. Questions such as, why did God give us a free will if we can sin with it and place our destiny in jeopardy? What is the greatest good in this life or our most valuable possession? Why does God give us goodness and happiness when we don't deserve it? How can we use pleasure or develop our talents and self-actualize our potential for the greatest good possible? Why is it important to know the goodness in every person? What do we get by giving? What should be the highest priority in performing any act? Under what condition can physical and intellectual pleasures be part of our highest priority? Where do we get the courage to do the right thing? Finally, what does it mean to die spiritually? We will see love is the answer to all these questions.

We have seen that the identity of God and human beings as living existence consisting of energizing relationships that may be directed internally or externally. This is revealed in the Bible, and confirmed by science. The Bible also reveals that **God is love, and those who abide in love abide in God and God abides in them.**[1]

Made in God's image, we too are made in the image of love! We now know as Christians the trait of love is our greatest trait. Our greatest spiritual need is love, and people of faith consider the spiritual need for God as the cardinal need. We now know God and love are one and the same. People call some of our specific acts "acts of love." We claim to love people or we can feel or experience love.

The word *love* is an abstract concept derived from our observation and experiences of individual acts of people. Love does not exist as an entity that can be seen in reality, just as the concepts "treeness" or "dogness" do not exist in reality. Like love, they are inferred by observing specific trees or dogs. Like love, they are universal spiritual ideas expressed in words and acts. *How do we reconcile our being both existence and love similar to God's being?* We will address an answer to this question in the pages ahead.

Our Destiny or Final End

An act of love is an end in itself. Our acts of love in this world provide us with an end that is merely a foreshadowing of our final end in our life to come. The kingdom to come is a spiritual existence with God, and it is a kingdom of love. This is why at the last supper, Jesus implied that His kingdom of love begins here and now. He said His kingdom would not come until He had eaten and drank and then proceeds to do so.

When asked by the Pharisees when the kingdom of God was coming, Jesus's reply was, *The Kingdom is not coming with things that can be observed for in fact the kingdom of God is among you.*[2] Of course, the kingdom of God is among us because it is a kingdom of love and Jesus is love. It is not a Kingdom with things that can be observed because love is spiritual. ***Love is our final end because when we possess it, we possess the highest good, God.***

We know to exist as human beings, our nature must have the attributes of intellect and free will. To love, a human being must have these same two spiritual attributes. We must first have the spiritual attribute within an intellect, which enables us to be aware of such things as the need to belong to each other, virtues and warm agreeable traits. *The intellect must be aware of its reason for acting to achieve these ends or goals associated with existence.* It enables us to be aware that satisfying this wonderful end of creating, maintaining, and enhancing life with the meaning or motive of love brings happiness. The happiness comes from the realization that we are living in accord with our nature, purpose, and destiny. We are happy because we are aware that we were made to exist by possessing God who is existence. We possess God by the process of love. *This awareness of our possession of existence itself by love is the greatest good, and so we are happy.* For those with an intellect incapable of such awareness God takes care of Her own.

The second spiritual attribute essential to love is free will. The motive of love is freely offered to a person who with a free will must be willing to accept or reject this gift of love. Love cannot be a fearful forced choice or it will not be love. It must be voluntary. If we consciously see clearly that love is the essence of our true nature, which is to exist as God created us to exist, we will love by our own free will.

We know that the process is somewhat similar in the basic way of existing for both living and nonliving beings. The process involves beings giving, sharing, and receiving parts of each other for the purpose of creating a union for existence. We wish to unite with our loved ones physically, psychologically, and spiritually. *Love is the "awareness" of the motive or meaning for this union to exist, so the act of uniting is not a random act of mathematical chance. Rather, it is a free deliberate act with meaning.* This meaning is only provided to living beings with an intellect and free will.

Human beings, with the help of God, can with motive create, maintain, and enhance the union of existence of all beings here on earth. ***The objective of love is union for spiritual, psychological, and physical existence.*** We possess God with love, but our possession is dependent on our motive for loving. *Without the right motive, there is no love*, no possession, and no existence. This is how we begin to reconcile our referring to God as *existence* in the Old Testament and *love* in the New Testament.

Love in Action

We've seen that love is a universal idea that involves a set of core traits consisting of thoughts and feelings that influence our behaviors to satisfy needs. The motive of love is primary and essential to our existence. The motive of love determines whether acts involving traits and needs are acts of love. The motive of love is always expressed as mental and physical acts. An intention or motive of love must enact works of love because physical and spiritual existence requires action. This is why the Bible states, "Be doers of the word and not merely hearers who deceive themselves but doers who will act will be blessed in their doing."[3]

This is why Paul writes to the Ephesians, "We are what He has made us, created in Christ Jesus for good works which God prepared beforehand to be our way of life."[4] Good works or doers of the Word are acts of love. *The "am" of action for existence requires the "I" of the intellect with the reason for the existence, which is love.*

However, if these verbal or physical activities of love are impossible to perform, then the *motive itself becomes an act of love and is enough!* Motive is a thought that is an intellectual and spiritual act that provides an understanding of reasons for our physical acts of love. With reason, we desire, and we act upon our desires. We may be able to mentally or even verbally express our reason and desire to act. Circumstances in our life, however, may make it impossible to physically act. As we saw with Saint Theresa of Lisieux, she wanted to go to the foreign mission but was prevented by poor health! As God revealed, her desire was enough.

→ Did you ever want to do something good, but circumstances prevented it? To God, the act of thinking your intention demonstrates your love if you cannot act!

Getting Started

The intellectual process of establishing the motive of love resulting in traits and acts of love to satisfy needs is quite interesting. Love starts by receiving with our intellect. Our experiences tell us knowledge comes from what is outside ourselves. To love someone, the one we love will enter our intellect by way of the senses.

This ideology of realism began with the Greek philosopher, Aristotle. He believes when we are born, our minds are a blank slate that we fill with ideas from our exterior experiences. Opposing realism is the ideology of Idealism started by the Greek philosopher, Plato. Idealism believes all ideas were present in the minds of all children at the time of birth as designed and created by God. These ideas that live in the shadows of our mind need exterior experiences to bring them out into the light of awareness. In either case, contact with the exterior world is essential.

Two Existences

We exist in two ways. The first is our *natural form,* which is the way we exist in ourselves within reality apart from anyone else. The second way we exist is in the mind of another person. Our existence in the minds of God, family, friends, and anyone who knows us is called our *intentional form*. Our intentional form is an image that is not a material existence, but it's a mental representation in our mind of anyone we know. We use these intentional images of people in our lives in the intellectual act of knowing and interacting with them.

In this world, we can only love what comes through our senses from the outside world (Realism). Or we can love the person God places in our mind at birth and we discover by using our senses in the outside world (Idealism). In Idealism, two people are destined to love each other from the beginning.

→ In matters of love, do you think you are a realist or idealist?

Within our intellect, an *initial surge of spiritual energy* imprints an intentional image, and we become conscious or aware of a person. We see nothing without the intentional image, and with it, we are aware of the person but not the intentional image. This intentional image is like a photograph we are not aware of, but we are aware of the image it projects. The process of love cannot begin without it. We can only love what we know, and this requires seeing or hearing or touching. The act of the intellect to be aware of the intentional image of a person can initiate physical and mental acts of love. The question is, why would the intentional image of a person generate acts of love? What is the reason or purpose for loving this person? The motive for love has still not been revealed!

→ To you who love, do you know your reason for loving?

The Motivation or Reason for Love

Love is the reason for existence, but what is the reason or purpose in loving? Without God's love, there is no existence. We know there are needs that must be satisfied to exist as beings or to exist as living beings or to exist as living human beings made in the image of God. To exist as living human beings, we need God, but God is love, so to exist in the image of God, we must love. But to love, we must be aware and understand the reason we love before we can physically act with love. As for the purpose for loving, it is simple: ***We now know we must love to exist as human beings, and we want to exist because existence as a spiritual being is a great good.*** This is very true and the heart of it, but there is much more we must understand!

Kinds of Awareness

There are two kinds of awareness with our intentional image. The first awareness is how a person affects us and how we affect a person or, for that matter, any beings. Animals have this type of awareness. The second type is an awareness of how a person is in himself or herself. This is a spiritual awareness, and animals don't have it.

Spiritual Awareness

Our intellect can focus upon the image of a person, including his behaviors, in different situations. Our image is enhanced with ideas and judgments, which provide information about him or her. This image of her within us is her intentional form. It tells us something about her as she is in herself or how she exists in her natural form. Our ideas about her may be attributes, such as beauty, trustworthiness, kindness, and patience; or it may be attributes such as plain looks, dishonesty, meanness, greed, and impatience. Perhaps she may or may not have the core traits of love or may consist of a mixture of these attributes. It can take time to know these attributes and core traits with certainty.

Sympathy and Empathy

Our spiritual awareness also focuses on his or her problems, suffering, and weaknesses as well as their ambitions, hopes, and dreams. Economic problems or weaknesses, as a result of physical handicaps or psychological fears, are just a few examples. If we have experienced similar problems or sufferings, we can identify with them and can be *sympa-*

thetic to their plight. Perhaps someone in our past helped us with a similar problem or weakness. If we never experienced the problem, we can *empathize* using our imagination and projecting ourselves into those with the problem virtually experiencing what they are experiencing. We ask ourselves, how would it feel to be in his or her place? And with an answer, we experience compassion, feeling pity for their suffering or misfortune.

→ Have you ever sympathized with someone who has a problem similar to one you experienced or are experiencing? You have some idea of what they are going through; what did you do?

→ Have you ever empathized with a person who has a problem you never experienced? Placing yourself in their shoes by using your imagination to answer the questions if you had this problem, what would you think? How would you feel? Or what would you do? What did you do?

Of course, with sympathy or empathy, you can reach out and help or you could run away. What do you think will determine which one you will do?

Active Identification

As we know, an initial surge of spiritual energy imprints an intentional image, and we become consciously aware of a person as he or she is within himself or herself. With a *sec-*

ond surge of energy, our intellect engages in active identification with a person's traits, problems, aspirations, attributes, dreams, and all the good we see in him or her. An example would be a young doctor who dreams about working in the inner city, healing poor sick people. She is afraid circumstances and obligations will prevent her from fulfilling her dream. Her dream is shared by a young male nurse who identifies with her dream. He sees her actions of healing with love and devotion. His identification is with her good traits and aspirations as well as her problems and sees a similarity or equivalence with his own. It means admiring the good traits, characteristics, and kind acts, which emanate from her. He wants to join and unite with her in the goodness of her mission. He loves her.

Another example is a man sees a woman's character traits of friendliness, unselfishness, and kindness displayed in her treatment of her mother and grandmother. He identifies with her traits and treatment because they are similar to his own. Or he does not possess these traits to such a degree, but he admires them and the woman who possesses them. Perhaps, united with her, he can learn to acquire them himself. He is aware that these traits are good and so is the woman who possesses them.

Because he is aware of her goodness, which perhaps others may not see, he feels good about himself. *With the awareness of her goodness, he loves her, which means reaching out to interact with her.* When he does, he is consciously possessing the goodness in her by being with her, giving her his time, his conversation, encouraging her, and expressing his admiration. He experiences positive thoughts about her. They interact together in acts of kindness and compassion toward each other as well as others. They are acting to satisfy the needs of each other and their neighbors, and in so doing, they are expressing their love, and it is good. It is the good end he seeks, and when he consciously unites with her, he possesses the good and he is happy.

As we see, when we are consciously aware or perceive the goodness within a person, our response is love. We want to possess the good in each other in a union of love. This is our *immediate motive* for loving. As we also see, our response in love is a desire to join and unite with people in the goodness of their mission. What they want becomes what we want. We love them by just "being" in their presence as we focus upon the goodness they are or can be. It's easy to see the good in people if we seek it. We are truly blind if we do not see the goodness or potential goodness in every human being.

We are motivated to love our fellow human beings because we are aware of their goodness and our desire to possess it. Since it is God our Father who created and placed all the goodness we find in each other, then when we love one another, aren't we loving, honoring, and glorifying the perfect goodness of God? We want to possess some of this goodness even in a limited way by living in a union of love with God. *If we love one another, God lives in us and His love is perfected in us.*[1] This is our *ultimate motive* for loving. This goodness we see in each other and in God we identify with. It is the goodness of living in accord with our identity and living the teachings of God found in the Bible, that is the end we desire. It is this end that motivates us to love by engaging in the process of love. When we do, we are living in love and possessing God. Remember, we act for an end because the end we perceive is good.

In the prior example, it is the goodness that man already has, would like to have, or wants to increase in himself. This makes him want to be a better version of himself. At the same time, the woman continues to exhibit the goodness he sees in her. When she does, she feels good about herself. Consciously aware of her goodness results in his replicating it by himself with parents and grandparents. *Consciously, the seeing is the doing, and goodness will always prevail.*

With love, we have the power to refrain from sin and be the person we want to be. The power emanates from thoughts expressed in action. It is called the process of love, and it involves our consciously seeing and doing good. *It is not how we feel but what we do and the reason for doing it that determines love.* Feelings have little to do with it, although I'm certain some people would disagree. They would argue the identification with sympathy, empathy, and compassion involves some degree of feeling. Certainly, love in most cases brings feelings and some degree of happiness, but here on earth, it is not always the case.

Her goodness, which he identifies with by recognizing it along with his being sympathetic and empathetic produces the motive to love! Identification or seeing the good is first in his intellect and motivates his acts of love. The conscious possession of her goodness is last in acquisition. It is acting alone or together with her that lies between his motive and his conscious possession of her and the good he seeks. *First is the motive to love by knowing or seeing her goodness, second are acts of love, and last is his possession of her in a love relationship.* This is the only way to possess her and God.

Of course, with human beings, we can love them not only by recognizing or seeing the good but also the potential good. We see goodness in the nature of people God created. In others we see with sympathy and empathy some of their evil ways we once had or could have here and now if not for the grace of God. This is the answer one might give to those who ponder how we could love such a terrible person.

The Essence of Love

Love is a process used by spiritual beings to establish a union of existence for surviving physically and spiritually. In a love relationship, two people will love each other to survive although they are usually unaware of it. We must also keep in mind that all existence created by God is very good.[2]

The objective of love is union, but what is the essence of love? As we know, love is necessary to exist. *We love so we can exist as human beings. This is the essence of love, to survive and exist as human beings.* Without God's love, there is no energy for acting or interacting, and without acting or interacting, there is no union for existence. We shout out to the world "it's good to be alive, it's good our love ones are alive and it's wonderful we both live in this union of love." God's love and the gift of God's love by virtue of our intellect and free will are responsible for all that exists. The Beatles were right, "All we need is love." The question is what actions and interactions unite us in love for the purpose of existence?

God is good, and since *God's identity is living in love, and our identity is living in love,* then living or existing in love must also be good.[3] This is the end we seek: to love like God so God can love and maintain our human living existence. This end is the true and perfect good. First and foremost, it is the existence of a love relationship with God. We are motivated to love God because we are aware of Her perfect goodness.

→ Do you identify with the goodness your loved one has, and you have or would like to have? Can you list the goodness your love one possesses? Or perhaps the potential goodness they have?

→ Do you act upon your awareness of their goodness by doing good? How do you feel when you do? Happy?

→ If you cannot identify or recognize their goodness or potential goodness and do not act upon your awareness, do you really love them? Perhaps you just think you love them.

Understanding of Goodness

A relationship of love, which is the result of their interaction, starts with the understanding of each other. Without understanding, there is no love! Understanding means the awareness of the goodness of our true nature and its similarity to every other human being. We are all bound together in our existence by our identities and interdependence. We are all one, created by God, and yet we are separate beings. It takes at least two to create existence which is a union of love. At least one of the two must act with the motive of love. One will always be God who is love. Will the other one be me? Without love, there is no living or nonliving existence. God is truly existence and love.

It is our focus upon our understanding of the intentional image of another person that produces the motive of love. This motive or rational idea generates the energy to act with love for the union of beings, enabling both to exist as human beings. *It is this focus of understanding with ideas that produces the spiritual energy.* For love to grow within us, we must focus our thoughts upon the goodness found in our loved ones. We cannot love anyone if our thoughts are scattered in many directions. We find it impossible to concentrate upon those we say we love. At lower levels of existence, God provides the understanding that motivates love and so maintains their existence. We are different. We have our intellect that is aware and a will that is free so we can refuse to love and reject God's love, but She will continue to love us because that is who She is. We can choose not to live by our Spirit of love and so not live as the spiritual human beings we are.

The two who love must understand what each desires and needs, and it must be accompanied with a perception of goodness. They must understand where to find the good in each other. They must understand how to get more of it by interacting together for the good of themselves and others. With the possession of goodness, the end of the love process brings peace and frequently happiness. Eastern ideology uses the word *mindfulness* to identify, be aware, and understand the truth about ourselves, our journey, and our destination. We must look deeply and see the truth of reality and to see that truth is good.

Now that we have considered the motivation to love, can we apply this motivation to love a man who physically lived thousands of years ago and claimed to be the Son of God? Can we love Him based upon what we read about Him and what people say about Him and His goodness? After all, this is one way in which we use the senses to acquire knowledge about a person. Or do we need to experience this man who claims to be the Son of God?

→ Have you ever loved someone you have never personally met but know about? Perhaps an ancestor, a historical figure, a saint, or Jesus?
→ Do we experience or know God more than only reading, talking, or hearing about Him?

My Brother's Keeper

There is another very important reason for loving. It emanates from the motive of recognizing and identifying the problems and sufferings of our fellow human beings with sympathy and empathy, which produces understanding and compassion for others and ourselves. We see and understand our similarities with our fellow humans in character traits, needs, suffering, and problems.

Interbeing

We realize that only another person or other people can satisfy our need for belonging. We see that all human beings are dependent upon air, water, plants, and animals for food and most of all each other to live in this world. Earlier, we briefly touched upon our dependency on each other and God.

Let us focus upon our dependency so we can see and gain greater insight into this basic truth. We are all interdependent upon each other, both living and nonliving beings in the here and now. There is no separate "material" existence even within ourselves. It is called "interbeing." It is a scientific fact.

→ Have you ever felt you were an individualist who didn't have to depend on anyone? Did you feel proud of your independence? It is an illusion.
→ Do you know people who consider themselves rugged independent individuals? How do you find your relationship with them?

We are all interbeings but know we have a separate spiritual existence which is the conscious awareness of ourselves as separate from all other beings, a conscious awareness that has us shout to the world "I am alive and it's good to exist."

Without God's spiritual energy of love holding us together materially and spiritually, we would fall apart. Revelation tells us we are all connected to each other because we all have the same God who created us in His image. God's image of love is placed at the core of our very being because we need it to exist physically and spiritually as human beings. When we unite with each other in the spirit of love, we are no longer alone; we belong to each other and to God. To Cain's question, "Am I my brother's keeper?"[1] we respond, "Yes! We are!" We are connected to our loved ones, but much more, we are connected to all humanity and to God who created us all to love each other and to love Him as He loves us.

The Bible is full of love stories in which we encounter God's love. With God's love, we respond to the needs of all others we encounter with love. In so doing, we are responding to our own need to know and fulfill our identity, our purpose, and destiny. The Bible, entreats us to "contribute to the needs of the saints and extend hospitality to strangers."[2] Early Christians were called saints because they were all expected to extend hospitality to strangers. The Christian sees every stranger or immigrant as a brother or sister! We all have the same Father in heaven, the same blood, the same identity, purpose, and destiny.

An old story from India tells of a teacher who asks his students, "How would you know when night has ended and day begins?"

One student answered, "When you look on the horizon and see the difference between an oak and palm tree."

The teacher responded, "No."

Another student, using the same approach, answered, "When you look in the distance and can tell the difference between an elephant and water buffalo!"

Again, the teacher's response was, "No."

The students asked, "Well, how then?"

The teacher replied, "Unless you can look into the eyes of any person and see a brother or sister, you are truly blind."

In the Bible, we read, "Whoever says, 'I am in the light' while hating a brother or sister is still in the darkness. Whoever loves a brother or sister lives in the light and in such a person there is no cause for stumbling."[3]

The Lord tells us in the first letter of Saint John, "We know that we have passed from death to life because we love one another. Whoever does not love, abides in death. All who hate a brother or a sister are murderers, and you know murderers do not have eternal life abiding in them."[4]

In the act of love, we do not experience enemies, the homeless, handicapped, or immigrants as strangers but as loved ones and friends. They are all our own kind, a part of our family of humanity, all brothers and sisters. They are all in need as we are in need. We care about them as we care about ourselves, and when we do, we know God by experiencing Her through them!

→ Can you look into the eyes of any man or woman, the people you give a sign of peace to in church, or those you work with and see brothers and sisters?

Immigrants

In the light of this ideology found in all major religions, how should we treat immigrants? Some will say welcome them if they come to our shores legally. If they come illegally, they have broken our laws, so treat them with compassion but send them back to their own countries. The only exception is if they seek asylum because their lives were in imminent danger, in which case, the courts and judges must decide.

Immigrants come to our country, seeking a better life. What shall we do? The Old Testament tells us God made all people equal in the nobility of our nature made in His image. God gives all of us the right to life, liberty, and the pursuit of happiness. It goes on to say we are all co-responsible with God in protecting the nobility and rights of everybody. In fact, the prophets of Israel revealed that our relationship with God is influenced by how we treat not only the immigrants but the poor, orphaned, widows, and the weak. We must treat them with kindness and generosity which is fair and just. We help them not out of charity but out of justice. The earth and all that is in it belongs to God, and God wants us to give and share fairly with everyone out of justice. This is love. In Matthew, Jesus made the practice of justice a part of the practice of love, the very standard used to determine our salvation![5]

Didn't our forefathers come to this country, seeking a better life, just like today's immigrants? Is it fair or just to turn them away? Of course, most of our ancestors came legally at a time when America had an open-door policy. All they had to do was pass physical and criminal background checks to enter. We have not had an open-door policy for almost 100 years, if we once again had one, how many should we or perhaps a better way to look at it is could we afford to let in?

We now have over 327 million people in our country. With an open door policy, we could take up to another 500 million (half a billion) over the next century or two. This would bring us to around a billion, including births and deaths. China right now has well over a billion. Our country is approximately the size of China. We have more natural resources and can grow more food than China, so we could certainly feed them. Why shouldn't we do it if we are truly religious people who love everyone as we do ourselves?

To admit large numbers of people into our country is not a simple thing and raises some important questions. First, what would the increase in number of immigrants coming so quickly do to the culture of our country? We may not be able to assimilate these large numbers of immigrants into our culture, and if they remain apart, it will bring a great number of challenges and difficulties.

Second, when most of our forefathers came to America, there was no welfare or free health service. How many of these immigrants would require these services, not to mention the strain on our school system?

Third, what affect would this number of immigrants have upon the job market for American citizens? With modern technology, the need for unskilled labor will diminish significantly in the years ahead. What will we do with large numbers of people and not enough jobs? A large number of immigrants can and will influence our economic and our political systems. Are we prepared to make the sacrifices that may be necessary to accommodate this number of immigrants that want to come to our shores? Are we prepared to help them financially with perhaps substantial increases in taxes that may lower our standard of living? If we truly love them, would this be too much of a sacrifice?

Right now, annually, we allow about one million legal immigrants into our country. This plan would increase that number significantly over the next couple of hundred years. Of course, the increase in number could be adjusted up or down, depending on the speed with which we could accommodate them. Who knows, we may reach a point where they may no longer wish to come in such numbers.

America is a country that wants to do what is right when it comes to immigration. We are exceptional because there is no other country in the world that admits one million immigrants onto its shores legally, let alone thousands more illegally! How generous should we or can we be as a nation? One thing is certain: if we don't secure our borders and stop illegal immigration, we won't have a country. What's your view?

What's Love Got to Do with It?

We reach out of ourselves into others to fulfill their needs. In so doing, we fulfill our own great need to belong and not be lonely. More importantly, we become what we are created to be: one who loves in a manner similar to God's love. ***We are to perceive love, behave with love, and become love, which is our very purpose for being and living.*** It is our identity and purpose! It is our final end, and we begin it here and now!

We can have a bit of heaven here on earth when we love. It is the highest good and the greatest happiness we will ever possess this side of heaven because in reality, it is possessing God Herself. This is why we do not run away, but we sympathize and empathize with the suffering and problems of people, especially the immigrants, the weak, and helpless. We see them as brothers and sisters, and our responsibility is to help them.

Responding to Goodness and Needs

One of the most important decisions we make in life is our response to what happens to us, whether good or bad.

Response with Love

We are free and have the ability to respond, or another way of saying it is responsibility. God, our Creator, loves us, and in the Old and New Testaments, we are called upon to respond by loving God and neighbors.

- "You shall love the Lord your God with all your heart and with all your soul and with all your might."[1]
- We are also called upon to love our neighbor. "You shall love your neighbor as yourself."[2]

- Jesus combines these two basic commandments together in His New Testament. *You shall love the Lord with all your heart, and with all your soul, and with all your mind and with all your strength. The second is this, You shall love your neighbor as yourself. There is no other commandments greater than these.*[3]
- Jesus goes on to define our neighbors as all humankind, including our enemies.[4] Jesus includes those with needs such as food, clothing, sick, and prisoners.[5] Prophets in the Old Testament affirmed that our neighbors include those with the least status in our society: widows, orphans, foreigners along with the poor and weak.
- Jesus gives us a new commandment: *I give you a new commandment that you love one another, just as I have loved you.*[6]
- God initiates His love for we who sin.[7]
- God gave us a spirit in our physical body with an intellect and free will along with His church united in love.[8]

Because of God's initiative of love toward us and His gifts of our Spirit, His Church, and the Holy Spirit, He makes possible our response of love.

→ Reflect on God's goodness and love for you, and ask yourself, "How should I respond?"

When we look at people, we see not only their good traits. but we see their physical needs for food, clothing, or shelter. We see their psychological needs for belonging, for achieving their dreams. We also see their spiritual needs for the love of God and eternal life. We are aware of their suffering, their experiences of injustice or misfortunes, and the fears their desires engender. Since they are good and we love them, we identify with their needs and suffering with sympathy and empathy. We know they are our brothers and sisters since we all have the same Father in heaven. We take responsibility by responding to their needs and struggles. Where there is a need, we supply it if we can. Where there is suffering, we comfort and heal, if possible. Where there is struggle and violence, we stop it. In so doing, we've helped the people and ourselves because we identify with them. Of course, if they identify with us and love us, they would respond in kind to our needs and struggles.

In an incident involving road rage, a man is cut off by another car. The driver who does the cutting off stops his car and confronts the man he just cut off. What will be the response of the man who is cut off? Let us say he is angry and afraid but refuses to get into a violent confrontation and takes the verbal abuse of the other driver. Refusing to fight is the right thing to do, the Christian way of handling it, but the essential question is for what reason does he refuse to fight? If his only reason to avoid fighting is because he is afraid of getting hurt, it is not good enough. He must refrain from fighting not merely for his sake but the sake of his adversary. He sees the suffering and struggle in this tormented man and identifies with him. He looks into his eyes and sees a brother and loves him and does not want to see his brother or himself hurt physically or spiritually. Is it difficult? Yes. Impossible? No. *Action alone is not enough; reason or motivation is essential, and feeling is secondary and not necessary*. Love is the way of and to God.

In a sense, we see ourselves a part of them and they a part of us. We intentionally unite with each other, giving purpose or meaning to our lives together. Knowing our loved ones as we know ourselves, we are concerned about their welfare, so our intellect transcends concern about ourselves and focuses upon them. *In a love relationship, each partner directs their energy of life to meet the needs of their lives as well as the lives of the spouses and families as completely and equally as possible.* However, in times of scarcity or extreme difficulty, the initial reaction of each partner in love is to use their energy of life for the other's welfare. If necessary, each would be freely willing to give their life for the others.

The need to nurture, affiliate, self-actualize, and achieve must have, as their primary motive, love. We want to nurture because we love. We want to affiliate and be with others and belong because we love. We want to self-actualize our talents because we can use them in the service of others because we love them. *In fact, any act we perform whether large or small is perceived and becomes the means of serving God by serving humanity with love.* This is the real measure of its importance.

Saint Therese of Lisieux talks about doing our daily activities, always aware of God's presence and our love for Her and all the people we know. When we love, we know it will contribute to their survival not only as animals but as human beings. When we love, we are living in accord with our identity, we are fulfilling our purpose in life, and contributing to our own spiritual survival.

→ What are the good traits or behaviors in your loved ones?
→ What are their weaknesses or struggles, needs and desires?
→ Do you value similar things?
→ Do you both work to satisfy each other's needs and desires?

If you can't answer these questions, especially those dealing with good traits, needs, and desires, perhaps you never loved him or her. If you no longer love someone, think back to a time you did and ask yourself what it was about him or her you loved. Do you think you can find it or help him or her find it again and rekindle that love? And if you can't find it, did you ever love the person in the first place?

Response without Love

There are relationships where the only purpose of one or both partners is to satisfy their need and not to love. Whether the need is fame, fortune, sex, or power, if the needs stop being satisfied, the relationship is over. This is not a love relationship because the motive for love was never present in the intellect. The partners were using each other, not loving each other. As an example, a woman marries a man because he can sexually satisfy her needs, but when the sexual appetites grow dim in advancing years, she divorces him. It's a similar story if a man marries a woman for economic security. If the money runs out or is lost, there is a quick divorce.

- → Do you know people who have this kind of relationship exclusively for their own benefit and satisfaction?
- → Would you enter into such a relationship without love? Perhaps you were desperate to fulfill biological needs or lonely for companionship, thinking perhaps true love would develop.
- → Would you enter such a relationship to have children if you desperately wanted them, thinking perhaps true love would evolve?

To marry someone, you must, at the very minimum, "like" them. Love can grow from liking a person. You can love a person you dislike but never marry the person.

Acts of Love

To Act with Love

What are the acts which constitute the process of love? Acts of love can be intellectual, verbal, or behavioral. **The specific acts of love involve *giving* and *sharing* of one's self as well *as receiving* for the purpose of joining together!** These acts can be one way with those giving and others receiving or it can be interactive with the two parties giving, sharing, and receiving from each other.

As one can see, they are the same acts essential at all levels of existence! Remember, atoms give, share, and receive parts of each other, joining in union to establish a new existence. ***The acts of existence and love are the same! In fact, our existence is an act of love by God. Love creates union, and union is existence. Love and existence are reciprocal in nature. You can't have one without the other.*** This is how the identity of existence and love are reconciled in our one God and in ourselves. With an intellect and free will, we are aware of the purpose for these acts, and we can cognitively, deliberately, and freely use them to create a new existence with God's help.

> → Do you think this wonderful process developed by chance and evolution? Or was it created by a divine Creator? Is this the same answer you gave to a similar question in chapter five?

For beings with an intellect and free will, acts of love are done with an understanding of the purpose! Purpose or motive is created by people who are aware of who they are and aware of the person to be loved. We are aware of what is being achieved with our acts or interactions with love. *We have a greater understanding of love because we have a greater understanding of God and ourselves.* With this understanding, we have a strong post to hold onto in times of trials and tribulations. We can create acts that share our ideas, our work, and the fruits of our work. We can give or share physically with an embrace or kiss, give psychologically by listening, or verbally praising and spiritually giving by praying, sharing thoughts from meditation, or encouraging a loved one to do the right thing. Love requires our giving and sharing for the well-being of everyone beginning with our family and extending our generosity to others.

All these acts of love require sacrifice of one's self for another. In sacrifice, we use a part of ourselves for the objective of uniting with another physically, psychologically, or spiritually. Any giving or sharing in the process of love, especially that which is considered of great value, can be considered a sacrifice.

To accomplish this sacrifice of giving or sharing of one's self for love, we must use our free will. With free will, we are able to freely step out of ourselves, renounce ourselves, and give ourselves over to our loved ones. Love is totally demanding. In fact, the more intimate we are with our loved ones, including our God, the greater the number of demands. We must lose ourselves only to find our goodness in the one we love.

Losing one's self is dying to self. By dying, we mean dying to the past by forgetting and letting go of our selfish desires and concerns only for ourselves. In short, this greedy, selfish part of us must die if we are to love. Luke talks about renouncing all possessions, and our greatest possession is self.[1] Even if we are willing to give and share with our loved ones to achieve a union, they must be willing to accept what we have to offer.

In the case of giving and receiving by communication, as stated earlier, our loved one must receive our thoughts by making room in her intellect to accept them. Often, it is a sacrifice to share our most personal thoughts and feelings about ourselves. A loved one's willingness to sacrifice her thoughts to accept our most personal thoughts could be considered a gift to us. It is an "intimate" process requiring an act of love!

This gift of sacrificing our ideas and replacing them with the ideas of another person enables us to listen and not merely hear. How many of us are willing to give to others material things, our time, and work, but not our ideas! In some cases, when a person asks to use our ideas without acknowledging the author, we refuse and get upset. We often give material things and our work unconditionally, but not what we think! Why?

Love and Energy

Love gives purpose or meaning to the energy of life. Life is also energy in motion. *Love provides the motive for using energy forces to unite energy forms to establish the union of existence.* The desire to live in love can draw upon energy from the Holy Spirit within us. If we access this source of energy, it will give us the strength to endure and overcome the greatest temptations, fears, and sufferings in our lives, even fear of death. *Our intention is to create existence by energy forces uniting energy forms because we truly see ourselves, everyone, and everything else through the prism or awareness of existence in love.*

What is this existence we create with the energy of love? It could be a friendship, family, church, or even a tribe or nation. We could create a song or painting or a house and bring them into existence. We could use them as gifts in the act of love.

→ Do you think the creators of nonliving objects such as a picture, song, or story love their creations?
→ Do they love themselves because of their creations?
→ Do they seek the fame or fortune such creations may bring them?

→ Do they use their creations in the process of love? Perhaps to help in the introspection and enjoyment of others?

→ Do creators love God for helping them create or for giving them the gifts that enable them to create? Perhaps it's a combination of factors.

In this process, we evolve into a better person. It is the acts of being with each other, interacting and talking with each other, thinking well of each other, and so trusting each other. Finally, it involves forgiving each other. We unite with each other physically, psychologically, and spiritually. *The objective of love is the union of energy forms by energy forces creating a spiritual and material existence.* We unite by intellectually and physically giving, sharing, and receiving from each other and acting together to establish an existence. We become a part of the other, and they become a part of us, not physically but cognitively, intentionally, and spiritually.

Specified in existentialist terms in the process of love, we *perceive* the goodness in each other, we *act* for that goodness we see, and *become* the goodness in each other in a union of love which is spiritual life. We also *perceive* their hopes, dreams, and suffering with sympathy and empathy. We *act* to verbally and, where possible, physically support their hopes and dreams and alleviate their suffering. In so doing, we *become* one with them in their successes and failures. We become one with them by sharing in their hopes, dreams, and suffering. *Love is in everything. It is in our hopes and dreams as well as our pain and suffering.* In existentialism, love is the only existence we can become by perceiving and behaving because it is what we were created to be.

Finally, we possess God in a union of love to exist spiritually as human beings. Love is the goodness we seek because it is with love that we possess God who is love. Here and now, love is the end. It is not a means to an end or an intermediate end but an end in itself. It is a part of our last end and greatest good. The only difference is here and now our love is imperfect, but in heaven, it will be as perfect as is humanly possible for all eternity. The most important words anyone can say are, "I love you." All too often, they are words that are misused, abused, cheapened, or misunderstood.

Acts of Love Are Spiritual

When we talk about the relationships of our identity as human beings, we are dealing with both the physical and spiritual aspects of our nature. Earlier, we learned since we have a human identity, there are these two aspects to it. We know we have acts that are physically good or bad and acts that are spiritually good or bad. There are acts that are both physically and spiritually good, but there are acts that are not.

A physically bad act may be thought of as evil for the body but not necessarily for the spirit or soul. Christ's crucifixion is an example of such an act. It was good for the spirit but bad for the body. *An act must always be spiritually good or indifferent, regardless of the physical consequences. Acts of love are spiritual.*

Summary and Review of Motivation and Acts of Love

We consciously see that love is a process beginning in our spiritual intellect and ending in action. It begins in the "I" and ends in the "am." In reviewing the motivation and acts of love, we see when we have a motive to love, we engage in the acts of love. The motive to love involves recognizing the goodness and needs in each other. We desire to identify and replicate the goodness in each other and satisfy each other's needs. Therefore, we become one with them by consciously possessing them with our intellectual and physical acts of love.

36

Receiving Can Be Giving

In the interaction of love, the one who receives can also be giving, depending upon the motivation behind the receiving. But what could the giver receive? If the receivers take the gifts for the benefit of those giving, then the receivers are helping the givers acquire that which is good for them. The good for the giver could be increasing their positive traits of kindness and generosity. It could help in the giver's salvation. In such cases, the act of receiving is also an act of giving.

In a true act of love, both parties are giving at the time of receiving! The psychologist, Eric Fromm, writes on this topic, "Giving implies making the other person a giver also and they both share in the joy of which they have brought to life." Fromm thinks the energy of life is reflected back to the giver as he writes, "But in giving he cannot help bringing something to life in the other person, and this which is brought to life reflects back to him. In truly giving he cannot help receiving that which is given back to him."

An example may help clarify this idea. I once had a ministry visiting the elderly in nursing homes. My visits were a ministry of love by giving to the elderly my time, attention, and talent, which means myself. My "I" identifies with them. With some of them, I could sympathize because I too had struggled with feelings of loneliness when I was away from my loved ones. With all of them, I could empathize by understanding that if I lived long enough, what they were dealing with I too would experience someday. On that day, I would want someone treating me as I was treating them.

My giving included my conversation, my prayers, and where possible, the Eucharist. In another sense, the elderly were giving to me. Their very presence was a gift to me because without them, I would not have a ministry. I am giving to them my acts of love, and they are giving me their time and acceptance by receiving the gifts of my ministry. Sometimes in my giving, a change comes over them, and it is good. The goodness makes them happy. Their happiness is reflected back to me. I am happy because they are happy, and they are happy because of the goodness in prayer and Eucharist they are experiencing. Hopefully, I could help them acquire an awareness that they are helping me by their presence and their willingness to accept me and the gifts I brought them.

The Bible says, "It is more blessed to give than to receive."[1] The Franciscan prayer proclaims that it is in giving that we receive eternal life. *It is clear that the process of love involves giving, sharing, and receiving by each party, and in every act of giving, there is always something a giver receives in return.*

The elderly would talk about days gone by or problems and concerns. They would thank me for our little service of prayer and the Eucharist. Grateful for the service, they would say, "You do a lot for us, and we have nothing to give in return." I would respond by telling them that the gifts they just received belong to God. It's what God wants, so they can show their gratitude by thanking Her and living a faithful Christian life for the rest of their days. In fact, any good we do or acquire belongs not only to us but to God!

In their receiving God's gifts, it is their act of love for me and Her. They are helping me acquire what is most important to me, which is simply my salvation. I would tell them an imaginary story of what may happen in the future when I go before the Lord, and He says, "Ralph, you've been a bad boy." I can say to Him, "Lord, what about my work in the nursing home? Perhaps my love for them can help me now." So I would say to them, "Don't thank me, it is I who must thank you." This remark puts a smile on their faces, and their smiles put a smile on my face. Their smiles make all my efforts worthwhile. The good I receive in their smiles increase the spiritual energy in my desire to continue to do more good.

What do we, the givers, receive when we do the right thing? In short, when we love? It is not something material nor is it recognition the Bible warns about[2], and it is certainly not gratitude from the receiver that we appreciate. It is an awareness about ourselves. The awareness that we have done something to help someone else and the good we do with God's help is in keeping with our identity. Do we think our goodness in such matters will be ignored by God who will not react to it?

As the Bible says, God will know and react accordingly.[3] We will not be satisfied and happy if the only benefit is for the common good. *No good act is totally selfless.* Ultimately, we all want to be loved for "ourselves," not for our fame or fortune, beauty, or talent. We want to receive love for who we are, the good we have, or could have. As Nat King Cole sang, the greatest goodness we'll ever experience "is to love and be loved in return." *Without giving, sharing, and receiving, there is no bond of love.* One could give with love, but unless it is received with love, there is no union of love.

→ Do you think the receiver in receiving helps the giver?
→ Do you think an act can be completely selfless? Or do you think an act of unselfish giving will always have some good for the giver?
→ Do you prefer to give or receive? Many people prefer to give rather than receive. Why? Could it have something to do with self-esteem?
→ Have you ever received a gift from someone, and you felt uncomfortable? Why?

Some of us must learn to receive from God and each other. There are those who want to be independent, in control, and may enjoy playing the role of philanthropist. When another gives with love, it is the incarnate God within that person who is giving to us, and we must accept with gratitude and love. In the process of love, we must be both givers and receivers.

→ Perhaps you prefer to give wanting to feel the enjoyment in being the power that controls and the benefactor? Or perhaps you feel you don't deserve to receive?

37

Two Kinds of Love

Perfect Love

God's love is perfect unconditional love. In the process of unconditional love, the acts must be done with a free will and never the result of any compulsion or force. A lover must freely give to the loved one without wanting or expecting anything material or psychological in return. The only return those who love unconditionally can expect is what they give to themselves and what God wishes to give them. God and all human beings who love unconditionally always receive the awareness they live in conformity with their created nature and with the divine nature of Jesus Christ. With this awareness comes their perception of possessing goodness, and with this goodness comes happiness.

Within God, the three divine persons living in a union of unconditional love for each other is a perfect existence and happiness. Within human beings, the three persons existing within each of us can also live in a union of unconditional love for each other and for God. This results in our existence being as perfect as our human nature allows. This is not very likely in this life but most likely in an eternal life to come.

There are interpersonal relationships of giving and taking, which are like reciprocal trade agreements. We give under the condition or expectation we get something in return. Conditions diminish love and make it imperfect. Unconditional love is called "agape" love. When we live in a state of agape love, we would never sin. Our existence becomes sinless and so we become holy. Like happiness, holiness is a by-product of love. It is not our last end. The possession of God is our last end, but to do so, we must be as holy as we can be and as holy as our finite nature can allow.

God's love is freely given to all creation without conditions. God unconditionally gives Her grace, even though we have no right to it and do not deserve it. Within the Divine Trinity, true unconditional love is always present and perfect. Here and now, it is difficult to love unconditionally because often in living, we don't want to change, but to be as perfect as possible, we must change often for the perfect goodness of agape love.

→ Do you think my work at the nursing home was agape love?

It would seem in the example given concerning the nursing home, my acts of love were not agape. I was expecting a return for my service. That "something" was some consideration concerning my salvation. I perform good acts of love because I dread the loss of heaven and the pains of hell. This does not seem to be unconditional because I'm placing heaven as the condition for my service. Let's take a closer look at my service. As explained earlier, any good done was not mine but God's good because I was doing His will. My expectations are also God's expectations. *Whenever we want to be good and happy, our will must be in accord with God's will!* God wants us in heaven along with every other human being He created. Since my expectations are nothing more than what God wants, it was not merely my personal desire but God's as well. Therefore, this is an example of agape love and not merely conditional love.

Agape Love and Fear

There is no fear in perfect love. In first John we read, "There is no fear in love, but perfect love casts out fear, whoever fears has not reached perfection."[1] As we know, fear comes from our will wanting something, and we're afraid of not getting it. In the nursing home example above, it is not my will but God's will that is essential. In agape love, we accept God's will, not our own in all matters. It is all about what God wants for us. We know She loves us, and we love Her.

When you truly love someone, you trust them. *Love involves trust.* Because She loves us, we trust that Her will for us is always for our benefit, perhaps not always physically, but most certainly spiritually. With this trust, we have hope in the promises of Jesus. *It is hope that conquers fear because it is stronger than fear.* The truthful answers to our three basic questions about ourselves and our future give us hope. The wrong answers can produce fear and despair. So we do Her will with trust and we are not afraid. Our love is perfect because we desire nothing except whatever God wishes. In prayer to His Father, Jesus says, *not what I want but what you want.*[2] How can we stop being afraid with true love? The following strategy is offered:

- Whenever we desire something significant such as a job, education, a spouse, or our life because it is being threatened, we take whatever loving action we can to acquire what we want, do the best that we can.
- Whatever happens respond by receiving the result with love and goodwill, knowing we did our best, and now the result is beyond our control. Of course, if we see some other alternative we forgot and could try, by all means try it, but eventually, we must accept the result, whatever it is, with love and goodwill.
- We can accept and respond with love regardless of what the result is because it is a part of life. We know the truth about life and we will live with hope in these truths we often can not prove and accept by faith. We know in life sometimes we are successful in acquiring our desires. At other times, shit may happen due to unforeseen circumstances

or the evil people do or the physically evil forces of nature that sometimes happen.

- We can respond with love because we love God, and so we trust Him. We believe whatever the result, God loves us and will make it benefit us, if not physically, certainly spiritually. This is all that really matters. Ultimately, it is God's will that will prevail if we truly love Him! If we truly understand, believe, and love, there is no fear.

The Bible is full of stories of the Jews not trusting God. They did not trust their God to help them in the Sinai when they crossed over from Egypt. They did not trust Him when Israel was being attacked by the Assyrians and Babylonians, even though their prophet, Isaiah, urged them to do so. On account of their lack of trust and love for God, the Jews crossing the Sinai never entered the promised land, and hundreds of years later, Israel was conquered by the foreign invaders. Once again, they became captives in a foreign land.

In conclusion, our response to God's love is our desire for a unity of wills; a union of our will with Hers and our acts are in accord with Her will. We respond to the goodness and love of God with this desire and action, which is an expression of our love. *If our love is pure and perfect, whoever we love, it is really God we are loving.*

→ Who in your life comes as close to perfect love as possible? Can you describe this love?

God's love is unconditional and wants our love to be the same. He does not demand it because He gave us an intellect and free will. Our love is often conditional, expecting to receive for our actions like when we buy, sell, trade, and work for what we desire or need. We act for what we need to survive physically and spiritually. It is God's desire that such acts should involve perfect love. Our desire is another story. It is a matter of how and why we desire that determines an act of agape love.

Imperfect Love

God needs nothing to stay alive. It is the love of the Father, Son, and Holy Spirit for each other that makes God alive and one. As His creation, we need life support systems, and most of all, love to live. God does not need love to live because She is love. We were created to love, but we do not have to love to stay alive! We do, however, need God's unconditional love to exist and live. Many of us are unaware of this truth or act as if we were not aware of it. The problem is, with the fall of Adam and Eve came the knowledge of good and evil. Original sin was born, which means a loss of God's grace, and expresses the sinful condition into which all humanity is born. All people share a like-mindedness in sin. With original sin, we can and often do exhibit imperfect love. In addition, with the fall of Adam and Eve, we became active participants in the acquisition of basic needs to survive. This truth can produce fear in the absence of perfect love.

Without agape love, we will fail to trust God, and so fear enters our lives; fear we will not acquire what we need to survive like the Jews crossing the Sinai. With fear, we can love conditionally, or even worse, we can sin. Jesus confronts our fear and worry about survival when He explains, *I tell you, do not worry about your life, what you will eat or what you will drink or about your body, what you will wear. Is not life more than food and the body more than clothing? Look at the birds, they neither sow nor reap nor gather into their barns, and yet your heavenly Father feeds them. Are you not of more value than they?*[3]

We must labor, buy, trade, or barter for things we need to stay alive. Unless we are extremely rich, most of us must work to earn our living. As we know, to acquire employment, we must barter with an employer. We can trade or barter our intellect, ambition, and willingness to work hard long hours. Those who are stronger in intellect and will or have valuable talents in the eyes of the world have more to trade with than those without. Some of them may think they are superior to those without strong intellects or wills and may consider those lacking these attributes weak and different. Their love is imperfect because they only love those like themselves.

This can occur not only with those with different attributes but those with different ethnic backgrounds. They classify humanity into groups and reserve their love for those in a particular group. There are not only attributes and ethnic groups but also social, economic, political, or racial groups in which they reserve their love for their own kind. Identity politics is subject to this danger.

→ Do you know anyone who has learned to only love their own kind, their own culture, or language group, etc.? Perhaps you've been exposed to this type of identity thinking?

We see our interaction and love with others can become conditional in our efforts to acquire the needs to stay alive or maintain a lifestyle in a particular class of people. This can be upgraded to our secondary higher order needs and traits. It can even be raised to the level of a religious group. We must have specific actualized talents, traits, or virtues to belong to a specific religion and receive our love. In all such cases, our love is conditional.

We are created to love as human beings. We are not animals. In this life, we can die to living as human beings and intentionally act like animals. To live like human beings, we need to love each other without conditions. Of course, there are organizations we belong to that are not necessarily based on love! A business unites people to produce a product, an athletic team to win, an army to protect, and even a particular club for social status. If we can't contribute to the production of the product, protect, win, or remain in a social economic status, we are removed from the organization or union. Our belonging to these organizations may have nothing to do with love. However, all these organized relationships can involve love if we choose to make them so. All who love God would choose to do so. Soldiers can love protecting each other in combat. Team members can support and play together in the spirit of love. Workers can help each other, and with love, produce a product they know will help people.

A family who truly loves will accept its members into its union without conditions. If a family requires certain character traits or prohibits members with certain traits, weaknesses, or sins from entry or reentry, it is not perfect love. If we are downtrodden or have done terrible things, we can go home and be with our families, provided they love us unconditionally. The only condition that must be enforced is to reject anyone that destroys the existence of the family. The family cannot accept a physical assault on family members or giving them drugs or stealing resources the family needs for their support and survival.

Remember the story of the prodigal son? The father welcomed back his long-lost son unconditionally with a celebration. The older son felt injustice because a son who had abandoned his father and squandered his inheritance was celebrated, and he who remained faithful was not. His love was conditional by thinking because of his faithfulness, his father owed him.[4]

→ Has a black sheep in your family returned home?
→ How was he or she treated or should have been treated?
→ Would you be like the father or older son in the story of the prodigal son?

How can love be imperfect and still be love? Imperfect love still unites with acts of giving, sharing, and receiving, aware of the goodness of loved ones. They are aware we are interdependent, and love is needed to survive physically and spiritually. However, we can be hesitant and reluctant to love those who are engaged in evil acts or who are different from us. Our reluctance to love someone due to imperfections or certain types of differences in people makes our love imperfect, yet we can still love others unconditionally.

The most perfect people in the world have imperfections, and so do we. At times, it's difficult to tolerate each other. Yet, we are to "bear one another's burdens, in this way you will fulfill the law of Christ."[5] This means we are to bear the burdens of one another's weaknesses and imperfections. *One mark of perfection in love is simply tolerating the imperfections of others.* We must live a moral righteous life and help others rid themselves of imperfection and sin. It is the Christian way. However, there are cases in which we can't help them, no matter how hard we try, so as Christians, we accept their imperfections and continue to love and pray for them.

Forgiveness: An Attribute of Love

We must not only accept imperfections in others and ourselves; we must forgive others and ourselves. Jesus said, *Forgive us our debts as we also have forgiven our debtors.*[6] *We cannot say we love someone if we are not willing to forgive them for anything they may do to us, whether they ask for forgiveness or not.* If we continue to love someone yet still harbor some ill feelings about a wrong he or she may have done to us, our love is imperfect. With perfect unconditional love, anything can be forgiven. The only exception is sin against the Holy Spirit. This occurs when we think we are so bad God will not forgive us nor can we forgive ourselves. We refuse to believe God's love is perfect. We refuse to believe She will forgive all our sins no matter how bad they are. We believe our case is hopeless, so indeed it is.

God will ultimately deal with our sins and imperfections. We must make an effort to correct our own sins and imperfections as well as help our loved ones deal with their sins. We must, however, recognize our own imperfections before we can do so.[7] *It is difficult to forgive someone if we can't forgive ourselves.*

→ Are you aware of your own imperfections?
→ Do you find it hard to love someone with imperfections and sins? Perfectionists do.
→ Do you love anyone unconditionally?

There is one truth all who love must know and accept. Only God is perfect. We must see and accept the imperfections in ourselves and others. *It is difficult to love another with imperfections or even see the goodness in them if we cannot recognize our own imperfections and goodness.*

More on Perfect and Imperfect Love

Since the intellect is fallible, its knowledge is imperfect. The intellect makes mistakes incidentally or accidentally, such as our perception of the apparent good as a true good. The intellect can be ignorant with inaccurate information, a lack of information, and doubts along with a weak will's inability to control appetites. Due to our wrong perceptions, lack of accurate information, or emotional control issues, our intellect will make mistakes. An intellect that can and does make mistakes can be the cause of imperfect love, even though we are created in the image of love.

Our love can be imperfect while God's love is perfect just as Her intellect is perfect and ours is not. For Saint Paul, knowledge is imperfect and useless if it is not animated by love.[1] Just as the intellect can be flawed in its intensity or strength, so too the will can be flawed. It too is flawed by the variation of its intensity or strength. Some wills are strong, others moderate, still others weak, and this intensity may vary from situation to situation. An encouraging fact is the will can be trained to increase in strength. This is one of the reasons Christians deny some of their appetites and desires, especially during lent.

→ Do you deny yourself something you want or like during Lent? Do you know why you do it? If it saves money, consider giving it to the poor.
→ What is the advantage of training the will to be strong?

We can place limits upon our love, and limits are conditions that make love imperfect. Any love that does not involve everyone, including our enemies, is not perfect or unconditional love! A love may demonstrate a great degree of perfection for some people and less for others. For example, we may love our family, willing to sacrifice everything for their needs, including our lives. For friends, we may be willing to respond to their needs up to a point. We would not exceed this limit, and certainly, we may not be willing to sacrifice our life. To our enemies or perhaps those we dislike or have wronged us, we would give nothing. With our family, our love is nearly perfect with friends, not so much and with enemies not at all.

→ Do you love your enemies unconditionally?

In another example, we may demonstrate our love for the poor by responding to their needs with donations at our church or volunteering to help feed them. On the other hand, we may own stock in a business that exploits the poor. Or we may vote for politicians who support policies and laws that financially enhance our well-being but are not very kind or just to the poor. At times, we may be unaware of this paradox, but if we are aware and do nothing to correct it, we are complicit in their unjust evil actions. The poorest and weakest people on our planet are unborn children. They cannot be seen, have no name, no power, and cannot act for themselves. They are completely dependent on their mothers. Yet, many mothers choose to kill their unborn children since an unjust man-made law gives them the right to do so.

Sometimes we are ambivalent, wanting to do what is right and just for the poor but are afraid to act further or do more than we have already done. Sometimes the spirit of love is willing, but the desires of our flesh are strong and influence a weak will. The will that is weak succumbs to the desires of the flesh. It acts contrary to what our conscious spirit knows is right. As Jesus said about His disciples who did not stay awake with Him in the garden of Gethsemane, *The spirit indeed is willing, but the flesh is weak.*[2]

This is why we must train the will to be strong. This is done periodically and deliberately, delaying gratification of the appetites and desires. Our unwillingness to delay gratification like little children can lead to failure and, in some cases, damnation.

→ Did you ever do something you knew was wrong but did it anyway because you wanted it so much?
→ How did it feel after you did it?

→ If you continued to do it, did the feeling change? The more you do it, the more you convince yourself it's all right, and you begin to feel a little better about the sin and less feeling of guilt.

Our intellect and will are flawed. The weakened intellect may reflect a weakened faith, which results in imperfect love. This weakened intellect may be overwhelmed with temptations of the flesh producing sinful behavior in the pursuit of apparent goods. *Greek philosophers talk about different loves such as filial, maternal, erotic, agape. In reality, they are merely different aspects of the one love. There is only one love because there is only one God, and God is love.* God's love is agape, and to love as God loves, our love must be agape, regardless of the venue we find ourselves in. Unfortunately, in the here and now, this is often not the case because of a flawed intellect and will.

Dealing with Imperfections in Our Loved Ones

Some of us become discouraged when we discover faults or sins in friends we love. We may stop associating with them or ignore their problem because it would be too uncomfortable to confront them. Evil prevails when good people see sinfulness and do nothing. There are good and bad ways to confront them. Our actions to correct a loved one must be based on the power of love. What does this mean? Our objective must be to show them the truth and the consequences when our loved ones persist in sin. Our approaches should not be to display our righteousness, but our humility in not being able to help sooner.

We must not judge but humbly invite them to look at the truth because we care about them. The motive of love propels the will to confront our family members and friends with faults that will hurt them. Love does not seek to win over loved ones or defeat them in any argument. Such an approach demonstrates judgment, arrogance, and pride. It often results in hardening their hearts for any change for the better. We are not trying to win over them but to convince them with understanding and love, using truth as our primary weapon.

This approach can also be used to help ourselves in our struggle to deal with our imperfections. Love doesn't spare our loved ones or ourselves if there is a need for correction, and there will always be a need. If our correction of ourselves or others hurts, it shows a sore spot has been touched. Even if our correction fails, our efforts test our humility and keep both ourselves and our loved ones accustomed to correction when we do wrong. *Any effort to try to help anyone, including ourselves, overcome sin is worth the effort whether we are successful or not.* Failure should not discourage us.

→ Did you ever make an effort to help anyone overcome an imperfection or sin?
→ Were you successful or did you fail? How do you feel with success or failure?
→ Have you ever tried to help yourself? Were you successful?

→ Have you ever asked someone to help you with an imperfection or fault? If not, why not?

Many of us struggle with imperfections and failures. Maybe it's a matter of how we see reality and the approach we use in addressing sin. We will deal with addressing the sin we find in ourselves and in loved ones in greater detail later on in the book.

Independence and Respect Essential to Perfect Love

Love unites two or more people, but this union is a paradox. As we have seen in their union, the two become one, and yet, in their uniting, they remain much of themselves. They are separate to a great degree, keeping their own identities. As we know, this paradox is reflected at all levels of existence beginning at the molecular level. Remember, a salt molecule can be separated back into sodium and chlorine atoms. In their union to make salt, the sodium and chlorine atoms must keep some of their individual identifying properties hidden. This can be proven by demonstrating that salt can be separated back into sodium and chlorine atoms with all of their original properties; therefore these atoms could not have lost all of their identifying properties in their union to make salt. Within the union they remain separated to a degree. If they were completely assimilated into the union to make salt, chemist would not have been able to separate them back into their original states of being. It is the same in the union of love!

Within a union of love between a man and woman, most of their properties are not suppressed or hidden. Each lover within the union is aware of the identity of the other and respects it. They are not only aware of their identity but their independence as well. They are free to enter or not enter a relationship and union or destroy it if they wish. *Within the physical and spiritual existence of love, each partner respects and preserves their own integrity and individuality, and each enables their partner to be themselves.* Love is not an assimilation of two into one as an inseparable unit with an inability to recognize the individuals within the union. Some who love fail to recognize this truth and smother each other in a relationship that becomes oppressive.

Each partner does change in a union of love. The changes are not significant in physical properties as they are with nonliving elements. The changes in a union of love are primarily spiritual, and by this, we mean the changes are in our intellect and consciousness, our understanding, and compassion. To all of His creations, God has given the gift of existence, which He maintains with His love. To some of His creations, He has given the gift of life, but only to human beings and angels has He given the gift of the ability to love. How fortunate we are and grateful we should be.

There is a separateness in the union of love, but at the same time, the energy of love breaks through the walls that separates lovers, overcoming their sense of isolation and loneliness. *In their individuality and free independence, they must unite in love for their own spiritual survival as human beings.* In any interaction establishing a relationship between people who love, there is no exploitation or manipulation of each other. There are some who believe life is exploitation where we use others to get what we want. Sexual exploitation is quite common now a days. There is no respect in exploitation. Couples engage in sex without commitment and without the sacred, fullest, and most beautiful relationship of marriage. *Exploitation is not the way of love.*

Each lover respects the person he or she loves. Respect means the lover admires and holds his or her beloved in regard, honor, and esteem. The beloved reciprocates with similar sentiments. With this respect for each other, each can grow and unfold as he or she is and not necessarily what their partner may wish. This occurs in a union in which each preserves their integrity and individuality. Each wants their loved one to develop for their own sake. *Every person has a God-given right to respect.*

→ Do or would you find it hard to respect someone who betrayed you?
→ Can you love someone you do not respect? Should you?
→ Do you believe every person has a God-given unconditional right to respect or do you think every person must earn respect?

Respect is essential in a love relationship, and it occurs when each lover achieves some independence with an awareness of our interdependency. Each must remain separate, allowing each to have some independence from the other. Partners in love must be secure enough in their relationship with each other that they can fulfill each other's needs without resorting to dominance, exploitation, or power. *Respect exists only on the basis of freedom and mutuality.* Romans states that we must "love one another with mutual affection and outdo one another in showing honor."[1] In first Peter we find these words, "Honor everyone, love the family of believers."[2] To honor means to respect our love ones.

The keys to unlocking love is *understanding* their true identity. As we know, we understand with *sympathy* and *empathy,* and when we do, we demonstrate our care for them. Because we care and love them, we take *responsibility* for them by responding to their needs. We respond to their needs with *respect* and a sense of *justice.* We must also have respect for ourselves. Every breath we take, our entire existence is dependent upon the love and generosity of the Lord. He has every right to expect us to live in accord with His wishes. Not only for God but for ourselves because it is the only way to live in the manner true to ourselves and who we are. The Lord respects us more than anyone could possibly imagine.

The Problem of Evil

Definition of Evil

Anything that diminishes good or attempts to destroy or dominate a rational living existence or relationship is evil. The problem of evil is simply this: God created everything that exists, and since everything that God created is good, then how can we explain the existence of evil in the world? The essence of all living and nonliving existence is good. If existence is good, then nonexistence is bad. *Evil is simply the absence of good, which is the absence of existence! Another way to look at evil is to see it as darkness or nothing as compared to the light of God,* which is existence by love that involves everything. Jesus said, *I am the light of the world.*[1] and we are "children of the light."[2]

This concept of evil appears contrary to Saint Paul's understanding of evil. Paul perceives evil existing as a universal force designed to oppose the goodness of God.[3] Paul was less concerned with the choices of a free will and more interested in the big picture encompassing an entire universal view. Paul's view came from ancient Jewish writings prevalent at the time and his own revelation.[4] He believes we are like actors and actresses on the world stage, involving a battle between good and evil. For Paul, sin is not merely the free choice of intelligent beings capable of love and sin but also an acting evil force that is the origin of evil.

Nothing created is bad because God is perfect goodness. We've seen existence is interaction or interpersonal activity or relationship, which is motivated by love. *Any act that diminishes or destroys a right relationship with God, humans, or our environment is evil.* A person who is good in essence can with an intellect and free will diminish or destroy his living relationship with friends, family, or God. This can be done by using a bad act or indifferent act illicitly.

As an example, a woman shoots her boyfriend and seriously wounds him. What is evil in its essence that one can find in this act of shooting. Certainly, not the body or intellect of the woman or her boyfriend. Nor would it be the gun or bullets that follow the natural law, and this includes the wound inflicted. There is no being in this incident whether the energy form or force of existence or the natural law that is evil in its essence. Natural laws are the laws of nature created by God.

The woman uses the gun in the illicit act. It is her "intention" to inflict harm by diminishing the goodness and physical existence of the man by killing him. This is evil! It is not the gun or the act itself that is evil! If the woman had permission from someone in authority such as God or governmental law, would it be considered an evil act? There are acts that are evil by their very nature; however, we must still intend these evil acts. Does this mean she is evil in her essence or very being created by God? No, because we are much more than our acts. She is good in her existence because existence created by God is good! What is evil is her intention to diminish his existence and goodness. In so doing, she diminishes her own existence and goodness. She will never be able to diminish all of her goodness and existence because if she did, she would be reduced to nothing, the absence of all goodness and existence.

No one can "totally" destroy with their intellect and free will the goodness of God's created existence. We may destroy or diminish physical existence but never spiritual existence. *Only we can diminish our spiritual existence as human beings by sin but will never destroy it totally.*

Can the government give us permission to kill? It can when a man is convicted of murder, and governmental law condemns him to death. It also can when it declares war. It gives its soldiers permission to kill. To defend our life and the lives of any other human being, it can be justified. Jews, Muslims, and Christians sometimes refer to a holy war. War is violence that involves killing with the loss of life, which is sacred. War is never holy. At best, a just war is a display of imperfect love. Perfect or agape love does not involve itself with wars that kill. It is sinful to fight in an unjust war on the side that is being unjust. If it is unjust, no government laws or declarations can make it just. Our abortion laws provide government permission for a woman to kill her baby, and in the eyes of the state, it is not a criminal act. These laws are evil because they permit acts that destroy the lives of human beings, which is contrary to God's law. We cannot claim self-defense against an innocent unborn baby! Abortion is an act of murder by its very nature, and no government law can change it.

At one time, I was in a religious training program. As part of the training, I had to attend classes for young adults preparing to become Catholics. This one particular class had to do with marriage. At the conclusion of the presentation, I reluctantly raised my hand for comment. I told the couple giving the presentation it was a very good talk, but they left something out. They asked what it was, and my response was, "Sex!" I went on to explain, "As Catholics, we believe we do not have sex without the solemn commitment of marriage, a commitment to love and be faithful to each other in sickness and health in good times and bad times as long as they both live. A commitment to have children if God wills it. Without commitment, the sex act is considered fornication and sinful." I went on to explain, "Casual sex can and sometimes does lead to abortion. One reason a woman will have an abortion is because the father of the child will not make a lifelong commitment to her and their unborn child."

I was denied entrance to the next class; I was told they didn't want my presence any longer. Later, I found out some of the couples in the class were not married and living together.

We may have laws that are evil in the sight of God and His ordinances but not evil or criminal in the eyes of the state and its ordinances.

→ If there is disagreement between God's law and government law, which law would you follow?
→ If there was a personal price you would have to pay to follow God's law, perhaps your freedom or even your life, would you pay it?

If we take something that does not belong to us without permission of the owner, it is an evil act by its very definition. However, if we were given permission to take it by the owner or if we were starving to death, and with no other way possible, we take bread that does not belong to us, it would not be an evil act. In the latter case, the right to life is a higher priority than the right to private ownership. In these examples, the act of "taking something that does not belong to us" is the same act as stealing. Stealing is a sin. However, "taking something" with the permission of the owner or as a right to life is not a sin.

The point is any being is a creation of God and good in its essence. With an intellect and free will, we can perform an act which is evil in its meaning. Evil acts can negatively influence and diminish the goodness of the essence of our nature or spiritual existence as human beings. It can destroy much of the goodness of our nature, reducing it to almost nothing. *An entity which would be pure evil in its existence or essence would be nothing and could not exist.* Remember, evil can be defined negatively, the absence of goodness.

Devil

The devil is good in whatever essence of his nature is left. After all, he was an angel created by God. So what makes the devil evil? He has the least amount of goodness. Taking everything that is good in existence, he perverts it, attempting to destroy, corrupt, or diminish physical and spiritual existence and goodness. The devil *deceives* us with untruths. With deception, he *divides* instead of our uniting with love. Consistent division can eventually *destroy* our existance as human beings and our unity of love.

The objective of the devil is to destroy our love relationships and reduce us to an animal existence. He uses our weakness and human desires, and if we succumb to his temptations, we reduce our existence as human beings. It is not people we are resisting when we resist evil, but the devil who is using them for his purpose.

Justice

What determines evil? The motive that specifies the fairness or justice of the act. To the Jewish people, justice is of paramount importance. The doctrine of an eye for an eye and a tooth for a tooth is essential to their law. It involves the fairness and uprightness of a just act. The just act is of high moral standard; it is true and honest. In the Old Testament, God's justice is often the same as divine fidelity and steadfast love.[5] The Jews lived by the laws given to them by God through Moses and the prophets. As Jesus revealed, however, the most important of all Jewish laws is the law of love.[6]

Love is merciful to any person in a love relationship who commits an unjust act, if the person repents. God is love; therefore, God is merciful.[7] Jesus said, *Blessed are the merciful, for they will receive mercy.*[8]

- → If everyone in this world loved each other, would we need any other laws?
- → Do you think in heaven, there are a host of laws we must obey? Or is there just one we live?

The trouble is we are imperfect; therefore, our acts can be imperfect. Sometimes we act willingly and with deliberation; at other times, without thorough investigation or thought. *By our motive and intent, we can transform an indifferent act into an unjust evil act. Motive is the key to acts of love and acts that cause sin.* An act of love creates and maintains rational living existence. An evil act destroys and diminishes rational living existence. It can transform a being to one with less spiritual or physical existence, perhaps no existence at all as human beings, living an animal existence without love.

Sin is a choice we make. When we sin, we are responsible for the choice. Paul perceived it a little differently. The wrong choice of a person's free will does not bring sin into the world. It comes into the world by an evil universal force or a being that imposes itself upon humanity.[9] Paul appears to be focusing less on people's choice and more on evil forces and God's desire to overcome them. God's desire that we live in love is because love not only saves us, but is like an umbrella that helps protect us from the rain of evil the devil brings into the world.

Two Evil Acts

We use indifferent acts with evil intentions or deliberately use acts evil by their nature. There are two kinds of evil acts. Evil acts that destroy and diminish the physical body and evil acts that destroy or diminish the spirit or soul. Jesus warns us to not be afraid of evil acts that kill the body but be afraid of evil acts that kill the soul or spirit within us.[10] Others as well as ourselves can kill our body with evil acts, but *only we can diminish the goodness of our soul by consciously and deliberately acting with evil intentions.*

Another Problem of Evil

Another problem with evil comes when we begin to place blame. Who is responsible for all the evil we experience and all the evil in the world? Certainly, we as human beings are responsible and to blame for much of the evil in the world. We cause war, genocide, injustice, poverty, and sickness with the pain and suffering that accompanies our evil acts. It is we, sinful ignorant humans, who may destroy this world with sin. This we can understand because we understand the nature of humanity.

The problem comes with natural disasters that cause tragedy in our lives. There are the physical evils of diseases and natural disasters, such as cancer and violent storms that kill so many. Many believe human beings are not responsible for these physical evils, so who are we to blame? When an innocent child dies of cancer, who is responsible? Unable to blame the human race, some blame God, or worse, reject their belief in God. They question a God who would cause such pain and suffering or at least allow it to happen. People become atheists because they are unable to resolve this problem.

To resolve this problem as a Christian, we must remember Jesus's warning about destroying spiritual life, which is infinitely more important than our physical life. This physical life is limited and exists only for a short time while the spirit is eternal. If there was no eternal life for those innocent people who die of disease or disaster, then their lives surely would be meaningless, and life would be unjust.

As mentioned earlier, because God has preknowledge of the evils in the world does not mean She determines it. Ultimately, it comes down to trust in a loving God who does the right thing for His spiritual living creations in this life but much more importantly in our life to come. We must always keep in mind this is not our home. This life is a journey, and a short one at that. It makes little difference if it is rough or easy, short or long; what counts is how we live this journey, which takes us to our true home of eternal life with God. This is the only thing that truly counts; nothing else really matters. The saddest thing in life is if we fail to get home!

41

More About Evil

To love people who behave badly, we must see them as they truly are and accept the fact some of their behavior is sinful. This does not mean we accept the sinful behavior. *We must make a distinction between people and their behavior.* Many people, including existentialists, believe we are what we do, but we know better. What we do is not who we are! Our behavior reflects what we are capable of doing and not who we are.

When we sin, we should feel guilt, not shame! Guilt has to do with feeling remorse because of our sinful acts. Shame has to do with disgracing or dishonoring who we are. We are Spirit, capable of a mental awareness of our nature and behavior. We see that sin and sufferings are conditions that can influence our being but are not the essence of our being or who we really are. The spiritual soul is more important than any of our behaviors and will continue long after our body and behaviors cease to be in this world.

→ Do you make a distinction between the sin and the sinner? Between the act and the person?

As we know, with our motive or intent, we can transform an indifferent act into an evil one. Eating or drinking are indifferent acts. However, they can become evil by overindulgent gluttony or the excessive drinking of alcoholism. Or we decide to perform an act, which is evil by its nature, for our own selfish reasons, acts such as stealing, lying, injustice, betrayal, and murder.

Causes of Evil and the Solution to the Problem of Evil

The question now arises, how does evil develop? What causes our evil intent or motive? We know evil doesn't exist in its essence. All that exists is real and good. An evil desire must perceive the end it seeks as having some goodness, but it is not a true good, which is in keeping with our identity and spiritual existence. As we learned, perhaps the person acting badly is getting the apparent good confused with the true good. The evil acts come from our failure to see clearly and has nothing to do with who we are. The original sin of all humanity is the cause of our having to experience all the physical evil in the world, even natural disasters and diseases.

Evils such as cancer and natural disasters which kill so many people have their origin in the sins of humankind, which emanates from original sin. Prior to human beings entering the scene, only animals had to experience the physical evils inherent in the laws of nature. When our original parents arrived, they were special. Made in God's image and a little less than God, they did not have to experience the consequences of the physical evils of nature, even death by natural causes.

Adam and Eve were the first human beings and, as such, were given free will so they could love God and each other. Unfortunately, their freedom gave them the ability to disobey God and acquire an awareness of evil because they wanted to be like God and know everything. With their freedom and now an awareness of not only good but evil, they were able to abuse their freedom and choose evil instead of good if they so desired. They are the initial parents or representatives of all humankind. Therefore, they became a source of sin for all generations to follow.

What happened to Adam and Eve could happen to any one of us. With awareness and freedom, they chose evil, providing all future human beings the ability to do the same. God permits this because She does not wish to take away our freedom and our ability to love. So with our sins, we become responsible for all the spiritual and much of the physical evils that can befall all the members of our species.

Because of their sin, Adam and Eve had to leave the Garden of Eden and live in a world subject to the laws of nature, including disease and natural disaster. Due to our ability to sin, our knowledge of good and evil inherited from our first parents and our fallible intellect, we too sin and so must live in this world with its physical laws which can be destructive. We can do something God cannot do! We can sin. God's free will voluntarily chooses good; to do otherwise would be contrary to His nature and very existence. Our choosing sin results in diminishing our existence of living in love and could ultimately result in a total loss of our ability to love. Our living without love is living completely alone and, as we will see a little later in the book, living in hell! *God is pure existence living in love. Unfortunately, with sin and evil in our lives, which we freely choose, we diminish our existence of living in love.* May the mercy of God save us from an existence without love.

Just as Adam and Eve were the source of all sin for the entire human race, Jesus Christ is the source of salvation for all people. All people including children who die of cancer, need salvation due to original sin, imprinted on our nature because of the fall of Adam and Eve.

Evolution and Humanity

Could we have evolved from lower forms of animal life? Possible our physical bodies could have, but not our spirit! God could have allowed evolution to produce a body that resembles ours, but it would not be human. It is only when He infuses into a body or many bodies the spirit of an intellect and free will does the animal become a human being. In the case of many bodies, they would all be our initial parents, all sinned by disobeying the Lord and all be the cause of original sin. In such a case, Adam and Eve would be a representation of them all.

We know this explanation of the evils that befalls innocence is not a satisfactory answer to our question "why?"

Perhaps all we can say is that we will never understand this mystery of why the innocent suffer and die. Ultimately all we can do is trust in the wisdom and power of God. There is a story about a man named John. Tragically, he ran over and killed his only son while backing up in his driveway. Being a man of prayer, he immediately turned his mind to God and asked the question "Lord, why did you allow my innocent son to die?" He got a response immediately in his thoughts. It was God standing at the foot of the cross asking him the question "John, why my innocent Son?"

God knows and permits this because all humanity has a natural propensity to sin. Although God allows physical evil to befall us, He never causes or allows spiritual evil to take place. We do this ourselves with sin. Innocent children are incapable of sinful behavior; therefore, a good spiritual end in heaven is assured.

We all want as much goodness and happiness as we can get in this life, but it is not obtainable with the apparent good or evil desires. True goodness can never come from evil desires or evil means. It's an illusion because sin is a distortion of reality. Any distortion of reality ultimately brings unhappiness and suffering because we are living a lie. We are not living in conformity to reality.

Trust and Sin

There are people who sin who are aware and not confused. They know what they are doing. They seek a lesser good, which is temporary and a distortion of what is truly good for our entire being. They know it is an apparent good or lesser good and is a sin, but they still seek it and pursue evil. Why? It is because we can see and touch the lesser good. We can experience it here and now. So we decide upon a lesser good, knowing it may distort or destroy what is truly good for us and others. As we explained earlier, one in the hand, the lesser good, is better than two in the bush, the true good. We do not trust God and do not believe She will keep Her promises. If we do not trust Her, how can we love Her. Trust, as we mentioned earlier, is an attribute of love.

At the root of this decision is doubt or another way of putting it is a lack of faith. There are some philosophers who believe ignorance is the only cause of evil. In fact, ignorance is evil. Ignorance is a factor. But as we see, it isn't the "only" factor. The lack of trust and a diminishment of love, the intention of evil for the lesser or apparent good, and a lack of faith makes us accountable for our sins. We do not have faith that what is truly good will ever come.

We trust God because He is truthful and loves us perfectly. At first, we trust everyone we love, however, we are a sinful people who can succumb to vices that can hurt us and others. We can love and forgive those with vices; however, in certain cases we cannot trust them until they prove themselves worthy of our trust! For example, we can not trust or reconcile with any person who abuses us or our children repeatedly until they repent and undergo rehabilitation to permanently eliminate the sinful behavior. In certain cases the consequence of the law may be necessary, such as prison time. *Everyone we love deserves a second chance, but in certain cases, they have to earn it!*

Ignorance

Ignorance does not necessarily alleviate responsibility. There are two kinds of ignorance, vincible and invincible. Ignorance either can or cannot be overcome. If it can be overcome, it is vincible, and if it can't, it is invincible. With vincible ignorance, we are aware of our ignorance and we can acquire the proper knowledge; however, we deliberately and voluntarily choose to remain ignorant. The results that follows from this voluntary ignorance are the responsibility of the vincible, ignorant person.

A vincible, ignorant man who likes to think of himself as an auto-mechanic knows he does not have enough knowledge to fix the brakes on a car and, if not repaired correctly, will put the driver in danger. Perhaps because of pride or for money, he tries to fix the brakes, they fail, and the driver is killed in an accident. Certainly, he did not intend the death, but he deliberately placed the driver in danger and is responsible for the death. Invincible ignorance may be an extenuating circumstance that could excuse people for the harm they cause; vincible cannot. The invincible, ignorant person is not responsible for their harmful acts; the vincible, ignorant person is.

→ Would you or have you sinned for an apparent good, even though you knew it was a sin and prevented you from acquiring the true good?
→ Why do you think you would want this apparent good instead of the true good? Perhaps you doubted the true good existed or could ever be acquired, which is a lack of faith. Maybe it was instant gratification due to the weakness of the flesh.
→ Why would a person commit adultery, knowing it was a serious sin that would place her or his immortal soul in jeopardy?
→ Do you think the auto-mechanic "committed" a serious sin? In criminal law, it would be termed negligent homicide due to his vincible ignorance.

Sin is an act that distorts and destroys a true good. **The true good is a relationship with God necessary for our physical, psychological, and spiritual existence.** We can freely and deliberately ignore what is true and good because we do not like the demands it places upon us. We lack the courage to leave our comfort zones and do what is true and good. This is a sin of omission. We don't want to talk about the evils of abortion or fornication because it upsets us, so we refrain from thinking or talking about it. We don't want to confront and tell people such acts are wrong or sinful because society will reject and punish us. *No amount of personal prayer or religious ritual is going to exempt or alleviate us from the responsibility of doing the right thing or following in the ways of God's truth.* We must refrain not only from sins of commission but also of omission.

Since we are responsible, justice requires us to face the consequences of our failure to act.

Ideology of Evil

A man may clearly see a good he desires, but it belongs to someone else. Because of his ideology, however, he has learned to take with the force of his free will what he wants from them. He may or may not know what he is doing is wrong. Perhaps he knows what he is doing may not be right or fair, but he has learned that life is not fair. With a strong will, he will take what he wants and needs. Remember, in the ideology of Nietzsche, the only concern is to be strong and wealthy, not weak and poor. We must intend to become strong with the virtues of power, cunning, ruthlessness, and most of all, a forceful free will. It is an ideology that dislikes the weak or poor who lack the courage or willpower to improve themselves.

They must "will" to become the ideal person who gets what they want by the power of their will and considers this the goal of human evolution. To these men or women of mental, physical, and material power, life is the exploitation or use of weaker or inferior people to get what they want. It was the ideology of Hitler. For him and many of the German people, it was a matter of the triumph of the will. It is not an ideology of love and is certainly not Christian. Many German Christians, even some clergy, embraced it or claimed invincible ignorance, which was really vincible. It was a matter of looking the other way for physical survival.

It sounds a little like Chris's story mentioned earlier. It's an ideology about getting what he wants, what he prizes and cherishes. Chris has chosen it freely, but not from an alternative because he sees no other way. This is what he learned and what he believed, and he acted upon his beliefs to get what he wanted at any cost. It was probably the one major cause of his bad behavior.

Just as we make a distinction between the person and their behavior, we must make a distinction between the sinners and their sins. We can understand the causes of bad behavior and perhaps can find some of these causes for sins within ourselves. We all have the potential of intending and acting sinfully. If we do not sin, it is because of the mercy, the help, and graces of a loving God. We too must love by showing understanding, forgiveness, and mercy to those who sin.

→ Do you recognize any of these causes for sin within yourself?
→ Do you attempt to find out the causes of sin by observing and talking about the possible reasons people may sin? Determining and understanding the causes of sin can help us avoid them.

Response to Evil

It is not only our response to the needs of those we love that determines our lives and destiny but our response to those who dislike and even hate us. They may ridicule, mock, and even inflict physical and psychological harm. How should we respond? We can respond by proportionally giving back in acts and words what they gave to us by their deeds and conversations. This seems just and fair. As the Bible says, "an eye for an eye" or evil for evil.[1]

Many in our culture believe in this idea of revenge. As the saying goes, "If someone hurts you, don't get mad, get even." We see it in many successful movies because people enjoy the violence and revenge. Perhaps it appeals to our sense of justice or karma.

→ Do you enjoy watching revenge and violence, seeing the bad guy get what he deserves, which is often a violent death? It is quite common in western movies. Moral film critics think it is quite acceptable. Good wins.

Returning evil for evil, we become like our adversaries. In so doing, we are harming ourselves as well as betraying the teachings of Jesus. As the Lord said, *Blessed are you when people revile and persecute you on my account (which means preaching and practicing His teaching) for your reward is great in heaven.*[2] When we take revenge, we are betraying God and who we are. Eastern ideology has a saying that if you hate someone because you're a victim of their brutality and you seek revenge, you had better dig two graves: one for your adversary and one for yourself.

→ How do you respond to evil?

How should Christians respond to evil? We can do nothing in return for the evil we experience, and in so doing, we are not diminishing our spiritual existence. In cases where it is possible, we can turn them over to law enforcement and let society administer justice. Or we could return their evil with acts of kindness, mercy, and understanding as disciples of Jesus. If we do, it will enhance our own spiritual existence. We must know, however, if we take this approach of love, three things could happen. Our persecutor may send us away. In extreme cases, this could result in their killing us. The persecutors may go away themselves or they may change and stop their persecution and injustice.

During basic training in the Army, there was an evangelical soldier who was being persecuted by a drill sergeant who hated him because of his religion. He would respond to the unjust treatment with a smile, without complaint, and whenever possible, with acts of kindness toward his persecutor. Eventually, the sergeant had him shipped out of the unit.

Always keep this in mind: we may pray that God changes the heart of the evildoer. She may answer our prayer by changing us, not the evildoer. She may give us the courage and strength to respond to the persecution we experience with Her love working through us. With love, the sinner who is persecuting us may change! With God's help, we are accomplishing Her mission and ours here on earth. Even if we fail, we have honored and loved God with our efforts, and personally, we are successful.

We can only respond to persecution with love if we truly know the answer to our three basic questions. It can be done if we truly love Jesus and have absolute faith in His teaching and in ourselves. But how can we have faith in ourselves if we don't know who we truly are? How did the Son of God respond to our evil? Paul writes to the Ephesians, "God who is rich in mercy, out of the great love with which he loved us even when we were dead through our trespasses, made us alive together with Christ. By grace you have been saved and raised us up with him and seated us with him in the heavenly places in Jesus Christ."[3] Death in our trespasses refers to the serious sins we have committed, and yet with God's mercy and love, our damaged relationship with Her can be repaired.

For Paul, the life and death of Jesus has set us free from sin and death.[4] A similar doctrine is found in Revelation.[5] Only Jesus can free us from sin and spiritual death. He gives us faith and the graces or gifts of the spirit to conquer sin if we so choose.[6] Salvation has more to do with the gift of graces from God and less to do with ourselves. Paul seems to suggest, God determines the destiny of all that exists, including human beings.[7] We believe we have some say about our destiny which depends upon choices we make and what we do. Within our Bible, there are many places that give us control over our destiny. In Chapter 25 of Matthew, we see that we will be judged by how we treat the weakest and poorest among us and how we exercise justice to the least of our brethren will determine our salvation. We can also look at the letter of James in the New Testament or the writings of Saint Augustine. Both doctrines have validity and should be taken into consideration in determining our salvation.

Righteous Anger

God does not address evil acts with anger, bitterness, or force but with love because She is love. Anger can be deceptive because some people believe in "righteous anger," but there are serious doubts about this belief. Anger can often lead to violence. If you are extremely angry with a person, you may hit him; if you hit him, you may knock him down. When he is down, you may kick him. If you kick him, you may kill him. Perhaps you may ask about Jesus in the Temple. Didn't he knock over the tables of the money changers? Wasn't this an act of violence done in righteous anger? As stated earlier, Jesus was not angry but perhaps sad, and He did not harm anyone. He knocked the tables over in a teaching moment, a symbolic act, to demonstrate and dramatize the point He was trying to make and perhaps briefly stop a sinful act.

→ Do you believe in righteous anger?
→ When you take your anger out on another person, how do you feel? Better or worse?
→ Did your anger ever lead to violence of some kind?

Passive Resistance

If you loved your enemies, you would never do anything that would hurt them physically, psychologically, or spiritually. We remain faithful in our love of our enemies to the end, and in so doing, we are showing our love for God. Jesus did not vanquish the men who killed Him. The men who committed the evil acts are not evil in their nature or essence. Acts are not the true identity of a person. They are only a part of someone capable of evil acts but also capable of good acts.

The Christian sees a person not only in the badness of their act but in the goodness they can become in keeping with their true nature. In the face of injustice, violence or any threat to the survival of others, we who love, have several choices. We can run away. We can fight not only verbally but, when necessary, with violence to defend the weak and defenseless. We can resist nonviolently with demonstrations such as picketing or striking. We can refuse to obey any unjust and sinful laws or commands and refuse to engage in any activity that could lead to violence. With this latter approach, we must be prepared to suffer martyrdom rather than harm anyone, friend or foe. Where possible, we would demonstrate kindness and obedience to any request that was not sinful.

Jesus taught us to love our enemies and do good to those who hurt us. Why should we obey this most difficult command? It seems Jesus is asking us to do the impossible. He teaches us to love our enemies because this is who we are! This is what He created us to be and do: to love everyone, both friend or foe alike. If we don't, we are not living in accord with our true identity. Jesus is telling us not to use violence in the face of evil. He goes on to say those who face injustice, poverty, and hatred on account of Him are blessed.[8] Yet not using violence and turning the other cheek does not mean we should accept evil. We must resist evil.[9] We can never obey nor submit to an evil command or rule of law, even if it means our physical death!

→ In Vietnam, if you were ordered to shoot innocent women, children, and old men, would you do it? Suppose hiding in the group might be terrorists or the people in this village had aided the enemy, would you do it?

→ If someone put a gun to your head and said, "Do it or I will shoot you," would you do it?

Gandhi used passive resistance and refused to obey unjust laws to remove British rule from India. He organized demonstration, marches, and strikes; he succeeded.

Gandhi was asked by a reporter during World War II what would happen if passive resistance were used against Nazi Germany; would it work? His response was, "Not without a great deal of pain and suffering." As Christians, we believe in the end, God will gently have the final say, and ultimately, His will is done. In freely giving of ourselves and sacrificing for the good in all people, we are following in the footsteps of love, Jesus the Christ.

The Martyr

A good example would be a shade tree whose purpose is to provide shade to humanity. It continues to provide shade, even as the woodsman is cutting it down. In its death, it continues to serve people, becoming furniture, homes, or firewood. This is true for us who live our Christian ideals by rendering service for the good of others, and when necessary, sacrificing ourselves. For a good end, Jesus sacrificed Himself. His sacrifice of love results in the salvation of humanity, the establishment of His Church, and the conversion of millions. *We can with our intention and will unite our suffering and sacrifice with His, and in so doing, become co-redeemers in the salvation of the human race.* Early Christian sacrifices of martyrdom assisted in the conversion of the Roman Empire. The Holocaust of six million Jews assisted in the creation of the Jewish State of Israel.

The martyr will suffer and die rather than renounce her beliefs. This does not mean suffering and death are good. On the contrary, they lack physical goodness, the goodness of being well and physically alive. They are not "ends" but can be the means to the greatest good end. They are the means of our salvation when done with faith in the service of love for God and others intentionally and actually. In the Bible, we read about those who suffered martyrdom for their testimony.[10] The death of Jesus is the primary example of martyrdom.[11] Martyrdom is of immense value considered by the Church as a" baptism of blood" that can replace the sacramental baptism! All the initial saints were martyrs.

If we can find value or meaning in our suffering or death, we can endure it. Prisoners in the Nazi death camps had a better chance of surviving if they could find meaning in their suffering. Suffering gives us the opportunity to endure with love. We have few choices. We can accept and endure or give up and die. By "endure with love," we mean working to diminish pain by helping ourselves and those who suffer with prayer, words, and acts of kindness using any skills we possess. The alternative is to exhibit anger and violence within and outside of ourselves, often resulting in greater suffering and quicker death.

At times, a revolution is the only acceptable alternative in the face of great oppression and injustice. A peaceful revolution involves not only passive resistance but active demonstrations, strikes, and working within the system to overthrow and change the unjust laws and leadership. Unfortunately, there are times we see violent demonstrations and intimidation tactics.

Jesus, Gandhi, Stalin, and Hitler were all revolutionaries! The difference is the first two placed their faith in the power of love and nonviolent action. The last two did not. Martin Luther King was a proponent of Gandhi and showed us the Christian way of nonviolent revolution and passive resistance in the Civil Rights movement. The way evil thrives is when good people do nothing to stop it.

There are some clergy who think that we should respond and resist evil with prayer and trust in the Lord, believing Jesus ultimately won the victory with His death and resurrection. In the end, God will have Her way. There are many sheep in the flock of these clergy who need guidance and direction in dealing with the moral issues of our times! There are issues such as abortion, fornication, euthanasia, injustice, and persecution of Christians here and abroad, terrorism, corruption in government, and most importantly, destruction of the family and single-parent households.

What is the Christian response to such issues in our lives? How do we decide what to do with unjust evil laws? How do we make decisions concerning candidates who must serve in corrupt governments? How should we feel and act toward homosexuals in our family who want to marry? What should we say or do with sons and daughters in our family engaged in fornication? Many of us need counsel on how to feel and what to say and do. But we are not getting it from some of our clergy. For whatever reason, these clergy have decided not to address such issues from the pulpit.

We unite our sacrifice with the sacrifice of Jesus, and with this union of love comes the highest good. We begin to see now why we should love our enemies.

- *We love them* because we see they are good in their essence or identity.
- *We love them* because we see not only the evil they do but the good they do or the goodness they can become.
- *We love them* because we see brothers and sisters in everyone since we all have the same Father in heaven. God made us "all" in His image.
- *We love them* because we have read Jesus's words telling us to do so. Jesus provides us with the *law of nonresistance. You have heard that it was said an eye for an eye and a tooth for a tooth, but I say do not resist an evil doer.*[12] Here, Jesus is talking about not resisting with force or evil.
- Jesus goes on to provide *His law of love. You have heard it was said, you shall love your neighbor and hate your enemies, but I say to you, love your enemies and pray for those who persecute you.*[13]
- *We love them* because we have read about Jesus's actions at the time of His arrest. He healed the soldier Peter had wounded, explaining to His disciples that if we live by the sword, we will die by the sword.
- *We love them* because we have committed similar sins or are capable of such sins but for the grace of God.

- We love them because we're created to love and love forgives. We are forgiven by God, so we must forgive every sinner even those who harm us.

→ Do you think you could ever love someone you disliked intensely? Perhaps someone who has done you or your family a terrible harm? As Christians, we do not have to like someone, but we must love them.

→ Do you think God loves people like Judas, Hitler, or Stalin? What else can She do? She is love and wisdom.

Heaven and Hell

There is a heaven and a hell. Christians accept this divine truth by faith. We believe in the teachings of the New Testament concerning heaven[1] and hell.[2]

Heaven

Heaven is a state of being. It is possessing God in a loving relationship. We live in conformity to our identity, and that is to create and maintain true goodness with the help of God. *Real goodness is to freely create and maintain existence with understanding; this is love.* Being in the state of love is our purpose for living. ***Our destiny as we know is to possess God with love, thus existing forever in love.***

In heaven, we live in this state of being in love with God in perfect goodness and happiness. Our love in this state of being will be as perfect as our finite human nature can experience. This is done to the capacity of our created nature. The philosophy of living for the common good in this life has only a part of the truth. The entire truth is we live for the common good and for our own sake and others because we love them and ourselves. It is the key to both of our survivals not only here and now but for all eternity. Heaven is the pure ecstasy of love without the agony that often accompanies love here on earth. There is no need for belief or faith because existence in heaven is "seeing" clearly and directly with conscious knowing. There is no doubt or confusion but an awareness of perfect truth and goodness without temptation or sin. No one who truly loves here and now goes to hell. Hell is for those who by evil intent refuse to love God and their neighbors.

Judgment

If heaven is our destiny, which is being in the state of possessing God in love, then hell is a state of being without love. In short, hell is our exclusion from the presence of God who exists in love. When we are judged by God, the criterion for judgment is love or specifically an attribute of love which is justice.[3]

The basic question we must all answer is, "Have we loved during our time on earth?" Another way of putting the question is, "Have we lived the identity of love we were created to live and be who we were created to be?" Or "Have we accomplished the purpose we were created to accomplish or fulfill?"

A corollary question would be, "Were we just and fair with others, especially the weakest, poorest, and those with the greatest need?"

Jesus tells us to love God with all our heart, soul, mind and strength and to love our neighbor as ourself. When we do, we are not far from the Kingdom of God.[4]

If we have not loved in our life, we've diminished our capacity to exist as human beings and we've failed to actualize the being God created us to be. Fortunately, for most of us, we have loved someone in our lives. It could be a parent, a spouse, a child, or friend. From all accounts, it would seem that even Hitler, one of the most despised people on earth, loved his mother and was abused by his father!

An Imagined Encounter on Judgment Day

On Judgment Day, we look into the face of God and see perfect love. Then we reflect upon ourselves, and if we see we have lived a selfish life without love with that one look, we know we can't be in a love relationship with God. As much as God loves us and as much as She wants to be with us in a love relationship, She can't. How can we be in a love relationship if we have become loveless and can't respond with love to the God of love? In this case, love must be a two-way interaction if we are to receive our heaven. However, we are not only judged on whether we have loved but on the quantity and quality of our love!

→ How many people have you loved and have loved you?
→ How close to perfection do you think your love is?

Hell

How can we love if the only way we respond is to focus upon ourselves and what we will get out of the relationship? So we must walk away to live totally alone with the fires of regret and despair consuming us with flames that burn from within. Imagine living totally alone with no one to see, talk with or touch, and no one to care for or be cared by. What is the meaning or purpose in such an existence? There is none. It is hopeless, you see. In eternal life, all the material possessions we thought were so important in our former lives mean nothing when we are alone. How can we have worldly power if there are no people to have power over? There is not fame because there is no one to recognize or admire us? What would be the reason for actualizing our talents or potential abilities if we could not use them to help others and no one to appreciate them?

In this life, living without love is an illusion, and almost everything we thought was important has no value unless it is used for love or related to love. In eternity, living without love is living alone without hope or meaning and with regret. Without love, we live alone because it takes at least two to love. *It is spiritual death or what some call hell.* No one can be sure, but if I had to guess, I would say there are few people in hell because as stated earlier, most people have loved someone. For those who have lived a loveless life, God will consider extenuating circumstances and reasons for our living our existence without having loved anyone! For some of these sad people, hell may have already started here on earth.

Of course, because we do not go to hell does not mean we will not face consequences for our sins. A God of justice will require it. Purgatory seems reasonable for our God who is just. What happens to any of us if we are judged by God and find ourselves in this terrible situation can only be left in the hands of a merciful God. Remember, the fundamental and effective force of God is His saving love for all.

→ What do you think of a hell in which you would have to spend all eternity alone? Does it frighten you?

Love Without Belief in Heaven

The interesting question is, if there were no heaven or salvation, would we continue to love or do any common good?

→ If there was no God, would you behave differently?

→ If you could commit any crime or sinful act as well as do anything you wished without any personal consequences or punishment, would you do it? If yes, why? If no, why not?

There were Greek philosophers and some in modern times without any belief in eternal life and no fear of punishment. Yet, they would still do the right thing! They seek the common good along with what is good for themselves. The question is, why would they seek the common good if they don't believe in eternal life or in any punishment. They seek it because *good is better than bad; love is better than hatred and evil. Living this truth results in a better life here and now.*

No Person Is an Island

As we know by experience, we are all interbeings. We are all connected to and dependent upon each other. In one sense, no person is an island. Therefore, to exploit, diminish, or destroy another human being's physical or spiritual existence is to diminish or destroy our own existence. This is because *we have no separate individual material existence. We are a part of everyone and everything, and they are a part of us.*

This insight into interbeings gives the nonbelieving philosopher the reason to do the right thing. There is some truth in our experience of interbeing, but it is not the total truth. Goodness and love always ultimately prevail over hatred and evil. In studying history, we find the evils of tyrants and dictators may be successful for a period of time, but eventually, they all fall and lose their power.

As we stated earlier, all existence is good, and even the most evil person has some degree of goodness, including the devil. If nothing else, there is goodness by virtue of our existence. Philosophers with the experience of love and reason can be aware that doing the right thing or being good is a basic truth placed into our nature. It is the best course of action for ourselves and this world. They think they can believe in love without God, but it's an illusion. God is love, so to believe in love is to believe in God. When an atheist does not believe in God but believes in love, he does not understand the divine truth that **God is living in love, and so are we**.

So we see our concept of who we are is much more than living existence; it is living in love. Our nature or identity involves the following:

- God exists in love, and so do we with a nature that has as its essence the ability to love.
- Love requires a nature that has an intellect and free will.
- The objective of love is a physical, psychological, and spiritual union by relating so we can exist as human beings. Love creates union, and union is existence.
- The process of love involves the giving, sharing, and receiving of ourselves to create the relationship of existence as human beings.
- The motive to love is the goodness we see in each other and in God that we wish to possess in a union of love for the purpose of surviving and receiving an eternal life spent loving God.

- Our purpose in this life is to do good and avoid evil by living in love. We are to perceive, behave, and become love.
- Our cardinal need is love, and traits of love are found in people of all nations, exhibited in acts of love.

Discovering the Soul

We are different from all other animals because we have the ability to think rationally. We think with our intellect, and it is within the very nature of this faculty that we discover the soul. If we were to ask someone what their idea of a soul is, what would their answer be? One possible answer would be that it's like a puff of white semi-visible smoke, which is a physical image. It is deep inside us, which gets soiled with sin and leaves the body at death to be judged. If it is found a just soul, heaven awaits. There is some truth in this concept of the soul. It does depart at death, it is judged and negatively influenced by sin.

Earlier we established with our intellect our spiritual existence, and the foundation of the existence rests within what the Bible refers to as the soul. The truth is the soul is within the nature of the intellect. We cannot see or study it directly, just as we cannot see or study our consciousness directly. It is our soul that provides spiritual energy to our intellect both in its intelligence and consciousness. It is the spiritual energy of the soul that enables our consciousness to reflect upon ourselves, our thoughts, and our actions. *We believe the spiritual energy expressed through the intellect comes from within our soul!*

We know the images derived from the senses are always singular, a specific object or event or a single group of specific objects or events. We know our ideas derived from the senses and images are products of our intellect, and they are universal. We have learned that *universal* ideas apply to everyone in the species. For example, the idea humanness applies to "all" different kinds and sizes of human beings. We know humanness does not exist in physical reality. There are crucial differences between images of sensations and ideas.

Therefore, there must be the same crucial difference between our senses or images and the intellect that produces these ideas. The difference is in their materiality. The senses are material, the soul which is the spiritual energy in the consciousness of our intellect is not.

The ideas do not involve quantity, space, or time as individual, singular concrete objects do here on earth. Our soul imparts immaterial intellectual knowledge in producing ideas. As we have learned, ideas are universal, abstract, and not subject to change or experience transformation in death. Since the soul produces ideas, we can infer the soul must also be universal, abstract, and not subject to change at death. *Some people think of our consciousness as our soul, and if not the entire soul, it is certainly a part of it.*

We cannot see the soul just as we cannot see the atom, but we can infer the existence of both by their effects upon activities we can experience. We are human beings, united body and soul, but it is the soul that animates the body. The soul or consciousness is at the core of our being and the essence of our self-identity, and it can see or create the essence or identity of other beings in our intellect. What does it profit us if we gain the whole world and suffer the loss of our immortal soul? *The soul is the foundation of our being.* It comes from God and departs at death.[1] This is why we talk about dying as giving up the ghost or soul.

Energy and the Soul

Existence is energy, and the energy for our existence is animated and controlled by the soul. The soul directs the energy of existence to hold the body together, and at death, when the soul leaves the body, the body disintegrates. The soul also directs the energy to push the body outward, causing it to interact and unite with other human beings.

The goodness of the spiritual energy of our soul is diminished by sin. The spiritual energy of life can be used for good or having lost faith in God and His promises, we use it to seek the evil of apparent good things and not what is truly good. Evil diminishes our relationship with God and so our existence as human beings. *Remember our spirituality is determined by how we use this energy of life.*

→ How does your soul use the spiritual energy of life?

In the New Testament, the soul is the principle of life.[2] In the Old Testament, we find that our human soul is not the same as the body because it has God-given immortality.[3]

Body and Soul

Yet, we know the nature of a person is twofold, body and soul. We are not pure soul or spirit as the angels. Therefore, Catholics believe not only in the resurrection of the soul but also of the body. They profess this in the creed they recite every Sunday for close to 2000 years. It is not our material body that is resurrected. It is our glorified body, which is enhanced, elevated, and illuminated with a majestic radiance, indicating God's presence within us. This dualism of body and soul is reflected in the New Testament[4] and the Old Testament.[5]

- → How do you conceive of your soul?
- → Do you believe there is a spirit world within and around us? Do you believe it's more important than the material world, which we can see all around us?

All who believe there is only sensual knowledge are materialists accepting the philosophy of materialism. We have shown our intellect has knowledge, which is immaterial or spiritual, dealing with generalities or universal ideas. Both the sensual knowledge of the body and the intellectual knowledge of the soul unite in their action to acquire truth.

Love and Power

The World's Power

Psychologists identify the elicited need for power as a major motive. We want to be powerful. Worldly power is a motive, which involves controlling people. *Power is using our energy to get people to do what we want them to do or not do what we do not want them to do.* This power gives individuals high status and a feeling of being stronger or better than the people because they can control them. It is a feeling of being stronger or better physically, financially, in status and position or intellectually. For many people, to seek power is the desire to seek this feeling of strength, which is perceived as good. This usually means that in peer interaction, one takes an active, assertive, and often controlling role in the interaction. This is caused by the motive to be better or stronger than others. It is not a love interaction because it lacks the motive of love.

→ Do you know people who seek worldly power? People who are actively assertive and controlling in their interactions with people? To see how worldly power works is to gain insight into the way the mind can work if we let it.

Winners and Losers

When we have aggression and conflict, we usually have winners and losers. It is the power of the will to attack, outwit, belittle in the interaction process so that the attacker emerges victorious, causing a feeling of strength and well-being. This is done at the expense of the other person in the interaction who is the recipient of the attack and the loser. What happens to the energy? It is transferred from the loser to the winner who feels good and strong while the loser feels defeated and weak. Other winners seek power for the purpose of exploiting a loser to acquire a fortune in the form of money and prosperity.

→ Do you know people with a great amount of worldly power and the need to win with all the symbols of power?
→ Do you think powerful people have a tendency to perceive their identity, at least in part, related to temporal power?
→ How do you respond when you win? Do you love the loser, encourage and treat them with respect and honor?

→ When you win at anything, how did you feel? How important is this feeling to you?

We are not saying winning is bad; it's how you win, how you perceive it, and what you do with it that can turn something good into evil.

Everyone Wins in Love

Love does not interact for the purpose of winning at the expense of another losing. There is no competition in love because competition involves the triumph of one individual over another. Neither do lovers interact for the purpose of feeling stronger, which in worldly terms means perceiving themselves as being better, smarter, and able to win in any competition with those they profess to love. One who loves does not exploit nor take advantage of a loved one.

On the contrary, we do what is right not merely for ourselves but for the benefit of our loved ones. We do this because our creator not only wants us to be righteous with God but with those we love as well. Our purpose in life is to help each other achieve this righteousness. *This means being in the "right" relationship with everybody and everything.* It is a love relationship. The power of love comes from our desire to be in right relationships, starting with ideas in the intellect expressed in actions. *It is the gift of being righteous in love which makes us acceptable to God.* It is the result of faith in Christ[1] and not only the good works of keeping the law.[2] Even if we do not start with an intellect that is righteous, keeping the laws of God with faith will eventually establish the motive of love within the right relationship. Everyone in love wins.

Materialism and Power

People with an intense need for worldly power surround themselves with the symbols of earthly power, which are seen as possessions associated with wealth, such as expensive homes, cars, clothing, and jewelry. Wealthy executives, professionals, politicians, successful business owners, and those holding high positions in government are often people who have a high need for worldly power. They also like to control the self-image they show to others. They want others to perceive them as powerful, authoritative, influential, and successful.

People who love are not impressed nor concerned with the symbols of wealth, power, or what people perceive them to be. They know who they are and how they should use wealth or worldly power if they acquire it. It is to be used in the service of people and not to buy unnecessary expensive toys as status symbols designed to impress people.

People high in temporal power tend to be narcissistic, absorbed with their own importance, and think mostly of themselves. These are usually selfish people who find it difficult to love. At times, they associate their identities with their earthly power, which is a cruel illusion. Their motto is those who die with the most toys (which are symbols of their power) are the winners. Jesus warns us that people with great worldly power and wealth are in enormous psychological and spiritual danger.[3]

As we stated earlier, Jesus turned over the tables of the money changers in the temple not out of anger but as a teaching tool to dramatically emphasize to the people that the house of the Lord shall be used and called a *house of Prayer for all people.*[4] It is not a place of business. It was not done in conflict for the purpose of winning so Jesus could feel stronger. Nor was it done to demonstrate His power to impress people. God's power is not worldly power in which He uses authoritative force to get people to believe and do what He wanted. Certainly, the Sadducees may have thought Jesus was asserting His power and challenging theirs.

In the desert, Jesus was tempted by the devil with worldly power to satisfy His physical needs if He would perform the evil act of worshipping the devil. In so doing, He would betray the essence of His very existence of love. He is tempted to satisfy His need for food by changing stones to bread. He was tempted to satisfy His desire for status and position in life by placing His life in peril so His heavenly Father with a host of heavenly angels would save Him.

The devil tempted Jesus by offering Him great possessions and the worldly power which accompanies it. The evil one offered Him all the kingdoms of the world! Many people are tempted with similar temptations certainly to a lesser degree. All they have to do is worship their creation of false gods in the form of fame, fortune, success, and worldly power. For some people, they can be the devil in disguise if we choose to make them so. Jesus did not succumb to these temptations. This indicates what the world sees as power such as the control of resources necessary for life, the status in occupying a certain powerful position, or the power associated with the possession of material things isn't what God considers power.

The Power of God (Love)

Love is the power of God in which He unconditionally gives Himself and His ideology of love to His disciples without conditions. When Jesus taught in the synagogue in Capernaum, the people "were astonished at his teaching because He spoke with authority." When He cast out demons, "they were amazed and said to one another, What kind of utterance is this? For with authority and power he commands the unclean spirits and they come out."[5] Jesus may teach with authority. He may command, with power, unclean spirits to heal the sick, but He does not rule with authority and power like an absolute monarch. In fact, He said to Pilate, the Roman ruler of Judea, *My kingdom is not from this world.*[6] As Jesus said, *The kingdom of God is among you.*[7] The kingdom is within the person of Jesus. It is within those who possess the Holy Spirit who interacts with their souls.

The power of God can never succumb to the wishes of the devil. The devil lies and cannot provide what he promises. Instead, he tempts and lures us with our motive of wanting to satisfy our selfish worldly desires. At times, to achieve our selfish desires, we must dominate and exploit weak inferior people with the superior power of a strong intellect and will. Superior and inferior are not concepts associated with love.

Love does not take power. Those who love give power with praise, encouragement, and with physical, psychological, and spiritual help to loved ones at the time of their need. Those who love, seek the good in each other, and bring it to the forefront for all to see and experience. ***The power of love is the power of thought or the awareness of the goodness in each other and the desire to possess it.*** We who love receive the power of the awareness that we are helping loved ones be their true selves. In so doing, we are helping ourselves be our true selves as we are both fulfilling our true identity, purpose, and destiny together, and it is good.

- God gives us this spirit and power of love.[8]
- She calls us into a community of love.[9]
- We are invited to share in this power of love found in the inner life of the Trinity.[10] *This power of love that God gives freely is the energy of life uniting us to Herself by our transcending ourselves and uniting with others. Its origin and norm are within the life of the blessed Trinity.*

Violence and Power

Dealing with our loved ones or our neighbor's bad character traits is one thing. Dealing with a violent person who is screaming in anger and disrupting our efforts to do our job is another story. It is not merely the problem of the person disrupting but our problem as well. Angry disruptive people are found in the home, school, neighborhood, and workplace. A teacher attempting to deal with a disruptive child in his or her classroom understands this. It is not only the child's problem but the teacher's problem as well. The angry and disruptive child can prevent a teacher from teaching and other students from learning, and it must be stopped.

How do we deal with violent people? How do we love them? We know that perfect love could never be violent. We believe one cannot love with force and violence. How can we become instruments of the Lord and change the hearts and minds of people we love who resort to the power of force and violence? How do we do this without resorting to force and violence ourselves?

Love would never use violence to change or convert anyone. Nor would it be used to repel any force that would harm those who love. Perfect love would never use force or violence to harm another, even if the person is trying to harm them. Jesus said, *But I say to you love your enemies and pray for those who persecute you, so that you may be children of your Father in heaven.*[11] To Gandhi of India, the worse kind of violence is poverty.

Tough Love

Violence is an external force compelling people to do something against their will. The normal reaction to violence is fear. Often, a person reacts to the threats of violence with force or violence out of fear, and this reaction is often done without a free will. As we know, unconditional love would never resort to violence under any condition, even under the condition of fear. One exception is when a mother has to threaten or forcibly remove a child from a dangerous situation. This is because the child lacks the wisdom to know better, and she acts for the sake of the child. Another exception is when a policeman must physically restrain or forcibly stop a violent criminal.

Some call it tough love. Tough love can also be used by adults when parents refuse to support or enable a son or daughter to continue in their evil ways. It could involve not only refusing financial support but turning them over to the police in some cases. This involves anyone who breaks a just law and includes clergy!

To love someone and refuse to have them face consequences for bad behavior is not love because it is not just, and love must be just. However, God is merciful as well as just. Most of us hope God's merciful side will be present in addition to justice when we all face our Maker. We too must be merciful. When it is a matter of others suffering from sin, the sinner must be confronted and face consequences. It is not merely for the sake of a victim who may be harmed by the sinner but for the sake of the sinner. We must try to prevent any person from doing evil that may harm others and themselves. *We must be merciful and forgive sinners, but we must confront their sins if we truly love them.*

The most appropriate consequences are logical ones. For example, whenever possible reparations must be made. If a person is not civil and is a threat to society, a logical consequence is that he or she may be isolated from society for a while. In school, it is called "time-out" from classmates. Being alone gives them the opportunity to calm down and recognize their bad behavior. With the help of a counselor, they realize they want to be with others to learn and socialize with friends. To accomplish this, they must behave in a civil manner.

The reason Egypt is primarily Muslim today is because the people were threatened with violence and death if they did not convert to Islam. Conversion was not done with love but with the threat of violence. In the Muslim religion at that time, force was considered an acceptable means of conversion, which is contrary to love. In the Middle Ages, the use of torture to get a person to confess and tell the truth or the burning of people at the stake are examples of Christian violence. Torture and death were done for the sake of getting sinners to repent. Of course, the Christian clergy did not do the actual execution. This was done by the state after they were found guilty of heresy by the clergy, but this was a mere technicality. It did not alleviate the responsibility of the clergy.

→ Did you ever force someone to face consequences for their bad behavior with tough love? How did you feel when you did it? How do you feel now?

Sometimes abusive spouses and parents use force to hurt children or other people. If we are aware of someone physically or psychologically abusing an innocent victim and we do not report it or do something to stop it, we are complicit in their abusive actions. If we vote for politicians we know support abortion or enact policies that are detrimental to poor people, we are complicit in any rules or regulations they support or enact that hurt the unborn or poor. Finally, if we buy stock in a company we know is exploiting the resources and riches of another country for profit, we are complicit in this evil.

46

Ways to Interact in Life

The psychologist Erich Fromm identified three ways we can interact and unite with other human beings; *surrender, worldly power, or love.* Why would one person surrender or submit to another person or group? They may wish to belong and overcome their separateness and loneliness or become a part of something bigger than themselves, giving meaning and purpose to their lives.

We can interact and identify with people because of power. The weak sometimes submit to the strong and powerful. Some weak admirers are impressed with the powerful and enjoy being around them. They gain pleasure in doing what they can for them and being considered their friend. This relationship enhances their feelings about themselves. The strong relate for the admiration they may receive for being friends with weak, inferior, less powerful people. This relationship also enhances their feeling good about themselves. Ultimately, they are not completely satisfied or happy with the relationship, and both the strong and the weak find themselves psychologically dependent on each other, losing their individuality and self-reliance.

- → Do you treat rich or what the world considers important people different from those with nothing? How?
- → Would your friendship with a US Senator or the CEO of a large corporation be more important than a common worker earning meager wages?

Only a love relationship creates a union that produces the satisfaction and happiness we seek. The ideology of power and submission is not enough to permanently hold us together. Only the ideology of love can do that.

Power of the Intellect and Will

As the saying goes, power corrupts, and absolute power corrupts absolutely. Sometimes people with a great deal of worldly power lose their sense of God and moral compass. They no longer think in terms of good and bad but strong and weak. They believe the strong should operate with a ruling morality over the weak with their slave morality. The common person for the common good does not count.

It is the duty of society to develop a race of superior people who by the power of the will and intellect will dominate and rule the weak. This morality is workable and profitable and developed by custom over time. The weak intellect and will mostly submit or surrender to the powerful who are stronger in intellect and will! As stated earlier, this is part of the philosophy of Friedrich Nietzsche practiced by Hitler.

To some extent, it is part of the ideology of some of today's politicians. They believe the masses should be ruled by a class of smart intellectuals. In general, the masses are mediocre intelligent people who are not concerned with the common good but live their lives focused upon themselves, family, friends, and their job. They have little concern about their government, the problems and challenges their country faces unless it affects them directly.

→ Do you think this is an accurate description of the average American?

Love Is the Answer

Morality cannot be based on an ideology of custom, power, and what works but on our complete identity with all our relationships existing with love. It is found in the person of Jesus and the Gospel He left us. *Only when we root our ideology in His Gospel of love will we find the right direction in this journey of life and the energy to follow it.*

We must not adopt an ideology based on custom over time. It is true some acts become good and others become bad by custom and our intention. However, there are good and bad acts independent of any custom. No amount of power or will can change or ignore the goodness or badness of these acts. As mentioned earlier, no custom can establish the goodness or badness of some acts, regardless of their being workable or profitable. Acts such as cheating the poor or bearing false witness are evil by their nature; they can never be good regardless of their use by the powerful for whatever reason.

Only human beings and angels such as Lucifer can take an indifferent act and transform it into an evil act. There are no evil beings. To be evil, our "I" would have to be evil by nature or essence, but this can't be because God created our nature. How can our "I" transform an indifferent act into an evil act? It is done with original sin and our succumbing to temptations of the flesh. An act is good if it creates, maintains, or enhances a relationship of existence. It is bad if it diminishes or destroys existence in all its relationships. Morality is based on existence by the love of God and the love of rational beings.

Perfect love is a democratic relationship, not autocratic. God is absolute goodness and His creation to a much less degree, but Jesus preferred His disciples call Him friend.[1] A friendship deals with a love that is democratic. *Some religions require their disciples to submit or surrender, but Christianity asks its disciples to freely choose to love.* It may be possible to love in an autocratic relationship. It can happen where one person exhibits dominant traits, and another is submissive and there is love, but it is not perfect or agape love. We could see this in absolute monarchs who may love their subjects imperfectly because they can exercise dominance over their possessions, work, and very lives with what they claim is God-given authority or right. Some do it with benevolence while others can be cruel without compassion or love for the common good. In the past, a benevolent monarch was considered the best form of government.

→ Do you think God our Father wants us to submit or decide that Jesus Christ is His only begotten Son by virtue of Jesus' revelations and miracles?

How would you feel about living under a monarch or dictator? Suppose they were benevolent and just, how would you feel? Many people in the world today live under the power of a dictator or the authoritarian rule of a minority not elected by the people.

Social status and class differences are not relevant if we love each other. It is not a matter of one being superior and another inferior. We are all different; some have more things, others less; some have greater intellect while others have less; some are strong, others weak; yet we must still love each other in our differences or diversity because we are all created human beings with the same Spiritual Father.

→ How important is social status and class to you?
→ How hard do you work to move up the social ladder and live the American dream?
→ Is the desire to move up into a higher economic and social class bad?
→ Can it be bad under certain circumstances? Explain.

Diversity

Society is diverse, and we must keep our diversity because in a love relationship, each person keeps their own unique individual existence. *These physical differences are accidental and not essential to our nature.* We know the essence or intrinsic nature of all human beings is the same. It is true we can diminish the humanity or spirituality of our essence by sin, but we can never completely destroy it. We can never destroy completely the goodness God placed in us at the time of our creation. The goodness is conscious living existence itself. *It is not our differences but our similarities in nature which unite us.* We have seen that when we identify with the goodness or potential goodness of loved ones, we connect and unite with them.

If diversity or identity politics seek to divide or separate people for devious reasons into victims and predators using race, religion, or culture, it is contrary to love. Only with God's love and our love for each other can we unite physically and spiritually and so exist. *All people share a common existence, a common nature, a common creator, God our Father. It is only in the giving, sharing, and receiving with love that we can exist with our differences.*

→ Do you believe in identity politics?

If identity politics advocates that the nature and identity of all people are similar and we are designed to love and unite with each other, it is good. However, if its purpose is to focus upon differences so as to divide people and have them not love but dislike or even hate others who are different, it is bad. We see this in news commentators who tell us "all" white people are racist or we live in a society of toxic masculinity. They dislike or even hate those with different ideologies and will not give them the opportunity to explain their beliefs or ideas. They will lie, cheat, and even justify violence to foster their ideology, believing the end justifies evil means.

Love Is a Democratic Relationship

In the relationship of love, we do not demand conformity from our loved ones. Consequently, we do not suppress expressions arising from their unique selves. Perfect love is a relationship that unites with two conditions? *Love is a union that must be entered into freely, and each partner retains some degree of separateness and integrity.* Of course, we must have the intellectual capacity and will to love. It's a communion of giving, sharing, and receiving, becoming one in love, and yet it provides the freedom to be different and separate. Love allows us to satisfy our need to relate and belong without abandoning our integrity and independent action. *When we are in love, the two become one in our union, yet we remain two!*

In a love relationship, we do not exploit our loved ones with authority that often comes with worldly power or status emanating from a position of influence. At one time, authority and status was given to the man in the family because he was the breadwinner. This viewpoint has changed in our society with women being the major breadwinner in almost half the households in our country. If any one man or woman uses their authority to exploit their spouse, it is not love. If authority figures dominate and control the behavior of weaker people who submit to their authority; these people become slaves. Jesus said, *Whoever wishes to be first among you must be a slave to all.*[1] In addition, He said, *I do not call you servant any longer, but I call you friends.*[2] We must, however, always keep this in mind: although He is our friend, He is also our God who rules with love. Sometimes it is tough love.

Slavery

What makes a person a slave? It is not wealth. Some masters have made their slaves rich. It is not social status because some masters have raised the status of their slaves, giving them power over people and land, provided they use their intellect and will at the service of their master. A slave is a slave because he or she is not free, yet God created everyone with a free will. Slaves do not have rights, except those the master chooses to give them, yet God created everyone with inalienable rights. A slave doesn't decide who he will serve or work for. He does not decide who his leader will be. For many years the church tolerated slavery because it was a way of life at the time. It was never intended by God because the practice of slavery is evil. No person has a right to own another human being like some beast of burden. We are spirit within a body created to be free to choose our own way in democratic relationships. God wants us to serve Her freely and select Her as our leader because in reality, She is. She is not the master of slaves because She loves us perfectly. To love Her, we must exercise our free intellect and will.

→ Do you think most people would give up a great deal of their freedom for security and guarantees of a good lifestyle?

As we know, a perfect love relationship is democratic, and God wants a perfect love relationship with all His created people. In a democratic relationship, all people have the right to freely go where they wish, select their work, serve who they wish, and select their leaders. Of course, we can freely choose to surrender our rights and freedoms in a love relationship. As we know, individuals in convents, monasteries, and to a certain extent all religious do this voluntarily to live in love. Religious are free to leave their community at any time without force or threats that generate and diminish freewill. Is living this way beneficial to our created nature? For some, it is most beneficial. For others it may not be. We all have the right to freely choose our vocation in life provided we are intellectually and physically capable of doing so. In a democratic relationship, all people have equal rights given by God that cannot be violated or surrendered! Unfortunately, this is not the case in many places in the world.

As we all know, we are not equal in our talents, traits, virtues, intelligence, or will, but we all have the same basic nature and consciousness with a right to life. We are all capable of love unless we are severely handicapped. We all have these rights by virtue of our nature and what God created us to be. God did not create us to be His slave but a friend who loves Him. We are free to act in any way we please, free to love or not love, but we must accept the consequences for our acts because in a democratic relationship, there are good and bad consequences derived from our acts.

If we were slaves, could we be free? Only if we love God and freely choose to live the way Jesus wants us to live. We voluntarily live the principles He taught. We can always do what God wants, not necessarily what we want. In so doing, we deliberately, voluntarily, and freely sacrifice our freedom to do evil. We live Jesus's way because we know what God wants for us is what He created us to be, and this is our greatest good and happiness. *When we freely choose not to do evil, we truly gain our freedom from sin.*

When we live God's way of life, we are truly free from the ravages of serious sin that can prevent us from being who we truly are. A slave can live "the way" and be truly free, provided the master allows it. In certain situations, if living the Christian way is contrary to the master's wishes, slaves may have to sacrifice their lives, but spiritually, they will live forever. Certainly, we can rebel or reject living the Christian way, but it can mean spiritual death. Each person has the God-given right to be free, even the freedom to choose evil, but in so doing, we lose our freedom. God does not command us like a child, employee, or soldier or slave but asks us to decide because as our friend, He knows us infinitely better than we know ourselves.

- As God's friend and not His slave, we can intellectually and spiritually be intimate with Him. He shares all of what His Father revealed about who we are and our purpose and destiny.
- As God's friend and not His slave, He does not command with the authority of worldly power but with the power of love. This power of love is driven by energy that emanates from His desire to enhance our well-being as His creation. God wants to guide us to our rightful end, but we must accept Her help.

Slavery is found in several places in the Bible. Romans talks about our not being slaves to sin but slaves to righteousness.[3] What does this mean? We know that righteousness means being in the right relationship with God, so we are a slave to a right relationship with God. Our relationship with God is a love relationship, so in reality, *we are slaves to love.*

In Jesus's time, the slave did the work of a servant. The primary difference is that a servant is free, a slave is not with respect to rights a servant has. The servant helps for one of two reasons. He works only for good things for himself, which is selfishness, or he works for others out of love, and in so doing, he helps himself. A slave can work for the love of his master and in so doing loves God! The process of love includes the work of a servant or slave who serve with love.

A politician is elected to serve the people. Unfortunately, many politicians serve themselves first; the people are second, if at all. For good servants, love for the people comes first, regardless of the physical outcome for themselves. Their service can be done out of understanding and their identification with those in need or suffering. Remember, we know this understanding involves sympathy and empathy resulting in compassion, a feeling of distress and pity for them followed by action to alleviate their problems or suffering.

Jesus said, *Whoever wishes to become great among you must be your servant; whoever wishes to be first among you must be the slave of all.*[4] We will be great when we are servants or slaves of love. If we wish to be selfish first, we fail to love and become a slave to sin and the least among all. Here, Jesus is talking about servants and slaves serving for the motive of love and nothing else. In the service of love, the slave is truly free because he or she is living their true identity and purpose. However, it is not the ideal or perfect relationship of love which is democratic. *To be truly free, we must live who we truly are and why we were created.*

Jesus spoke about slavery because it was a fact during His time on earth. It was evil because it denied every person their God-given rights, and God did not intend or determine it. Slavery is an evil creation of human beings, not God.

We reach out to Jesus in love; we seek to know more and more about Him. When we reach out to know Him, the knowledge of His goodness grows in us. We obey God's commands out of love for Himself and ourselves. Our love comes from our knowledge and understanding of God and ourselves and not from any of Her power or status. We do not fear God's power or wrath because we know she is not a tyrannical autocrat. She is merciful. What we do fear is the consequences of justice and the reality of not living the way we were created to live. In societal justice, consequences are only administered for our criminal acts. God's justice involves consequences for both mental and behavioral sinful activities. As stated earlier, a follower of Christianity must be a true believer to be a good disciple who is engaged in a democratic love relationship. Agape love is always democratic.

- → Are you afraid of God?
- → What are you afraid of when it comes to your relationship with God?
- → How important is freedom to you? Do you take it for granted? I'm afraid many do.

Communication of Love

Introduction

We know a good or indifferent act can be transformed into a sinful act by evil intent and can be harmful to others and ourselves. How do we address the evil done by our brothers and sisters in Christ? *Any sinful behavior which hinders people from growing and surviving as human beings must be addressed in a good way.* Unfortunately, most people do not want to get involved in the sins of others. In many situations, our reason is fear; fear of reprisal in different forms. We're afraid the sinners will take revenge if we witness their crime, so some of us refuse to testify in a court of law.

A sin can affect us directly or indirectly. For some people, they will confront the sin of a parent or friend when it directly affects them. If it doesn't, they look the other way. If we truly love them, we will not ignore the sin. Jesus said to His disciples, *If another member of the church sins against you, go and point out the fault when the two of you are alone.*[1] Ezekiel takes this directive much further when he says, "If I say to the wicked, 'O, wicked ones, you shall surely die' and you do not speak to dissuade the wicked to turn from their ways, the wicked shall die in their iniquity, but their blood I will require at your hand. But if you warn the wicked, trying to turn from their ways and they do not turn from their ways, the wicked shall die in their iniquity, but you shall save yourself."[2]

How are we to deal with sin? We can run from the sins we see in others because we are afraid. We no longer want anything to do with them because they are sinful. We can resort to arguments and judgments which are not the Christian way of love. Or we can interact with them by communicating with love and truth in an effort to help them. If a family or friend is struggling with sin, who owns the problem? Not just a friend or family member, but we do as well because we love them. We help them overcome sin because we see the goodness and potential goodness within them. We are co-redeemers with God, trying to save our brothers and sisters along with ourselves from the loss of heaven and the pains of hell.

Communication is a two-way activity that can be an activity of love. Love often requires at least two rational beings interacting. The communication must be done freely by both parties. We give our thoughts and feelings to loved ones by talking or in writing. They receive our gift by listening without interference or judgment. Sometimes we can be so involved in thinking about how we will respond to what are loved ones are saying, we miss much of what they are saying. The interaction of giving and receiving in communication can be love if done with the motive of love.

Introversion: Internal Communication

Communication can be interior, involving the spirit world within us. This interior world consists of God, angels, dead prophets and saints, demons, and all our deceased relatives and friends. They are real separate entities in our intellect or psyche, and psychologists call it "psycho reality." We communicate with these spirit entities by using our thoughts, and they communicate back to us through our thoughts. Our imagination is the vehicle we use in this internal communication.

We can imagine a deceased friend, family member, or we can imagine God and we can ask them questions in thought. We wait for an answer, and it comes in the form of a thought we have. It's an internal dialogue we are having with a spirit we cannot see nor touch but only experience using our imagination. One morning, upon awakening, I said to the Lord, "It is dark, cold, and rainy this morning and I am tired. I'm scheduled to visit the nursing home to give the residents communion, but my bed is warm, and I need to sleep." So I asked Jesus if I could put it off for the day. His response came immediately into my thoughts, "I did not want to go to the cross either, but I did because I loved them. These people are expecting you, so if you love me, love them and go."

These thoughts from Jesus could have come from an imagined picture of Him or they can stand alone. This type of communication can happen with anyone in the spirit world, and if we want to use our imagination visually, we can even see them in our mind's eye. This type of prayer we call meditation.

→ In my example above, was Jesus talking to me or was I talking to myself? Many psychiatrists would say I was talking to myself.
→ Have you ever conceived of a person in your imagination, talked to that person who answered you through your thoughts? Did you ever have an imaginary playmate when you were a child?
→ How would I know if it was a good Spirit or a demon talking to me?

We will know it is the Lord or a good spirit talking to us if they encourage us to act with love. God and those who are from God are good, and their words bear good fruit. Words that will be for our benefit because they will be in accord with our identity, mission, and destiny.

- Jesus tells us, *No good tree bears bad fruit nor again does a bad tree bear good fruit for each tree is known by its own fruit.*[3]
- John the Baptist reveals to us, it must be "fruit worthy of repentance."[4]
- Paul talks about bearing fruit that responds with good works.[5]

Formula Prayer

Any conversation with God is prayer. In the form of prayer mentioned above, God was responding and interacting with me. It was a two-way conversation. However, we could have a one-way conversation in which we do the talking internally or externally, and God does the listening. When the thoughts in our communication are already established and we repeat them from memory, it is called formula prayers, such as the Our Father and Hail Mary. When we pray formula prayer, we don't expect an answer. These one-way prayers are acts of love in which we give and God receives, but God isn't responding directly or immediately to us. We are using our time to talk to God, and this is an act of love.

Extroversion: External Communication

Communication is external with others who are alive in the physical world. This involves verbal or visual communication in written or visual forms. God can respond to us by Her written Word found in the Bible. She can also respond by the events or happenings in our life. In this form of prayer, we review the events of the day and ask ourselves, "What is God trying to tell us with these events?" It may be something or nothing. Many people who engage in this type of prayer do not believe in coincidence. Everything that happens to us has meaning. It is not a coincidence but God communicating with us. I was once involved in several motorcycle accidents. Upon reflection, it occurred to me that perhaps God was telling me to stop riding motorcycles!

Of course, God could also speak to us through a person we know, perhaps admire and love. She could be using a person's thoughts and speech to communicate with us. In such cases, it is not the person talking to us but God Herself; however, we must recognize the source of the communication is God and believe it is possible. *We cannot say we love someone, including the Lord, if we are not willing to talk to them or read what they have written.* People who love one another communicate with each other verbally, in writing, or even in sign language or gestures. Can you imagine living in a house with any person you say you love and never communicate with them? Would this be a sign of love?

Time and Love

In any communication, we are not only giving and receiving thoughts but also our time. Our time is limited, so it is a "precious" possession. When we use the energy of life to be with anyone, we are using our time; this indicates the value we are placing upon the person. We are giving the person we love the gift of our time. *We cannot say we love someone, including the Lord, if we are not willing to give our time and be with them, especially in their time of need.* Praying is nothing more than communication with the Lord in various ways as an act of love.

→ Do you believe the spiritual beings are real and exist?
→ How much time do you take from your busy day to have an internal conversation with the Lord? Or is it formula prayer?
→ Has the Lord ever spoken to you through another person?
→ Have you ever reviewed the events in your life at the end of the day and asked yourself, "What is the Lord telling me with the events?"
→ Do you believe everything is a coincidence? Or do you think all happenings have a design and purpose to them?
→ What is your higher priority, the realm of physical existence or the realm of spiritual existence? Is your answer reflected in the life you live? The decisions you make? The way you use time?

People also talk to God with a petition. Many expect an external response by events that occur in their lives. For example, we may ask God for a healing. If there is a healing, we would conclude God answered our prayer. If there is no healing, we conclude God has Her reasons, even if we don't know what they are. For the true believer, sooner or later, God answers all prayers in one way or another. It will always be a way that benefits us spiritually if not physically. *We are all where God wants us to be; how we respond is our decision.*

Communication and Forgiveness

We ask God for forgiveness. We know God sees our hearts and knows us better than we know ourselves. We know some of God's thoughts by reading the Bible and the writings of the church Fathers. By reading His written Word, we know what His response would be to many of our questions and our request for forgiveness. God is love, and we've read about His forgiveness. We read in Ephesians, "Be kind to one another, tenderhearted, forgiving one another as God in Christ has forgiven you."[6]

This is what love does: forgives even when the offender doesn't ask for it. Jesus said from the cross, *Father, forgive them; for they do not know what they are doing.*[7] Many women might say, "I could love and forgive my husband anything, except his being unfaithful. He betrayed me and the commitment he made to me and God when we married." The same could apply to a man with an unfaithful wife.

→ Is there anything you could not forgive?

As stated earlier, forgiveness of all sinners is an essential aspect of "perfect" love. We love "imperfectly" if we forgive some people but fail to forgive others. Forgiving people does not necessarily exempt them from having to face consequences for their sins in this life or the next. To ask for forgiveness, we must be aware of our sins, take responsibilities for them, and repent if we are to be saved. We could love and forgive a loved one but decide we cannot associate with him or her because of an abusive or destructive relationship.

God knows and understands our needs and desires without our telling Her. She satisfies our needs in ways that help us without our asking because that is what love does. We don't have to ask a "true friend" for help. In most cases, those who love us know we need help and respond to our need with compassion.

Yet, in Mark's Gospel, Bartimaeus, the blind man asks Jesus for mercy. Jesus asks him, *What do you want me to do for you?*[8] Jesus knew he wanted to see but asked him anyway. Why did He ask this blind man if He knew? Jesus asked not for Himself but for the sake of Bartimaeus. Jesus's question is designed to have him be aware and voice out loud what he considers his deepest need. This is why we exercise prayers of petition for forgiveness, health, or our daily bread. We are made in Jesus's image, so our inner witness is symbolic of our own true identity. God made us and gives us the power to ask for what we need without relying on external authority. Even when we are aware of our inner needs as part of our nature, do we have enough faith to ask and, if possible, act to satisfy our needs? Or do we allow our inner critic to silence us? Bartimaeus did not allow his inner or outer critics, who rebuked him, to stop him from asking Jesus for help. How often do we allow our inner or outer critics stop us from asking for what we need or doing what we need to do?

→ Have you ever allowed your inner or outer critics stop you from asking for help?

Communication as Acts of Love

Certainly, God hears and accepts our praise and thanks if they are sincere, but She knows them even before we utter them. This does not mean we should not express our love and make petitions because the very act of asking can be an act of love. It all depends on our intentions. The very petition indicates our belief in God and Her existence! Private prayers of praise and petition are not enough. To express our gratitude is not enough. To exercise personal devotion or engage in church ritual is not enough. *We must repent our sins and love God by loving others through our daily actions starting with communication.*

We can use our intellect in communication to acquire information about our work, people and the environment. Communication provides knowledge about the goodness of people. It also provides knowledge of their weaknesses, needs, and desires in life situations. We now know our understanding of people, derived from knowledge obtained by communication leads to love. *We know communication is essential to the activity of love.* Love in the act of communication can be used to express our love by doing such things as thanking, praising, forgiving, sharing our most intimate thoughts or feelings and dealing with loved ones who are sinners or maybe experiencing problems. The question is, how do we confront sinners with the process of love?

Communication with Sinners and People with Problems

We start this topic by specifying what not to do in talking with sinners. The psychologist, Carl Rogers, identified mistakes we can make in our approach.

- We do not use God to threaten hell.
- Nor do we treat the sinner like a subject or student by lecturing or arguing.
- We do not instruct nor persuade with logic like a teacher or politician might do.
- Nor do we treat the sinner like a patient, interpreting, analyzing, and diagnosing like a psychiatrist does.
- Nor do we treat them like a suspect, interrogating with probing questions, criticizing or threatening as policemen might do.
- Nor do we evaluate, compare, or make judgments as judges might do.

Sins that are Crimes

If a serious crime has been committed or the sinner is engaged in activity that is harmful to others, like selling drugs or abusing children, we must try to convince them to turn themselves in. If the sinner refuses, we must turn them in to the authorities no matter how hard it may be. Then we should help them all we can. The best way to handle this is to explain to the sinner before the conversation that if they reveal a crime that is hurting or has hurt others, we would be obliged to turn them over to the authorities if they don't do it themselves. Our conversation with a sinner is not equivalent to a confession to a priest where the bonds of silence are sacred. If we do not report them to the police, we will be complicit in any crimes they may continue to commit!

Remarks to a Sinner

Your Remarks	Your Intention
You could say to a sinner, "When you lie to me, I feel sad and frightened"	You just identified how you feel when someone lies.
"I feel this way because I love you and when people love each other, they trust each other"	You just identified why you feel this way.

"People who love talk to each other, but how can we talk if I'm never sure you're telling me the truth. I'm afraid it's going to hinder our relationship, which is very important to me."	You just identified the effect it may have on your feelings and behavior.
"Just as important, it may hurt your conversation and friendship with others because sooner or later, they always find out"	You just identified the effect it may have on the behavior of others.
"I care about you and would not want to see this happen."	You expressed your concern for the sinner and would not like to see him or her hurt.
"Do you see the problem?"	You just asked if he or she recognizes this and will admit they have this problem.

The reason we confront sinners is because we love them. Our acts of talking and listening are acts of love. The example provides some good opening remarks because they do not threaten, lecture, diagnose, interrogate, or judge. They do not treat sinners like children by our ordering, scolding, or moralizing the way parents or bosses might. We start with how we feel about their sinful behavior and why we feel this way. We go on to explain to them the bad effect their sinful behavior has upon us and others. We tell them we love them and are sad because they will have to suffer the consequences of their bad behavior. We ask them if they will admit they have a problem.

Two Key Determinations

It is our job to get the sinner to see the truth about the problem they have. We must always expose a sin or a problem with the truth because *the truth can heal. If they do not see or admit their problems in spite of our efforts, we cannot go on!* Once the sinners see their problem or sin and the negative effect on themselves, others they hurt, or those who love them, we can move on. Our next task is to determine if the sinners think they can possibly stop sinning with our help. Do they want to change? *If they do not want to change or do not think they can change, we can't go on.* Our job is to encourage them. Ask them to give change a try and see what happens. Tell them we believe they can do it with a little help. In short, try to convince them that they have a problem and can solve it.

We must get the sinners to see the truth about their sins and believe they can solve their problems and change with the help of others and God who loves them. Unfortunately, some people like being helped, so they don't change for fear that we may stop helping them if they do. It's like a person who needs attention and love. If some people cannot get it for being good and acting appropriately, they will sin or act inappropriately. If we fail to help them see and admit their sins or convince them that they can change, we must stop our efforts. All we can do is continue to pray to God to help them see.

→ Have you ever confronted one of your family or friends with sins? If not, why not?
→ How did you feel? Did it help the sinner? Did you ever do it again?
→ Are you afraid to help a sinner? What are your fears?

Attitudes and Solutions in Communications

We love the sinners, so we must treat them as equals and not assume any position of authority or superiority. Pope Francis, in *Rejoice and Exult*, parallels Jesus's thoughts when he writes, "If we regard the faults and limitations of others with tenderness and meekness without an air of superiority, we can actually help them."

Paul indicates we should correct with the spirit of meekness and gentleness. We should not assume any position of authority by speaking to them like a policeman or judge who knows better. If we wish to help a sinner we love, we must never forget we too are sinners. They may have sins we too had or could have had but for the grace of God, so we respond to their sin with sympathy or empathy.

After our opening remarks, we must carefully listen to what the sinners say to perhaps determine not only their thoughts but feelings attached to certain thoughts, helping them identify these feelings and the needs or desires they are trying to satisfy by sinning. We can encourage them to offer solutions to their problem, the sinners own plan to alleviate the sinful behavior. Hopefully, we can help them find ways and formulate a plan that may satisfy their needs or desires in ways that do not require sinful acts. They would be more committed to achieving the plan if it was their own. We can offer our services to help implement the plan. The sinners can be encouraged to share their thoughts and feelings about the plan and our involvement in the plan.

We can also help the sinner acquire good virtues! We know when we constantly repeat a mental, verbal or physical act, it becomes a habit. When the acts are good the habit is a virtue and when the acts are bad a 'vice.' A virtue will always eliminate a vice with the help of the Holy Spirit through prayer. We can help the sinner identity the good thoughts, verbal or physical activities they will do and the number of times they will do them within a period of time, ie day or week. The number must be large enough to establish the habit or virtue. Of course as the virtues are established the vices will dimish and stop. *Remember when we repeat good acts, they become virtues and along with prayer they can conquer any sin or vice.*

To help them stop sinning or behaving badly, we must encourage them to hold to their commitment to the plan. Simple say, "You said you will do it. When are you going to do it?" It will seem like nagging and probably is, but it is necessary. If failure persists, we may have to renegotiate a modified version of the plan which may be less stringent and more achievable. We must love the sinners and remain with them in all their efforts, helping, encouraging and praying for them.

This is the way we can help anyone with a sinful problem or any problem, for that matter. It is the way of *love* and *truth*, the only way! *Ultimately, it is our love that will help change the sinners if they are receptive. Love is the change agent.* More specifically, in our love for God, we must have a deep trust in God's commitment to save us from our sins and ability to accomplish it in those who love Him. Those who wish to help sinners as well as themselves must have the love and trust in God's promises and power. Remember in your conversation with the sinner, God is always present. Don't forget to ask Her for help.

→ Do you love and trust God and believe He will keep His promises? Do you believe God is capable of fulfilling His promises?

In confession, we acknowledge our sins and commit to God to sin no more, to do penance, and to amend our lives. Within confession, most priests do not have time to explore the harm the sin is doing to us and others. He does not have time to get to the causes of the sins. There is no time to identify needs we are trying to satisfy, no time to establish a plan to satisfy these needs without sinning. The priest is not available to encourage or be with us when we are being tempted and need someone to talk with or encourage us.

At these difficult times, we need communication with God in psycho reality and meditation. Unfortunately, many Christians do not engage in this type of prayer. The church has established a program of lay counselors to help people with problems and spiritual difficulties. It is not certain if people would be willing to address their most intimate feelings and sins, especially serious sins with lay counselors. The sacraments, especially the Mass and Confessions, along with prayer and the help of family and friends who love us are crucial. Of course, the sinner must believe in prayer and the sacraments.

Saint Francis of Assisi belonged to a group called "Penitents of Assisi." They supported each other by prayer, manual labor and begging for themselves and lepers. They may also have helped each other refrain from sin as was done in convents and monasteries. This was similar to Alcoholic Anonymous that helped its members remain free from alcohol and drugs. Ultimately, we understand sin will be conquered by love and our working together as brothers and sisters with the help of God. Our sacrifices must be made in an atmosphere of love and respect for each other. We must believe in the presence of God who is aware of our struggles and ready to help if we ask for Her assistance. We must always keep in mind God is always present during our deliberations with a brother or sister. We must have enough faith to not let our inner or outer critics silence us.

Perhaps many Christians do not believe it is their job to deal with the sins or addictions of acquaintances and friends, and in some cases, even family members. They are wrong. If we love them, and we should love our brothers and sisters, we must try to help them, even if we are not successful. *When we make an effort to help our brothers and sisters refrain from sin, we are being faithful to our God of love, regardless of the outcome.* Unfortunately, many of us are afraid of rejection or we may be afraid of losing a friend, perhaps a family member, and we may be embarrassed to get involved. We may think it is none of our business; we would be wrong! Love provides the courage to overcome our fears and act.

Clearly, we must confront the sinners *with "love" and "truth," giving them these two great gifts.* We also give sinners the gift of our intellect, fully concentrating upon them. We can help them see they are very special and loved by God as well as seeing their sinful ways and their need to repent. In communication, we help our loved ones discuss their thoughts and feelings, encouraging them to talk about their problems and sins. It is our job to listen. It may also work in reverse; we talk about our sins, and they listen. The interaction is giving and receiving with love!

Resolving Conflicts

Previously, we considered assisting sinners with love and truth. Let's now consider how to help two people who may have a conflict of desires or needs. What we learned about helping sinners can be applied in this type of conflict.

Responses to Conflicts

There are times when one partner in a love relationship submits to the other in a conflict of needs or desires when he or she feels like strongly objecting. In the past, the church may have considered this a virtuous act, suffering for the sake of peace. This could be a mistake. In some situations, a partner might lie or run away to avoid any confrontation over a conflict of needs or desires. These responses are a mistake. They are not proper responses in the interaction of love.

An exception would be when a person is being abused by an authoritarian partner who needs to win any conflict at almost any cost. Abusers in such relationships seek to enhance their need to feel a sense of power at another's expense. In such abusive relationships, we don't lie or rationalize to ourselves. We seek resolutions to conflicts by getting professional assistance from counselors, and if necessary, law enforcement or moving away from the psychological or physical abuse.

In confronting a sinner we love, there is no name-calling, no assigning blame, ordering from a position of power, lecturing, or preaching. The interaction must not be viewed as competition in which one party wins and the other loses. Emotions must be controlled to avoid arguments. Failure to confront and resolve conflicts can result in feelings of guilt and low self-esteem. Sometimes we blame ourselves or others for our failures. We learn to repress our need to express ourselves, so we suffer in silence. This is not what the Lord intended when Jesus said, *Wives, be subject to your husbands as you are to the Lord.*[1] He follows up by saying, *Husbands, love your wives.*[2]

Those who love understand that all who love have legitimate needs and desires such as life, liberty, respect, dignity, and the pursuit of happiness. They have a right to have their primary needs and some of their secondary needs and desires satisfied, provided the desires are not sinful. Some of their secondary desires may not be completely satisfied, such as the need to fully develop their talents or achieve all they desire. They have the right to express these needs and desires because that may be extremely important to them. When there is a problem satisfying certain needs or desires, those who love must commit themselves to resolving their differences democratically and peaceable.

Sometimes lovers are capable of satisfying their own needs and desires without interfering with others such as introverted activities like prayer, reading, and other solitary activities. At other times, we will need the help of those we love. There may be times when the behavior of one partner in a love relationship interferes with the other partner satisfying a need or desire. The partners whose desires are being frustrated must be free to express their thoughts and feelings openly and honestly without fear of reprisals of any kind. We trust our loved ones will accept our most intimate thoughts and feelings with respect and understanding. We know they would help us satisfy our desires if possible. We would also be willing to sacrifice for them if the situation was reversed. We would be willing to modify our behaviors for the sake of our loved ones needs and desires. This is the way of love and is a democratic way of working to solve a problem.

Conflict of Needs or Desires

There will be times we reach a point where neither one of us can modify our behaviors to meet the needs of the other. There is a conflict of needs in our democratic interactions with each other. At this point, we must resolve to seek a solution that does not resort to the use of power or violence resulting in a diminished or destructive relationship. Resolve to respect each other's needs if they are in keeping with our human nature.

The process for resolving the conflict could be as follows:

- Initially, the needs must be identified.
- The reason and importance of their needs must be specified by each partner.
- Next is the focus upon brainstorming for solutions that will satisfy one another's needs and desires provided, of course, the solutions are for their mutual well-being.
- Finally, they should agree upon a solution they will try. If this solution fails, they are free to brainstorm others and try them.

How do we use this process in resolving a conflict of needs? For example, a man may want and truly need a vacation because if he doesn't get a break, he is liable to go crazy. His spouse wants and needs a better car because the one she has is on its last legs, and she needs it to get to work. Their funds are limited, and they don't have enough money for both. Each partner who may be frustrated must be free to express themselves and *respect* each other's opinions by carefully listening to each other. In such cases, each must see not only from their perspective but the perspective of their partner by exercising sympathy or empathy. In brainstorming a solution, they may settle on one of the following:

- They may be willing to *prioritize* their desires with respect to their mutual and individual well-being.

After talking it out, they both agree upon pursuing the higher priority.

- They may both decide to *negotiate* and *compromise* accepting a solution in which each gets a least a part of their desires satisfied.
- It might also be that after they both have said all they wish to say, one will freely decide to sacrifice their desire for their love one.

An Attitude of Love in Democratic Conflict Resolutions

- We are in a love relationship, which we both believe is of great value and wish to keep.
- We know that we are to some degree separate in our union of love. We each have unique needs and desires and we have the right to try and satisfy them.
- When you have a problem and share it with me, I will listen with acceptance and understanding in a way that helps you solve your problem. The solution will be yours, not mine. If I have a problem, you will respond in a similar manner.
- If my behavior is interfering with your needs and desires, causing you a problem, I encourage you to tell me honestly and freely how you feel and think. I will listen and try to modify my behavior because I love you. If I need your help in modifying my behavior, I will ask for it.

- If your behavior is interfering with my acquiring my needs or desires, I will respond in a similar manner. We both agree to be honest and open with each other when it comes to interfering with each other's needs and desires.
- We resolve to share our sins with each other and help each other refrain from sinning. These are sins harmful to each other and perhaps to others.
- When a situation develops where we both have trouble modifying our behaviors because of a conflict of needs or desires in our relationship, we will commit ourselves to resolve our conflict without resorting to power with one of us winning and the other losing.
- We agree to always strive to seek solutions in our conflict that we both can accept, and whenever possible, both needs and desires will be satisfied at least to some degree. In this case, there are no winners or losers; we both win.
- In any situation where a solution cannot be found, then those with greater perfection in love will resolve the problem. At this point, the one who loves more deeply will make the sacrifice and relinquish their needs and desires for the sake of the one he or she loves. In so doing, we who sacrifice for love are aware that we become a little more of what we were created to be, and that is love. This conscious awareness should bring us peace and happiness. We make this sacrifice in a democratic process, knowing we were given the opportunity

to express our needs and our reason for them. We know we worked hard to find a solution that would satisfy as much as possible both needs but failed. There is no threat or intimidation to people who listen to each other with empathy, understanding, and compassion. Our decision to sacrifice our lives or a part of our lives is done freely, without reservation, and with no regrets.

- In our relationship of love, we promise to help each other live up to our true nature in all its relationship, coming as close as possible to what God wants us to be. We promise to help each other follow the teaching of Jesus by our continuing to unite with each other in mutual respect, peace, and love.
- Finally, in our communication with each other and God, we agree to always be truthful in expressing our true feelings and thoughts. It is only with honesty that we can be free to change and grow in our relationship of love. Lying is sinful and damages relationships. Suppressing our true feelings, desires, and thoughts can lead to lying, and if not, it could bring pain and suffering. Truth heals.

→ Have you ever sacrificed for the one you love in a conflict of needs?

→ How did you feel? And what did you think? Were you happy and at peace? Or did you feel cheated and resentful because the outcome was not fair or to your liking?

→ Do you think your feelings about your sacrifice could be different if you had experienced the democratic process mentioned above and the attitudes that should accompany it?

Truth

Introduction

To love, we must understand what truth is. Since we seek goodness and goodness is existence, we are really seeking existence. However, existence is real, so in seeking reality, we are seeking truth. As stated earlier, the objective of our intellects is to acquire the truth about reality or existence. *To love, we must understand the goodness in people. Understanding is essential to truth.* This means understanding the truth about our loved ones and ourselves. *Without understanding, we do not know the truth!*

What Is Truth?

"What is truth?" Pilate asked Jesus this question.[1] Jesus refers to Himself as the *way, truth,* and *life.*[2] Jesus is truth because *truth is the reality of existence.* Jesus is the Word that exists, the way of existence, the life of existence. We have the truth about a person when our idea about the quality or characteristic of the person conforms to the characteristic that exists within the person. The standard of truth does not rest within us but with the reality that exists outside us. Truth is not always in the eyes of the beholder. Only when our ideas are in conformity with what exists in reality is truth present in the eyes of the beholder. For example, when our intellect tells us a person is greedy, but in reality, the person is generous, then our understanding of the attribute of generosity in the person is not true. It is an illusion or falsehood.

When our concepts about a person are true, our relationship with respect to these concepts is true. If the concepts are false, our relationship concerning these concepts is false. We can have several false concepts and many true ones. We do not measure a relationship with a single or several false concepts. It does not mean the entire relationship is false. It all depends upon if or when we become aware of our false concepts and more importantly once aware, how we respond to them. Our concept of a person may be true or false; however, it is our truth concerning love that must guide our interactions. If the characteristic or quality of a person is evil, we must confront it with goodness and love if our interaction is to be true and valid concerning this quality. *Love* is *always truthful and remember truth can heal because God is truth.*

Since we were created to love, Christians should always tell the truth. Christians should not swear falsely or even swear an oath to tell the truth since it may give the impression that we only tell the truth when we take an oath; otherwise, we may lie. There can be no division between an oath and common conversation. Lying is a sin because we are living an illusion not the truth. The Bible says:

- "Do not accustom your mouth to oaths."[3]
- "A lying mouth destroys the soul."[4]
- "A faithful witness does not lie."[5]

Love Without Knowing the Truth

There are times when a wife finds that the man she married isn't the man who courted her before the marriage. She thought she knew all his characteristics and moods, but apparently, she didn't. Their interaction before marriage was better than after. Some might say you never really know a person until you live with them. It is important to get as truthful a picture as possible prior to marriage. This includes goals, primary traits, economic, moral and religious values, etc. This does not mean she didn't love him prior to marriage when she didn't know certain truths. *We can love someone completely even if we lack certain truths about them.*

We do not stop loving them when we find out the truth. We Christians love people with all their weaknesses, imperfections, and sinfulness, even if we do not know the reasons for their sins. We don't necessarily divorce a person we love because we were unaware of their sins prior to marriage. Nor do we stop loving them when our efforts to help them fail or when we do not know how to help them or even when they don't want the help we have to give!

We as Christians know no one is perfect; we are all sinners and we all need love and forgiveness. As noted earlier, this does not mean we must or should live in an abusive relationship. We can limit our relationship or sever it completely for our sake or for the sake of others. As Christians, we can love them spiritually with intellectual acts. We would never speak ill of them, forgive them, pray for them, wish them only what is good, and would always be willing to help them if the opportunity presents itself. We can do all this and be as good a friend as possible without being intimate or living in close proximity.

We can love someone without knowing certain truths about them or with a limited amount of information! How can this be? Don't we have to know someone to love them? *We do know the most important truths about everyone!* We are all children of God our Father. We are all created with the same identity, purpose, and destiny. As we know, we were all created with the same image and potential for goodness and love, even if we have not yet learned to actualize it! We are all brothers and sisters in Jesus the Christ.

→ Could you continue to love someone if you found out he or she has weaknesses or sins you didn't know about? No matter what the sin?

→ Could you love them if they do not have the qualities you thought they had?

Truths About Ourselves

As we have seen, we can conceive of God's creation or God Himself, but our conception may not be true. Our concept of God can determine how we will behave. If we conceive of God as violent, vengeful, full of righteous anger and retribution, we may think our acting in a similar manner may be considered acceptable behavior when living in love! It isn't.

→ What is your concept of God? How do you perceive Him or Her?

This can also apply to the concepts people have about themselves, their self-image. As we know, this is because our intellect can and often does make mistakes, or at times, we just don't see clearly. Some people conceive of themselves as intelligent animals, act like animals and, for the existentialist, become intelligent animals. They believe their purpose in life is to take what they need and live as happy as possible until they die and return to the cosmos from whence they came. These ideas about who they are, their purpose in life and destination are all illusions. They are living a lie! When we know who we truly are, we love God, ourselves, and our neighbors.

When we know the revealed truth concerning who we truly are, we are free to live the life we were created to live. As Jesus said, *The truth will make you free*[6], free to be who we were truly meant to be. We have the right to life, freedom to love, and to pursue being happy. These are God-given rights found in our Declaration of Independence. To be or not to be that is truly the question.

→ What do you think you were meant to be?
→ Do you believe you are free to be what you were created to be? Or are there obstacles preventing you?
→ Do you know what these obstacles are?
→ Do you know how to overcome them?

If we truthfully understand our loved ones, we understand ourselves better. If we truthfully understand ourselves, we better understand our loved ones. *In understanding others, we can love them, but how can we love them if we do not understand our identity, and in so doing, love ourselves*? Since we are made in the image of God, then as we stated earlier, this principle of understanding applies also to God. *The more we understand God, the better we understand ourselves, and if we truthfully understand ourselves, we have a better understanding of God.*

→ Do you know the truth about yourself? Many do not have a truthful self-image.

God and Truth

It has been revealed that the Word of God is truth. The remarks of Jesus about truth are as follows:

- To His disciples who believed in Him, He said, *If you continue in my word, you are truly my disciples, and you will know the truth and the truth shall make you free.*[7]

- Jesus asks His Father to *sanctify them in the truth, your word is truth.*[8]
- The Bible also reveals: "All God's commandments are true"[9] "God is true light which enlightens"[10] "For the fruit of the light is found in all that is good and right and true."[11]
- Finally, Truth should be obeyed,[12] should be loved,[13] and should be manifested.[14]

God's ideas are always true and all reality is merely an expression of the concepts of His perfect mind. *If we know the teachings of God, we know the truths because God is truth.* Certainly, truth is an attribute of God,[15] and the devil is devoid of it.[16] Since truth is of God, it is essential to our sanctification and freedom. Truth is to be obeyed, loved, and manifested because it is essential to our existence as human beings. **Since God is love and truth, to live in love is to live in truth.** The intellect desires truth, which is a desire to see reality as it exists in itself, and it is good. *With seeing the truth about reality comes understanding. With understanding comes love that includes freedom and justice. With love and justice comes happiness and peace.* Happiness is the God-given right of every person. *I've never seen a truly happy person who does not love and is not free in spirit and truth.*

→ Do you think love should make us happy? Does it?
→ Do you think freedom should make us happy? Does it?

Belief and Truth

There is a saying most of us are familiar with: "In here, we never discuss religion or politics." What is the reason for making such a rule? We all know the reason. It is because such discussions often end up in fierce arguments that can lead to fights, indicating intense emotion or energy. They are what some people call emotional trigger issues that set off strong emotions. Why the arguments? Because religion and politics are topics that involve beliefs. Beliefs can sometimes lead to violence in which no one wins. By this, we mean no one is convinced or accepts an opposing belief as true. Families who argue over opposing beliefs can end up with hard feelings sometimes severing family ties.

In the Gospels, Jesus explains that belief can divide families.[1] *Beliefs are ideas which may or may not be true and have strong emotions attached to them.* Whenever we find ourselves willing to proclaim our ideas, argue, fight, or in some cases even die for them, we know we are dealing with a belief or a whole system of beliefs. Wars are fought, and people die because of beliefs. *Often, to be in a state of belief is to be in a state of internal violence.* Look at the actions of Muslim terrorists or the Christian Crusaders in the Middle Ages to confirm this. Beliefs are either true or false; we can't prove they are true at this time. Once a belief is established as a fact, it is no longer a belief but a truth. Once we have a belief, we are usually convinced it is true, even though we cannot prove it. At one time, people believed the earth was flat until it was proven to be round by men like Columbus.

Earlier, we considered how ideas were placed into our memory by authority figures. Some of these ideas may be facts while others may be an opinion or belief. An opinion is similar to a belief. One difference is energy strength. A belief has a very forceful energy or emotion attached to it, an opinion significantly less. In addition, a person with a belief is absolutely certain their belief is true; there is not as much certainty with an opinion.

People prize, cherish, proclaim, and will sacrifice for their beliefs. Sometimes proclaiming them can result in pain and suffering. People with strong beliefs consciously or unconsciously make a commitment or Covenant to keep them. Beliefs can cause us to change the direction of our lives, and sometimes, we replace old beliefs with new ones. In Matthew, Jesus said that new wine, which are new beliefs, are not put into old wine skins, which are people with old contrary beliefs.[2] It is extremely difficult to put new beliefs into a person with old contrary beliefs, and in some cases, the person who tries to do so can be destroyed.

Jesus goes on to say otherwise the skins burst and the wine is spilled and the skins destroyed; but when new wine is put into fresh new wineskins, both are preserved. With some beliefs, however, it may not be a matter of replacing or destroying our old beliefs but enhancing, modifying, or fulfilling them as Jesus did. Of course, living or dying for one's beliefs requires physical and, most important, spiritual energy and courage. It takes courage to live our beliefs.

- → Can you list your beliefs?
- → Can you identify a belief contrary to your own for the purpose of possibly learning something that could enhance and so modify your beliefs? This is extremely difficult.
- → What are your most passionate beliefs?
- → Do you prize and cherish your beliefs and the behaviors they produce in you?
- → What is the Apostle or Nicene Creed that Catholics recite every Sunday at Mass?

If you can't think of any belief you're willing to proclaim and live at the cost of your prestige, fortune, or even your life, then perhaps you don't have beliefs but merely useful ideas or opinions.

People who desire and acquire what are real beliefs will always acknowledge and live them. They are convinced their beliefs are true and important for people to know and accept. They are afraid their beliefs will be rejected. For example, many people believed the Vietnam War was an unjust war. During the Vietnam War, we could quickly determine if a person was in a belief for or against the war by raising the topic and observing their reaction. The question is what does one do if they are being forced to fight in a war that they "believe" is "morally" wrong? They could run away to Canada as some did. They could stay home and engage in protests. If they are called upon to enter the conflict, they can refuse and face the consequences such as jail-time as some did. Some who protested the war at Kent State University were shot and killed!

Franziska Jägerstätter was an Austrian farmer who refused to be inducted into Hitler's army. He believed it was an evil war initiated by an evil ruler and contrary to his Christian beliefs. To take such an oath and participate in an evil war would place his immortal soul in jeopardy. All his critics, including his neighbors, priest, and even his Bishop urged him to join and fight! He refused, remaining true to his beliefs and conscience. Consequently, he was beheaded by the Nazis

→ Are you willing to proclaim or affirm your beliefs when asked to do so in a company with some people who have opposing beliefs?
→ Are you willing to accept consequences for proclaiming and living your beliefs, even if the consequences mean jail-time or death? Fortunately, most of us will not be put to this test.

Jesus blessed those who are persecuted for their belief in Him, those disciples willing to proclaim Him as The Son of God, His teachings, and to act upon them, regardless of the consequences![3] If we love someone and believe in a way of life, aren't we willing to sacrifice and, if necessary, die for our beliefs? Jesus did, and so must we if circumstances require it!

Dangers in Beliefs

A belief can be dangerous or even deadly. This is because *once we are into our beliefs, in most cases, all objective investigation concerning them stops*! *All learning stops.* We will not consider any ideas contrary to our beliefs. We only accept those ideas that affirm our beliefs. We will select and distort facts to support our beliefs and reject or modify facts that minimize or cast doubt on our beliefs. Many with political beliefs respond in this manner.

Beliefs can cause us to think we have truths others lack, and this can bring pleasure because to have our beliefs makes us feel better or superior to them. We may pity them because we have something of immense value they lack. We may think it is better to be a Christian, Jew, Democrat, Republican, capitalist, communist, or even belong to a particular race or culture. We are better because those who do not share our beliefs are wrong, and we are right! We are sorry for their ignorance and have an intense hatred for their beliefs because we think they can be destructive to the person and perhaps our culture and way of life.

We see this happening today in our country with people divided by liberal and conservative ideologies. We've seen the division between these ideologies in the past but never with the degree of intense animosity we find not only in the Halls of Congress but within many of our universities and within our homes. It would be all right to have these differences in beliefs if people realized their political or philosophical beliefs may not be true and so be more tolerant! It would be fine if we could proclaim our beliefs without experiencing violence, intimidation or threats. Unfortunately, at many prestigious universities today, this is not the case. We must respect the right of free speech in a civil atmosphere because only in such an atmosphere can people disagree with each other and still be friends.

As Americans, we have the right to peaceful protest and demonstration. It is part of our culture. Protest is quite acceptable, provided we respect the rights of others to live their lives and go about their business without being disrupted, their property destroyed, coerced, or physically in danger. As Christians, we love those who disagree with us and even hate us for our Christian beliefs.

In the past, universities were the bastion of free speech and debate. Both sides of an argument were presented. Students were encouraged to think about both sides of the argument. They were encouraged to decide if they were for or against a belief. Perhaps they may make a decision to suspend their judgment for more information. Or they may take a little bit from each of the opposing positions and synthesize them into their own belief or position. Unfortunately, this is not the case in many universities today. Professors present only one side or ideology, and sadly, it is no longer free independent thought but indoctrination.

→ How do you feel about people who do not agree with your beliefs?
→ Do you listen objectively to opposing beliefs?
→ Do your beliefs bring you pleasure? Should they?
→ Do your beliefs make you anxious or afraid? Why?

→ Have you experienced teachers who indoctrinate instead of educate?

Source of Beliefs

As we have seen, our beliefs can come from authority figures in our youth such as parents, teachers, clergymen, older siblings, or grandparents. For Christians, the most important sources of our beliefs are the words of prophets, apostles, disciples, Wisdom (the Third Person of the Holy Trinity), and especially Jesus, all recorded in the Bible.

To children, authority figures often appear larger than life, godlike protectors who must be believed. The beliefs these authority figures place in us as children are accepted unconditionally without questions. They are not chosen from alternatives or after careful consideration of consequences. Most importantly, they are not chosen freely. For example, in my youth, my father taught me two of his core beliefs. *First,* "everything comes from work," and "hard work never killed anyone." *Second,* "the big fish eats the little fish." My father was not thinking about fish but of powerful people who exploit the poor and weak. He proclaimed both beliefs. He lived the first by working hard all his life. However, I never observed him living the second.

Perhaps it was because he was not a powerful man or a big fish. To my knowledge, he never admired or wanted to be one, nor did he think of himself as being a victim of one. He was stating what he perceived to be a reality or truth. As an adult, and after careful consideration of both my father's beliefs, my conclusions are as follows:

My father's first belief I accept. This is because what my father meant was that a man or woman must work hard to supply the needs required for the survival of the family. My father loved his family and his country. He worked hard to maintain his family and his country by paying taxes and voting. This was an expression of his love for both. As an immigrant who became a citizen, he loved America because it gave him the opportunity to work and support his family. His children could grow up in a safe environment and live the American dream.

My father's second belief I could not accept as a truth I could live. This is because it is contrary to my Christian beliefs. It might be an apparent good, but it is not a true good for all people. We should not "eat," which means exploit or take advantage of our fellow human beings. We should love them because we are all brothers and sisters in God our Father who created us all. Many people may think this belief is true in our reality and yet will not accept it or live it. Perhaps this was the case with my father.

Another source of beliefs about ourselves may be acquired by repeated experiences in our lives. For example, a man who is constantly turned down when he asks a girl for a date will experience emotional pain and may adopt the belief that he is not lovable or perhaps capable. This belief may have been adopted without properly investigating the causes for the rejection and considering who he truly is.

As we know, we must carefully examine not only the ideas and opinions we acquired from authority figures in our early lives but the beliefs we acquired by our experiences. Perhaps after careful consideration, we may decide to reject them. It is not only because they are no longer useful to us as mentioned earlier but on account of their being contrary to other more important beliefs we have accepted in later life.

→ Have you ever had a belief you acquired as a child that you rejected as an adult? Or do you still believe it?
→ Have you had a belief about yourself acquired by repeated personal experiences that you have now rejected or changed? Or do you still believe it?

In the past, boys and girls were taught early in life the belief that people engaged in premarital sex are committing a serious sin. Unfortunately, today, we live in a promiscuous culture. Sadly, this belief about the evils of premarital sex is not being taught in many homes, schools, and is not being reinforced by the Church. Consequently, many of our teenagers and young adults are engaged in illicit sexual behavior.

Deviant sexual behavior is rampant in our society, yet you seldom hear clergymen talk about fornication or adultery. Seldom do you hear clergymen make the argument against it. One thing is certain, without these teachings, our young people have little chance of refraining from sex before marriage. The sex drive is extremely powerful in young people. Don't you think our youth should be informed of the argument against premarital sex, not only in their homes but in their churches? Perhaps fornication is no longer a sin or is no longer relevant. We know this is not the case. Remember premarital sex can lead to pregnancy and abortion.

54

Belief in Jesus's Ethical Teachings

President Thomas Jefferson accepted Jesus as the greatest moral teacher of all times. As Christians, we believe Jesus was not only the greatest authoritative teacher of moral theology but the Son of God. Jesus said that His Father's Words are truth and that He came into the world to reveal the Words of His Father. Whoever hears His Words hears the Words of His Father because He and the Father are one.[1] Jefferson accepted Jesus's teachings as great pragmatic truths perhaps because he observed them working in the lives of others. Or maybe because he personally experienced them working in his own life. He did not believe Jesus was God nor did he believe Jesus's ability to perform supernatural miracles, including His own resurrection. Nor did he believe in any revelations concerning God!

Jefferson was a Deist who believed in God. He created his own Bible by cutting out all supernatural miracles by Jesus or any supernatural revelations about God or humanity! As a Deist, Jefferson believed in a God in heaven who did not become a man in the incarnation nor reveal any supernatural beliefs or truths about God.

His Teachings

The Bible states you will "know" them by their fruits. When it uses the term "know them," it means we will know they are His disciples because they will bear the fruits of love by living His teachings. When we are deeply living the teachings of Jesus, we no longer have to be engaged in beliefs. We are aware of the principles Jesus taught, and living them, we know they are true. Can we have belief in the teachings of Jesus without living them? It is doubtful because "Faith by itself, if it has no works is dead."[2] *We must practice what we believe, and we will have pragmatic truth.* The belief we have in them is now confirmed by intimate firsthand knowledge and understanding. As we know, by pragmatic truth, we mean they're true because they work in real-life situations.

Earlier we asked those who read this book if they could state the teachings of Jesus. If we do not know them, how can we live them? To truly be a disciple of Christ, we must live His teachings and go where He leads. The following are some of His fundamental ethical teachings that Jefferson admired and affirmed. First who we are to love?

- We are to love God with heart, mind, and soul.
- We are to love our family and neighbors as ourselves.

- We are to love our enemies and not exact retribution or seek revenge against those who hurt us.
- We must love and respect all human life from conception to death.

Second, how do we love and follow Jesus's teaching?

- We love by refraining from sinful thoughts, words, or deeds contained in the Bible.
- To love, we must forgive others as we ourselves have been forgiven by our God.
- We love by reconciling with people we have hurt or who have hurt us.
- To love, we must tell the truth and honor our commitments.
- We must love and be faithful to our spouses.
- In love, we are to be compassionate and generous to those in need of our help.
- In love, we must be peacemakers and not be angry or violent to any person.
- When we are persecuted because of our love for God, we consider ourselves blessed.
- We love by treating everyone with respect, dignity, and with justice. This is especially true of the weakest among us. This means feeding the hungry, clothing the naked, sheltering the homeless, caring for the sick, and visiting those in prison.

We are aware that everything belongs to God, and all we have are gifts from God, and with our love, we use our gifts as God wants us to use them. As we can see, it all boils down to love. To live these truths is not easy, and it all must be done without complaint, humbly and anonymously! Obviously, these truths are not supernatural revelations or activities.

→ Consider each truth and ask yourself, "Do I believe this truth? Do I live this truth in my thoughts, words, and actions?

Faith

Faith is very much like belief. In fact, the Latin word for faith means a belief. Faith, like belief, is an idea accepted as true without proof. Like belief, an idea based on faith can be true or false. *We often use the word* faith *to believe in events that have no basis in reality and may be contrary to scientific facts.* It's a scientific fact that people cannot walk on water, calm a storm, or rise from the dead, but by faith, we believe Jesus did! We have faith these supernatural events happened because of our most fundamental faith in Jesus as the Son of God capable of controlling the laws of nature.

Saint Paul, writing to the Galatians, explains that through the spirit by faith, we await the hope of righteousness. Hope is the expectation of a future blessing.[1] This hope rests upon faith that expresses itself through love.[2] Remember, it is hope that comes from faith in the love of God and trust in His promises that overcomes fear, *even the fear of death, because hope is stronger than fear.* What really counts for anything is faith working through love.[3] *When we love, we have faith and trust in the one we love.* There is much Jesus revealed about Himself as the Son of God and the kingdom of God that we accept by faith.

So to have faith in God's teachings, we must trust Him, to trust Him we must love Him. To have faith, we must live in love. *Remember trust is an aspect of love and so is faith.* Faith comes with the grace or gift of love from God to the people He created including ourselves!

One thing is certain when we live Jesus's ethical teachings and see they are true: we find it easier to have faith in Jesus's miracles and supernatural revelations. If Jesus's philosophical and moral teachings are true because we have established their pragmatic truth, then his supernatural teachings and miracles can also be true. However, in the end, we will never have faith in them without the grace or gift of love from the Holy Spirit.

- *Faith* is made possible through the help of the Holy Spirit.[4]
- It is our rational and totally free response in *faith* that we confess the truth in the disclosure of the divinity of Jesus.[5]
- Through our obedience to *faith*, we make a subjective personal commitment to Jesus the Son of God because we are called to belong to Him.[6]

The revealed truths of God's miracles are truths based on faith. However, some prior church doctrine based upon their interpretation of the Bible were not true.

Faith and Science

There can be no disagreement between the truths of revelation and science. The disagreement comes with the *interpretation* of the revealed truths contained in the Bible. *Whenever there is disagreement between scientific truths and the interpretation of the Bible, scientific truths will always triumph.* A case in point was the discovery by Galileo who scientifically proved, with the use of a telescope, that the earth traveled around the sun. This was contrary to church doctrine, which maintained the sun traveled around the earth. The church had to modify or change its doctrine or interpretation; however, it almost cost Galileo his life. Science deals with objective knowledge and truth while religion deals with subjective theological knowledge and truth. In both cases, it is the truth. There is a difference between religious truth and an interpretation of a religious truth. Religious truth is never wrong, interpretation can be.

→ What would you do if one of your beliefs was contrary to scientific fact?

An example in our times would be beliefs involving abortion. Some women believe they are not killing a child that is alive within their bodies. It is merely a bundle of tissue. The medical science of fetology clearly demonstrates beyond a shadow of any doubt that what is being killed is alive, a little person. If the mother of an unborn child who is contemplating abortion could examine the facts of fetology, things might be different. If they could see the child within them with ultrasound, they might be convinced of the fact that the child is alive and a human being.

Another example is the age of the earth and the number of days to create it. The Bible states God created the earth in six days and rested on the seventh which is contrary to scientific facts. The Bible was not written to reveal scientific truths, but to reveal theological truth. To ancient people, it made little difference how long it took to form the earth. They would not understand scientific facts associated with the earth's age. It is the theological truth that is most important. The theological truth is there is only one God, not a multitude of Gods which was the prevalent belief at the time, and He created all that exists.

As for faith in the existence of the spirit world and life after death, there is some evidence. There are people who were scientifically dead and were resuscitated or brought back to life. They relate to having experienced a spirit world. Many have testified to their account of the spirit world, and most have had similar experiences in the hereafter. Faith can also rest in trusting and accepting the testimony of these people about the spirit world, provided their revelations are not contrary to theological truth. As Christians, we are not required to believe their testimony.

Power of Faith

The Centurion in the Bible who asked Jesus to heal his servant without Jesus, even seeing or touching the servant,[7] had faith and trust in the power of Jesus. It is difficult to live by faith, believing what many very intelligent scientists think is impossible and our own experiences also tell us is impossible. *When our mind lives in a box of intelligent thoughts, our hopes and expectations are extremely limited.* Often, faith is rejected, and with it, the "power" of faith, which is stronger than reason. When we open ourselves up to God by faith, with love, we are opening ourselves up to the power of faith and love.

With faith in God, we are no longer subject to the circumstances of life we often find ourselves having to deal with. We are free from anything good or bad happening to us. We are detached and no longer dependent on these happenings because with complete love and trust in God, we are subject to Her will for us, not our own. We are no longer afraid of death, poverty, sickness, or failure. We are free with the power of faith to live our lives with the purposes for which we were created and the destiny for which we were ordained. *Like love, faith not only provides the truth that makes us free but the power to live our salvation here and now.*

56

Faith unto Total Truth

True love survives in good times and bad times, in sickness and in health, being faithful to each other until death. We must live faith-filled lives if we are to remain united in love. Without faith, love doesn't last. Our love remains faithful, even when we fail to see the bad traits in our partners at the time of our courtship. Our love remains faithful when we experience frustration, disappointment, or discouragement when our efforts to love fail to get a response. Our love remains faith-filled and constant in the midst of problems, suffering, and failures, including tragedy with its unhappiness and loss. We remain faithful, even when our love is not perfect, and in this life, it seldom is. The Bible speaks about faith this way.

- Motivation for our *faithfulness* is because "God is faithful."[1]
- If we are *faithful*, we will abide with Him in love.[2]
- *Faith* requires the action of living it. "The righteous live by their faith."[3]

- *Faith* can save us if we do the work of love as it saved the woman who ministered to Jesus's needs out of love.[4]

Natural and Unnatural

Faith is something that is very natural in our daily lives. Many of us believe with faith in the information people reveal to us, even when there is little or no personal evidence or proof. We accept it as true because we trust, admire, have faith and often love the people who reveal it to us by spoken or written word.

Even when strangers or people we don't know very well give us directions to a place, tell us what the program of an event will be or the food on the menu, we believe it is true without proof. Much of what we think and do is based on the faith we have in people. It is true we could substantiate what they tell us as true, but at the time they tell us, we accept it with our faith in them.

We must believe with faith the supernatural miracles performed by Jesus. His disciples did not have to believe because many were witnesses to these events. We were not, so it requires a much greater degree of faith because the events are supernatural. Jesus recognized this and blessed us for it. He said to doubting Thomas who had seen Jesus after His resurrection from the dead, *You believed because you have seen me. Blessed are those who have not seen and yet have come to believe it.*[5]

There are mysteries in the Bible that no one can explain how they could happen; things like the virgin birth, incarnation, and resurrection. Remember, these are not "interpretations" of the Bible but supernatural events and revelations recorded in the Bible. Many people accept them as mysteries with faith and trust in God and His son. A lot of scientists think that all the mysteries of today will eventually be solved by the science of tomorrow. They point to flying with airplanes, space travel, and medical wonders as just some examples. As for supernatural miracles, they may attribute it to mass hypnosis, hysteria, magic tricks, or exaggerated writings.

Many people will never believe God became man in the person of Jesus the Christ, nor can anyone overcome the forces of nature by faith, using commands and willpower. Jesus revealed it was possible to move a mountain by faith.[6] Some would say He was speaking symbolically, not literally, but if one truly has the spirit of God within, anything is possible. As someone once wrote, "For people of faith, no evidence or proof is necessary. For people without faith, no evidence or proof will suffice."

Truth by Sense Knowledge

We have learned that we acquire some truths by our intelligence which can think and reason and our consciousness which sees truth and acts upon it. We are aware that much of what we know begins in the senses. Without information from the senses by reading, listening, touching, seeing, and experiencing, there is no sense knowledge. Many people, including some scientists, believe only the senses are capable of giving us truth. We only have sense knowledge.

Our intelligence thinks by using sense knowledge, so intelligence is the sum total of our senses. They believe all ideas, including truthful ideas come from images derived from the senses, and what enters the senses comes from the outside world. With intelligence, we think using the images from the outside world, we can discover truths about reality. As we know, these truths are used to create new beings, which are designed to maintain and enhance our lives. It is the philosophy of many scientists who believe sense knowledge organized and used in experimentation is responsible for all human progress. Earlier, we identified it as the philosophy of materialism.

→ Do you believe thinking with sense knowledge is the most important source of truth, responsible for all our progress?

Supernatural Truths by Faith

We know now we can acquire truth by faith. Faith provides us with truths our intelligence and consciousness could never provide. It is difficult for some to accept truths acquired by faith. Saint Paul warned that natural people do not accept what pertains to the Spirit of God, for them it is foolishness and they cannot understand it, because it is judged spiritually.[7] Most Christians accept many religious beliefs as true and factual. Other people including some proclaimed Christians do not. For them, these beliefs may or may not be true or they see them as false ideas.

The spirit knows with consciousness and with faith. *Faith has a greater energy than reason. We cannot restrain a strong belief with reason.* It is greater than reason. Suppose someone asked us what proof we have that Christianity is true; how would we answer? The answer is simply that the testimony of God is greater than the testimony of a person! As the Apostle John proclaims, "Those who believe in the Son of God have the testimony in their hearts."[8] This inward testimony given by the Holy Spirit is greater than the testimony of a person or reason. This inner testimony does not require the senses!

→ Have you ever experienced this inner testimony by the Holy Spirit?

To accept truths by faith, we must put aside sense knowledge and thinking. Even our consciousness cannot affirm the supernatural truths. To our intelligence these truths of faith are impossible to prove! What are some of these truths that Catholics accept with faith? Many Christians accept most, but not all of them.

- We believe in God the Father, almighty creator of heaven and earth.
- We believe we were created in the image of God.

- We believe in the one God who is three persons: Father, Son, Holy Spirit.
- We believe the Son of God was incarnate, became man, and was born of a virgin.
- We believe when alive, the Son of God performed supernatural miracles by faith such as healing the sick, walking on water, changing water to wine, multiplying food to feed the people, and raised people from the dead!
- We believe the Son of God suffered and died, in atonement for our sins, thus saving us from eternal damnation.
- We believe the son of God was crucified, died, and was buried, on the third day He rose from the dead, and so we too will rise from the dead and live eternally with our God.
- We believe bread and wine consecrated at Mass to be the actual body and blood of our Lord Jesus Christ.
- We believe in the Holy Spirit, the Holy Catholic Church, which is the mystical body of Christ with God the Son as its head.
- We believe in the Communion of saints, forgiveness of sins, the resurrection of the body, and life everlasting.

None of these religious truths can be proven nor will they ever be disproven. They have been proclaimed for 2,000 years without change because truth cannot change. *By faith, we who believe have the total truth!* Saint Paul describes faith in these divine truths this way: "So also no one comprehends what is truly God's except the Spirit of God. Now we have received not the spirit of the world, but the spirit that is from God, so that we may understand the gifts bestowed on us by God. And we speak of these things in words not taught by human wisdom but taught by the Spirit, interpreting spiritual things to those who are spiritual."[9]

→ Do you really believe beyond a reasonable doubt in these supernatural spiritual truths? Or do you believe they may be true? Or would you like them to be true?

→ How many of us seek the help of the Holy Spirit within us, talk to that spirit, and listen for a response? Or do we pray to a God whom we only perceive as residing outside our being?

If at times you have doubts about these truths and you sincerely ask the Spirit within you to help you with them, the spirit will.

57

False and True Beliefs

False Beliefs About Life

We know some of the reasons a person commits evil acts. It comes from confused thinking and desires that produce fear. *Much of the confused thinking comes from beliefs that are simply not true.* Illicit desires create the false beliefs which are apparent goods, not true goods. They are created to satisfy the desires and diminish the fear.

These false beliefs are evil thoughts because they are contrary to what is true in existence. These illicit desires initiate sins of commission or omission to achieve the apparent good from evil beliefs and what we may acquire from them. The following is a list of illicit desires creating false beliefs, which can initiate sinful acts:

- We desire or want to live in this world with this life forever. Living in this world forever is a false belief, an apparent good we know is an illusion. *The truth is we are all going to die.* We are afraid of dying, and fear can have us commit terrible sins.

- We desire to live our lives without pain, and this creates the false belief that pain shouldn't happen to us! *But the truth is we will never completely eliminate pain from our lives, especially psychological pain.* It will always be a part of our lives, and fear of pain can cause us to sin in an effort to escape it. Addiction to drugs and our sinful acts to maintain this evil habit is one example of our effort to escape it.
- We desire to live without problems, and we have the false belief it can be done. *The truth is there will always be times in our lives when we will have problems and difficulties.* We can live in fear of their arrival in our lives. In an effort to avoid problems, some people will resort to sin like lying and cheating.
- We desire to always want to be happy, and we have the false belief that possessions or avoiding certain things will result in happiness. *The truth is possessions and avoiding problems will not make us happy.* Nor can anyone achieve perfect happiness in this life, and yet some people will spend a lifetime searching for it.
- Our desire to be perfect creates the false belief that we can and must be perfect. *The truth is no human being can be perfect.* Yet, there are some people who spend a lifetime searching for perfection. Some even think they have it, but they are chasing or

living an illusion. They want to be right, and this initiates the false belief that they must be right. *The truth is our intellect can and does make mistakes*. They fear mistakes and are usually intolerant of those who make them, including themselves. It can make loving those who make mistakes difficult if not impossible.

- Our desire to be successful in this world initiates the false belief that worldly or material success will make us as happy as we will be in this life. They are willing to do anything to achieve it, sometimes committing the gravest of sins. These people believe failure is bad and a disgrace. *The truth is they spend their lives pursuing and achieving an apparent success yet fail to recognize true success and the happiness it brings.*
- Our desire to keep things the same and keep change to a minimum produces the false belief that there can be serenity and permanence in this changing world. Many of these people are afraid of our changing world and the unknown. *The truth is this world and everything in it and almost everything we are is changing.* Almost everything, but not everything! These people fail to accept or embrace change but instead resist it and live in a state of unrest, anxiety, and fear.
- We desire to be totally good, and it produces the false belief that we must be totally good. We must seek it and are intolerant of the evil found in all people. Some fail to see *the truth is we are all a*

mixture of good and evil. They find it difficult if not impossible to love their enemies. They are afraid to look at the evil within themselves.

- We desire to be completely independent, and this desire institutes the false belief we are or can become an independent individualist. For these people, "security" is their highest priority. They want security in their primary or secondary needs, and the way to acquire it is in the possession of wealth and power. They believe wealth and power will give them independence from fear of not having what they need and want. It's an illusion because people have lost all worldly and personal possessions, including wealth and power. *The truth is we are all dependent upon each other and the elements that surround us.* These people find it difficult to love because they are reluctant to receive help or admit they have needs only others can help them acquire or fulfill.
- We all want many, if not all, people we know to love, like, and accept us. It's an illusion because *the truth is there are few, if any of us, that will be accepted and liked by everyone.*

To resist these truths is living an illusion that will always bring fear, frustration, and suffering. We fear the illusion is not true and we will have to accept what is true. *We must embrace the truth or suffer the consequences.*

→ Do any of the desires producing false beliefs and illusions sound familiar to you?
→ Do you know people seeking to always satisfy these illicit desires to their own detriment?

Most people do not want to die, and many refuse to think about it. Others want nothing to change, and some people believe they should live without pain or problems. Still others want perfection, complete independence, security, success, or to be always right and good. Seeking to satisfy these desires is an illusion, some will pay any price to achieve, and they always lead to suffering and sometimes sin. These illusions could prevent us from being our true self, stop us from fulfilling our purpose, and interfere with our acquiring our true final end. *To live with a desire that is satisfied by a false belief that is not true is to live a lie.* Lying to one's self means suffering the possibility of sin and the loss of heaven and the pains of hell.

Truthful Beliefs About Life

The truths needed for our survival are grounded in reality so we can live in the here and now without illusions. To deal with these illicit desires seeking satisfaction with the illusions of false beliefs, we must be aware of the illusions and replace them with truthful beliefs and live properly by loving God and neighbors. What are truths we know are real with faith in divine revelation or our own experiences in life? Truths that are accepted and lived in love.

- We believe dying is merely a transition from this life to eternal life. *The truth is if we live and believe in Jesus and His teachings, we will never die.*
- If we can understand and find meaning to our pain and suffering, we can survive it. Holocaust victims who found meaning in their suffering had a better chance of surviving the death camps. *The truth is we as Christians find meaning in our suffering by uniting it with the suffering of Christ crucified for the atonement of our sins and the sins of the whole world.* In so doing, we are co-redeeming ourselves and all our brothers and sisters in the world. We are fulfilling our purpose or mission, which is the same as God's mission!
- Many people try to avoid problems and believe failure is bad. *The truth is problems and failure can be a force for good.* Problems can present challenges we can overcome or learn to accept, and failure can be good if we learn from it. When we do, we can become stronger. Problems also give others an opportunity to help us, and by our acceptance, we are helping them.
- All people are good in their being because God who is total goodness can only create people who are good in their being or existence. The *truth is in our essence or identity, we are all good and we all desire to be totally good.* This desire to be perfect and to seek as much goodness within ourselves and others is a noble ambition. *The truth is we are all capable of good and bad behavior.* It is our duty to love everyone, focusing

upon the good and encouraging it to grow. With free will, anyone can diminish or destroy some goodness or existence with bad behavior. This can emanate from the illusion or false beliefs we harbor. If we look hard enough, we will always find some evil in the best of us and some good in the worst of us.

- *The truth is we are all created by the same Father in heaven; therefore, we are all brothers and sisters.* We can see we are all different, yet looking deeply into each other, we find that we all have the same humanity. If we look hard enough, we see the same identity, purpose, and destiny.
- We are not independent but experience the fact that we are all dependent on each other and nature to survive in this life. *The ultimate truth is we are totally dependent on a merciful God for all the good we possess.* God loves us and takes care of us in every good way. Some gifts we receive, whether we wish them or not, such as living existence. Others we must freely request and accept to receive them, such as the grace of virtues.
- Since we are all brothers and sisters, *the truth is we all want love and we are all created to love each other.* We know the capacity to love is at the heart of our soul and existence because God is love and we are made in Her image. Love is the only way God wants us to relate to each other and to Herself. True happiness comes from love.
- *The truth is, some people are happier than others.* Those whose love is closest to perfection are the

happiest because God, the Supreme Good, is perfect love and, therefore, perfect happiness. As bad as we can become within every person, there is the capacity to love at the core or essence of our being. God's love works through us in service to others who depend on us to fulfill their primary and secondary needs. In turn, we depend on others to fulfill our primary and secondary needs.

- *The truth is everything, including our lives, is a gift from God.* Everything in this world belongs to God and is, at best, a temporary gift to be used in the service of love. Those people who are truly aware of this never forget it, use it as their reason to be grateful, and are poor in spirit and truly blessed.
- It is fact that everything is changing, and there is no security because we can lose anything and everything. *The truth is although almost everything is changing, what is constant is our spiritual existence* or conscious awareness of ourselves and true perfect love. The only absolute certainty is God's perfect love for us which never changes.
- Finally, when we look at history, we know evil has always been with us. We've always had dictators, tyrants, and leaders who oppress bringing all manner of evil upon the people. Yet, sooner or later, they all fall naturally or unnaturally. *The truth is in the end, good always prevails over evil, love over hatred, truth over untruth or deceit, and peace over violence.* In the end, God will have His way.

Summary

We all want to live forever in a life without pain or problems and with a lot of success and happiness. This is natural, but *the hard truths of life must be accepted because we know to desire what is contrary to reality can bring a lot of sorrow and pain.*

We must also accept the ugliness and injustices found in life as well as the illusions and imperfections within ourselves. With an awareness and understanding of the truths of reality, the ethical teaching of the Bible, and faith in its supernatural truths, we can deal with the injustices and ugliness. We can deal with any problem stemming from false beliefs. *With* faith in the supernatural truths revealed to us in the Bible, we have the "total" truth about ourselves and our destiny. *We accept both the problems and the truths with compassion and acts of love to reduce or alleviate many of the problems and much of the suffering which goes along with them.* Love involves not only the ecstasy of giving, sharing, and receiving to alleviate the problems of those we love but at times the agony of suffering. Sometimes the ecstasy and agony happen at the same time.

We are animals with physical and instinctual drives we must learn to control. It is necessary to acquire the things we need to survive as an animal, and this is good. We are also a spiritual being with an intellect consisting of a conscious awareness and reasoning that we must use if we are to survive as human beings, and this is also good. *When we talk about our survival as a human being with all of life's problems, we are talking about the survival of the essence or core of our identity as spirit, regardless of the corruption in this world.* We must live in accord with our true identity as *spirit.* When we do not, we are moving away from our destiny and diminishing our spiritual nature's ability to establish good relationships.

Dealing with Life and Problems

Dealing with Perfection

We can experience the truths of life and love about ourselves and all others. When we do, we see in those we love some of ourselves. We want to be as perfect as possible, the best version of ourselves. We have seen for some people this means seeking perfection and not willing to accept imperfection in themselves and others.

We see the signs of the perfectionist: They can't forget mistakes; mistakes are their fault; compared with others, they feel defeated when they come up short; when they make mistakes in front of others, they are embarrassed; they are reluctant to ask for help because it reveals their weakness as a person; they must hide weakness from themselves and others; and they find it hard to admit mistakes. Perfectionists believe in the falsehood that they must be perfect, and if they are not, they consider themselves failures, which produces pain and a lot of negative feelings.

To diminish the pain and negative feelings, they engage in the following: drug abuse, overeating, constant self-abasement, inflicting physical harm upon themselves, and to be perfect, they submit to a grueling regiment. Sometimes perfectionism results in our desire to be God! This endeavor to be God was precisely what alienated us from God, others, and ourselves, which causes pain.

In dealing with perfectionism, we must gain insight or the awareness that it may hinder our capacity to show compassion and love for ourselves and others. This type of awareness helps us constructively deal with perfectionism. Another insight or awareness is the fact established by experience that we are imperfect, and imperfection is a part of humanity. We must realize this while living with the fact we want to be perfect. Finally, we must all accept the facts of our own participation in the human experience. This includes losing our health with suffering, the ills of old age, the fact of our making mistakes, committing sins, the death of our friends or family, and finally, our own death with the loss of all our material possessions. Often, we judge others by the very things we hate about ourselves

Dealing with Suffering

The truth is at times, we all experience pain, sorrow, unease, grief, disappointment, and despair. We know by experience that suffering is a normal part of the lives of all people. We must accept this truth when it enters our lives and the lives of everyone we know and love. We must respond with sympathy and empathy. With this response, we gain the insight and an awareness that it is not my suffering or their suffering; there is just the suffering of humanity.

As mentioned in the prior chapter, with this understanding, when we suffer, we can choose to unite our suffering with the suffering of Christ and with all who are suffering for the redemption of all humanity. With this understanding, we can reach out to all humanity with love and compassion to alleviate the suffering of others. When we do, we are happy because we feel good about the meaning or purpose for our lives and are satisfied with ourselves. We also experience compassion for ourselves when we acquire insight into our compassionate feelings and treatment of others.

Dealing with Change

We live in an impermanent world, but we want it to be permanent. How do we deal with this? We deal with it the way we dealt with perfectionism, pain, and suffering. We become more "aware" of reality. We practice this awareness in prayer. *To be at peace, we must be aware of the reality of what is and to accept who we really are.* We are aware of the impermanence of this life and accept it with the awareness that we have no control over it. All we can control and change is the awareness of reality, contained in our "I," and expressed in behavior, which is our "am," with the help of the Holy Spirit. All we can do is ask God to give us the insight to know what we can change and with the power of love influence our "I" and the behavior of our "am" to change it; the insight to know what we cannot change and accept it with faith, hope, and love in a merciful God. And most importantly, the wisdom of God within us helps us to know the difference between what we can and cannot change. With these insights comes peace.

There are many things in our lives we cannot change. *One thing we can deliberately change is ourselves through our thoughts and actions.* We can either become more righteous or destructive to our being. I've prayed many prayers of petition. Sometimes God would answer promptly while on other occasions, He would answer in His good time, not mine, in one way or another. In my experience, there is one prayer He always answered with clarity and speed. It involves my asking God to change my attitude (traits) or perception with respect to a given person or situation such as asking Him to help me act with forgiveness, compassion, patience, and tolerance. God will always love us, but when we love God, our reality changes, and we become more of who we were truly created to be.

We use our enhanced awareness to bring us closer to the true reality of ourselves without illusions. To get closer to reality with awareness and prayer brings us closer to God because our reality is created existence, and God is existence. It also brings us to a life of greater holiness or closer to pure existence. To see reality as it truly is and to see ourselves as we truly are is to be aware that God is permanent and our conscious awareness of ourselves and God is also permanent. God is eternal existence, and His total existence is in the eternal present without a past or future, so there is no change. Our awareness of God's eternal existence makes our awareness permanent. Our conscious awareness and a glorified body that contains it will live forever. Our existence, regardless of any changes in this world, and possibly the world to come, is permanent. Since God is existence by love, we are aware that both love and spiritual existence are permanent.

Dealing with Corruption and Injustice

We can feed the hungry, clothe the naked, shelter the homeless, minister to victims of violent attacks, and pray for those who suffer because of the evil present in our society. All these acts of charity are essential to our salvation.[1] But have you ever asked yourself these questions: What are the causes of poverty? What are the *causes* of abortion and war that produce the victims that need our comfort and ministry? The follow up questions would be, what can we do about it? How can we address these *causes* and eliminate or, at the very least, reduce the evil? These are social justice questions.

These questions have us look and acquire a greater awareness of the reality of the political, social, economic, religious, and cultural institutions to determine if they are at least partially to blame for the evil. When our awareness based on reason and consciousness determines they are, we are morally obligated to work for change or modification of these institutions. Since we live in a democratic form of government, we elect the people who govern us. If we vote to elect or vote to continue to elect people who we are aware do evil, we are complicit in the evil they do. It is our sin of commission. If we do not vote while aware of the evil these leaders do, we are complicit in the evil they do. If we are unaware of the evil they do but can be aware, we are still complicit in the evil they do. It is our sin of omission.

→ Is failing to vote or being vincibly ignorant in a vote a sin if we know or should know leaders are corrupt?
→ If we knowingly vote for a corrupt leader, is it a sin?
→ What if both candidates running for office are evil and corrupt? We can vote for the lesser of two evils if we can establish there is a difference.

We can lobby our leaders to change or enact better laws and regulations. We can elect leaders who can bring about change or make necessary modifications. Peaceful protests and demonstrations may help leaders move in the direction of reducing or eliminating corruption. We can refuse to participate in any injustice or obey any unjust law. We can expose any corruption or injustice that we experience. We can educate our children so we can produce a better future culture with children who grow up to be citizens and leaders with a greater sense of God and justice. Only when we are aware of the causes of corruption and injustice in our government and society can we work to alleviate the evil. This is social justice.

→ Can you identify the corruption and injustice in our society? Are you aware of the causes of such evil?
→ Have you ever peacefully tried to change or improve the political system by voting, demonstrating, or petitioning?
→ Have you ever lobbied to change bad laws and enact better ones designed to improve the lives of people? For example, removing abortion laws, funding of projects helpful to poor people, improving education, prison reform, etc.?

Power of Thought

We must be realistic in our desires because desire is associated with power. We understand the hard truths of life that we may never get what we desire, or we may get some of it, a lot of it, but never all of it. It doesn't matter! We must see that it makes little difference to our identity, purpose, or destiny unless we allow how much we get in life to harm us. What can make a significant difference is how we use what we have, how we respond to what we get or do not get.

Regardless of how much we desire to have and never get, our response must be with the power of love. When we love in the here and now, we will get the good God wants us to have now. We also get the ultimate or final good we know comes later. We accept and respond to the outcomes in life with the power of love, the truths, and teachings of the Bible. This helps us understand others and treat them as we want to be treated. The Golden Rule is to love our neighbor as ourselves or treat others as we want to be treated. *As Christians, we must always be first in initiating fair treatment whenever possible.*

We have considered the power of the intellect and will, truth, love, and faith. All provide power, but how is it done? Simply put, it works through the focus of thought, especially desire.

What to Focus Upon

We must be aware and accept but never focus on our imperfections, delusional desires, evil thoughts, the ugliness, and the injustices in life. Instead, we must focus daily upon the truthful beliefs listed earlier about ourselves, our purpose, and destiny. We must focus daily upon the truths of the Bible and what we have learned about the truths of love. It's called the power of positive thinking. *Focus gives power to thought which results in action.* Without insight and understanding of these truths about reality, it may be more difficult to live in love. Insight into the truths about reality and how we exist provides us with understanding to live the Bible teachings we believe are true. To summarize, we *focus upon the positive truths and the goodness of God and His creations along with our desires to possess this goodness. The experience of this awareness produces understanding. Remember with understanding comes the energy to actualize love. With love comes existence as human beings with freedom, justice, happiness including peace and our salvation.* These truths we focus upon must be truths that come not only from science and experience but from faith.

At the heart of our intellect are ideas concerning desires. In previous chapters, we read about "motives of wanting to satisfy our selfish worldly desires" or "the power of love emanating from God's desires." Most of the Bible stories about love, belonging, sex, adventure, longing, or searching involves some form of desire. This desire is like the fire within us that burns and can consume us. Desire is responsible for the energy or power that pushes us outward in pursuit of happiness, pleasure, and most of all, the satisfaction that comes when we get what we desire. We must access this energy if we are to be successful in achieving any end we seek. Desire is a key to energizing the power of faith and love.

A story will demonstrate this energy of desire. There was a young man who wanted to know the secret of being successful. He was told an old wise prophet who sat under a palm tree near town could answer his question on how to be successful. The young man approached the prophet with his question. The wise man told the young man if he really wanted to know the secret of success, he should follow him down to the river.

At the river, the wise man asked the young man to put his head under the water. Trusting the wise man, he did what he was asked at which time the wise man placed his hands on the young man's head, holding it under the water. As time passed, the young man struggled to lift his head out of the water. The harder he struggled, the more force the wise man used to hold his head under.

Now the young man used all his strength to lift his head up to save himself but still could not lift his head out of the water. Just as he was about to lose consciousness and drown, the wise man lifted his head out of the water, threw him on the ground, looked into his eyes, and said, "Young man, when you want or desire success as much as you wanted that breath of fresh air, you'll get it!"

→ How much is your desire to do His will? It is the key to your salvation and the energy you will need to accomplish your mission and achieve your goal.

The basic truths in reality are that everyone has some degree of goodness. We all have the same nature and we are all connected and dependent upon each other and God. Without the mindful awareness of these truths, it becomes easier to dislike or even hate those who sin or harm us. This is contrary to the teachings of Jesus. Insight from deep reflection into these truths and the revelation about the brotherhood of all people can provide us with the "desire" to comply with Jesus's command to love our enemies and do good to those who want to hurt us. The truth in reality is we all have a propensity to act in unwholesome or evil ways. We experience this truth, and it was at one time considered a self-evident truth.

As mentioned earlier, this ability to do evil is a part of our nature and was the basis for the doctrine of original sin in all of us. A corollary truth used by psychologists is that some of us are blind to our own sins, and at times will project them on to others we dislike. A reflection into this truth provides us with an understanding of why Jesus proclaims, *You hypocrite, first take the log out of your own eye and then you will see clearly to take the speck out of your neighbor's eye.*[1]

Ultimately, we must focus upon this thought which is a divine truth: *All our power comes from God. We must have a strong desire for God's presence and guidance if we are to use His gift of power for the common good.* To think this thought is to be poor in Spirit. In the Sinai Desert, Moses did not have or focus on this divine truth when he struck the rock to get water for his people. Moses thought it was he and Aaron alone who were expected to get water for the people! He did not acknowledge that it was God's power they must rely upon. Moses did not think or trust and so did not expect God to keep His promise to help His people survive in the desert and get to the land He promised them. Because of his failure to be poor in spirit, Moses never entered the promised land![2]

→ Are you poor in spirit when it comes to any power you exercise for the common good?

Dealing with the Doubts and the Temptations of Evil Thoughts

We must admit we all have doubts at one time or another, including the Saints. Perhaps they are temptations from the devil. When we have doubts, we are uncertain about a particular Christian belief or we suspend our assent of it. There may even be times we have doubts about our faith as a whole. Doubts and questions do not amount to sin. It all depends on how we respond to them. The same applies to any evil or negative thoughts. If we give in to doubts or evil thoughts, they can become sinful.

Responding to Doubts and Evil or Negative Thoughts

To doubts and sinful thoughts, we respond with good thoughts. This is how we fight doubts and sinful thoughts. We develop an awareness of these negative and destructive thoughts within our intellect. Once we identify evil thoughts, doubts, and negative ideas, we can make a choice on how to handle them. Then we must ask ourselves, are these doubts or sinful thoughts conducive to happiness? Or do they promote suffering, often in the form of fear and anxiety? Consider whether they come from an evil force, a force that encourages our selfish desires, and what we could have if we were not prohibited by the divine laws and truths of the faith.

We must be aware and identify these thoughts as unwholesome and detrimental to our well-being and do not lead to freedom and peace. They produce pain, suffering, anxiety, and fear. They are related to selfish desires, hatred, and delusions of reality. Wholesome thoughts enhance our well-being in all our relationships as human beings. They do not produce pain and suffering but are conducive to peace and freedom. *Once aware of evil thoughts and doubts, we turn away and replace them with good thoughts.* Conscious awareness, our seeing truth and righteousness usually means doing what is true and righteous.

To identify these doubts and evil thoughts with their affect upon us, we must honestly know ourselves with ruthless observations devoid of passion. To deal with these doubts and evil thoughts, the following summary is offered:

- *Make a solemn commitment or covenant with God* to live the teachings of Jesus in the spirit of our beliefs we know are truthful and not illusions.
- *Replace* the evil thoughts and doubts with good thoughts and an assent of faith. Read and reflect upon the disclosure of God's saving power and

self-revelation in Christ crucified and risen.[1] This entails a personal promise to Christ as God[2] and a confidence in the resurrection to come.[3] With an assent of faith and with the power of the Holy Spirit, we cast out doubt and evil thoughts.

- *Reflect on the consequences if we succumb to doubts and evil thoughts* becoming nonbelievers. Think about the kind of person we could become and what our eternal life will be like.
- *Rely on impermanence.* Resist doubt and evil thoughts by always keeping in mind the fact that almost everything in this world is changing, including our thoughts. Let this fact of impermanence be a source of comfort and peace to you. Wait, and the evil thoughts and doubts will pass.
- *Find the cause of these thoughts.* Go into our memory, and see if we can determine what gave rise to these thoughts. Perhaps a conversation, something we've read or seen, maybe our own selfish desires. Something perhaps we can avoid in the future.
- A series of good thoughts can become a good mental habit which is a virtue. A mental virtue can lead to verbal and or physical virtue. We fight a bad habit or vice with a virtue and we replace an evil act with a good one with an awareness of the causes and effects of sin and the help of the Holy Spirit through prayer.

If we don't act on our bad habits or vices, they will disappear. If we establish good habits or virtues, we are less likely to commit a sin or maintain a vice. Remember an act or virtue must be based upon the intention of love and if it is, it becomes an act or virtue of love. Recall how a person can be kind or generous to sell a product or to have a person or a group of people do his or her will. Hitler gave the German people jobs, vacations, the arts and restored their pride in themeselves as Germans and their nation. He did this so he could control and manipulate them for his own purpose which was wars of conquest.

With an ever increasing number of good acts and virtues, we become more and more the love we should be.

Repeat acts of giving, with the motive of love, until they become virtues of love.

Repeat acts of sharing, with the motive of love, until they become virtues of love.

Repeat acts of receiving, with the motive of love, until they become virtues of love.

With enough virtues and the right motive, we fulfill the essence of our nature, existence by love. We possess God and eternal life in heaven which can begin here and now on earth in a limited way.

By using these methods, we can overcome these evil negative thoughts that can dominate our thinking. Remember, doubts or evil thoughts or desires that at times push into our thinking are not sinful unless we give in to them. If we do, we become tragic figures because we are rejecting reality or the truth.

→ When you had doubts about your faith, how did you deal with them?

→ Have any negative or evil thoughts or temptations dominated your thinking? Can you identify them? How did you deal with them?

Conscience

As Christians, we should examine our conscience daily to identify our sins or if any evil negative thoughts have crept into our thinking. What is our conscience? Paul tells us, "All who have sinned apart from the law will also perish apart from the law and all who have sinned under the law will be judged by the law. For it is not the hearers of the law who are righteous in God's sight, but the doers of the law who will be justified. What the law requires is written on their hearts to which their own conscience also bears witness."[4]

What Paul is saying here is that conscience is not a separate faculty of the mind. It is the ability to evaluate and choose our actions based on the law God has written in our hearts. Conscience is not, however, synonymous with God's law. Our conscience can fail by becoming careless or too lenient. On the other hand, it may become too careful or scrupulous. It can also become insensitive or hardened to the guidance of the Holy Spirit.

With the working of our conscience, we repent of the evil we have deliberately done, repent of the good we deliberately failed to do, repent with awareness the evil thoughts and doubts we fail to overcome. We resolve not to sin with the help of God's grace.

61

How to Be a Better Me

Where does the desire to want to be a better Christians or better version of ourselves come from? This desire was placed in our nature by God and reinforced by the teachings of our parents and Jesus: *Be perfect, therefore, as your heavenly Father is perfect.*[1]

Reasons that Stop Us

People want to change and improve for the better, so what is stopping them? We live in a materialistic world with a lot of good but also a lot of evil. Earlier we learned that we can have false beliefs, and at times, we can be confused with an intellect that makes mistakes. We can be confused about what is the real or apparent good and unclear on how to act for a good with negative consequences. Perhaps we are afraid of the unknown future and think changes may be too hard, or in change, we may find ourselves in worse circumstances. It could be we just don't want to leave our comfort zones and the security of knowing what we have and may lose if we change.

Maybe we do not have a clear understanding of the truth concerning our identity, purpose, or destiny. So we have doubts, false beliefs, or illusions about ourselves and the world. We see, it could be a host of reasons. All of this brings struggle, fear, mental violence into our lives as we try to cope with an imperfect intellect.

→ What prevents you from changing and being a better version of yourself?

Change

How can we change? To change, we must first and foremost change our thinking, and consequently, our verbal and physical behaviors. To accomplish this, we must know and believe the truth about God, ourselves, and the world. We have attempted to address this issue with sources of truths by the natural use of our intelligence and experiences and also by using the natural truth revealed by Jesus along with the supernatural truths revealed in the Bible that can only be accepted by faith.

We can change by learning to control our thinking by first identifying negative thoughts. We must identify beliefs, conditioned habits, desires, sins, and untruths that produce negative destructive thoughts so we can teach ourselves not to focus upon them and deny them any power. Remember, *focus gives energy to thought, and when we focus on a good thought, we give power to that thought.* On the other hand, negative thoughts can diminish power and produce fear, resulting in discouragement and hopelessness, if allowed, to dominate our thinking.

Gospel Living

We start living the Gospel by focusing upon the moral teachings of the Bible, especially God's teachings on *love.* We replace evil thoughts with Christian ideology. To live God's moral teachings can be very difficult. When we do live them, we see they are true because they work and establish the truth about our purpose for being here and the way we are to live if we wish to be at peace and to be truly happy. *They must be lived in love.* Living them holds the solutions to many of our problems as well as the problems of a corrupt and unjust world. Living them also makes it easier for us to have faith in the supernatural truths of divine revelations.

To change, to be our better self, to be the person we were meant to be, we must have *faith* in Jesus Christ and the promises He made. What does Jesus promise? He promises the destiny of eternal life for those who live and believe in Him,[2] for those who are righteous,[3] and for those who follow Him.[4] We must *know* and *believe* who we are, our mission in life, and our destiny. We must "desire" to live a life of love so we can acquire those promises and be the person God created us to be!

We know we all have the same basic nature or essence. If we desire to live a righteous life of love, we can fulfill the created nature we were all given. We can be more and more of what we were created to be.

→ How much is your desire to possess God in a love relationship and to be a better you?

Your desire is reflected in the time you spend with God, talking to God, focusing your thoughts upon God, trusting God, and forgiving your neighbors and yourself. If you really want to change:

- You will *make time* to be with God every day, not just on Sunday.
- You will *talk to God* throughout your day with meditative or contemplative prayer or simply a "Good morning or goodnight, God," "God help me," "Be with me," "Forgive me," or "Show me the way."
- You will *talk about God* when the opportunity presents itself.
- You will *focus your thoughts* daily on the teachings and sayings of God in the Bible and the *way* of the Christian.[5]
- You will *trust* God because you love Her and resolve never to be afraid because She is with you, and Her will is always done.

- You will ask for God's *mercy* and *forgiveness* for your neighbor and yourself. You will forgive your neighbor as you forgive yourself.
- You will help your neighbor as you would help yourself.

If we implement acts of love with family, friends and strangers, but not with God, we do not have a sense or awareness of God. We don't have a knowledge or direct personal relationship of love with God, but an indirect one with a longing we can't explain. If we do not have a love relationship with anyone, we become tragic figures. With a personal relationship of love with God, our love is fulfilled, complete and closer to Agape love. Our lack of knowledge or sense of God and our failure to have a direct personal relationship of love with Her is the most serious problem facing our generation today. *Do you have a relationship of love with God or are you just going throught rituals or motions without a real love affair?*

If you really want to change, your desire must be "determined" and "persistent" in bringing about change. You must implement these seven acts of love.

Summary Review

We have discussed controlling our thoughts by replacing negative thoughts with positive thoughts and focusing upon the positive thoughts. Remember, we can control negative thoughts by determining their causes and reflecting on their consequences. *When we truly see and understand how bad they are for us, how sad and fearful they have us feel, we can suppress negative thoughts and replace them with positive ones.* We must keep in mind that in our efforts to suppress negative thoughts, impermanence will sooner or later cause them to leave us.

We have provided some of the answers associated with our identity, purpose. and destiny. To establish the answers, we have investigated science, psychology, philosophy, our experiences using our intellect, and accepted divine revelation with faith. It is now time to investigate our complete and true identity.

62

Our True Identity

To know who we truly are, we must look outside ourselves to divine revelation! To change by knowing who we truly are, we can use much of what we learned about our identity, purpose, and destiny. For some, this would be enough, but it is not nearly enough! We know we are spirit with a soul existing within a material living body with an intellect and free will capable of love. Love is our purpose for being. We are motivated by love to focus upon good thoughts and generate energy that creates, maintains, and enhances our existence as human beings. Made in God's image, our love is similar to His. In so being, we are destined to possess Her in a loving relationship here and now and for all eternity. **We perceive God's purpose in life as good and true, we act upon God's mission, and in so doing, Her mission becomes our *mission*. It becomes our mission because we love Her. Yet our identity is still not complete!**

Grace

To change to the person that we want to be or to move closer and closer to what the Bible entreats us to be, we need grace! We must ask for grace in prayer. When we ask for grace, we are asking for a supernatural revelation. It has been revealed that God gives us grace because She loves us. We received grace within a love relationship. What is grace? It is:

- a gift of salvation through faith;[1]
- a gift of salvation for everyone who comes to a knowledge of the truth;[2]
- a gift that brings us a new birth from above;[3]
- a gift of the Holy Spirit who pours God's love into our hearts;[4]
- a gift that enables us to become adopted children of God;[5]
- a gift of being individual members of the body of Christ.[6]

Who We Truly Are

It was Peter who answered the question Jesus presented to His disciples concerning who He was. Suppose Jesus, however, asked this question, "Who do I say you are?" He might say, "You are human beings who exist by living in my love."

We now know so much more about ourselves with the gift of grace! We know by faith, we are beings who have been saved from the effects of our sin by the undeserved gift of the crucified Lord and Savior, Jesus the Christ! He loves us, made us adopted children of God and individual members of His mystical body, the church! We have the Holy Spirit dwelling within, providing us with God's love! We are created to inherit the kingdom of heaven, imperishable, undefiled, and unfading![7] Believers are invited to share in divine love found in the interior life of the blessed Trinity![8]

If we really believed this and were absolutely convinced it was so, would we worry about fulfilling any of those primary or secondary needs? If we believe our true identity and destiny, would worldly success and self-actualization and many of the things we think are so important have the same meaning or value? Of course, we could give them a meaning of love by using them in the process of love.

Imagine being the child of one of the wealthiest parents in the world who were kind and loving. They give you a meaningful life, which includes anything you want that was good for you. You will have a wonderful future, a great inheritance, and the absolute assurance you will have nothing to worry about in this life because all your needs will be met.

→ As that child, do you think you would be "perfectly" happy? Some people believe they would be.

→ Do you think that all of your needs would be satisfied? What about your need for God? Some people in such a position might not give God a thought.

What the Lord has given us and is offering us is infinitely more valuable than anything such wealthy good parents could provide. But it gets much better! We are made in God's image,[9] and now we are designated by grace to share in the divine life! Peter tells us with grace and the promises of Jesus, we can escape the corruption in this world, moreover we can become "participants in the divine nature."[10] Some theologians define grace given by God's love as *the gift of divine energy in our souls that enables us to participate in the divine nature.* It raises us to a higher level of relationship with the Lord. **With the Holy Spirit within us and our deification with Her grace, the Lord is incarnate within us!** *The incarnation continues in the world today in individual members of His mystical body!* God is present here and now within us and working through us. What a magnificent obsession!

The Holy Spirit is within us, but is not a part of out being! We are His creation, She is not, She is a separate entity within us, equal to the Father and Son. She provides us with the wisdom to use our energy of life for the good, if we allow Her to do so. We must always keep in mind we are not God or a part of God. We are members of the Body of Christ which is a body of love. We exist within our body, united by the spirit of love with God and our neighbors, but we never lose our identity in this union. As a creator who loves His creation, He shares Himself with us by creating us with life and capacity to love similar to His own. We can freely become God like in a union of love with Him. This union is established when we give and share our love and life with each other and our Lord, Jesus the Christ.

When we pray to God for something good, if it is possible, aren't we supposed to work to answer our own prayers with the help of the Holy Spirit within us? When friends pray for something truly needed, if possible, aren't we obligated by love to help them acquire or achieve it with the help of the Holy Spirit? Isn't it really God who is answering their prayers and ours by working in us and through us? This is one way God works through His incarnation within us!

We know the amazing fact that our identity is a little less than God's identity. God's purpose here on earth is our purpose, and our destination is to be with Her. Now we can add to our belief God loved us so much, He has given us His gift of grace so we can love one another. If we love one another, God lives in us, and His love is perfected in us. With the love of God perfected in us, we become holy. For it is written, "He who called you holy is holy, be holy yourselves in all your conduct; for it is written You shall be holy for I am holy."[11]

Holiness is pure and total existence as full of existence as our identity or nature will allow. Holiness fulfills the purpose for our existence. Since we have the incarnate God within us, our human life becomes deified, equipped to conquer sin and share in the divine life! If we are truly "aware" of these graces concerning us and we have absolute faith in them, we would know how to act and react in our lives and be a better person.

→ Were you aware of these graces? Do you see your identity in the light of these graces?
→ Do you have faith in these graces?

If you answered both questions affirmatively, could we tell your answers were true by seeing the way you live, acting, and reacting to life's situations?

63

Our Identity and Gospel Living

Focus on Humility

If we had faith in what has been revealed to us about our identity and destiny, what would we focus upon concerning ourselves? Some Christians would focus upon humility. It is true that with self-knowledge comes gratitude and humility. We are insignificant compared to God and we are totally dependent upon Her and others for our lives. There is much truth in this.

An example of this humility is expressed in the life of a Franciscan, Antonio Margil. He established six missions in Texas, including the Mission of San Antonio. When he became a Franciscan, he chose the nickname "Nothingness Itself." In fact, he would sign all of his letters with this nickname. He would say, "We must never forget our nothingness and never fear any demons greater than that called I." As you know, we are much, much more than "nothing itself."

Jesus said, *For all who exalt themselves will be humbled, and those who humble themselves will be exalted.*[1] In the eyes of the world, humility will not bring success by the worldly standard of fame and fortune. To acquire worldly success, we need our "I" to focus upon the traits of assertiveness, ruthlessness, and without compassion; for after all, it's not personal, only business. Those who exalt themselves with worldly power, fame, and fortune will be humbled. The pride that comes with such exaltation often comes before a fall from grace and a possible loss of heaven and the pains of hell.[2]

It is good to have talents and success. To deny or minimize them is to deny and minimize reality. However, we must always acknowledge and praise their source who is God. Thanks to a loving God we have them. This is humility. What is also very important is how we use them.

Focus Upon Our True Identity

On the other hand, we can also focus upon our identity that reveals we are made in God's image, a little less than God, an adopted child of God, and part of His mystical body. In short, we can focus upon our "deification" and "incarnation" of God within us. There is much truth in this also. If we focus upon these revelations, we are more likely to face the challenges of Gospel living. We are more likely to be successful walking the straight and narrow, keeping our sins in proper perspective, and increasing our love of God. With this awareness of who we truly are and the graces and goodness God gives us, we become grateful. With gratitude, we are more likely to remain faithful during those times we suffer with pain, failure, and injustice. We must not only be aware of Bible revelation but must believe we can communicate with God in a very special relationship and receive Her many gifts and graces.

If we believe we can live a Gospel life, we will find ways to accomplish it. In addition, others are more likely to have faith and confidence in us. Jesus said if we have faith, we can move mountains.[3] If we believe, we can move the mountain of Gospel living. But we must be careful because there will always be people or our inner critic, perhaps inspired by Satan, who will cause us to doubt ourselves and discourage us. We can always rationalize to ourselves that we must focus upon our humbleness as we accept the facts of our weaknesses, lack of talent or strength, determination and, of course, our failures.

Doubt could indicate a core disbelief and a desire not to succeed, perhaps because we are too much of a sinner. As we now know, this indicates sin against the Holy Spirit by doubting Her ability to help us succeed in Gospel living. We may want to fail, and so we punish ourselves with failure!

Gospel living requires balance as we have seen between individualization and socialization. It requires a balance between justice and mercy as well as between a focus upon our True Identity and humility. Living the Gospel can be very difficult and requires the help of God.

→ Do you really believe or have faith that you can succeed in Gospel living with the help of the Holy Spirit? Do you really believe you can be a better you?
→ Do you really want it, as much as that boy wanted that breath of air to live?

Judgment

How often do we compare? Quite a bit, one suspects. We compare ourselves with others in a whole host of areas such as our possessions, talents, and activities. Comparing leads to judgment, and Jesus says, *Do not judge, and you will not be judged.*[4]

What should we judge? When we judge, we should not judge the person but his or her acts. Contrary to some ideologies, people are not their acts. We are not what we do nor do we become what we do. As we now know, acts are only a part of who we are. The complete acceptance of the awareness of this idea, which is true, ultimately gives us the ability to love our enemies with the help of the Holy Spirit. When we do something wrong, we feel guilty. *The guilt is associated with the act, not the person.* Guilt is a feeling of responsibility and our deserving punishment for our sinful behavior.

Guilt is not shame. As we know, shame is a painful emotion associated with our nature or identity. Shame deals with "honor" or integrity. It involves failing to adhere to the moral teachings and revelations concerning who we are. Shame deals with honesty. To be dishonorable has to do with going against what we perceive ourselves to be and what our true nature is. We now know what our true identity is, and to go against it is to be dishonorable. Yes, we will sin and make serious mistakes, but we will never betray God by denying who we truly are and failing to acknowledge Him as our Creator. *Guilt is associated with what we do; shame deals with who we are. We must never be ashamed of or doubt who we are, only guilt for what we do.*

We will never say, "I've tried so hard, so often, but I cannot change. I cannot be what God created me to be. I've failed so often; there is no sense in going down this path of changing for the better in my thoughts and efforts. Frequently I've asked the Holy Spirit for help, but She does not seem to give it. This is because my case is hopeless. My very nature is sinful and by my evil actions, I reveal my evil nature." This is a sin against the Holy Spirit, and this kind of thinking and attitude can lead to our damnation!

Instead, we should pray this: "My nature is a gift from God and is good by its very essence at its very core. I am lovable and capable because God will always love me no matter what evil I do. Therefore, I can and will change, be a better me, refrain from sin with God's love, and help no matter how long it takes. I will never give up thinking and working to do God's will because I am Her child, destined to share in Her divine kingdom. Sooner or later, little by little, I will get closer and closer to that perfect love She wants and created me to be."

The first approach is pessimistic: *focusing* our thoughts upon our guilt, our weaknesses and evil acts, our natural tendency to act sinfully, not trusting God or believing She can and will help us. The second approach is optimistic: *focusing* upon who we truly are and God's love without shame but with hope and the trust found in love.

→ Do you make a distinction between guilt and shame? Have you experienced and can you describe any difference?
→ Are you optimistic or pessimistic?

Never Compare

We should never compare ourselves to Jesus, the saints, or any person we consider holy. Instead, we should focus upon our small successes in spite of the sins we may have committed. *We must not measure ourselves on whether we reached our goal but by how much progress we make no matter how small.* Remember, we can love and learn from Jesus, but we can't compare ourselves with Him. We will always be imperfect in this world, no matter how perfect we become. Jesus is the Son of God, and God is perfect. When we compare ourselves with perfection, we can become very discouraged and stop making an effort. Keep in mind, if we focus upon this type of comparison, in most cases, we lose energy, and failure often follows quickly.

We must focus our mind upon believing we can live the Gospel life, thinking we are lovable, capable children of God. We are a part of His mystical body with His *mission* to redeem people in the world by our love with the help of the

Holy Spirit within us. Ultimately, we will live forever with God in a union of love. If we believe this is our identity, purpose, and destiny, we will act accordingly. If we don't believe and think it, we will most likely not act in accord with Gospel living. Good thoughts reflect good acts, and good thoughts along with good acts result in Gospel living.

→ Do you believe you are a lovable, capable child of God?

Look into a mirror or into the eyes of a friend and say out loud, "I am a child of God who is lovable and capable. Made in Her image, I am good and created to love. God's mission is my mission. He created me to redeem the world with His love within me, and I will live forever united to Him in love." If you feel uneasy or awkward or ashamed in saying it, then ask yourself this question, "Do I really believe what I have just said about who I am, why I am now here, and where I am going?"

Many people do not feel themselves lovable, capable children of God and of extreme importance. If they really believed in their true identity and destiny, they would feel otherwise. We are so important Jesus sacrificed Himself unto death for our sins. If we were the only person in the world, Jesus would have died for us! This is how precious we are. If we have faith and love for Jesus and His revelations, we must also have faith in ourselves to live His Gospel and practice His teaching with His help. *Faith in ourselves means believing in our true identity, purpose, and destiny. This results in believing and accepting ourselves as lovable, capable, and important.*

Remember, there is some good in all of us, and when we focus upon the good, we get the power to love and minister to people. Focus upon the good in people no matter how small. We must direct our minds to believe in the truths about God and ourselves so we can live the Gospel teachings of love with the grace of God. *Good thoughts in us produce spiritual energy needed to act with goodness and succeed in living the Gospel.* It is the power needed to succeed in living the Gospel.

We are living a life based upon faith and grace. Keep in mind, however, to think you can live a perfect life, accepting and obeying all the teachings of Jesus is an illusion for most people. No one is perfect in holiness, which means without sin. It is true with the Holy Spirit, we have the power to conquer sin, but there will always be some sin no matter how small in this life but not in the next.

Live in Love

Replace destructive thoughts with constructive ones, and always look for opportunities to help. To do this, you must train yourself to recognize the needs of others and respond. Albert Schweitzer, the great African missionary doctor, arrived at a train station in California to a cheering crowd. Standing on the train platform, he could see over their heads. He saw an old woman struggling to pick up groceries knocked to the ground by the rushing crowd.

Instead of speaking to the people, he immediately rushed through the crowd to help her pick up her groceries. St. Francis of Assisi once said that we must preach with our action and, if necessary, with speech. Unfortunately, the only Bible some people will ever know is what they see us doing and, at times, saying.

→ How good are you at recognizing the needs of others and responding to them? When you do, how does it feel?

The ideology of Jesus's teaching is lived by responding to our needs and the needs of others. We can know any ideology whether it is Christian, communist, liberalism, or capitalism. Knowing ideologies does not mean we will live them or we may live them for a while then walk away. To live the Christian Gospel is to love Jesus, and to love Him is to believe His teachings. We cannot walk away from love! To love Jesus, we must practice His teachings, which is the process of love for all that exists. Jesus is God, and God's teaching is love. Every time you read the word *God* or *Jesus,* replace it with the words *love* or *existence,* and you'll see what we mean.

Gospel living is simply this: ***doing good and avoiding evil by living in love.*** It is driven by love of God and love of neighbor as we love ourselves. It is not driven by knowledge or truth unless they are understood with compassion and generosity. Remember to live in love is to live in truth. It is not only doing big things but simple things with love that any person at any age in almost any condition of health can do. People will always find excuses related to their health, age, job, intelligence, or failure not to serve with love. We can always find people to help on our job among our friends, at school or church, our clubs and any organizations we belong to. All we have to do is deliberately look for them. Love has nothing to do with failures but everything to do with effort! *Love does not require complex thinking but awareness. Once the need is recognized, consciously seeing is the doing.* The success of Gospel living comes with the process of love, regardless of the outcome in this life. Mother Theresa of Calcutta was once asked by a reporter how she felt after laboring so hard in India for so many years, yet it resulted in relatively few converts to Christianity. Her response was that God does not judge us by our successes but by our effort in acts of love. She explained that to know God is to love Him and to love Him is to serve Him by serving others regardless of the number of converts.

In the business world, success is measured by the amount of economic profit. In the world of love, we measure success by the process of love. The process will always have a good effect but may also have a physically evil one. When the one we love suffers psychologically, we suffer. Or when we sacrifice for a loved one, we may suffer. Love is always our primary end with a good effect while the evil effect, if present, is a secondary or collateral one. In heaven, love is our final end with only a positive effect. In heaven, love is only ecstasy, not agony. Here on earth, we are laborers in the field; we leave judgment of success in the hands of God.

We can love a person who ends up killing us, and we would be successful. This is what happened to Jesus. We are created to love, and love is at the core of our identity and purpose. *There is no excuse for not loving.* Even the excuse of selfishness is an illusion because if we truly understood and cared about ourselves, we would love! To care about ourselves is to love ourselves along with everyone and all of God's creatures. People who do not think they are lovable, capable, and important must change their thinking.

→ In the light of what you now know about yourself and about God, could you change your thinking?

When doubts or evil thoughts arise, just focus upon your identity and destiny and smile! It may not be a matter of intellectually knowing who you are but the *faith* to accept this knowledge in your heart and truly believe it and make it your own; just sincerely ask the Holy Spirit to help you.

→ Can you think of any excuses not to love? There are none!

Courage to Live the Gospel with Failure

For some people, fear is the reason they do not live the life they would like to live. Fear prevents them from changing. They fear embarrassment, ridicule, and insults. When they proclaim the good news or attempt to do the right thing, they are often afraid of those who have not heard it and do not want it. They are afraid of being different and not fitting in. They want to go along with what everyone else is doing. We need courage to face and overcome our fears so we can live righteously.

Like Saint Peter, they are high self-monitors who are outward directed. Some of us do not love some people for fear of being rejected and getting hurt. Often, it is not physical but psychological suffering. At other times, it may be fear of our physical well-being. As we remember, a person may not run into a burning building to save a child because she is afraid of dying.

Often, it is not the giving or sharing in the process of love that is of concern but fear of the possible outcomes. Anticipated outcomes could prevent us from loving or living the Gospel. We lack the courage to proclaim the good news to others or do the right thing because we fear failure. It takes courage to be different and to be contrary to what the majority of people around think or want. Courage is a virtuous gift from God, which is used to conquer our fears and sins. Love of what is good and hatred of what is evil provide the courage to overcome fears and act.

There are times we use failure as an excuse to not respond with love but with sin. At times, it is not our failures but the failures of others, such as parents and other authority figures in our lives. Parents may tell young adolescent children not to drink or smoke, but they do! They tell us not to cheat, but they do on their income tax! Instead of listening to our parents and not drinking, smoking, or cheating for our own good, *we use our parents' failures as an excuse to join them in their vices or sins.* We feel betrayed and may respond with acts of vengeance. As we get older, we may discover the truth that our parents are human beings, not Gods and we all sin and make mistakes. Instead of adopting the vices of authority figures or parents, we should strive to do better, which is what our parents want because they love us.

Many Catholics leave the mystical body of Christ, the Church, because of the failures and sins of priests or church leaders. Children will not forgive their parents, and some parishioners will not forgive their priests. Sometimes it takes courage to forgive. *God tells us He forgives us, so we in turn must forgive others.* If we don't, we will face consequences. Remember the parable of the landlord who forgave his servant's debt. Recall how he punished his servant when he found out the servant would not forgive those who owed him a debt. He forgave his servant his debt and expected his servant to do the same.[1]

→ Have you found it hard to forgive authority figures in your life who have sinned or violated the very principles they expect you to follow? Parents, teachers, or clergy encourage you to do the right thing, then they do the opposite.

Sometimes to do good, we must come out of our comfort zone. Many of us will not stand up and speak out against the evils of abortion, fornication, and adultery or the sanctity of marriage between a man and a woman. We are afraid of leaving our comfort zone. We lack the courage to face what Shakespeare calls "the slings and arrows of outrageous fortunes." If we truly love God, Her will is of paramount value and prevails over our will as well as all who may want us to act contrary to Her will. This includes what the world considers the most powerful people.

Look at John the Baptist and his stand against Herod who took the wife of his brother. It cost John his life, and Jesus proclaimed of him, *I tell you among those born of women, no one is greater than John.*[2] If we love God, we will trust Her to help us and save us from those who persecute us; if not physically, most certainly spiritually. If we focus our minds in prayer, the Holy Spirit will give us the virtue of courage to overcome fear.

Failure

The outcome most people fear is failure. We may fail in our efforts to live the perfect Gospel life or live as sinless a life as possible because we are fallible, prone to ignorance and sin.

→ How do you perceive failure? How do you feel when you fail?

We have needs we strive to satisfy, and if necessary, some of us will sin to satisfy them. Failure is seen as bad and to be avoided at any cost. In some cases, even at the cost of self! The truth is sooner or later, many people fail at something.

→ How do you respond to failure?

If we fail, do we have the presence of mind and courage to not give up but to keep trying? It's all in the way our mind perceives it. Failure could be considered good, not bad, if we learn from our failures. Have the courage to share your sinful failures with a friend you respect, trust, and love. Often, from such sharing comes the wisdom and encouragement that can help you grow and succeed in your next effort. When we fail, we must pray to God for the wisdom to face failure in a positive way. We may have failed with our method or approach, but there may be a way that we can be successful, and it's our job to find it. Focus more upon the process than the product. It's natural to feel guilt but not shame. Forgive yourself and move on, and never blame others for your sins.

"The devil made me do it" is not an excuse. Leave the judgment and consequences to God. We must critically observe what we've done or could have done. Look at it as a trial and error approach until we find the right approach to doing the right thing and avoid sin. Finally, and this is often not easy, do not attack the messenger who confronts you with your sin. Do not try to cover up, ignore, or rationalize the sin away. Instead, thank the bearer of bad news, understanding that it takes courage to do it, and the motivation for doing it is most likely love.

Establish an atmosphere in which it is acceptable to confront each other with sins or share our sins with each other. Certainly, it will be extremely difficult but could be an important ingredient in our salvation. At times, we may have to move on to the next opportunity to do what is right or help someone with love. If we truly believe what we are doing or hope to accomplish is good and just, we will be motivated by love to go on and continue to do, in spite of any failures or obstacles to success we find in our path.

Earlier in chapter 52, we asked a question concerning how we can overcome obstacles that prevent us from being what we were created to be and lead a righteous life. The method listed above, along with responding to evil thoughts (chapter 59), conflict resolution (chapters 50, 51, and 60), and Gospel living (chapters 61 and 63), all may help find the answer to this question. Of all these methods, Gospel living is the most important. Put simply, love is the answer!

In fact, if we love, we have already succeeded because there is not failure in love. The only failure there is would be our failure to love! Even if the outcome is not to our liking, our effort to do what is right, just and good, is worth it. *To God, our efforts bring us personal success in living the Gospel life.* As a school principal, I would counsel students who had been sent to me for fighting. My key question to the students would be, could they have done something to avoid the fight? If they answered yes, then I wanted to know what it was and if they did it. If they didn't do something they could have done to avoid the fight, then they must assume some of the responsibility and face some of the consequences, regardless of who started it. Certainly, the one who started it would most likely face greater consequences. On the other hand, if they did something to avoid the fight and it failed, it would have been worth the effort. With such an effort, there would be no consequences.

Often it takes courage to make an effort to solve a conflict peacefully. *The lesson is any effort to avoid sin and violence is worth it, regardless of whether it is successful or not.* Our objective is to teach our children to do the right thing and to solve conflicts or disagreements peacefully without physical violence, threats, extortion, or exploitation. It's the Christian way, and considering the number of wars we've had in the last century, it is not the way of the world.

Peace

Yet, in spite of all our efforts, we will experience failure, violence, and evil in this world! The Lord wants to give us peace. Jesus said to His disciples at the Last Supper, *Peace I leave with you, my peace I give to you.*[3]

What is this peace Jesus wants to give us? It is not the peace of the absence of violence or the peace after a war or military victory. It is a gift from God for our complete well-being: the gift of grace, an inner peace that conquers fear so that we no longer want what we want but only what God wants for us. We know it will be for our total well-being because He loves us. As the angel said to Gideon, "Peace be to you, do not fear, you will not die."[4]

Trust God, and in our final end, everything will be all right.

65

Experiencing God

We have seen that we acquire truths by experiencing reality and truths revealed by authority figures in our lives. Truth is the objective of the mind, and with it can come understanding. The focus on our desire for truth and the understanding that comes produces the energy to love. ***The essence of our identity, purpose for living, and our destiny is living in love.*** It's the key to our continued existence and survival as human beings. It's the secret to freedom, peace, and happiness. We've described it with ideas, words, and images. Yet we cannot know love by a definition or any description in ideas or pictures we might use. We can't know love by reading this book, listening to a lecture, engage in a debate or conversations about it, or look at pictures depicting it. Not even watching a movie or good play will do the trick. *The only way to know love is to live it.* To experience love, we must practice love.

Experience

No matter how much we hear about a steak or see pictures of a steak or watch someone eating steak, we will never truly know a steak until we experience it by eating it. Certainly, many of us have heard this before. The critical point to keep in mind is this: *we may believe in ideas or have faith in them, but we don't love ideas!* If ideas are true, they are accurate representations that can emanate from specific human beings we experience in reality. Ideas do not exist outside our minds. Can we love spiritual, living beings that are no longer physically present in this world? We can because they are specific beings living a spiritual existence; they are not merely ideas in our heads!

As human beings, we are made to see, hear, and feel what we love. In other words, personally experience our loved ones. We love Jesus because He has given us the words of eternal life and teaches us to love by loving us, and we love Him. How do we personally experience Him? How does God reveal Herself? It is done through the Bible, meditation, the Eucharist in which Jesus makes himself present in wine and bread. Here and now, Jesus acts through the sacraments, which reveals and communicates grace. He gives the Holy Spirit and God's body the church, which we experience. Most of all, we experience God in each other since God is incarnate within us.

In previous pages, we read about the different aspects of love. It begins in the intellect, seeing and identifying with the good, followed by the process of love consisting of giving, sharing, and receiving, which brings about the union of the two which is the objective of love. We will not experience love without consciously doing it. Love creates and maintains existence. The purpose of our union of love is survival because the essence of love is a *living relationship of intellectual beings, which is existence.*

We can know and believe any religious, political, or philosophical ideology. We love, however, the person who teaches the ideas and lives them. We can witness a person as a living example of His teaching or we can read about God's teachings and action in the Bible. Witnessing is a better teacher. We can experience Jesus by living his teachings and traits. This means exercising the process of a loving union with other people based on an ideology of love they share and practice in common.

If we experience the Holy Spirit within, we can relate and communicate with Her. We are in a better place than if we only read or listen to Jesus's words. Communicating and listening to God in conversation is better than studying His Word. Of course, it would be ideal if studying the Word results in communication. Both are essential in relating to God.

Unless we experience the actual relationship by living it; unless we give or share ourselves in activities such as intimate conversations, interaction with someone and help them; unless we work with someone to accomplish some true good for others and ourselves, we will not know love. We must be willing to sacrifice our wants and needs for the benefit of someone or some worthy cause we both believe in. We suffer when our loved one suffers and experience their joy when they are happy. We act with love to help brighten their lives with a smile, a compliment, embrace, or any gift of ourselves. Sometimes we may receive gifts in return from loved ones. Love always returns goodness to those who love; if not in this world, most certainly in the next. At times, love brings happiness, and at other times, sadness. For those who love, they know what is written here is true.

If we want a relationship with God, to possess Her in a union of love, we must practice the way of love. When Jesus says, *I am the way.*[1] He means His life of love is the way. Early Christians used "The Way" to describe Christianity. Religious people know our nature is a soul within a physical body. The intellect has to know and understand people to love them, experiencing them by hearing, seeing, and touching them here and now in a union of love.

Experience is an essential ingredient in understanding. The question is, "How do we understand something that happens to a person if we personally never experienced it?" One way is empathy. For example, in the book of Kings, we read about a widow and her son who are starving to death. Trusting in God, she gives the small amount of food she has left to a prophet who promises God will provide for her needs and those of her son.[2] Obviously, we have never experienced such a situation. Yet as we have seen, with empathy, we can place ourselves in the women's shoes with our imagination and ask ourselves questions like, "How would I feel?" or "What would I do and why?" Another way is to perform the same acts the person did, as mentioned earlier by living Jesus's teachings as He Himself did. *We experience God in His temple of love.*

66

God's Presence in the Eucharist

God was present in the world as a historical person, Jesus, born of a woman. God is present and reveals Himself in Jesus's spoken Word, which was recorded in the Bible. He and She are also recorded in the words of the Old Testament prophets who professed the truth disclosed to them by God. God is present and reveals Himself in the Eucharist. He is present in the entire mystical body of Christ, His Church, and within people containing the presence of the Holy Spirit.

The doctrine of transubstantiation, which means "change of substance," results in the Eucharist, which is central to the Catholic faith. The change in the substances from bread and wine into body and blood is one of the most difficult doctrines to accept as true. It can only be believed by absolute faith in a supernatural God, faith in Jesus as the Son of God, and His revelations.

Foundation of the Eucharist in Judaism

The Eucharist is similar to the Jewish priest eating the physical parchment upon which the law is written. Was this a symbolic gesture? Or was there more to it? Did it involve his living the law of God and the law becomes a part of his very being at least for a while? We read in Ezekiel that God stretched out His hand with a scroll and told Ezekiel to eat it! Then He told him to go and speak to the house of Israel. Evidently, the scroll had changed in substance because when he ate it, it was "as sweet as honey!"[1] Not only had the scroll changed, but the prophet changed as well.

God's ideology is now written on Ezekiel's heart, giving him a great ability to speak the word. And his forehead was hardened so not to fear the people or be dismayed of their looks for they are a rebellious house.[2] This procedure was repeated in the book of Revelation.[3] Once again, the author was asked to eat a small scroll by God that tasted as sweet as honey, and then he was to prophesy. This time, however, the scroll turned the stomach sour! Was this a symbolic gesture or much, much more? What do you think?

In addition, in the Jewish religious ritual, an animal such as a lamb could take on the sins of the people and was slaughtered in atonement for their sins. Christ becomes the lamb of God and by His death takes away the sins of the world which is enacted and recalled at each mass.

The Eucharist

We are human beings, and as such, it is a part of our nature as body and soul to want and need to experience by our senses. The Lord understands our created nature, so the Eucharist was established. The Eucharist refers to Christ's real presence under the appearance of bread and wine. It was instituted by Christ at the last supper. It involves our sacrifice by giving praise and thanksgiving in which God is present as priest and victim. The Eucharist is a new covenant,[4] and by Jesus's death and resurrection, we are reconciled with God. As a meal, we are guests at God's own banquet and assert our unity or communion with the mystical body of Christ, His Church. As a meal and sacrifice, the Eucharist effectively symbolizes our giving by self-sacrificing service to others as Jesus gave us the sacrifice of His life.

The Eucharist was instituted by the process of transubstantiation so we can physically experience by seeing and touching Him. The priest recites Jesus's saving words at the last supper and invites the descent of the Spirit of God into the bread and wine. This is done at Mass in the presence of the congregation who unite their praise and thanksgiving with his. There is a change in the substance of bread and wine, and they become the actual body and blood of Jesus; however, the appearance of bread and wine remains. Unlike the Jewish parchment that tasted as sweet as honey, the Eucharist does not change its physical properties.

The Fourth Lateran Council (1215 AD) used the word *transubstantiate* in the Eucharistic section of its professions of faith. The Council of Trent restated very clearly that it was not symbolism but our "belief that by the priest's consecration, bread and wine are transubstantiated into the body and blood of Christ and should be adored." St. John Chrysostom wrote that it was Christ who was responsible for transubstantiation. The priest pronounces the words, but the power and grace are from God.

During the reformation, Ulrich Zwingli (1484–1531) advocated a symbolic impression of the Eucharist and did not believe that any change took place. Ultimately, transubstantiation was rejected and the real presence denied. Martin Luther held that the substance of bread and wine did not change but remained; however, Christ does become present for the believer. He is present "only" for the believer, and this view is called consubstantiation.

Sadly, enough surveys reveal many baptized Catholics, especially the young adults, no longer believe in the real presence in the Eucharist. They believe it is symbolic and not to be taken literally. Surveys also reveal the American society is becoming more and more secular and losing their sense of God because they do not have a loving relationship with their God.

Foundation of the Eucharist by Jesus

The Gospel of John, sixth chapter, contains the foundation of the Eucharistic doctrine in addition to Christ's words at the last supper. In John's Gospel, Jesus states, *Unless you eat the flesh of the Son of Man and drink His blood, you have no life in you. Those who eat my flesh and drink my blood will have eternal life.*[5] Those who heard His remarks interpreted them literally, saying to Him, "This teaching is difficult (offensive). Who can accept it?" Because of this doctrine "many of His disciples turned away and no longer went about with Him."[6] On this day, Jesus lost a great deal of His popularity with many of the people who were present.

If Jesus was speaking symbolically, he would have called back those walking away and explained that their literal interpretation was wrong. He would have explained He was not speaking literally but symbolically, but He didn't! Jesus is the Son of God who always speaks truthfully. It would be impossible for Him to do otherwise. Why would He allow His disciples to walk away with a doctrine that was not true? Their literal interpretation was true; they refused, however, to believe it.

Jesus lost many disciples that day. Their decision to stay had to be based on a supernatural truth they would not believe, so they left. Almost two thousand years ago, the Romans believed Jesus's words were to be taken literally because those who followed the Christian way must have believed in a literal interpretation. This is why the Romans wrote on the walls of the catacombs the word *cannibals* in describing Christians.

I was once teaching this doctrine to a very intelligent adolescent boy who wanted to be a scientist. He could not accept this doctrine because the host did not taste, look, nor feel like flesh! In fact, it has none of the physical or chemical properties of flesh. For the boy accepting this host as the actual flesh of Jesus is to deny the truths or facts of reality and science. I asked him if he would eat this host if I exposed it to a high dose of radiation. He laughed and answered, "Never." He didn't want to die. I asked him if it had changed, and he answered it had. My response to him was, "But it looks the same and it has many of the properties of bread!" The Eucharist changed internally in its essence, but not in its physical properties or appearance.

Appearances can be deceptive in nature. Jesus gives us His flesh to eat and His blood to drink and receiving it with faith, we experience an intimacy beyond any other union of love.

→ There are people who believe Jesus is the Son of God but do not believe in transubstantiation or His real presence in the Eucharist. Are you one of them? Do you believe in the real presence?

Bread of Life

What is this bread of life Jesus talks about? How do we give meaning and understanding to eating the flesh of Christ and drinking His blood? Some will say we can't because it's a mystery, and it is, yet God gave us an intellect to know, understand, and love Him. We must seek to understand, to always search for answers to the important questions in our lives. Communion bread, like all regular bread, provides the energy to move and do things, which means to live. Communion bread is bread that has become the physical Body of Christ and remains so until it is digested.

God's spirit is present in the Eucharist. God's spirit can only be activated within us by our faith and engagement in the process of love for God and neighbor. When the presence of the Eucharistic bread is activated within us, the energy which emanates from it is not merely physical but spiritual energy. It is used to unite us with our neighbors by the motive and process of love. God gives us Himself, love, so we can willingly give, share, and receive it from each other for the benefit of others and ourselves. Not only physical benefits, but the spiritual existence of love and peace within us.

Consuming the Eucharist, we will change if we truly believe it is the body and blood of Christ. We identify with Christ, and our identification is exhibited by a greater love. With love, we carry within us two persons of the blessed Trinity, spiritually the Holy Spirit, and physically, at least for a while, the Son of God. God is incarnate within us and acts through us. *We share in the divine nature as a conduit for God's goodness.* Any good we do with love is really God working through us. It is not a matter of goodness coming from us but the goodness we allow to pass through us emanating from God. We do this because we use the love given to us to love God and our brothers and sisters. We want the Lord's goodness of love for ourselves and our neighbors with the ecstasy and peace which emerges from it.

There is a vast difference between regular bread and communion bread. Regular bread gives physical life. Communion bread as the actual body and blood of God gives physical and spiritual life. Christ is the bread of spiritual life everlasting. Eating communion bread is similar to the marital act of a husband and wife. It can be much greater than a married couple sharing themselves with each other in a physical union of love. For those who truly believe with faith, communion will be an intimate physical and spiritual sharing with God to establish an existence through a union of love.

As for our physical body, we believe it will also be resurrected and remain but in a different way. After all, we are not angels but human beings with a body and soul. Our bodies will continue in the same way Christ's body continued after His resurrection in a glorified form. We will be recognizable but different as Christ's body was recognizable but different.[7]

67

Born Again in the Spirit

We are not physically born again, but we do experience a new birth through the spirit from above. As Jesus said to Nicodemus, *You must be born from above.*[1] This demonstrates our spiritual essence is of paramount importance because it is through the spirit that we can partake of the divine nature. It is the *Holy Spirit within us and God working through us that we are renewed by our birth from above into the newness of life.* God's mission in the world now becomes our mission and our destiny to be with Her in a union of love for all eternity.

We must bring forth the Holy Spirit born from above by the mindful focus of our intellect, believing we have a new birth of the spirit that is real and within us. We are living a new life. With this belief in Her presence within us, we can evoke a conversation with Her. We can use our thoughts and feelings and perhaps cause Her to respond to our remarks and questions by Her using our thoughts. With our new birth from above, the Holy Spirit can help us become more understanding, and with it, more loving. Since we have a spirit of love that is our essence, we can become incarnate beings with the new spirit from above, sharing in God's divine existence.

→ Are you born again in the Spirit?
→ Do you pray and focus your thoughts to experience a new birth from above?

The mystic, Caryll Houselander, was an English woman who was born in 1901. She was given a vision of Christ within all the people she met. She describes it as wonderful images within her mind. Christ means anointed. Anointed one could refer to God the Father, the Son Jesus, or the Holy Spirit. Perhaps she was seeing the traits of God the Father working through the parent person in every individual; or the Son Jesus working through the child person in everyone; or the Holy Spirit working through the adult person in all the people. She saw God who is in her fellow human beings as loving and living, rejoicing with joy, saddened with sorrow, suffering and dying with all the people in the world. It is the agony and ecstasy of love.

The Holy Spirit within us that is born from above can counsel and direct us. As we know, we are members of God's mystical body, and as such, "we" are His real presence in the world today. We are commissioned to carry out His mission. We find God within us with prayer and meditation, and when we do, we see Her presence in the world in other human beings. This is Jesus's new commandment to us that we love each other as He loves us. In so doing, with the help of God, we save each other from the ravages of sin, thus ensuring heaven.

What is unique about this commandment, what makes it new, is not merely that we love one another but we love our neighbor as God loves us.

- With our presence comprising the mystical body of the Son of God, which is the Church, God is present in the world today.
- With our incarnation of the Spirit from above and our loving everyone as Jesus loves everyone, God is present in the world today.
- With the Eucharist and the Word of God found in the Bible, God is present in the world today.

With God's presence in us, Her mission continues in this world. This is how important we are and our mission is, and we must never forget it.

→ Do you now know what your mission or purpose is here and now?

To experience this mystical birth from above, there must be an inner transformation by the power of God's love. *By mindfulness, we must die to the illusions of being our false self, which is self-centered and self-sufficient.* To eliminate the illusion of a self-sufficient ego, we must be aware of our impermanence in which almost all of our being is changing. We must also be aware of our interbeing in which we are dependent on each other for our existence, and we are all a part of God's creations.

Transcendence

To die to our self-centeredness, we must transcend and choose to totally surrender to God. It is much more than surrendering our will to the will of God.

- We transcend by extinguishing all delusions, which are not true along with the anger, fear, and desires or cravings that cause them.
- We transcend all notions associated with worldly concerns. Things such as origin or ends, individual or group, going or staying don't concern us anymore. It's not denying them; it's a matter of going beyond them.
- We transcend the notion of death, mindful there is no terminal death, only transformation from one existence to another.
- We transcend notions of a lifetime because life is no longer limited by time and space.

Surrendering to the will of God is complete acceptance of ourselves and any situation in which we may find ourselves. We are no longer self-centered with any illusions of ourselves or any exaggerated ideas about our abilities. We are free to obey the will of God whenever and wherever it comes to us in the here and now.

Focusing the Mind with Meditation and Contemplation

To have the experience of this mystical renewal of the mindfulness of transcendence, we must quiet the mind and not lose ourselves in daily activities. Unfortunately, many people do. How do we train the mind to focus so we may experience the renewal and presence of the Holy Spirit?

- We can practice meditation on the Scriptures. With our imaginations, we can place ourselves in any Bible scene. We can assume the role of any of the characters with an intellectual image and interact with others, including Jesus. In our imaginations, we can express our feelings and thoughts about ourselves and others. We listen in our thoughts for responses from God and other people in the scene. God is spiritually present in the scene we create in our minds.
- We can practice contemplative or "centering" prayers in contrast to meditative prayer. It does not use imagination but goes beyond thought and image, beyond the senses and the rational mind to our center where we'll find God. God has the greatest degree of respect for us. God would never encroach upon our freedom; He would never force His way into our lives. God says, "I am standing at the door knocking."[2] Free from all thoughts, images, or emotions, we can open ourselves to God who responds by making Herself present to us. We can repeat a word or phrase, which centers

all our attention and desire on God and nothing else. In our quiet mind, God speaks to us through our thoughts. They are no longer our thoughts but His, and we just listen within the quietness. In the quiet of our mind, we experience the presence of God in our feeling and being peaceful and content.

- We can read the Bible. The amount we read we leave up to God. We read it slowly, peacefully until thoughts from our intellect like a voice tell us to stop on a word or phrase. Memorize the word or phrase, and allow it to interact with our ideas, worries, or concerns. If our ideas or concerns are distractions to us, just give them over to God along with the rest of ourselves. Hopefully, that inner pondering invites us into a dialogue with God.
- We can use our imagination to enter into a dialogue of thought with God the Father, Son, or Holy Spirit. It is conversation without images, just our thoughts, and God who uses our thoughts to express Hers. We interact with God as we would a loved one who knows and accepts us.

One final example of meditative prayer and most painful to this father: My daughter was dying of colon cancer, so I turned to the Lord in prayer. I said to Jesus, "Lord, save her. Take my life, but spare hers. The children need her." His response was immediate and as follows: "Ralph, I created MaryAnn with the help of Sally and you. I love her infinitely more than you or Sally possibly could. I would never harm her. Trust Me."

At first, I thought He was telling me He would save her. Perhaps it was wishful thinking because when I once again thought about His words, He said He loved her and would not harm her, not necessarily heal her. Was I talking to myself? Or was it God? The believer might answer one way and the nonbeliever another. My daughter wanted to live and fought her illness. My prayer changed from healing to asking God to give her the graces to face whatever happens with hope, faith, and love along with His peace. He answered my prayer. She now rests with Him, enjoying a goodness and happiness she has never known.

The love of God through prayer gave me the strength to carry the pain and suffering I was experiencing. With the loss of my daughter, I was living a new life without her. I mourned my loss, but eventually, I had to accept the fact that she was gone. Her spirit rests with God from whence it came. I embraced the new life I was already living without my daughter, just as King David did after the death of his son.[3] Only after I let go of my old life with my daughter and embraced this new life did I receive the blessing from above and a renewed spirit to live it.

It was at this time that I realized or understood we all experience many deaths in our lives. I experienced the loss of loved ones and my youth with its ability to do things I once took pride in doing. I experienced the loss of much of the good health I once enjoyed, the loss of being whole and fit, and the loss of my singing voice and the hearing and seeing I once had. I can no longer run, having two artificial hips, and much of my strength is gone. I experienced the death of my dreams of being a graduate of West Point and of being a doctor and a deacon. I've also experienced the death of many of the rituals of the old Catholic Church and some of my preconceived notions of God. I miss the twentieth century with its great Broadway musicals, talking on the phone instead of texting, writing a letter instead of punching keys, reading newspapers you can touch and smell, and finally attending classes and meetings instead of experiencing it on the computer screen. I prefer real instead of virtual.

Almost everything dies or changes, and all that remains of the past resides in memory. We have been resurrected into this new life. In fact each morning, we are all resurrected into a new life, and so we have a choice. We can cling to the old, which is no longer real, and be unhappy, fearful, and trapped. Or we can embrace the new life, which is real here and now, and experience God's graces and renewed spirit for the stage of life we are living. This choice enables us to live a new, rich, and full life.

Although I will always remember my daughter with pictures and fresh flowers daily, I have chosen to live the new life that has been given to me. There was a time I wanted to be twenty again; I was young and had my whole life ahead of me, dreaming of the great things I was going to do. Now I say it's great to be eighty-five with a renewed spirit. I take every day as it comes and do the best I can with faith and hopeful expectation that I have my whole life ahead of me. I will experience great things to come, maybe not as much in this world but in a glorious life to come.

Formula prayer such as the Rosary is good if it helps focus the mind to go beyond itself to real communication and a relationship with God. If not, then prayer becomes merely a set of words we repeat with little or no meaning. The mass too can become a ritual stereotyped activity without experiencing God in ourselves, those around us, and in the Gospel and Eucharist.

Whether we use ideas, images in meditative prayer, or silent listening in contemplative prayer, we can find God at the center of our being. We seek Her in the glow of faith or knowing with love. It is only in the repeated submitting to prayer and total self-giving will we slowly die to our false self and ultimately realize more and more fully the experience of our true selves through our union with the God of love. As Paul writes, anyone united to the Lord becomes one in spirit with Him, a mystical union of love in which we remain individually separate or distinct, but by experience, we become one Spirit![4]

Contemplative prayer can help us acquire an awareness of our true identity. With this awareness, we realize that we already have what we are supposed to have. We are aware of the purpose of our creation. As we know, our perception of the goodness of the nature of God invokes or brings forth a response of love. The purpose of our creation is with the love of God, we share in the goodness of the Lord's nature with joy and peace. In contemplative prayer, we do not seek enlightenment. What we desire is to give ourselves completely to our Lord. This includes our intellect and feelings, focusing our minds completely upon God. With focusing, we experience an identity with our Lord in a Godlike manner. By grace, the Holy Spirit is incarnate within us so that the love that unites us with Christ is similar to the love of Jesus for the Father and the Holy Spirit.

Focusing our minds through prayer aims at our being who we truly are. It is difficult to perceive and grasp our true selves. This is because with the power to love comes the power of free choice. With this power of choice, we can choose something that is not God. When we choose something less than God, we make these things false gods. In short, we do not seek God but ourselves, and when we do, we become a cause of sinfulness for others as well as ourselves. Prayer can also help us be aware and exercise our free will appropriately, uniting us to God in the process of love and the energy and determination to live the life of Jesus the Christ. Turning to God in prayer in the depth of our being, we discover our true selves. We have revealed our true selves in this book, and put simply, it is a participation in the Divine Being through love.

→ Do you lose yourself in daily activities and fail to establish a relationship with God?
→ Do you now know and experience your true self? Or are you still clinging and grasping at false identities?

Living Our True Self

We do not have the intellect to make a judgment about what is happening in contemplative prayer because it goes beyond thought and reason. How do we discern with contemplative prayer, or any prayer for that matter, whether we are making progress in living our true selves? As we mentioned earlier, we make such a discernment by using the criteria established by the Lord.

- Jesus said, *For the tree is known by its fruits.*[5] We know we are living in love with the Holy Spirit, which is the spirit of love by the fruit She creates in our lives.
- Jesus explains His norm for discernment, *By this everyone will know that you are my disciples, if you have love for one another.*[6]
- If we truly love God, then all the other fruits of the Holy Spirit shall accompany our love, such as "joy, peace, patience, kindness, generosity, faithfulness, gentleness and self-control."[7]
- The Bible goes on to say, "If we live by the Spirit, let us also be guided by the Spirit. Let us not become conceited competing against one another, envying one another."[8]

We now know what we want out of life and how to get it. To live the Christian way is to be in touch with both our true physical and spiritual self. To live as Christians, we must be humble, and yet, we must not think too little of ourselves. We seek what will fulfill and satisfy us, and we want to be all we were created to be. It is pointless to see an ultimate goal or end to our lives with anything less than

God. Only God can satisfy our desire for perfect love and as much knowledge as our nature permits.

In life, we make choices because we do not see clearly. All our choices and seeing must ultimately embrace our union with God because we are partakers of the divine nature and made to be one with Her. As a saint once said, we are made for God, and our souls will not rest until it rests with Him. Nothing else will ever satisfy or make us completely happy and indeed will lead to frustration and sorrow. Only in the possession of God or perfect love will our life have its full meaning.

There are three roads to our union with God, but in reality, all three become one. One is the *study* of revelation, the attainment of wisdom, and the perception of the Lord's infinite goodness. The second leads to *prayer* with faith and intellectual acts of love. Finally, this in turn leads to *physical acts of love* or corporal works of mercy.

Summary

As we now know, God can't be reached by notions, thinking, or concepts alone. We also know God by consciousness and human experience in the here and now. We can experience God by prayer or by living as She lives, which is loving. Whenever we see someone who is loving, mindful, caring, understanding, compassionate, we know we are experiencing the Holy Spirit. We experience God in each other.

We can experience God by mindfully looking deeply into the realities of our true selves and being enlightened by God in prayer. We can experience God by the mindful reception of the Eucharist. We experience God by loving all our brothers and sisters in Christ because in loving them, we are loving God. By experiencing God, we are born into a new liberated true self who lives and acts in the Spirit. The objective of our daily spiritual experiences in prayer is to possess God in a mystical union of love.

Final Thoughts

If you have carefully read this book, you know who you really are, what you were created to do, and where you are going. One final time, we are spirit existing in an animal body with a soul within our intellect consisting of intelligence and consciousness. Created by God in His image, we are His children, members of His mystical body who share in His divinity and in His mission to love. We exist by a relationship of love. The objective of love is union, the process of love is generosity, sharing, and receiving. The purpose of love is our existence and salvation, surviving as human beings in this world and the next. Our destiny then is possessing God in a mystical union of a loving relationship beginning here and now and continuing on for all eternity.

→ If you truly believe what is written in this book concerning your identity, mission, and destiny, how do you think you would feel, act, and be?

We have provided false ideologies concerning our identity, purpose, and destiny in the hope you will not fall victim to their error and succumb to them as many have.

We provided you with the truths about our reality with the hope that you will focus upon them, and with mindful understanding, make these truths your own; and with faith, act in accord with them in the process of love. We have used theology, philosophy, psychology, and science to help you see God's revelations can be found in all disciplines because they are true and are to be believed and lived.

We can know who we are, our mission, and destiny in life, but knowing is not necessarily understanding and experiencing the God of love. Without understanding and experiencing love, knowledge means very little. The intellect without love has no real meaning. As Saint Bernard once said, "Knowledge for the sake of impressing others or controlling a situation for your own benefit is vanity. Knowledge for the sake of serving others is Godly." It is true living in love with and for God gives meaning and purpose to our life. It is the way to live, but it does not guarantee a life without problems and suffering where everything in this world will be wonderful.

Hopefully, this book has given you an understanding of love, why we love, and how we do it. With what you now know, why not give love a chance by practicing it with greater understanding, making it the essence of your life, which it is?

Don't think about it. Just consciously see the good that can be done in your family, friends, church, job, community and do it for God, the people and yourself. If you have not already done so, start with God and then move on to others. Do it even if you have fears or doubts, focusing upon who you are and where you are going. Continually do good until it becomes a virtuous habit. Love of God is the most wonderful thing that ever existed and will continue to exist forever. Once you experience it, you won't turn back.

→ What do you have to lose? Nothing.
→ What do you have to gain? Everything.

To the Christian who truly believes chapter 25 of Matthew, if we lose the battle with evil, we have lost "everything"; and in winning the race, as Paul would say, we have gained "everything".

Bibliography

The New Oxford Annotated Bible, New Revised Standard Version. Edited by Bruce M. Metzger and Roland Murphy. New York: Oxford University Press, 1994.

Give Us This Day. Liturgical Press.

Catechism of the Catholic Church. Liguori, MO: Liguori Publications, 1994.

Alexander, Eben MD. *Proof of Heaven*. New York, NY: Simon and Schuster Paperbacks, 2012.

Carver, Charles S. and Michael Scheier. *Perspectives on Personality*. Boston: Allyn and Bacon, 2000.

Collins, Gerald, S. J. and Farrugia, S. J. *A Concise Dictionary of Theology*. New York/Mahwah, NJ: Paulist Press, 1991.

Dennis, Marie, Cynthia Moe-Lobeda, Joseph Nangle, OFM, and Stuart Taylor. *St. Francis and the Foolishness of God*.

Fromm, Erich; *The Art of Loving*. New York, NY. Harper Brothers, 1956.

Mary Knoll, NY: Orbis Books, 1997.

Dewey, John, *Human Nature Conduct*. New York: Holt, 1992.

Donceel, J. F., S. J. *Philosophical Psychology*. New York: Sheed and Ward, 1955.

Escriva, Josemaria. *The Forge*. Princeton, NJ: Scepter Publishers, 1988.

Fagothey, Austin, S. J. *Right and Reason, Ethics in Theory and Practice*. St Louis: Mosby Publishers, 1953.

Farrell, Walter OPSTM, and Martin J. Healy. *My Way of Life Pocket Edition of St. Thomas Aquinas, Summa Theologica.*

Brooklyn, NY: Confraternity of the Precious Blood, 1952.

Fiest, Jess, and Gregory Feist. *Theories of Personality*. New York, NY: McGraw Hill, 1998.

Hanh, Nhat, Thich. *Living Buddha, Living Christ*. New York, NY: Riverhead Books, 1995.

Gordon, Thomas Dr. *Teacher Effectiveness Training—Teacher Notebook*. California: Effective Training Associates, 1972.

Gula, Richard MSS. *Reason Informed by Faith*. New York/Mahwah, 1989.

Harris, Thomas, MD. *I'm OK—You're OK*. New York, NY Avon Books, 1973.

James, Muriel, and Dorothy Jongeward. *Born to Win*. Addison-Wesley Publishing Company, 1975.

Kant, Immanuel. *Critique of Practical Reason*. University of Chicago Press, 1949.

Kelsey, Morton. *The Other Side of Silence: A Guide to Christian Meditation*. New York/Mahwah, 1976.

Kramer, Joel, *The Passionate Mind*. Celestial Arts, 1974.

Kreyche, Robert J. *Logic for Undergraduates*. New York, NY: The Dryden Press Publishers, 1956.

Lisieux, Therese, translated by John Beevers. *The Autobiography of Saith Therese of Lisieux*. New York, NY: Image Books, Double Day, 1989.

Marcel, Gabriel. *The Philosophy of Existentialism*. New York: The Citadel Press, 1971.

Nietzsche, Friedrich. *The Genealogy of Morals*, translated by H. Samuel, Edinburgh, TN: Foulis, 1913.

Prather, Hugh. *Notes to Myself*. Utah: Real People Press, 1970.

Rolheiser, Ronald. *The Holy Longing*. New York: Doubleday, 1999.

Schwartz, David, PhD. *The Magic of Thinking Big*. California: Wilshire Book Company, 1971.

www.amazon.com/Rejoice-Be-Glad-Gaudete·Exultate/dpl

Notes

Chapter One
[1] Exodus 3:14
[2] Genesis 1:26
[3] Psalms 8:5
[4] Psalms 8:6–9
[5] Genesis 1:31

Chapter Three
[1] Matthew 28:19
[2] John 10:30
[3] John 10:15–17
[4] Luke 22:42

Chapter Five
[1] Luke 10:38–42

Chapter Nine
[1] 2 John 1:9

Chapter Eleven
[1] 1 Corinthians 2:12–13
[2] John 6:63

Chapter Twelve
[1] Jeremiah 1:5

Chapter Thirteen
[1] Matthew 5:27–28

Chapter Sixteen
[1] Exodus 20:13

Chapter Eighteen
[1] Matthew 13:10–13
[2] Matthew 5:48
[3] John 14:27
[4] John 14:2–3
[5] Psalm 84:11
[6] Sirach 1:13
[7] Ecclesiastes 3:12
[8] John 11:25
[9] Romans 12:2

Chapter Twenty-One
[1] John 6:27
[2] Luke 12:15
[3] Matthew 7:15

Chapter Twenty-Three
[1] Sirach 17:32
[2] John 8:14
[3] Isaiah 6:3–5
[4] Leviticus 19:2, 20:26

Chapter Twenty-Four
[1] John 1:9
[2] John 8:31

Chapter Twenty-Six
[1] John 4:24
[2] Matthew 25:40

Chapter Twenty-Seven
[1] Micah 2:1–3

Chapter Twenty-Nine
[1] 1 John 4:18

Chapter Thirty
[1] Matthew 26:52, John 18:10

Chapter Thirty-One
[1] 1 John 4:16
[2] Luke 17:20–21
[3] James 1:22, 25
[4] Ephesians 2:10

Chapter Thirty-Two
[1] 1 John 4:12
[2] Genesis 1:31
[3] Ephesian 5:2

Chapter Thirty-Three
[1] Genesis 4:9
[2] Romans 12:13
[3] 1 John 2:9–10
[4] 1 John 3:14–15
[5] Matthew 25

Chapter Thirty-Four
[1] Deuteronomy 6:5
[2] Leviticus 19:18
[3] Mark 12:29–31
[4] Matthew 5:44
[5] Matthew 25:35–36
[6] John 13:34
[7] Romans 5:6–8
[8] Ephesians 5:26–30

Chapter Thirty-Five
[1] Luke 14:25–33

Chapter Thirty-Six
[1] Acts 20:35
[2] Matthew 6:2–4
[3] John 10:14–18; James 2:13

Chapter Thirty-Seven
[1] 1 John 4:18
[2] Mark 14:36
[3] Matthew 6:25–26
[4] Luke 15:11–32
[5] Galatians 6:2
[6] Matthew 6:12
[7] Matthew 7:3–5

Chapter Thirty-Eight
[1] 1 Corinthians 13:2, 8–12
[2] Matthew 26:41

Chapter Thirty-Nine
[1] Romans 12:10
[2] 1 Peter 2:17

Chapter Forty
[1] John 8:12
[2] 1 Thessalonians 5:5
[3] Ephesians 6:10–13
[4] Galatians 1:12
[5] Jeremiah 9:24
[6] Mark 12:31
[7] Deuteronomy 4:31
[8] Matthew 5:7
[9] 2 Corinthians 4:3–4
[10] Matthew 10:28

Chapter Forty-Two
[1] Exodus 21:24; Matthew 5:38
[2] Matthew 5:11–12
[3] Ephesians 2:4–6
[4] Galatians 5:13; 1 Peter 2:16; 1 Corinthians 15:3
[5] Revelations 1:5
[6] Ephesians 2:5; Wisdom 3:9
[7] Ephesians 1:4–5; 1 Thessalonians 5:5
[8] Luke 6:20–26
[9] James 4:7
[10] Acts 22:20; Revelations 12:11
[11] Acts 3:13–15
[12] Matthew 5:38–39
[13] Matthew 5:43–44

Chapter Forty-Three

[1] John 14:3; 1 Peter 1:4
[2] Matthew 13:36–43; Matthew 25:41–46
[3] Matthew 25:31–46
[4] Mark 12:30–31, 34

Chapter Forty-Four

[1] Genesis 2:7
[2] Matthew 10:28; Hebrews 4:12
[3] Wisdom 3:1–4, 9:15, 16:13
[4] Matthew 10:28
[5] Wisdom 9:15

Chapter Forty-Five

[1] Romans 1:17; 9:30–31
[2] Romans 3:27–28; Galatians 2:16
[3] Mark 10:23–25
[4] Matthew 21:13
[5] Luke 4:31–37
[6] John 18:36
[7] Luke 17:21
[8] Romans 5:5
[9] Ephesians 5:25–30
[10] John 17:26
[11] Matthew 5:44

Chapter Forty-Six

[1] John 15:15

Chapter Forty-Seven

[1] Mark 10:44
[2] John 15:15
[3] Romans 6:16
[4] Mark 10:42–45

Chapter Forty-Eight

[1] Matthew 18:15
[2] Ezekiel 33:7–14
[3] Luke 6:43
[4] Matthew 3:8
[5] Colossians 1:10
[6] Ephesians 4:32
[7] Luke 23:34
[8] Mark 10:51

Chapter Fifty-One

[1] Ephesians 5:22
[2] Ephesians 5:25

Chapter Fifty-Two

[1] John 18:38
[2] John 14:6
[3] Sirach 23:9
[4] Wisdom 1:11
[5] Proverbs 14:5
[6] John 8:32
[7] John 8:31–32
[8] John 17:17
[9] Psalms 119:151
[10] John 1:9
[11] Ephesians 5:9
[12] Romans 2:8
[13] 2 Thessalonians 2:10
[14] 2 Corinthians 4:2
[15] Deuteronomy 32:4; John 14:6
[16] John 8:44

Chapter Fifty-Three

[1] Matthew 10:34–35
[2] Matthew 9:17
[3] Matthew 5:11

Chapter Fifty-Four

[1] John 10:30
[2] James 2:17

Chapter Fifty-Five

[1] 1 Corinthians 15
[2] 1 Corinthians 13:13
[3] Galatians 5:1–6
[4] Romans 8:26; 2 1 & 2 Corinthians 3:16–17
[5] John 20:31; Romans 10:8–9
[6] Romans 1:5
[7] Matthew 8:5–13

Chapter Fifty-Six

1 1 Corinthians 10:13
2 Wisdom 3:9
3 Habakkuk 2:4
4 Luke 7:47–50
5 John 20:29
6 Matthew 17:20
7 1 Corinthians 2:14
8 1 John 5:10
9 1 Corinthians 2:10–13

Chapter Fifty-Eight

1 Matthew 25

Chapter Fifty-Nine

1 Matthew 7:5
2 Numbers 20:2–13, 22–24; Deuteronomy 32:48–52

Chapter Sixty

1 Romans 10:9
2 Roman 10:9; John 20:31
3 Romans 6:5–8
4 Romans 2:12–13, 15

Chapter Sixty-One

1 Matthew 5:48
2 John 11:26
3 Matthew 25:46
4 Mark 10:21, John 14:6
5 Joshua 1:8

Chapter Sixty-Two

1 Romans 3:21–26, 4:13–16
2 1 Timothy 2:4
3 1 Peter 1:3–5; John 1:13
4 Romans 5:5
5 Romans 8:14–16
6 1 Corinthians 12:27
7 1 Peter 1:4
8 John 17:26
9 Genesis 1:26
10 2 Peter 1:4
11 1 Peter 1:15–16

Chapter Sixty-Three

1 Luke 14:11
2 Proverbs 16:18
3 Matthew 17:20
4 Luke 6:37

Chapter Sixty-Four

1 Matthew 18:21–35
2 Luke 7:28
3 John 14:27
4 Judges 6:23

Chapter Sixty-Five

1 John 14:6
2 1 Kings 17:8–16

Chapter Sixty-Six

1 Ezekiel 3:1–3
2 Ezekiel 3:7–9
3 Revelation 10:8–11
4 1 Corinthians 11:25; Luke 22:20
5 John 6:52–55
6 John 6:60–66
7 Luke 24:13–42; John 20:11–28

Chapter Sixty-Seven

1 John 3:7
2 Revelations 3:20
3 2 Samuel 12:19–25
4 1 Corinthians 12:13, 27; Ephesians 3:16–17
5 Matthew 12:33
6 John 13:35
7 Galatian 5:22–24
8 Galatians 5:25–26

About the Author

Dr. DeGruttola's career spans thirty-five years in public education in the state of Connecticut. He holds four college degrees, including a PhD in psychometrics from the University of Connecticut. He has taught in middle, high school, and universities. He has served as a guidance counselor, school psychologist, principal of an elementary and middle school, and director of Pupil Personnel Services.

Dr. DeGruttola is a Secular Franciscan who has worked in a host of church ministries, including religious education, soup kitchens, prison and aid ministries, as well as Respect Life. He has three children and is presently retired in Florida with his wife, Sally.